Second Chances

To Mick & Jo Ellen
good luck & best wishes

Bill Ellis

Second Chances

BILL ELLIS

FirstPublish, Inc.
Orlando, Florida

ISBN
1-929925-70-0

Library of Congress Cataloging in Publication Data
2001090329

Bill Ellis
Second Chances

FIRSTPUBLISH, INC.
170 Sunport Ln. Suite 900
Orlando, FL 32809
407-240-1414
www.firstpublish.com

Printed by QUESTprint
Orlando, Florida

Dedication

To Joan, my second chance and "ideal reader."

Acknowledgments

Several years ago, my good friend Ruth Anderson invited me to speak at the West Rockies Writers Club in Grand Junction, Colorado. My topic was plain English writing, a subject I had vainly tried to teach to Federal government writers for about 20 years. After I spoke, a couple of members asked me to become a member. They sincerely encouraged me to start writing the fiction I'd said was a lifelong goal earlier in my presentation. A month or so later, I joined with four members of the club to form a critique group, and thus began my real education in the craft of writing. Virginia Jenson, Val Horton, Linda Armstrong, and Phil Neal skewered my writing for 18 months and taught me plenty. So I thank the membership of West Rockies for pushing me and never letting up on their encouragement. Especially, thank you Ruth, Virginia, Val, Linda, and Phil.

Duane Howard and Caroline Morrell, also of West Rockies, read this story and gave me invaluable comments. Thank you both. Special thanks to Monika Todd, Mesa County Clerk and Recorder for making it possible to use the image of the state "designer" license tag for background on the cover. Sometimes the best choice is right in front of you.

Phil Neal deserves his own paragraph. I have read and critiqued his work, and marvel at the maturity of someone in his mid-20s who can express feelings as if he had lived a full lifetime already. He edited this story with his heart. I have his margin notes to prove it. I also have many marks indicating lost commas, errant clauses, and questionable word choice. Thank you, Phil.

Finally, even though my wife Joan has the book dedicated to her, she deserves more praise here. I didn't write a single word without thinking about her reaction. Her positive reinforcement boosted my morale and encouraged me to write on. Her silence, accompanied with a scribbled note or two, meant I was off the mark. Miraculously, she became my compass in writing as she has always been in everything else. She says it is her gift to me, and she wants no thanks for it. Fortunately, I get to put my gratitude in here, in print. Her love is something I appreciate more each day.

ONE

Winter, Douglas Pass, Colorado

A cold sweat chilled Jack Marshall as he struggled to see out of his iced-over windshield. He followed his target up the winding mountain pass in blizzard white out. Fierce winds created hurricane-like conditions within the snowstorm. Anyone who had lived on the Western Slope of the mountainous state of Colorado knew to stay away from Douglas Pass in the winter. Being here was a mistake. Yet, here he was. Jack Marshall, an experienced and supposedly intelligent Secret Service Agent. He drove with his lights off, hoping to catch a payoff bribe in midstream somewhere up ahead on the winding two-lane county road.

Douglas Pass perched at the crest of route 139 as it struggled over the Bookcliff range. It was a straight line on the map that had fooled many tourists who thought they could save time by taking it from Loma to Rangely. The best the Colorado Highway Department could do was remove the larger boulders that continuously slid onto the road. That is, when there was a road, for entire stretches often disappeared under avalanches and mud slides, crushing animals, vehicles, and people down into treacherous ravines. Once there, they remained until search and rescue teams could find them during the spring thaw, usually under ten feet of icy snowpack.

Jack had been tailing the Durango SUV for over two hours in the whirling blizzard. No other idiots were out. The wind chill was far below zero. Jack had gotten the case because phony money had been traced to the area, and to Willard Shupe's bank account in particular. Tonight, Shupe, a Mesa County Commissioner, had dramatically changed his vote at the last minute to allow development of public lands that encroached on the Colorado National Monument. The monthly Commissioner's meeting had erupted in chaos when Shupe had cast the deciding vote.

Jack sensed the vote was a break in the case. He suspected whoever was bribing local officials had used the counterfeit money to do it, knowing there could be no retaliation. He had anticipated the double-cross by Shupe, but not tonight. He had tailed Shupe from downtown Grand Junction across the

partially frozen Colorado river to Shupe's home in the Redlands neighborhood. Jack had not waited long before his target had hurried back outside
and headed to Loma, ten miles west on I-70. From there, Shupe had driven
due north towards Douglas Pass on route 139.

Both vehicles traveled farther and farther up the snaking road. Jack kept
Shupe's tail lights in view from a safe distance and knew the location for the
payoff would have to be at the top of the pass over 9,000 feet above sea level.
That was the only place within miles large enough for more than one car to
stop. Unless Shupe was going to Rangely, another 35 miles north.

The road had so many 180-degree turns that Jack had to run with his
lights off or risk being spotted from above. Fortunately, he was driving a Jeep
Cherokee equipped for hazardous mountain driving. He had his cell phone
programmed for emergency calls, but transmissions were uncertain in these
mountains.

Douglas Pass topped the Bookcliff range, which stretched east from Utah
into Colorado for several hundred miles. Route 139 was a pathetic excuse for
access to the wilderness crowning the range. It looked like some drunken
cattle had moseyed up a dry creek bed, and the road crew had simply run a
steam roller over the cow paddies. One side of the roadway was always a
sheer drop-off with no shoulder and few trees to halt sliding objects.

Willard Shupe's SUV slowed as it neared the top of the pass. Brake lights
indicated he had stopped at the small parking area on the crest of the pass.
Jack pulled to the opposite side of the road, up against the body of the
mountain and stopped. This was as far as he dared drive. The rest of his
journey was going to be on foot. He checked *Snoopy*, the pistol he had taken
with him from the Army Intelligence Service. He had named it because
Navy seals had used this gun to silence vicious attack dogs in Vietnam. Its
official name had been the *Hush Puppy*. It was powerful enough to knock a
man down, yet light and easy to conceal.

God, please don't make me use this tonight, Jack thought as he glanced
up at layers of curtained snow and ice draped along the slope behind him.
One significant sound, like a gun going off, and a wall of snow could cascade
over the road. Then, collaring bribe-takers and counterfeiters would be his
least concern.

He waited a minute to see if another vehicle had tailed him as he was following Shupe. Stillness. He walked ahead, sticking to the safe side of the
slippery gravel at the shoulder of the road. When he stopped to peek around
a mammoth boulder at the edge of the road, he saw two sets of headlights
and two men gesturing in the collective spotlight.

This was not a happy reunion; Shupe and another man who towered
above him waved their arms and shouted. Jack crouched and duck-walked

toward the light, keeping close to the side of the mountain. When he was within fifty feet of the men he could pick out some of their conversation.

Shupe: "Who cares if I called you at home? I don't dare show my face back there until Hell freezes over. They're bound to suspect something after I changed my vote at the last minute. Give me the money now and I'll be out of your hair."

Big Fellow: "Don't screw with me, Shupe. You know I don't like sudden changes. I promised you half when you made the vote and the rest when the permits were issued. Don't crap out now."

Shupe: "This is too much. I'm in trouble, and you're screwing me with this shit. Give me my money now."

Jack waited for an envelope to appear. There! Big Fellow reached in his coat and pulled out something.

Three shots exploded into the blizzard. Jack ran toward the two figures, the smaller now slumping to the ground.

"Freeze! You're under arrest," he shouted, closing the distance to the big man holding the gun, who began to turn toward Jack.

At the same time, the big man shouted. "Drive, Bull!" The SUV beside him roared to life and turned, fixing Jack squarely in its bright lights, blinding him. Jack tried to shield his eyes but the damage had been done. When he looked back at the huge man, Jack was greeted by a sinister laugh. The man raised his other hand and gestured with a small box like a remote control device. With a flick of his wrist, a deafening explosion shattered the stormy night, quickly lost in the roar of rocks, ice, and snow thundering down the mountain.

Avalanche! In the split second Jack needed to turn his head and take in the awesome sight of the disaster up on the mountain, the big man had jumped into the waiting SUV and sped away back down the northern slope escaping the rumbling snow. Jack kneeled and fired at the SUV, but it was too late.

He got up to try for a better shot, but stopped in his tracks as rocks and snow slid in front of him, blocking his path. A deep rumbling noise cut off all sound as Jack looked back and up at the avalanche gaining momentum and coming straight at him. He tried to scramble back to his vehicle, but it had already been pushed over the side of the road by the immense wall of snow. He was caught in the open with only one direction to go: straight down the mountain.

He had time for one breath before the wave of snow picked him up and catapulted him out into a black void. One word screamed in his head as he tumbled with the torrent of whiteness-swim! Teeth clenched, Jack began waving and pumping his arms and legs, frantically exaggerating a swimming stroke, the recommended method for riding out an avalanche. He could see nothing and felt little as he rocketed into frozen space. All sensations were lost in a numbing freefall of whiteness. He had little chance at escape, with a hard landing guaranteed. Jack felt akin to the pilot who had climbed on top of a nuclear bomb to personally guide it to the ground in the final scene of "Dr. Strangelove." Like that crazy man, certain death seemed to await Jack as he navigated his own snowy bomb.

Like an overgrown, arctic tsunami, the monster avalanche slowed gradually and came to a rest with Jack's legs sticking straight up into the night air. He started kicking and began sliding deeper into the icy cold. He moaned. Not a good idea. Dig sideways first, then gradually turn. He tried to scrape his hands into the wall of snow. It was slow going to dig out and keep from sliding down to whatever lay below.

One more stab at the snow and the slide started all over again, only faster this time. Yet there was a God, and this one took the shape of a blue spruce that rammed sideways into Jack's waist just ten feet into the new slide. Breathless, Jack hugged the tree and hoped he could hold on until the mass of snow flowed by beneath him. He gripped ferociously with frozen and lacerated hands as the slide settled around him.

Miraculously, he saw the front bumper of the Jeep Cherokee sticking out of the snow 20 yards below him. His SUV had landed tail down and formed a perfect location finder. All Jack had to do was crawl very carefully down to it, dig his way inside and turn on the lights. Then he could use the cell phone inside to get help, if he wasn't too far down in the ravine for the signal to get through.

Jack began inching up the tree to ease his body out of the hole that had formed around him. Then, foot by foot, he worked his way down the slope. He knew that at any moment another slide could take him farther into the yawning ravine over a thousand feet deep.

Hand over hand, he crawled across the snow to reach the Jeep. Now dig, he commanded his numb hands. When he reached the front windshield, Jack realized he would have to break it to get inside. The driver's side door was crushed into the frame and probably wouldn't open. Jack stood on top of the windshield and kicked at the glass. The Jeep uttered a metallic groan and burrowed deeper into the mound of snow.

Oh great. Now what? A well-placed shot from his pistol might do the trick if he knew where it was. Saving Snoopy had not been a priority when the avalanche had buried him. What the hell, he reasoned, and jumped onto the glass with his full body weight. His six-two frame and 200 pounds of muscle did the trick. Simultaneously, the Jeep's windshield shattered and the SUV sank even deeper, disappearing down a funnel of icy snow. The Jeep stopped suddenly, lodging on the side of the slope, and Jack was sucked into a ready-made, leather-upholstered casket.

On the way in, his head nipped the top of the Jeep, knocking him out. He was unaware of the rush of snow, blanketing him with enough insulation to let him survive the night.

Hank Smithers grimaced at the destruction on route 139 the next morning. This was getting monotonous. Every week, he and his crew spent several days clearing a path through the slides going up the southern approach to Douglas Pass. But this morning was different. As the crew crunched its way to the top, pushing massive rocks and mounds of snow over the side, Hank noticed early sunlight breaking against the trees far down the ravine.

Hank raised his hand to halt the big machines. He had supervised this crew for twenty years and sunshine like this was something new.

"Hold up!" he shouted. "Look down there! Lights on the trees! Stop the tractors, now!"

All five men stepped gingerly to the side of the road and stared at the miracle down below. Although the sun was just topping the eastern slope of the pass, twin streaks of light illuminated a huge blue spruce tree in the otherwise complete darkness.

TWO

Cottonwood Estates, Front Range of the Rockies

Helen Marshall loved living in Cottonwood Estates. Each home was custom-made, and from the outside, at least, the neighborhood appeared to be idyllic. She and Jack had built their home at the end of a cul-de-sac, and their back yard disappeared into a greenbelt. It was one of the last undeveloped natural parks and wetlands on the Front Range, an environmental paradise. The greenbelt bordered the South Platte river as it snaked its way north towards Denver and the eastern Colorado plains. South of their backyard, bike paths wandered into Cromwell State Park. The park surrounded a man-made lake formed by a dam built to prevent another 500-year flood like the one in sixty-five.

Today her surroundings brought little comfort from the intense pain Helen suffered as sharp spikes pounded through her head. She watched the peaceful snowfall outside her family room window. How could it be so calm out there, she wondered. Everything inside her brain was scrambled. Ice picks stabbed against her skull.

This was the worst migraine yet. Helen had been to a neurologist. The CAT Scan had showed *extra stuff,* she'd told Jack when he had called from the Loma Medical Clinic, 15 miles west of Grand Junction. He had been plucked from his premature grave by the highway crew and taken to the nearest urgent care facility.

Jack was scratched and bruised all over, but had no broken bones and would be home in a day or so. He had told Helen to stay put. It was too treacherous to drive or fly over the Rockies in this storm. So it was Helen's turn to hurt. The two previous attacks had left her blind for hours. She knew to stay home and call for help. Soon she would be incapacitated and under covers in a dark room. Someone had to be there for her children.

Helen reached for the phone and called her good friend Martha Riddle at the Recreation Center.

"Martha, hi. This is Helen. Can you come here quickly?"

"What's up, Helen?" Martha asked.

"My head is about to come off, and I need someone to be with the kids." Suddenly, Helen felt sick. She dropped the phone, clutched her stomach and vomited. She collapsed on the kitchen floor.

"Helen! Helen!" Martha yelled frantically into the receiver.

Upstairs, Tommy Marshall picked up the extension and started to dial his buddy Andy Schmidt over on the next cul-de-sac. He heard nothing at first, then drew back the receiver from his ear as Martha shouted his mother's name a final time.

"Hello," he said to Mrs. Riddle, the neighborhood mom for all the kids. "This is Tommy, what's the matter?" But Martha Riddle had already hung up.

Tommy was scared. Something was wrong. He ran to the stairs and yelled. "Mom! Mom! Where are you?" Dead silence. Tommy ran down the stairs and skittered into the kitchen, his sock feet sliding on slick linoleum. He stopped short when he found his mother lying by the phone, very still, a trickle of saliva at the corner of her mouth. Her eyes were glazed, wide open and sightless. He knew she was dead.

Tommy automatically picked up the phone, hung up, then dialed 911. He gave out their address mechanically as he stared at his mother's inert body, afraid to look away. It was too much for the six-year old, and he began sobbing and clutching at his shirt front in a vain search for comfort.

When Martha Riddle ran into the house a few minutes later, Tommy was sitting on the floor beside Helen's body. Martha went to Tommy and hugged him, trying to turn his head away. He relaxed in her arms but continued sobbing against her shoulder. Martha could not move him from his mother's side. He had become Helen's guardian, even in death.

"Mommy, I'm hungry." Kathleen or Katie, as the family nicknamed her, wandered into the kitchen, awakened from her afternoon nap.

Martha let go of Tommy and gathered the three-year old in her arms before a permanent image of her lifeless mother could register. Martha carried Katie into the living room and called to Tommy.

"Honey, please come to me. Your sister needs you." Martha knew Tommy was proud of his protective role as Katie's big brother. He was nearly twice her size and fearless in her defense.

Tommy came immediately and sat silently beside his sister and Martha to wait for the paramedics.

•••

Several hours later, a crash awakened Becca Schmidt on the family room sofa. She was groggy at first, then realized the noise had come from the garage. Malcolm was home and probably drunk. Thank God she had decided to sleep downstairs tonight and could try to calm Malcolm before he reached her children.

"Mom, what was that noise?" Six-year-old Andy appeared at the top of the stairs, rubbing sleep from his eyes. Thankfully, Missy, his younger sister by three years, had not gotten up.

"Please go back to bed, Andy. That's just your father coming home. He probably dropped something in the garage."

"I want to see what that noise was," Andy persisted.

Andy was no dummy, Becca thought. He knows Malcolm comes home in a drunken stupor and runs over anything blocking his path. She had to get her son out of sight before Malcolm's rage started.

"Please, Andy. I mean it. Go back to bed. Your father will be angry, and I don't want you up when he comes in." Mother and son exchanged a sorrowful look. The rage was totally illogical, all-encompassing, and Malcolm's way to demand obedience. So far his actions had amounted to vile threats, shouting, and emotional abuse, all heaped on Becca. She had managed to keep the children out of it. But she knew Andy was aware of the turmoil, had been caught in the crossfire. She also knew he listened for his father's tantrums on nights like this.

"Motherfuck! Who left that goddam bicycle out there?" Malcolm shouted as he entered the house. He crashed through the door and bounced off the family room wall.

"Rebecca, where the hell are you?" He shot vicious looks around the room, not seeing anything through his drunken rage. His eyes came to a stop and focused on her.

Becca had not moved.

"I'm right here in front of you, Malcolm." She dared not say anything else until he had gotten this out of his system. She shivered under her housecoat. There were so many buttons that could set off an explosion, and she never knew which one it would be.

Malcolm tried to stand straight but wavered before her. He placed a supporting hand on the L-shaped sofa and lumbered across the room. His face became a leer, then turned nasty. He swung his right arm in a vicious arc, smashing his fist into her face. Becca's head jerked backwards, and she fell to the floor.

Malcolm circled Becca like a prizefighter taunting a victim on the canvas. He yelled, "Get up, I know you're awake. I got more to say."

Becca's head was ringing. She could not see clearly, and there was no firmness in her body. She lay boneless on the carpet, shaking, and mercifully lost consciousness.

Becca felt a coolness on her brow. Tiny hands smoothed her hair back and washed her face with a wet cloth. She opened her eyes to Andy kneeling beside her, tending her like a second in a boxing match. Her first thought was to wonder how he knew what to do. She tried to smile her thanks, but the strain hurt her face. Malcolm had never hit her before. He had threatened many times but had never gone this far.

Andy whispered frantically.

"What's wrong, mom? Please get up. He won't hurt you now. He's asleep over there." Andy pointed to Malcolm's sprawling heap on the striped sofa.

Becca stared at the miserable sight of her abusive husband. She often rested there herself, waiting for him to stagger in after a drinking binge. In that short reflection, Becca decided: the sofa would become his bed in this house, if he stayed there at all. Yes, that was her course, as years of anger filled her. She glanced at Malcolm again, and determination set in like cement. She wasn't going to leave her children. But she would no longer share her bed with her husband.

She raised herself to a sitting position, then rolled over on all fours to check her dizziness before it turned to nausea. Steadied, she used the back of a chair for leverage and pulled up to stand with Andy's help.

Like two combat veterans, mother and son wobbled arm in arm upstairs.

•••

Years before, a little boy had stared up at the gruff juvenile court judge towering behind his bench. The boy was only nine, yet this scene had become routine. Initially, he had been abandoned and turned over to county social services. Today, he would be placed in yet another foster home with another pair of well-meaning parents. But Malcolm was what the social workers called "incorrigible," and peace with a new family would last only a short time. Shorter, it seemed, with each new home.

He knew the standard lecture he would hear from each parent. "We have rules in this house, young man, and they must be obeyed." He would answer "Yes sir. Yes ma'am." And then go about dancing to another tune, one he seemed to have no control over. The longest he had lasted had been six months in one place. He wondered who would be the lucky people to deal with him this time?

There was that familiar expression again, "*Young Malcolm is incorrigible, your honor.*" The social worker had just wrapped up his life's story for the judge.

"I think I've heard enough," the judge droned in a dull monotone. "This boy needs to learn discipline. Send him to the state school in Hansford. A few years in the military academy will straighten him out."

The judge glared down at the unsmiling, emotionless face of the boy. There was no fear, no respect, no hope.

"Next case." The judge dismissed Malcolm.

For the next five years, Malcolm Schmidt learned to obey rules and to expect everyone else to do the same and without feeling. That was what Hansford Military Academy taught. Adherence to rules; no questions asked. Commandant Oleander was the supreme authority, and he used a special wooden paddle to enforce the rules.

On his fifteenth birthday, Malcolm escaped and never looked back. He neither sought help from anyone nor expected any. He was already forged into a hardened man, vowing to set his own rules.

THREE

Jack and Deputy Glen Russell watched several Grand Junction TV minicam crews standing in the hallway outside his hospital room. They were practicing their interview techniques on each other in the Loma medical clinic, waiting for Jack's attention. Jack had instructed Russell to tell them some lucky man had miraculously been saved from an avalanche on Douglas Pass. He had been brought to Loma and examined by a Dr. Michaels, who had pronounced him fit for consumption by the news teams. The Mesa County Sheriff's Department had first crack at him, though and the freshly-rouged media neophytes were forced to bide their time.

Officer Russell glanced at his watch. He had finished taping Jack's information about the shootout on Douglas Pass, and seemed ready to call it a day.

"I botched the sting, Officer Russell," Jack said from beneath a mound of blankets. "Shupe argued with the big fellow and got shot before I could reach him. I couldn't identify the man, never saw him before. Then the avalanche took over, and you know the rest."

Russell wasn't following the trail that easily. "Sir," he said, "how come a Secret Service agent is all the way out here tailing a local politico taking a bribe? Don't you guys guard the president back in Washington?"

"Yes," replied Jack, "but we also chase counterfeiters, and someone out here has been passing around phony fifties like candy. I live on the Front Range and got the assignment to check things out."

Barry, a male nurse, came to the door looking worried.

"Excuse me, Mr. Marshall, but I have an emergency call for you from someone named Martha Riddle." Barry was not smiling. Jack's heart sank. He had felt uneasy since his call to Helen earlier this morning. She had told him she wasn't feeling well; perhaps another "spell" was coming on.

"Thanks, Barry. Excuse me, Deputy." Jack reached for the bedside extension.

"Hello, Martha. What's going on?" He was chilled inside as he heard the tragic news about Helen.

"She had an aneurysm, Jack. She was gone in an instant. Tommy found her on the floor. Jack, I'm so sorry."

He sat in shock and anguish as Martha's words washed over him. This couldn't be happening. Helen was the heart and soul of their family. She was his safe harbor, one he had counted on for a dozen years. Helen made it possible for him to work in a dangerous career. Jack shuddered as his world collapsed.

He tried to speak yet could only manage a low moan. A saddened *no* kept reverberating, audible only in his mind. For the first time in his life, he shut down emotionally. His ears were ringing from the shock as Helen's death slowly seeped into his consciousness. Suddenly the sound cut off and he plummeted back to the hospital room, immediately concerned for Tommy and Katie. How could they survive this trauma?. Thank God for Martha Riddle. His thoughts kept him silent until Martha spoke again.

"I have both kids at my house. Don't worry about them, Jack. How soon can you get back here?"

Jack looked at the impatient deputy, then at the flock of budding journalists waiting to interrogate him. He hurt all over on the outside, and now a deep ache chewed at him from within.

"Soon, Martha. I'll call from the airport. Thanks for what you've done. Those kids worshipped Helen, Martha. I don't know how I'll get along without her."

"You'll be a good father to them, Jack. Like you always have. Be careful coming home."

Jack hung up and motioned Deputy Russell over.

"Deputy, my wife died this morning. I need to get out of here and back to my kids. Can you get me by that mob out there, and to the airport?" Jack nodded toward the crowd outside. Russell returned his nod grimly.

"Tell them you're taking me into custody," Jack said, "and there will be a press conference at the jail or something. Send Barry in on your way out. And thanks."

Russell left to follow his orders. When Barry came back in, Jack told him about Helen and asked for his help getting out of the hospital. Barry left quickly and returned in a few minutes with remnants of the avalanche, an armload of scruffy, torn clothes.

"Figured you'd want these, Mr. Marshall, uh, Jack. Fresh from the nursing home laundry upstairs." Barry pulled the privacy curtain around Jack's bed and helped him with the clothes. Jack struggled to dress himself and keep back tears.

"It's okay, Jack. Let it go." Barry wrapped his big arms around Jack, and the sobbing began. In a moment, Jack backed away and turned to wipe his face with a towel.

"I called Walker Field, Jack. They'll have a charter flight waiting. I'll skip the lectures about staying in bed and resting."

Outside Jack's room, cameras flashed and four local news teams beamed their questions and strobe lights in his face. Jack only shook his head and looked down. He was almost unrecognizable with two days' growth of beard, two black eyes, and a bandage encircling his head. Both hands were wrapped in bulky bandages covering slices and abrasions from his swim through the avalanche. No one noticed that Deputy Russell and Barry helped him walk down the hallway and opened the door for him, unusual gestures for someone going to jail.

"What crime are you accused of?" "Are you sorry for what you did?" "How do you feel going to jail right after your ordeal on Douglas Pass?" "How did you get caught in the avalanche?" Inane, uninformed queries bombarded him from all directions, and microphones were pushed at his face.

Barry had seen enough.

"Back off! This is still my patient and he's a sick man. Leave him alone!" Barry glowered at the youthful mob. He towered over the pathetic bunch, all hoping for a big news break to catapult them to a larger market.

Jack slipped into the back seat of the deputy's cruiser and looked back. He mouthed a thank you to Barry and turned away, praying for the strength to last all the way to the Front Range.

After calling Martha, Jack sank into the cushioned chair on the executive jet and let himself sink under a flood of memories about his twelve-year marriage. The 60-minute flight to Centennial Airport was long enough for Jack's grief to deepen as he remembered Helen. He had met her when his life was rudderless. As a young intelligence officer in Germany, he had grown bored analyzing routine message traffic about East German spy activities. His nights were spent at the local *gasthaus*, soaking up liters of warm beer. Each successive morning found him less willing to drag himself from bed and go to work. As a good friend had described it, he was in a rut and needed someone to toss a bowling ball down the middle and force him up one side or the other. Helen had rolled the ball.

She had come to Heidelberg to work as a secretary at the Headquarters of the Commander-in-Chief for European Forces. Jack met her one Monday morning as he waited to present an intelligence briefing to the Chief of Staff. One look and he forgot his meeting. She was exquisite. He lost himself in dark brown eyes that sparkled with mirth, seeing through his attempt to appear uninterested.

He gave his briefing - later not remembering a word of it - and left the conference room hoping to talk to her. Instead, her seat was occupied by an old battle ax with gray hair twisted in a bun. She fixed him with an icy stare.

"Here, Captain. She left you a message." The woman held out a small card as if it were tainted by sin.

Jack thanked her and walked down the hall to read his note in privacy. It had few words, but they were good ones: "Helen Matthews - 244-7869." He learned later that Helen had been a last-minute substitute that morning for the older woman. Funny, Jack had also been a stand-in for his commanding officer, General Bill Conley.

His first call to Helen had been rocky. No, she wasn't seeing someone else. Yes, she would like to go to dinner some night. Yes, she knew of him, and she thought some changes were in order before they met socially. He had stammered out, "What changes?" He'd barely seen her a minute, yet something told him this was important. Listen to this woman. Pay attention.

"Your appearance, Captain, suggests late nights and excessive drinking take too much of your energy."

"What do you mean?" He had asked, anxiously.

"The secretarial grapevine," she said, "reports that a certain intelligence officer is not being very smart. You're adrift, muddled, and not a particularly good catch at the moment."

The phone buzzed with silence from her end as Jack struggled to take in her sobering words.

"What, uh, what about you?" His palms were sweaty holding the phone and he swiped at his pants leg to gain a better grip. "Do you think I'm a lost cause?" He realized his words had come out in a quick frenzy of desperation.

"Oh, I'm not sure," she said coyly. "I might be willing to take a risk. Think about it and give me a call after you decide."

Jack had been shaken. This was not audacity. She had spoken with genuine concern, and there was no doubting her interest. She had told him to clean up his act. The decision was his.

No one had ever talked to him that way, not even his parents. He was stubborn, perhaps arrogant according to one close friend. He had always laughed it off. But Helen had nailed him with one look. She knew he needed something, and she had challenged him.

Not a day had passed in the last twelve years that Jack hadn't thanked Helen for saving him. She would only laugh and say he'd have snapped out of his doldrums sooner or later on his own. Jack wasn't so sure. She had been strong enough for both of them. He had come around quickly in a month-long hiatus before she agreed to a date. He had been anxious to just be with her, to soak up her vitality. Helen saw him as her own unpolished gem. She had stuck with him as if crazy glue and Velcro were part of her chemical makeup.

It was true love. The first sight, storybook kind. And the beauty of Helen's affection was that she had risked everything. She had known Jack needed to change. He saw that today on the flight back more clearly than ever.

These last few years had been tough. Her headaches were diagnosed as migraines - incorrectly, it now seemed. The CAT Scans had not picked up the blood vessel that had weakened and eventually burst. Martha told him death was immediate; the paramedics pronounced her dead at the house.

Jack tried to be stoic. An old friend's mother had died the same way. A splitting headache, vomiting, then sudden death. It would have been over quickly for Helen, and for that he was grateful. He didn't search for blame. He stared out over the ridges of the Rocky Mountains passing below, not seeing them, grieving for his wife with an ever-deepening sadness. Helen didn't deserve this. She had been too young. Their children would be devastated without her.

He did his best to remember better times, to be thankful for his good fortune to have spent twelve years with her. He remembered feeling lucky to have found her - or, in truth, for her to have found him. When the plane landed, he would hold his grief in check and be strong for Tommy and Katie. When he stepped off the jet he was determined to start healing some of the hurt in his children. He would do his very best to be a good father.

His best friend, Dave Mendes, was waiting in the airport lounge when he arrived. They had served together in the army and both settled in Denver, often working on special assignments together undercover.

They exchanged looks and greeted each other with giant bear hugs. Embraced by Dave's linebacker strength, Jack lost control and sobbed again. He gave in to the comfort of friendship and silent empathy. He had been there for Dave when his wife Kathy had lost her battle with cancer. Now they were both widowers at 37. Both were too young to have lost lifemates. He wondered how Dave had managed to deal with such crushing tragedy. Had he recovered? Or, did he mask his sorrow by throwing himself into his job? Jack didn't have that option. Tommy and Katie needed him more than ever.

"I made calls to some friends for you, Jack." Dave spoke with a husky voice, working to keep from breaking. "We can swing by Martha Riddle's and get the kids and go to my place for the night. Tomorrow is soon enough to go home."

FOUR

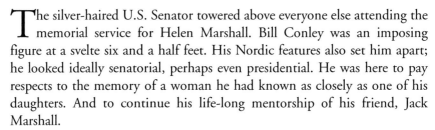

The silver-haired U.S. Senator towered above everyone else attending the memorial service for Helen Marshall. Bill Conley was an imposing figure at a svelte six and a half feet. His Nordic features also set him apart; he looked ideally senatorial, perhaps even presidential. He was here to pay respects to the memory of a woman he had known as closely as one of his daughters. And to continue his life-long mentorship of his friend, Jack Marshall.

Senator Conley fondly remembered his days as the Army's so-called "master spy" in Europe. In the closing days of the cold war, General Conley had recruited a brash Captain Jack Marshall from the dull administrivia of army life. He had needed someone with guts to work behind the East German border retrieving records about the spy network the Soviets had established throughout Europe. Captain Marshall came to his attention when the word spread that he had become an excellent intelligence analyst. General Conley discovered that Helen had been the catalyst.

He plucked Jack from obscurity and almost threw him over the Berlin wall. Time was running out, and he needed Marshall in place quickly. After months of silence, Conley tossed another agent across the line. This time Captain Dave Mendes got the call. Again, silence.

General Conley had given up on ever seeing the young officers again until one day his secretary appeared at his office door. She was grinning like she had won a prize.

"Excuse me, general." Betty almost giggled before continuing. "There are some characters out here to see you, and they look pretty scruffy."

Sensing something was out of kilter, General Conley had replied, "By all means, Betty, send the, uh, gentlemen in."

Two of the dirtiest people in the European military theater walked into his office and saluted. One was well over six feet tall and vaguely resembled Jack Marshall. The other fellow had obviously crawled through a sewer, and had the build of a linebacker. He was shorter, about medium height, but filled the doorway as he entered. That had to be Dave Mendes. They had been dressed as chimney sweeps, an occupation highly respected in Europe. Their stovepipe hats were crushed in around the sides. U.S. Army combat fatigues had been dyed black, and the pants were pulled out of airborne boots as a means of carrying off their costuming facade. The dirt had been real and particles of dust and mud quickly decorated the office carpeting.

Their American soldier status was further disguised by several months' growth of scraggly beard. Marshall had developed a rat tail of hair down to the nape of his neck. Mendes' hair sprouted wildly from beneath his hat. Each man held the typical broomstick covered in chimney soot. Soon though, a terrible stench wafted into the office as the air currents passing the two officers carried to the general and his secretary. Betty backed out of the room holding her nose and waving her other hand in the air to swoosh away the foul odor.

"Sir," Captain Marshall said, "we have the information you requested. Just don't ask how we did it." He tossed a roll of film on Conley's desk. "That's a breakdown of their entire network with names, code names, and locations."

"Gentlemen," Conley had begun to reply, but his air gave out, and his eyes were beginning to water from the overwhelming stench. Gasping for breath, the general had managed to say, "Good work. Get cleaned up and report back in the morning," before he ran out in the hall for air.

When he had recovered, Bill Conley found two distinct piles of dust and dirt on his office floor and a faint trail leading back to the hallway. Betty had opened the windows, but she still held a handkerchief to her nose.

Senator Bill Conley met with his two friends after the service. He had groomed Dave and Jack to be good officers and had watched each lose his wife. Dave Mendes had overcome his grief to become one of the best anti-drug task force leaders in the country while earning his law degree at night. Family was not a consideration for Dave, due to fear of losing again what he had loved so much. His job was hardly a safe one either.

Bill Conley studied the bleary eyes of Jack Marshall closely and noted a glimmer of determination buried in the man's deep sorrow. He knew Jack would put his children first now. After all, he had drilled into Jack's head the need to be close and bond early with his kids. The retired Major General knew first hand what it took to be a dad and a career man. His wife Elizabeth had delivered five beautiful babies with him right beside her. He had fought hospital administrators, doctors, and nurses for his right to be with her during delivery decades before it became common practice.

Only hours after hearing of Helen's death, Bill Conley had contacted some friends in the Secret Service. He was going to make it easy for Jack to be a full-time dad while continuing to work as an undercover agent. He owed Jack this helping hand, just as Jack had come through for him during their service together in West Germany.

Bill Conley reached out a big hand to grip Jack's shoulder firmly. In the eyes of his protégé he was gratified to note a strength of character that surpassed even this enormous grief.

"Jack, I called in a few favors." A flare of anger lit up Jack's face at the senator's words. He had always bristled at the thought of someone managing his life, and he was still a stubborn mule, Conley thought.

"No. Wait and hear me out. Whether you recognize it or not, this is a time to retreat and regroup. Take some time to set up a routine with those kids and forget about your job. It'll be there when you're ready to come back."

"General, I can't do this work anymore. I appreciate the favors, but I have my kids to consider, and I have to figure out how to run a household. Then there's that jackass Strothers bugging me about following up on the quote-unquote blown assignment on Douglas Pass. I told him to stuff it and resigned yesterday."

"I personally tore up that resignation, Jack. I also tore Strothers another asshole. He won't bother you again. Now, here's the deal: call me in thirty days, no sooner, and we'll talk. If you want more time, you'll get it."

"But, Bill," Jack's voice broke, "I can't travel anymore. Tommy is six, and Katie is only three. They need me here." Jack's frustration was clearly about to boil over.

"Hold on, Jack. I envision your working right out of the house, with minimal time away from the kids. Colorado has become an international state right smack in the middle of the country. There are crimes being committed here that you can solve for us, simply by being in place and doing some analytical work. That's all I'll say for now. Concentrate on those kids and reach out to your friends here."

The big man gave Jack one of the confident smiles that had won him reelection. His independence and honesty had gained the attention of both political parties. He was a strong force in the Senate, and getting steadily stronger. Some had suggested he might be the man to snap the country out of its leadership malaise. But Bill Conley was an avowed independent, though a strange one who could form coalitions across the political spectrum and still maintain his statesman-like qualities. A rare combination.

Jack watched his good friend and mentor say his good-byes. The senator gathered Elizabeth close to his side as if he were protecting a precious gift. He opened the car door for his wife. It was a long drive to their home in Colorado Springs, but the car was barely away from the curb before Elizabeth scooted across the bench seat close to her husband. It was a bittersweet scene for Jack. Senator Bill Conley had shown by example how to be a strong yet caring and sensitive man. His close friends knew that his wife was his foundation. Now Jack faced life without that foundation, and he shuddered in his loss.

FIVE

Always true to his word, Senator Conley had helped smooth the way for the newly widowed secret agent. Henry Strothers backed off immediately with the threat of a transfer to a distant, cold environment. Jack discovered his assignments were mostly routine analysis and short-term stakeouts the first few months after he returned to work. He was able to drop Katie off at her play group and get his field work done easily. He could then write up his reports on his new computer at home and transmit then electronically.

Managing the housekeeping was another matter. After several months of waiting for repairmen to show up on time, learning to cook something besides pasta, and keeping his multiple phone lines straight, Jack had settled into a routine.

He was still working to smooth out some rough edges. For example, he had forgotten to bring a dish to the potluck PTA meeting last Tuesday night. He had gotten several nasty looks when he went back for seconds, but hey, the food was good and he had apologized for his lapse. As penance, he had volunteered to lead a field trip to Rockhill Park this Saturday.

Katie missed her mother, but she was overjoyed to have Jack in the house with her most days. Her daytime play group suited her just fine, and she had made several new friends. As long as she could crawl into bed with him when she couldn't sleep, she was okay.

Tommy was another matter. He was at an age where his mom had been his idol and he was furious with her for dying. No amount of hugs and playtime could staunch his misery and anger. He had nightmares regularly, most centered on the trauma of finding his mother on the kitchen floor. The doctor prescribed lots of loving and a commitment by Jack to be there. Tommy needed time to heal.

When Jack thought about himself, he was miserable. Dave Mendes came by often, and Martha Riddle was a savior. At 55, Martha was like a grandmother to his kids and a second mother to him. Both Dave and Martha tried to keep his spirits up and assured him the pain would fade someday. He heard them, but most of the time his mind and heart replayed the same lonely thoughts of the perfect mate gone forever. He tried to get outside and take walks through the neighborhood to get over his lethargy and despair. He was fine until he passed young couples holding hands, smiling. How could they be happy? Why wasn't the rest of the world sad like him?

Tonight Jack tossed around in his king-sized bed for an hour before he gave up and went downstairs. He turned on the TV to distract his mind away from the depression and loneliness weighing down on him. He shuffled into the kitchen like a man twice his age to look for something to eat, but as usual, when he opened the door to the fridge nothing appealed to him. He had no appetite, no energy, no enthusiasm. He could not remember times in his life when he hadn't been sad.

Mealtimes had become a drag. Three dreary souls sat around a table meant for a family of four. No one spoke. Finally, the kids had drifted in front of the TV to eat. Jack had let the custom start in spite of his unspoken desire to throw the set out the back door.

Now he sat down to watch TV, but soon turned it off. There was too much lovey-dovey kissing and hand-holding. He sat in the dark, thinking. His doctor had diagnosed mild depression. It would go away with time, and participating in activities with his children was supposed to help. He also needed to reach out to adults and make friends.

Long and dreary winter weather followed by a tumultuous Rocky Mountain spring hadn't helped. It was either too cold or too wet to go outside. None of them had the heart for it. Somewhere within his soul, Jack had to find the strength to pull out of this morass. His children saw his sadness and emulated him perfectly. Like Scarlet O'Hara, he kept saying he would worry about it tomorrow.

The entire week had been clear and sunny. Daytime temperatures had soared into the mid sixties. Trees had a greenish tint at their edges and a few daffodils had broken through the ground with bright yellow blossoms. Stray bushes of blooming forsythia peppered the yards in his cul-de-sac. Even the iceberg along the gutter in front of their house had begun to thaw, making it possible for a visitor to get out of a car without risking a broken leg. Also, wonder of wonders, just yesterday a street sweeper had been spotted working its way into the southwestern suburbs of Madison County, cleaning up the mounds of sand and gravel used to fight winter's snow and ice.

Well, old buddy, Jack Marshall's tomorrow was now. There were no more excuses. There was no better time to break out of the doldrums, snap out of this blue funk, get his act together, or whatever cliché seemed to fit best. By golly, he was determined to fight his way out of this putrid state of mind.

Saturday came with a bright blue Colorado sky and brilliant, therapeutic sunshine.

"Let's go, let's go. Everybody up," shouted Jack as he roused his drowsy children from their beds. "I got special pancakes ready to be eaten downstairs, with bacon on the way. Up, up!"

Jack set out some jeans and a pullover sweatshirt for Katie alongside her new hiking boots. Then he wrestled her out of the cocoon she had burrowed into the bottom of the bed trying to gain another five minutes sleep. He gazed at his daughter with a mixture of love, admiration, and wistfulness. She reminded him so much of her mother. Her frizzy red curls seemed to sprout in every direction as she rubbed the sleep from her green eyes. Her eyes, it seemed to Jack, were the only sign of his parentage. Katie was slender, soft, and sensitive, like a little girl should be. She was curious beyond belief and into everything that wasn't nailed down. This morning her curls settled around her ears, and Jack felt a pang of grief hit him in the gut. Katie's ears, like Helen's, always flopped out of her hair and away from her head. Jack thought it looked cute, but realized that Katie, like her mother, would eventually rue the day she first looked in a mirror and saw those big ears.

In Tommy's room Jack found his son sitting in the window seat angrily staring out at nothing, refusing to get dressed. Tommy was big for his age, like Jack had been. He was already growing out of the chubbiness that had marked his body until earlier this year. Tommy would be bigger than Jack and weigh more too. Probably had some of Helen's father in him. He'd be big around the chest, yet have long and strong legs like Jack. He wanted to play nose tackle on the football team, but Jack hoped he would gravitate to wide receiver as his body gained some of Jack's leanness.

Tommy had Jack's reddish-brown hair clipped short, almost like a crewcut. He had inherited deep brown eyes from Helen, and today they almost unraveled Jack's resolve to yank his family out of its despair.

Tommy wore his emotions on his sleeve and blurted out his feelings.

"I'm not going," he huffed in a snit. "I'm not interested in a silly old hike to look at flowers. That's sissy stuff. You can't make me do it." Tommy crossed his arms defiantly, as if daring his father to attempt to handle him.

Jack stopped his whirlwind schedule and kneeled in front of his angry son.

"Tommy, I know you don't feel like it. I don't either, but we can't sit inside all year and feel sorry for ourselves." A tear rolled out of the corner of his son's eye. "Your school buddies will be there, including Andy Schmidt. They'll miss you if you don't show up."

"No they won't. They just feel sorry for me because I don't have a mom anymore." Tommy turned his head to hide more tears welling up in his eyes.

Jack pulled his son into his arms. He let Tommy cry it out, then stood him beside the bed and left the room.

Miraculously, five minutes later the revitalized family of three was settled around the kitchen table devouring Jack's specialty pancakes. No one noticed that there was too much baking soda again, or that he had missed a few lumps when stirring the batter. Heck, Jack figured, that's what syrup was for, to cover stuff up and make it taste good.

This had been one of their best meals in months, but the jangling phone interrupted the tranquillity.

"Hello," Jack answered cheerfully. "Oh, hi, Martha. What's up?"

"Jack, are you coming or not? The entire group is out here in the park waiting for you to lead them. Did you forget the time?" Martha sounded perplexed, yet sympathetic. She seemed to understand that Jack was struggling with his new role of single dad and homemaker.

"Ohmygosh!" he said, barely stifling a curse. Jack glanced at the kitchen clock and stood up quickly. In his efforts to comfort Tommy and get everyone to the table, he had forgotten his schedule altogether. They should have left a half hour ago.

"Sorry, Martha. We'll be right there. Don't leave without us." He threw the phone down and looked at his two hiking buddies, syrup dripping from fingers and mouths.

"We're late, gang. Wash up and let's hit the road." For once he got an immediate response, as both kids dashed to the bathroom to clean up.

Within fifteen minutes the Marshall family pulled into the parking lot at Rockhill Park and got out to join their hiking group. Jack was greeted by a mixture of smiling, sympathetic parents along with frowns from some who had grown tired of his always being late and unprepared.

Tommy and Katie left him immediately to join Andy and Missy Schmidt, who were there with their mom. Jack felt relief. Being on call 24 hours a day was tough, and playmates gave him some respite.

Martha Riddle came over to him. Jack fought to appear happy to be there.

"You're improving, young man." Martha said. In another month or so this will be old hat, and you'll be the one out here waiting for the rest of us. Uh, by the way, are those new boots I see on Katie?"

"Yeah, picked them up yesterday on sale. Just her size and half off." Jack was proud of his growing knack of checking out bargains and anticipating the kids' needs.

Martha winced. "Just watch out for her, Jack. This is a two-mile trek down the lower loop of the park and back. The return stretch is all uphill, and those new boots might cause her some trouble with blisters."

"Just when I thought I was getting in a groove. I may end up carrying her back."

"Well, the lunch break will give her a chance to rest her feet some. What did you bring to eat?"

Jack turned red. He hadn't packed a lunch and had forgotten to bring water. He turned away from his friend and raised his hands to the sky, then slapped them on the top of his head.

"Damn. Damn," he muttered. Another screw-up.

"It's okay, Jack. I brought enough to feed an army, plus plenty of water."

Jack broke out into a sheepish grin, then a smile, and finally he laughed so loud the rest of the group turned to stare.

"Marry me, Martha," he said jokingly. "What would I do without you." Then he gave her a big hug and kissed her on the cheek.

"Get away from me you big oaf," Martha chortled and pushed him away. "You're too young for me."

Jack looked over to Tommy and Katie, who both gaped bug-eyed at the scene he had created with Martha. He hoisted Martha's bulky backpack and went over to his suspicious kids.

"We're just having fun and kidding around, gang. Let's get going." Thankfully, they shook off the incident and plodded after their father to begin the hike.

Indian paint brush, blue bells, and columbines sprinkled the sides of the pathway with a profusion of bright colors. The background of red sandstone monoliths gave stark contrast to the new growth. Part of the *new* Rockies that once towered over 40,000 feet in altitude, the red rocks all seemed to tilt backwards to the west. Time, wind and water had reduced them to these miniature formations. Crevasses opened at odd spots where porous sediment had washed down to nearby creek beds in earlier times. Thickets of scrub oak promised a sighting of white tail deer. There were no clouds, only bright blue sky and crisp air.

Jack strolled along, admiring the scenery and enjoying his day out. He needed the sun and fresh air to cleanse the grief from his system. He could never forget Helen, but Lord, he sure needed to move on with his life. Today seemed a perfect time to start over. He stretched out his long legs and picked up the pace, beginning to feel more human.

"Mr. Marshall? Jack? Could you please slow down a minute?" Jack snapped out of his reverie at the sound of a melodious voice behind him. It purred with a softness that reminded him of fine silk chocolate. He turned to find Becca Schmidt five yards behind him, rushing to catch up. The rest of the hiking group was another fifty yards behind her. Jack realized he had daydreamed his way beyond the range of the group.

Becca was carrying Missy and Katie under her arms like two sacks of pinto beans. She was out of breath and struggling to catch him.

"I'm sorry, Mrs. Schmidt - Becca. I kind of lost myself out here in the fresh air and took off."

"You lost the rest of us," she huffed. "You started walking faster and faster. Pretty soon Katie complained that her feet hurt, so I picked her up. Then Missy wanted a ride, and now I'm done in carrying them. It's your turn." She unloaded the two cherubs and sat down on a park bench to rest. Missy and Katie automatically jumped in Jack's lap when he sat beside her.

"I'm sorry, Becca. I'll gladly take over." Jack watched her from the side as she looked away to some unseen point up the ridge. She gave no response. Apparently she had slipped into her own daydream.

Becca Schmidt was a very attractive woman. That is, what little Jack could see of her was very attractive, but some imagination was required. Perhaps that's what intrigued him. She wore huge, black-framed sunglasses that covered most of her face from the nose up. Still, he could see a finely sculpted face and full, luscious lips that kept his attention. Her rich, coal-black hair was hidden under a tightly-wound scarf. Only a few velvety strands had escaped. She wore no makeup, and her mouth was set in a grim frown that bore no optimism. She had on baggy pants and a jacket that gave few hints of shape or proportion, yet Jack pictured soft curves on a slender frame.

Jack was definitely intrigued, and not just by Becca's beauty. She seemed weighed down, troubled in a way he found familiar. Jack caught himself staring, but Becca ignored his perusal. Finally she nodded her head at him, got up, and continued hiking, leaving Jack to tote the two giggly girls the rest of the way.

There goes another story, he thought. A real deep one. He realized he was concerned about her, and that was new to him after months dwelling on nothing but his own sadness.

SIX

Three Years Later

The Cottonwood Estates neighborhood was part of a bedroom community southwest of Denver. It had no city limits, no police force, no city hall or courts. Fire protection came from a special district taxing authority managed out of Fullerton to the east. Police services were provided by Madison County and managed out of Taylor City, the county seat 20 miles northwest.

The school district was a jumble of administrative levels. As new residents came through the neighborhood searching for a home, Realtors proudly showed them huge vacant lots developers had earmarked for new schools. Parents beamed at each other when they saw the potential building sites.

They had yet to learn about bond issues defeated annually by conservative voters in other parts of the county.

Decided character flaws detracted from the neighborhood, yet, the Cottonwood Estates Recreation Center made up for them by acting as the heart and soul of the community. Fact was, most residents thought of Martha Riddle, Center Director, as their leader. Whatever fell through the cracks, Martha fixed.

One summer, litter had crept out of the gutters surrounding the perimeter of the Estates. Martha got tired of driving by the unsightly mess. She also got tired of calling the county to have the trash picked up. So, she advertised summer jobs and hired two teenagers to clean it up.

Martha's empire consisted of all parks and recreation facilities in a five-square-mile area. She oversaw an Olympic-size pool, tennis courts scattered around the neighborhood, and several parks containing soccer and baseball fields. Lotto money had been used to build picnic shelters and bike paths. When it was added up, Martha Riddle managed the largest collection of parks in the county.

The center of activity in her empire was the pool. Every summer she hired lifeguards from the Swordfish swim team that practiced and competed in her pool. In turn, the older Swordfish swimmers gave inexpensive swimming lessons to the younger kids.

Martha gathered many kids around her and loved them all. They were all substitutes, she knew, for her son Jason. He had been killed by a drunk driver 15 years ago. Ever since, Martha had worked 16-hour days making life nicer for other kids.

She had to be a tough lady at times, but all the kids thought of her as their second mom. As a result, Martha heard many stories of real home life in Cottonwood Estates. She knew who got a promotion and who got fired. She was aware of drinking problems and absentee parents who dropped their kids at her pool, expecting Martha to watch them. She also had a pretty good gauge on general happiness. People smiled or frowned, laughed or shrank back from view. She saw everything.

Priscilla Huff pulled up to the one-story pool house and parked her mammoth SUV. She entered the building and saw an older woman - she appeared to be a clerk of sorts - fretting over a printout.

"Darn it, where does the money go?" Martha muttered, not realizing she had an audience. "How can we spend $200 for lawn fertilizer in January? Why do we need $125 worth of pool cleaner now? We don't use it until May."

To Priscilla the harried bookkeeper seemed a grandmotherly woman, probably in her late 50s, with blonde curls succumbing to gray. Pencils poked out of her frizzy cap of hair like darts in a board. Somewhere on the top of her head, bifocals were entangled, impossible to use until all the pencils were removed.

Martha sat back in her chair, looked up and saw Priscilla.

"Oh! Why hello. Can I help you?" Her glower changed quickly into the friendliest face in town.

"Yes, I'd like to speak to the manager about joining the recreation district." Priscilla used an official voice. "My husband Orson and I have just moved in down the street with our daughter Sharon. Our next door neighbor advised us to stop by the Center first thing."

Martha read her right away. Here was another upwardly mobile professional mother hoping to bypass this clerk and deal with the top man.

"Well, you've come to the right place. I'm Martha Riddle." Martha came around her desk to the waist-high counter and held out her hand. When there was no response, Martha continued with her routine spiel. "I run the center. Would you like to pay your fees now?" She reached for her receipt book. At this early hour the kids were in school and she had all her jobs under her belt. Her office staff of 25 part-timers came and went freely, and no one knew quite how Martha kept track of their time and pay.

Priscilla looked skeptical and appeared uncertain of her next move.

"Could you tell me about the recreation programs you have and the education and training certifications of the instructors.

"Come over here and I'll explain what we have." Martha guided Priscilla behind the counter, around boxes of office supplies and file cabinets set at odd angles. Martha stopped before a large map of the neighborhood tacked to a bulletin board.

"I apologize for the mess, but my cleaning crew won't be in until after track practice." Martha pointed to the map. "We're here in the poolhouse, which holds my office, locker rooms for the swimmers, and a concession stand during the summer. Right outside is the big pool. Next door is the main park with playground and open fields for football, soccer, and softball practices. See right over there in the corner? That's the first set of tennis courts. About three blocks south of here is Blue Heron Park, where we have four baseball fields, two soccer fields, some small bleachers set up for spectators, 16 tennis courts, and several shelters for picnics and meetings. These other green splotches on the map are parks with mainly open space we haven't developed yet."

Martha let this information sink in as she noticed the surprised look on the young woman's face. As yet she hadn't offered a name. The tall, slender woman seemed taken aback. She would have been attractive if not for her dour expression and air of skepticism.

"Beside the map is a chart of neighborhood sports associations that operate from this building. We have football, soccer, swimming - last summer's state champions - baseball, and just about any other sport you could ask for. As for training and certification, you'll have to ask each organization. Everything runs off volunteers. Parents work afternoons, evenings and weekends to make all this happen. I just sort of sit on top of it and pay the bills."

"I'm sorry." the young woman seemed to remember her manners. "My name is Priscilla Huff. We just moved here from Baltimore. My six-year old daughter, Sharon, is interested in playing soccer and needs to learn how to swim. How much will all that cost?"

"Family membership is $100 a season. That covers use of the pool, tennis courts, and all the parks. Each association has small fees, mostly to cover costs of leasing fields for their games. If you join the center, you'll have another $50 fee for the swim team and $15 for the soccer association. Swim lessons are $6 each, and they're taught by certified lifeguards, usually seniors on the swim team." Martha could tell the prim young mother was debating what to do.

"What if we don't like it and want our money back?" Priscilla seemed intent on demanding options, as if she were negotiating a contract for buying a sports franchise.

"Fine with me," Martha replied. "But I suggest you ask around the neighborhood first before you commit to the fees for membership." Martha knew this woman would back out as soon as she felt her daughter was not being properly *trained*. She had seen dozens of over-protective parents who expected little Johnny to be a future Olympic star. They demanded better coaching. Some even tried to get the volunteer coach fired if he didn't play their child more often. Many of those parents had never played a sport competitively, yet they expected their child to be the best, to excel, to win.

"I'll discuss this with my husband." Priscilla turned and left.

Martha watched her leave and worried. More and more parents expected to pay for professional services without contributing the most important element, themselves. There was a corps of parents, just under ten percent of the total, who ran everything, volunteered all the time. They were dependable, committed, and wanted nothing more than to see their children participate. Winning was nice, but it was icing on the cake. Learning sportsmanship and how to get along was more important.

Martha felt a tug on her heart for Sharon Huff. She didn't even know the child and already felt lonely for her.

SEVEN

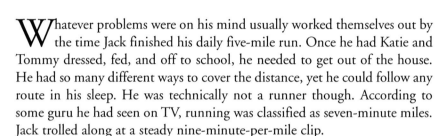

Whatever problems were on his mind usually worked themselves out by the time Jack finished his daily five-mile run. Once he had Katie and Tommy dressed, fed, and off to school, he needed to get out of the house. He had so many different ways to cover the distance, yet he could follow any route in his sleep. He was technically not a runner though. According to some guru he had seen on TV, running was classified as seven-minute miles. Jack trolled along at a steady nine-minute-per-mile clip.

He was in great shape from the daily runs and visits to the health club over on Copperhill Road. He was the same size he had been in the army 20 years prior - "A lean, mean fighting machine" - only not quite as agile. The knees creaked occasionally, but he was addicted to his jaunts around the neighborhood. He knew he could load a problem into his subconscious and have it solved before two miles were up. He didn't care how this happened. It just did.

Jack never remembered running while his brain was chugging away on his latest dilemma. He moved on auto pilot, and less than a quarter mile down the street his mind would click into super overdrive. Thoughts swirled with options, answers, strategies, details, diplomacy, scripts for conversations, on and on. His gray matter sifted through information at warp speed until he stopped running a few hundred yards from his front door to cool down. Supernaturally, he felt, answers came to him. His mind had taken over like a computer's central processor and worked through whatever was bothering him. The same thing happened in the shower, minus the sweat.

After a run, Jack's next step was to rush into the house to write everything down. About 99 percent of the time, his initial gut reaction matched the answer generated by the running. He called it his internal feedback mechanism. He had yet to develop the requisite government acronym for it. It just worked.

For the three years since Helen's death, Jack had run every day. He guessed at a total of roughly 5,500 miles and a dozen pairs of running shoes. People all over the neighborhood saw him and waved. Jack waved back but didn't know half their names. He also didn't know that he had created an anonymous society of housewives and divorcees who secretly coveted his body. Many of them managed to find yard work to do when he was scheduled to pass by their houses. Some took out the trash in increments each day, others pulled weeds along the sidewalk. Most wore halter tops and short shorts in the summer. A lucky few were positioned near the end of his trek and could actually converse with him while he walked the last quarter mile home.

Jack was oblivious to the covetous glances and occasionally obvious come-ons. He had no idea that he could get into bed with several women each morning, wives who were left to cook and clean while their workaholic husbands toiled 15 miles away, 60 to 80 hours a week, and their children were in school. Opportunity was rampant but unseen. Jack thought only about his kids, his job, what to cook for dinner, and doing the laundry.

Once he had stopped to talk to a middle-aged mother because he smelled something scrumptious cooking near her house. "Ummm, yummy," he exclaimed to her. The woman wilted on the spot and was about to invite him inside. "Can I have the recipe?" he asked. Her tongue was tied, and she could only nod. Fortunately, Jack said he would pick up the recipe in the morning on his next run, and she was saved more embarrassment. Still, she had waited until everyone was out of the house the next day before showering and dressing in her most provocative shorts and a top tied in a slip knot just below her breasts. But Jack had taken another course that day, forgetting completely about her recipe.

Those lucky enough to speak to Jack during his cool-down focused at first on his green eyes and reddish-brown hair. A few stole glances at heavily-muscled shoulders and arms, or those legs that seemed like hairy tree trunks.

Jack Marshall was an anomaly, partly because he was above average in looks and build, but mainly because he was just there, the only single male in the neighborhood during regular working hours. He was a single dad who stayed at home - doing what, nobody knew. He cooked, cleaned, did laundry, attended PTA meetings and always found time to be with his kids doing something. He was part of that ten percent who volunteered to coach, time swimmers, referee games, or whatever it took to make the community work. And to many women, he was a mystery they craved to unravel.

As he ran today, Jack concentrated on Katie, his six-year-old child prodigy. She was more than a handful. Her behavior had been atrocious before Helen's death, so Jack wasn't searching that trauma for an answer. Katie had always been unmanageable. Every teacher had complained about her lack of attention. Jack found himself being called into meetings to explain why his daughter was such a holy terror.

Finally, his pediatrician had recommended Ritalin, a drug successfully used to treat hyperactive kids like Katie. It had turned her to mush within a few days, and Jack had thrown the bottle of pills away. Back to the doctor's he went, dragging Katie with him.

"Okay, Jack. Let's try something else," Dr. Vasquez had said. He watched little Katie scamper around his examining room, touching everything, opening drawers and taking out whatever was in them. He and Jack exchanged a look of concern.

"Let's do an evaluation, Jack. Maybe that will give us some answers."

"What's an evaluation, Doc?" Jack was at the end of his rope, dangling without a clue.

"We'll schedule an appointment with a team - a medical doctor, a nurse, a social worker, a psychologist, and a psychiatrist. Each of them will spend time with Katie. They'll observe her and have her try some tests to determine aptitude, interests, IQ. They'll also talk to you about her family life. Afterward, you'll get written and oral reports on their findings and recommendations." Dr. Vasquez reached out his hand and grasped Jack's arm. "Don't worry, my friend. Katie will come out of this unscathed and you might finally get some answers."

Jack was still struggling to implement the evaluation team's recommendations. Yes, he had a real prize in Kathleen Mary Marshall. At four, when the evaluation took place, she could read at fifth grade level. At six, she was writing essays and poetry in a journal she kept beside her bed. Her IQ had tested at just this side of super bright, well above genius but in a comfortable zone that left her capable of communicating with normal human beings. Some super bright people, he had been told, needed an interpreter or buffer between themselves and the rest of the world.

Katie was interested in everything, which was the source of her behavior problems. She might see a picture across the room and head towards it, but on the way she would be attracted to so many other things that she would lose focus and get into mischief. In preschool and kindergarten she had been so bored that her teachers would often find her asleep on the floor in the back of the room. She learned the lesson ten times faster than the average child, got bored, and simply wandered off for a nap.

The evaluation team had prescribed getting her into outside activities and keeping her busy. They thought perhaps she would find one special talent she liked and concentrate her energies there. Finding playmates had been a chore, but Jack had discovered a play group through Martha's help. That had worked during the summer and when Katie didn't have some class or school to attend. Lately she had spent a lot of time listening to CDs on his stereo, especially new wave jazz. Jack had begun searching for a music teacher in the neighborhood. He had also signed her up for beginning soccer with the Cottonwood Estates Soccer Association, or CESA. Jack had never played soccer and was curious about the game. As a college football player he had considered soccer a rather puny sport.

Today his run gave him no new answers. Yet he also felt good about what he was doing for Katie. It was hard to go wrong with music and sports.

That night Jack was working on a spreadsheet analysis of counterfeit money that had been reported along the Front Range. Henry Strothers, his official supervisor in the Denver area, thought his reports "looked" more professional if they contained a spreadsheet. It was one of Jack's home office duties to collect reports from field agents and compile them into a more formal report for Strothers. It was boring stuff, but kept him near his kids. The phone rang, breaking his concentration.

"Hello," he answered in a neutral voice.

"This is James Craig from the Soccer Association calling. Could I speak to Jack Marshall, please?"

"You got him, what's going on?"

"Well, er, Mr. Marshall, I see you registered your daughter Kathleen for spring soccer. Is that correct, sir?"

"That I did, Mr. Craig. Are you going to be her coach? When does practice start? Sounds like an interesting game with six kids running around on a half-size field chasing a ball into a net." Jack chuckled as the image of six Katies came into his mind, all of them trying to kick the ball at the same time. Boy, what a job it must be to coach a bunch of active little girls. He didn't know whether to respect or pity the man in charge of such chaos.

"Actually, Mr. Marshall, I had hoped to talk you into becoming the coach." Craig hurried on before Jack could decline. "You see, Mr. Marshall, we run this association on the good will of volunteers like yourself. Each team has to supply its own coach, assistant coaches, a referee, and a team mother. Without these volunteers, the team can't be allowed to participate. The children won't be able to play. See what I mean?"

Somehow, in the back of his mind, Jack had expected this to happen. The ten-percenters in the neighborhood were stretched thin at this time of year. Parents were coaching softball, baseball, swimming, hiking, you name it. Whatever folks wanted to do, Martha Riddle got someone to start a team and the activity would catch hold because of the ten-percenters. Jack had never coached his daughter, and his number was up.

"Okay." Jack replied.

"Wha, what did you say, sir?" Craig's voice sounded stunned over the phone.

"Please call me Jack, and I said okay. You can count on me. I coached Tommy's football team last fall, so I'll give this a try. But I don't know the first thing about soccer. Played football though, if that'll help," he added. "You'll have to tell me what to do step by step, Jim. But, I'll give it a shot." Jack heard a sigh of relief over the phone line.

"That's the easy part, Jack. Just call a team meeting of all parents and get them to volunteer for the other positions. Once they see you're the coach, they all relax and do what it takes to make the team a success. You may have some difficulty finding a referee, but you have several weeks to figure that one out."

"Maybe you didn't catch on to the part about not knowing a thing about soccer, Jim. How do I learn what to do?"

"We have coaching clinics starting this weekend. Drop by the poolhouse, and Martha will have a coach's packet for you with a list of team members and phone numbers. Our schedule is in there too. Say, thanks again, Jack. Got to go now. See ya."

The line buzzed as Jack sputtered further questions. Apparently Craig had hung up to pursue his next victim.

EIGHT

There was no play group this afternoon and Katie had time on her hands. Time to curl up in bed and add to her journal. She didn't know if other little girls did this sort of thing, but Katie needed to talk to her mom. Since she couldn't really talk to her, Katie wrote letters to her in her journal.

Dear Mom. It is starting to look like spring. We have some flowers in the yard. Tommy is mean sometimes. I try to ignore him. Dad signed me up for soccer. All the parents are coming here tonight so he can get help. I want my best friend Missy to be on my team too. Dad says she will be. Her mom is so pretty and lonely. She looks sad a lot. She lets me play her piano when I go over to Missy's house. We have fun. Mom, I love you. Tommy and dad don't say much, but I know they miss you too.
Love, Katie.

She couldn't tell her mother how badly the kids treated her because she was smarter. Katie also couldn't write about waking up scared and crawling into her father's bed for comfort. Tommy really was mean sometimes, but he also looked after her and made sure the neighborhood kids didn't pick on her when he was around.

She knew she was different. Other children her age were just learning to print the letters of the alphabet and write simple sentences. Katie wrote long letters to her mom and to Missy. More and more she was finding it easier to hide her intelligence and not raise her hand to answer every question. It just caused too much trouble. Sometimes she would lie and tell her friends that she had missed questions on the simple tests they were given.

Her dad always asked her how she felt about things, and her answer was always a happy one. He had too many other things to worry about, and she figured she had caused him too much trouble already.

NINE

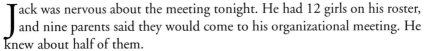

Jack was nervous about the meeting tonight. He had 12 girls on his roster, and nine parents said they would come to his organizational meeting. He knew about half of them.

Roger Hamilton lived down the street. His little girl Susan came up to play with Katie sometimes. Jack remembered her, because she wouldn't eat any candy or drink a soda when Katie offered them to her. Still, she played on the jungle gym he had put together in the backyard and looked like a potential soccer player.

Becca Schmidt had reluctantly agreed to come, if the meeting didn't last too long. Her husband was known in the neighborhood as a stickler for routine, and he expected her to be there when he got home from work.

Jack's roster included one new family. Priscilla and Orson Huff had signed up their daughter, Sharon. They were both coming. They had also let him know over the phone that they wanted some answers about soccer training, rules, and so on. Jack hadn't a clue what to tell them.

He had mentioned to each parent that he needed volunteers and had been greeted with silence. All were noncommittal except Gloria Ashworth. She came on strong over the phone and even began to flirt with him. Perhaps she could be the team mother if she was going to be that outgoing. Their whole conversation puzzled him. When he had mentioned he needed a referee, everyone ran from that job quickly like he was imposing a death sentence. Jack wasn't worried. He had an ace up his sleeve and would call in a marker to make this team work.

After dinner, Jack sent Tommy and Katie over to Becca Schmidt's. They would play there until his meeting was over. This had gotten to be a routine, since the kids were best friends. Their cul-de-sacs backed up to the greenbelt and their two back yards were only a minute's walk away. The kids had worn a path through the sparse woods from backyard to backyard.

Becca waited until the four kids had settled in front of a movie, then left for Jack's house. She was taking a risk doing this, but it was time to make her

move. Malcolm wanted her to stay in the house and practically be his slave.
Cook his meals, clean his house, take care of his kids, do his yard work, and
the list was endless. One step out of line, and she could count on more
abuse, usually put-downs and heaps of guilt. He had only hit her that one
time, yet the threat of another explosion of rage was always there.

Becca felt drained, depressed. At 37, she wondered if this was as good as
it was going to get. What was there to look forward to? She wore over-sized
sunglasses when she did go out to hide the dark circles from lack of sleep.
She had moved Malcolm's belongings into the study downstairs after he had
knocked her out that awful night three years ago. He slept on the couch
whenever he was home, which had become less and less over time. Becca hid
his pillow and blankets each morning so any visitors wouldn't suspect. She
had made it clear that she was no longer available as Malcolm's bed partner.
His reaction had surprised her. He had smiled and shrugged his shoulders as
if it were no great loss.

He was supposed to be in Utah until the weekend visiting sports stores to
promote his company's line of snowboarding equipment. She thought he
must be a pretty good salesman, but she had no idea about their finances
because Malcolm managed all the money. She didn't even have a checking
account. He gave her an allowance each month and expected her to live
within it. She had been forced to call the Gondo Ski Company headquarters
in Boise once to find out why their health insurance wasn't accepted at the
Fullerton Clinic anymore. Malcolm had failed to tell her he had switched to
an HMO and they needed to change doctors.

What a way to live. It wasn't a long walk to Jack's house, but Becca's mind
traveled a thousand miles trying to understand how her life had drifted away
from her.

The parents gathered in Jack's living room. He had arranged kitchen
chairs between the sofa and rockers to form a circle.

"Okay, thanks for coming, everyone. I'm giving each of you a roster with
names, addresses, and phone numbers. Please keep this handy, as we may be
calling you frequently to schedule practices and verify game times. Our main
job tonight is to get organized. We have one volunteer position filled, mine.
I'll be the coach."

"Excuse me," interrupted Orson Huff. He was a balding man around
Jack's age, medium height with hawk-like features. He wore black-rimmed
spectacles over which he peered as if examining a tax audit.

"What are your qualifications to coach soccer, Mr. Marshall?" Huff
straightened in his chair and studied Jack like a prosecuting attorney.

"I said yes, Orson. Nobody else did. I'll go to a coaching clinic this weekend and you're welcome to join me and learn while I do. I need an assistant coach anyway. How about it?" Officious bastard, Jack thought.

Orson Huff sputtered and backpedaled. He turned red and trembled slightly at Jack's put-up-or-shut-up challenge.

"Er, uh, I'm afraid that won't do. I have some work at the office this weekend. I'm sure I'll be pretty busy."

Jack turned off his attack-mode attitude and smiled at the group.

"Folks, I have never played this game. I admit to being a complete novice when it comes to soccer. But my little girl wants to play, and it seems that the only way she can is if I coach."

Jack saw a few heads nod in a positive way and went on.

"If I don't get volunteers, the association will break up this team. Chances are none of our girls will get to play then. So how about it? I need a team mom. That job requires a lot of phone calling. That's the person I'll depend on to get the word out about changes in practices, game times, what field to go to, and a million other things."

Gloria Ashworth spoke. "I'd be delighted, Jack. You can count on me." Her voice puffed at the air, low and husky.

Boy, would he have his hands full with this one, Jack thought. Mrs. Ashworth had silenced the pre-meeting conversation with her entrance. She was tall, nearly six feet, and built like a Playboy bunny, with golden blonde hair to her shoulders. Her micro-skirt hitched to just below the "danger zone" when she sat down. All the fathers in the room had trouble keeping eye contact with her.

"Thanks a lot, Gloria." Jack managed to say at last. "Your daughter's name is Gina, right?"

"Right, Jack," she replied, with a look that meant more than he could handle at the moment.

Jack cleared his throat and the rest of the men glanced around nervously to see if any of the wives had noticed their stares at the new team mother.

"Now we need an assistant coach volunteer. Who's game?" No one moved. This was not as easy as Jim Craig had said. "Come on now. We'll get through this together. Who will help me out here?" As Jack looked from one parent to another, they all turned their eyes away. Except Becca Schmidt.

"I'll do it, Jack." Her voice was unsteady, and her hand trembled slightly when she raised it to loosen her collar. She had kept her sunglasses on for the whole meeting, but now she removed them.

Jack was surprised. "Thank you very much, Becca. I think we can make this work." He was grateful she had volunteered but was shocked at her appearance. She obviously did not sleep well. Her hands skittered nervously from her lap to her throat and back. He wondered about that. And, she had made an enemy of Gloria Ashworth, who seemed to be checking her out with a stony glare. Oh well, onward.

"How about a referee?" Jack offered his best smile, but he might as well have suggested they jump in the South Platte during spring runoff. Heads shook negatively all around. There were no takers. Not unexpected, he thought.

"Jack, I've got to go." Becca surprised the group as she stood up and reached for her coat. "I'll call you about the clinic this weekend. Bye."

"Thanks for coming," he managed to say before the door shut behind her. Darn, thought Jack. She was out the door like a shot, not bothering to stay for his rehearsed speech on sportsmanship. He turned to the remaining parents.

"Folks, I have read over the rules, and they sound good to me. Each girl must play half of each game. That's at least two of the four quarters. The policy is to encourage recreation and playing for fun, not just to win. Competitive soccer comes later, when they get bigger and older. For now, we just want them to enjoy playing on a team and learning what sportsmanship is all about. Any questions?"

Priscilla Huff raised her hand as if she were attending Sunday School.

"Mr. Marshall, what will you do if one child turns out to be better than the others? Will she get to play more of the time?"

Jack caught himself before he gave a smart-ass reply. He had just answered that question as plainly as possible. The Huffs, he could see, were not going to be fun.

"No, Priscilla. Not if I can help it. I coached my son's football team last fall using the same rules. It's too soon for kids to sit around and watch other kids have fun. They all need to play. As they get older, some may turn out to be better, and those girls can move over to the competitive league."

Most of the parents, the Huffs excepted, nodded in agreement.

"Well, okay, that's about all I've got to say. Unless someone wants to volunteer to be referee, let's call it a night."

Small conversations broke out around the room as new friends were made and the tension of the meeting dissipated. Once again, Jack thought, the ten-percenters had stepped forward. Oh, oh. Gloria was sauntering across the floor toward him.

"Do you have any special instructions for me, Jack?" Gloria spoke in a soft voice and stood too close for a soccer team mother. Close enough for Jack to get a big whiff of her perfume.

Jack checked out her deep blue eyes and perfectly applied makeup. This was one good-looking woman. She was actually prettier than a Playboy

Bunny, yet nothing ever clicked for Jack when a woman was this aggressive. He was curious, though, about her obvious, teasing manner in front of the other parents.

"Not really. Does your husband like sports, Gloria?" Jack figured the guy was probably too tired to get out of bed.

"Oh, him. Let's just say he travels a lot. He's rarely home these days." Gloria stepped back a comfortable distance. Her face seemed to shut down, and her shoulders slumped. Flirting stopped.

Struck a nerve, Jack thought.

"Gloria, thanks for volunteering. I'll call you after the clinic if I have more information about your duties."

"Certainly," she replied, and turned to leave.

Jack exhaled. Then he shook hands with the other parents, and closed the door on a successful and interesting night.

TEN

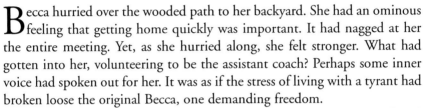

Becca hurried over the wooded path to her backyard. She had an ominous feeling that getting home quickly was important. It had nagged at her the entire meeting. Yet, as she hurried along, she felt stronger. What had gotten into her, volunteering to be the assistant coach? Perhaps some inner voice had spoken out for her. It was as if the stress of living with a tyrant had broken loose the original Becca, one demanding freedom.

When she reached the gate to her yard, lights came on over the deck and the double-wide doors opened. Tommy and Katie hurried out, still putting on their coats, almost scrambling to get away. Becca met them half way across the patio.

"Hey, kids. Why are you in such a hurry?" Becca searched their faces for some clue. She hoped the boys had not upset the girls, who were getting to be super-sensitive lately.

Tommy spoke. "Mr. Schmidt told us to go home right away. He was mad. He sent Andy and Missy to bed." Tommy was bug-eyed and his voice squeaked with his anxiety. Becca noticed that Katie hung back, gripping Tommy's coat tail as a sort of safety line.

"It'll be okay, kids." Becca spoke calmly, even though a queasiness began to gnaw at her stomach. "Sometimes Mr. Schmidt gets in a bad mood. He didn't mean anything by it." She embraced them and soothed their trembling. Damn the man for scaring these children.

Becca walked the two Marshall kids to the gate and watched them run through the woods to their house. Her anger increased, turning her queasiness into a steely resolve. That was the last time Malcolm Schmidt would frighten children - hers or anyone else's. Becca gathered her courage and entered the house.

Malcolm stood in the center of the living room, feet spread, arms crossed, ready to do battle. He huffed in and out as if he were a bull who had just spotted a red flag.

"What were you doing over at the neighborhood Casanova's house?" Malcolm spit his words as if he were sheriff, judge, and jury rolled into one.

He stood as tall as his five-feet-nine allowed in an attempt to tower over Becca's five-six. At this point in their previous confrontations, she had cowered, cried, and apologized for whatever concocted crime he accused her of.

Becca ignored his accusation and went to the heart of the matter. "How dare you frighten the Marshall children? And scare your own off to bed like criminals? You have no cause to act like we're all guilty of breaking your almighty rules whenever we breathe. You expect me to put my life on hold and sit around waiting to serve you. What kind of father are you?" Becca paused to catch her breath. She was shaking with the terror of having stepped over an imaginary line, one Malcolm had been etching skillfully for years.

"Answer my question, Rebecca. I fully expect you to be here when I come home. Why did you leave the house?" Malcolm's tone of persistence showed that he had not recognized the new wife standing in front of him. He merely continued on in his usual manner.

But Becca was determined. "You're not paying attention, Malcolm. I am not going to stay in the house waiting to serve you when I never know where you are or when you're coming home. But, that's a minor issue. Again, why did you scare the kids? Andy and Missy never see you anymore and you don't spend time with them. The Marshall kids have been through enough trauma for several lifetimes. They were frightened by your nastiness."

Malcolm's eyes bulged from his face. He shook with fury and lost whatever control he had before his wife had challenged him. He growled and struck out using the only form of communication he knew.

Becca had been glaring at her husband's face, waiting fearlessly for an answer. She didn't consider that he would strike her and took the blow squarely on her left eye. Her head jerked back. She sagged to the floor, landing on her knees at first, then slowly sank down to the carpeting.

Andy and Missy had watched the scene play out from the stairs. When Malcolm hit their mother, the two children reacted differently. Missy screamed and stood up crying. Andy was furious. He raced down the stairs and ran at his father, tackling him around the waist. But with less than a hundred pounds on his wiry frame, his heroic efforts had no effect.

"Get away from me, you little brat," Malcolm shouted. He grabbed Andy by the shoulders and tossed him aside. "This is my house and I demand respect, do you hear me? Ouch!" Malcolm yelped in pain. Missy had followed her brother's example. She attacked her father, kicking his shinbone just like she did to the mean boys on the playground.

Malcolm lost it completely. He grabbed Missy by the shoulders and started to shake her. But, he was stopped cold by two strong hands that gripped his own shoulders like a vise.

"Set her down gently, Schmidt." Jack spoke menacingly from behind. There was no please in his tone.

Malcolm put Missy down next to her mother, who had risen to a sitting position beside Andy. Becca reached for her daughter and collected both children in a comforting embrace. The three of them watched as the master of their house was marched outside by the man who had saved them.

Once outside, Jack slammed Malcolm against the side of the house. He smashed his fist into Malcolm's eye, matching the blow Becca had received. Malcolm dropped to the deck like a stone.

"You sorry piece of shit. You scared my kids then beat up on your own family. Well I'm here for you now, butthead. It's time for you to pick on somebody your own size. Get up. It's just you and me out here, pal." Jack glowered at Malcolm. He had come over to vent his anger at the louse for upsetting his children. But he wasn't going to stand by and watch a man abuse his family. What Malcolm had done was so disgusting and low that Jack was ready to wipe up the deck with him.

Malcolm cowered on the deck and held up his hands feebly in defense. He stuttered wildly. "Wha, what are you doing in my house? This, this is my business. You have no right to be here."

Jack decided the fool in front of him was both crazy and stupid. He grabbed Malcolm's shirt front and jerked him up to his face.

"You dumb prick, you don't talk to kids like they're pieces of garbage. And you don't speak to my kids again. Ever." Jack shook him as if he was getting the dust off a rug.

Malcolm's face was frozen in fear. He managed to nod his head and mutter a tiny, "yes."

"Sit down," Jack commanded. "Don't move out of that chair." Jack let go of Malcolm's shirt and wiped his hands on the side of his pants as if he had just handled filth. He went back inside to see about Becca and the kids.

Becca was lying on the sofa, with Andy and Missy tending to her as if they were regular nurses. Missy held her mother's hands, while Andy gently pressed a wet cloth to her swelling eye. Jack was struck by the scene. A cocoon of unconditional love seemed wrapped around the three on the sofa as they tried to rise above this shattering experience. Her children stroked and cooed over Becca as if they could absorb her pain. Their caring had a tragic beauty transcending the deep hurt Malcolm had leveled on them. In that moment, Jack sensed that Malcolm Schmidt had lost his family forever.

Jack moved a chair to Becca's side and spoke softly. "I'm not leaving until I know you're safe. What do you want me to do? Call the police? Throw him out? You name it. Anything to help out."

Becca shook her head. "Just bring him in here, and stay with us, please." She struggled to sit up and hugged her children to her sides.

Jack got up to fetch Malcolm. He returned dragging the master of the house in front of his abused family and stepped aside. Malcolm cowered again, this time before his family turned judge and jury. He held a hand to his swelling eye.

Becca looked at her husband of ten years with disgust.

"Pack a bag and get out."

Malcolm flinched. "You can't throw me out of my own house. I pay the bills here. You three belong to me."

"No. You must leave. When you're ready to act like a normal person, come back and apologize. For now, we don't want you in this house."

"Becca," Jack interrupted. "Call the sheriff and get a restraining order. I'll be your witness."

"No, Jack. I don't have the energy for that now. I just want him out." She turned to Andy and sobbed on his shoulder.

Malcolm deflated on the spot. He turned and went upstairs to pack. He was gone in ten minutes. Jack watched the tail lights of his car disappear down the cul-de-sac. Then he called his house and spoke to Tommy, who picked up the phone before the second ring.

"Tommy, watch your sister. I'll be over here a while longer. Everything is fine now. Be cool." He went back into the living room.

Jack sat down on a chair in front of Becca and her children. He reached out to touch her, but she drew back.

"Please don't say anything about this, Jack." Becca whispered, choking back tears. "I feel hurt and embarrassed at the same time. All mixed up. Like I did something wrong, then again, I was right." She looked straight into his eyes. "You saved us tonight. I've never seen him like that. We need to get some rest. Please, go home to Katie and Tommy. We'll be okay."

He didn't want to go, but he knew she had to pull her family close to her. Quiet privacy was the answer in the short term. He left for home remembering the loving touch of those kids and their mother's courage. He wanted to do more than protect them, but he couldn't get a handle on his feelings. But they were safe, and that would have to be enough for now.

ELEVEN

Washington, DC

Bill Conley had seen the old axiom proven many times: once a spy always a spy. No matter how hard you tried to leave the work behind, it seemed to stay attached to your tail. This was especially true for Senator Conley, who had run a massive network of spies. Because of his background, Senator Conley discovered his job in the Senate required a split personality. One person was the silver-haired grandfather, the scrupulously honest man the voters had overwhelmingly sent back to Washington for another term. The other person still kept his finger on the pulse of the intelligence business. It was a rare combination. The voting public ignored his background as an intelligence agent. The intelligence community counted on him for solid advice, never considering the possibility that Conley might use covert information unwisely. It wasn't in his makeup.

Bill Conley had expected to retire to Colorado Springs and play some golf after his army career, but he hadn't counted on Senator Garth Mattox dying in a plane crash near Telluride. The governor had searched for a neutral person to complete the two years left on Mattox's term. He had hoped for a man who would happily step aside and make way for the governor, himself, to run for the senate seat when he vacated the Governor's Mansion in Denver. But the governor hadn't counted on Bill Conley's popularity.

Bill Conley was a true American military hero. He had been wounded winning a battlefield commission. As a much decorated retired major general, he had been called back to duty to serve in the Senate. The people of Colorado loved and respected him, and the feeling seemed to be threading its way across the country.

Then there was his lovely wife, Elizabeth. Who could resist her? Mrs. Conley was an attractive mid-westerner who had maintained her slender figure and good looks through hard work and exercise. She was the real head of their family of five children and six grandchildren. Elizabeth Conley exemplified family values by keeping her family grounded. With her husband's help, she cooked and cleaned, even drove herself to the market. First her children, then her grand children helped her with the chores reserved for butlers, chauffeurs, and gardeners in other homes of the rich and famous. Expensive trappings the public had come to expect from people in their position were not allowed in the Conley home.

But the Conley's were a team in every sense beyond their simple home life, never apart if it could be helped. Always her husband's best friend and closest advisor, Elizabeth easily shifted from wife and lover to political confidante. They were affectionate in public to such a degree that the tabloids wondered out loud if they were on some sort of drugs. Their honest humility was admired by a public too often exposed to the excesses of the rich and famous.

Popular magazine reporters and TV talk show hosts approached her for interviews, but had been politely turned away. Elizabeth always refused, stating that her husband's monthly press conference provided enough information for the press to chew on. Mr. and Mrs. Conley believed theirs was a normal home. They were average people who didn't care for the attention. Frankly, she always answered, both she and the senator were public servants not celebrities.

If this perfect American success story wasn't enough, no one could have imagined what the senator would do when he got to Washington. Most expected him to be a back-row freshman in the Senate chamber. Political pundits figured he would do no more than attend sessions of Congress and vote. They were the first to be shocked at his active stances on major issues. The quiet patriot had become a fighter on Capitol Hill and a force for the common man.

He rode the subway to work. Refused appointments with lobbyists. Refused freebies of any kind. Free tickets to games, plane tickets to boondoggles overseas? Not a chance. He spent his free time with Elizabeth and his family back in Colorado. Senator Conley refused to join a political party, remaining an outspoken independent.

He ran the most efficient office of any Member of Congress. He had one secretary and a staff assistant in Washington, and the same in Denver. He didn't need a bunch of Capitol Hill staffers to tell him what to think. He rarely paid attention to pollsters to tell him what issues were important and how to "tweak" his positions to best advantage with voters. He simply said what was on his mind, straight out, and the people loved it.

The Senator also didn't need administrative support when he had friends and contacts all over the world in the intelligence field. These connections still viewed him as a master intelligence agent. They valued his opinion enough to keep him apprised of domestic and foreign affairs.

Information came to him from many directions. People asked his advice and his opinions about sensitive matters, whether it was part of his work in the Senate or not. He knew where the cold war intelligence networks operated and was a chess master in manipulating the lines of communication to get results.

Senator Conley looked at the two men sitting across from him in his spare office. One was an FBI agent, the other from Secret Service. They had requested this meeting under the guise of reporting certain "criminal activities" back in Colorado. Bill Conley knew there was a deeper reason for their visit, and he was determined to get a straight answer.

"Mr. Allen, Mr. Bloomberg, what's your business here? I don't like to get scheduled for secretive meetings like this as if I belonged to your inner sanctums. If you want something from me, come right out and ask for it." Conley drilled both men with his Nordic stare, his gray-blue eyes turning icy. He grew tired of the coy games being played behind the scenes inside the beltway, and this smelled like one.

"Sir, er, Senator," Allen stumbled into his remarks obviously unsettled by the formidable giant behind the desk. "We need to brief you on a scam being played out back in your home state, one that has crossed wires at our agencies. We were ordered to get you involved before you got wind of it and grilled one of our bosses in an open hearing. Sir." Allen was out of breath, and Bloomberg took over.

"Plain and simply speaking, sir, a plot to grab open space is infiltrating local governments in Colorado. It involves some counterfeit money, thus Secret Service's interest. It crosses state lines, thus my agency, FBI, is also concerned."

"What do you mean, grab open space?" Conley sat up straight, taking immediate interest. He did not hide his agitation. Nothing, with the exception of water rights, was a more volatile issue in the west than open space and what to do with it. No one agreed on any approach. If the wrong person suggested a plan, dozens of organizations objected, and compromise was nigh on to impossible. The Interior Department had stewardship over federal land, and it couldn't even give it away without stirring up trouble. Opposing groups fought for every square inch of dirt whatever the circumstances.

"To put it bluntly, Senator," Allen had gotten his voice back, "local politicians are being bought. Shady operators convince them to put land out for bid. Land that was ceded to them for public use. A series of transfers from one institution to another unfolds. Eventually a commercial developer manages to take possession, paying pennies to the dollar. They end up making a ten-fold profit almost overnight. Basically it's money laundering with political bribery at its core."

The Senator reflected on this information. He had a distant memory of just such a caper going on several years back. It became clearer now as he focused on it. Yes, Jack Marshall had almost been killed in an avalanche, then his wife had died a few days later. It had been on the Western Slope of Colorado. Bill Conley relied on his encyclopedic memory to keep track of the many details that came to him from his sources.

"You have my attention, gentlemen. What can I do for you?"

"Sir," Bloomberg was speaking again, his voice more confident. "We hoped you could enlist the aid of some of your contacts out there to give us a hand."

"You mean, of course, Marshall and Mendes, right, Bloomberg?" Bill Conley grinned at the two men as their smiles formed.

"Well, yes sir. Those two would do great, but when we spoke to their supervisor, Henry Strothers, he was not very cooperative. In fact, Strothers said to talk to you and wished us good luck in a sarcastic way." Allen had relayed this to Conley with a distasteful smirk when he mentioned the administrative supervisor of operations in Denver.

Bill Conley sat back in his big chair and grinned. Strothers again. Some day he would shoot the bastard.

"Gentlemen, let me deal with Mr. Strothers. Now what do you want Marshall and Mendes to do?"

TWELVE

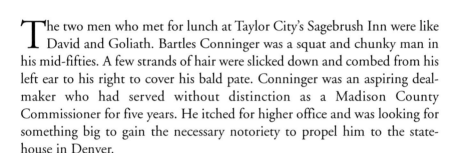

The two men who met for lunch at Taylor City's Sagebrush Inn were like David and Goliath. Bartles Conninger was a squat and chunky man in his mid-fifties. A few strands of hair were slicked down and combed from his left ear to his right to cover his bald pate. Conninger was an aspiring deal-maker who had served without distinction as a Madison County Commissioner for five years. He itched for higher office and was looking for something big to gain the necessary notoriety to propel him to the state-house in Denver.

Conninger stole small glances at his host across the table. He cautiously eyed Rafe Stalker and shivered. He was a giant of a man. In his mid-sixties, Stalker stood well over six feet and weighed over 300 pounds. His features were blunt and doughy, giving the impression he had been a prize fighter several bouts too many. His face and ears appeared to be made of bronzed cauliflower. Stalker spoke in low growls that demanded attention, and his black eyes showed no depth or feeling. He was not a subtle man in either appearance or demeanor.

The man reeked of danger. Stalker had invited him to lunch but Conninger felt like he was going to be the main course. Still, he had called some friends, gleaning interesting information. Word was, several commissioners to the west of Taylor City had fallen into tidy profits when Stalker's company worked their counties. Bartles wished for his chance to dance with the devil.

"Your food good?" Stalker rumbled at Bartles. His tone scraped like sandpaper across the void at the stumpy politician. It carried an undercurrent that said the food had better be good, or some cook would be minus a hand.

Conninger jumped. "Yeah. Yeah, it's fine," he answered. It was hard to screw up fries and burgers. It wasn't like they had ordered something at a four-star restaurant. The Sagebrush Inn served the typical greasy food of the town bars. Calling it a restaurant was an upgrade.

Conninger's appetite escaped him. He put down his fork. "What can I do for you, Mr. Stalker?" He figured to play the first card and maybe see what aces Stalker held up his sleeve.

"There's some land I want to build on, and the county zoning department is not being very cooperative." Stalker exhaled mightily and shoved his dinner plate to the side, his food half eaten.

"This is what I want." Stalker's thick, hairy hands spread a paper napkin in the middle of the table and roughly scratched out some lines with a pen. Conninger understood the preliminaries were over and slid his plate to the side as well. Stalker continued his clumsy drawing until it became plain to see what he wanted.

"Here's the river coming from the dam. Go along here a ways, and there's pretty level ground on both sides of it that would be cheap to develop."

Conninger felt a depressing coldness seep into his body as he recognized the area on the drawing. Tree huggers, all sorts of wildlife enthusiasts, half the state government, and anyone with common sense would object to this plan. He gulped as Stalker sketched in shopping centers and tract development zones on both sides of the South Platte River from Cromwell dam to the Fullerton city limits. The man wanted nothing less than to scrape away the five-mile-long greenbelt containing the most popular parks and recreation area in the metroplex. He would also bulldoze and fill in the most extensive wetlands on the front range.

Conninger used his napkin to pat at the trickles of sweat forming on his forehead. How could he respond in a way that expressed concern for the environment - a hot election button, and still hold the door open for negotiation on such a stupid plan?

"That certainly does look like a fine piece of property, Mr. Stalker." The big man had not offered his first name, and Conninger doubted anyone used it. "There would be several rather large hurdles in the way, though, don't you think?" The other man's puffy face expanded and wrinkled as if a rolling pin were massaging it from the inside. Then Stalker's mouth curved up a few degrees at the corners in a sinister smile. Conninger froze in mid-thought.

"Maybe a few, but nothing too big." He glared at Conninger, then added, "That's where you come in, Conninger." Stalker actually chuckled before continuing, and Conninger felt his belly tighten as if two big hands had gripped his short hairs by the roots.

"The county owns this land, right?" Stalker pointed at Conninger, demanding a positive response.

"Right, yeah sure, of course." Conninger was stumbling through a script he felt unprepared for.

"The County Commissioners control that land, right?" Again the stare and unspoken demand for agreement by Conninger.

"Of course they do, but - ," Conninger was interrupted before he could object.

"So, you'll figure a way to get us that land, and I'll slip you something on the side, say a good amount of cash." Stalker sat back in his chair, appearing satisfied his message had been clearly received. He looked sure of getting his way.

Bartles Conninger didn't share the big man's confidence. He could use some extra cash, and this could be his ticket to the big show. He knew the obnoxious man sitting across from him had won similar battles out in Colorado's back country. Stalker needed someone on the inside, and he had picked Conninger. There was money in it, of course, but dangling just within reach were connections that could get him much more. Was this his lucky day? His hesitation lasted all of five seconds.

"What do you want me to do?" Conninger answered the glare from his host, stepping over the edge. He felt like he was falling into the two-thousand-foot deep Black Canyon of the Gunnison.

Stalker gave a sarcastic smirk and reached a mammoth paw across the table to shake on the deal. He crushed Conninger's hand, grinding it to the bone.

"I'll tell you what worked in Glade Park a while back. It'll do for this place, too."

Bartles listened for another thirty minutes as his new business partner out-lined a strategy that smelled worse than a dead skunk in the middle of the road, but that just might work.

Rafe finished talking. The little man nodded, then excused himself to scutter out the door. County commissioner or government worker, they were all the same - slimy bastards making rules to stop him and take what was his. The unfortunate ones got in his way and paid a steep price.

The giant waved the waitress away like a pesky fly and finished gobbling up the rest of his food and the remains of his guest's. His thoughts turned inward.

•••

"Steady, boy," Rafael's father whispered roughly as he cuffed the gangly ten-year-old on the side of the head. "You make too much noise with them big feet. That buck's coming closer and we'll kill him for dinner."

Rafael held back tears from the blow and nodded at the sickly man who could barely walk. His mother was in worse shape back in the cabin. The two of them were always sick over something. They couldn't afford a doctor and had resigned to dying anyway.

There was nothing to do since the mine shut down. Men were out of work all over this part of Montrose county in the San Juan River valley. Rafael's schoolmates talked about it every day. Other people were sick too. Some claimed it was from the tailings left out in the open from the uranium mines. Heck, the stuff never bothered him and their cabin was less than a couple hundred feet from a big pile of the yellowing rocks. Still, his folks were bad off.

Rafael's attention was drawn to his father's arm as it raised the gun. He scanned in the direction of the rifle barrel, and spotted the mule deer prancing into the glade. The proud animal stepped into a patch of sun as if it knew hunting season had ended a month ago.

Blam! His father's gun exploded. The buck went down in a heap. Rafael and his father hugged each other at their success. They would eat tonight. Rafael left their cover of downed branches and started for the deer.

Rafael dragged the animal over to the nearest tree, tied rope around its hind feet, and pulled it over a branch so the lifeless form hung vertical in mid-air. This is why he had come. His father had just enough strength to pull the trigger, then sit down and rest in the trees. Rafael had to finish. That meant slitting the throat to drain the blood, skinning the dead beast, and cutting off chunks of meat.

"Young man, hold on there. You're under arrest for hunting out of season." Rafael jerked his head around to see a forest ranger standing not 20 yards off to the left. His shiny badge reflected the sun sharply and announced his authority over these woods and anything in them.

Rafael glanced around nervously for his father but couldn't see him. He returned the Ranger's demand with a plea of his own.

"Sir, we don't have no food, and we killed this deer for our supper." He hated that his voice went high and cracked in the wrong places. The tears had come back to clog his throat.

"Doesn't matter. The law's the law, young man. Hunting season is over. I'm confiscating that deer and arresting you."

Blam! The big deer rifle exploded again, silencing the forest. Rafael dropped to the ground shaking and confused. Who shot? Why? Then he looked up to see his father standing by the trees, smoke wafting from the end of his rifle barrel. Rafael looked over to the spot where the ranger had stood and saw nothing. He got to his knees and looked again. A Smokey Bear hat lay on the ground, a body lying beside it.

"Go to the house, boy, and get the shovel. Ain't nobody taking food from us. Never. Damn the gov'ment to hell."

Rafael dug a grave for the ranger. Before the next spring, he repeated the act for both parents. Then he simply walked away, looking for work. He had developed a burning hatred for authority, especially government folks who took what he needed.

Rafael Stalker worked construction digging ditches, doing whatever physical labor was demanded for the next ten years. He was smart and learned all the other jobs of the trade, finally rising to the position of project superintendent. He had a way about him that no one challenged. He was bigger and stronger and demanded obedience.

He only dreamed a short while about owning his own company. Then he put aside those dreams when he realized it would be easier just to take someone else's. So he did.

Today he owned one of the largest construction and real estate development companies in the state. He had fought his way out of the mines of the dreary San Juan River valley, a forgotten land on the Western Slope. Stalker's memorial to his parents had been a vow that he would build on whatever land he could take without regard for the public's concern. After all, no one had been concerned enough to protect his parents. Why should he care about anyone else?

THIRTEEN

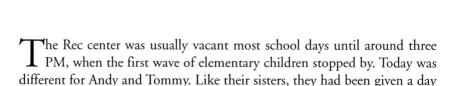

The Rec center was usually vacant most school days until around three PM, when the first wave of elementary children stopped by. Today was different for Andy and Tommy. Like their sisters, they had been given a day off after the excitement of last night.

Martha had seen this before - kids skipping school and expecting to come into the center and hide out under her good graces. But this visit had been preceded by a phone call from Becca Schmidt canceling her afternoon tennis match at the main courts. Her call had been followed by one from Jack Marshall granting the boys "dispensation" so they could play under Martha's watchful eye while he worked on a report. She knew something was brewing in the neighborhood. Both boys had ambled into her center around mid-morning and had been huddled in the corner of the game room since then, whispering, not competing at ping pong or any other game.

Martha decided to get at this directly by talking to Jack. She knew him well, whereas Becca was rather reclusive and still a mystery to her. Martha picked up the phone and dialed.

Jack answered on the third ring.

"Jack, it's Martha. Can you enlighten me as to why I have two whispering boys down here? Why are they really skipping school?"

There was a hesitation as she waited for Jack to answer. Finally he spoke.

"They got underfoot, and I had to get some work done, Martha. I promised Becca I'd look after Andy, and before long there was just too much noise in the house. If they act up, send them back to me."

"Well, why aren't they in school, Jack?" She would get to the bottom of this yet and persisted.

"Uh, they were up late last night horsing around, and I decided to let them sleep in. That's all. Hey, it's spring. The sun is shining, birds chirping. Whoa, my other line is lit up, Martha. Got some business to work on. See ya." He hung up.

A likely story, she mused as she checked her personal directory for Becca's number. Something was fishy. She had her own reputation to consider. Some parents had accused her of harboring kids who just wanted to stay out of school for a day and hoped their parents wouldn't catch on. Martha knew the precise time each school let out for the day, and loitering children in her center before those times could count on Inspector Riddle to do some investigation.

First, though, Martha went to the game room to check on the boys. The room was located down a narrow hall leading from her command center. Large sliding doors led out to the pool deck and were always open in the summer. Boys' and girls' locker rooms were on either side of the game room. Bean bag furniture was draped around the floor affording kids the space to create their own domains.

Martha stopped at the entrance and watched the boys over in a corner. They had tossed bean bag chairs in a semi-circle out from the far corner and had climbed inside, partially concealing themselves behind a makeshift fort. She walked closer and snooped at the whispered sounds coming from the invisible boys.

Tommy spoke: "I never saw my dad so mad, Andy. He was red in the face and looked like he could bust something."

Andy replied: "He did bust my father. I'm glad. Mom was hurt bad."

Tommy again: "Is she okay now?"

Andy: "Yeah, sort of. She cried most of the night. Me and Missy slept in her bed and tried to calm her down." There was a pause until an angry voice came from Andy this time. "I hate him! I don't want him for a father anymore!"

This was enough snooping for Martha. She returned to her office and called Becca immediately. The phone rang for a long time before a small voice answered in a rushed and breathless response. Martha heard Missy say, "My mother can't come to the phone now. Call back later." Click. The line went dead.

Something terrible had happened and she was determined to help. This was her neighborhood and she had intervened before when she discovered that families were in trouble. This sounded like one. Some folks thought of her as a busybody, but most just appreciated her care. Martha considered the entire neighborhood her family. She watched everybody's kids at one time or another in her unofficial day care center. She solved problems that no one else could deal with. What's more, she had heard before about Malcolm Schmidt, the traveling salesman who demanded his wife never leave the house. But she had never seen the man. He did not come to the pool with his family. His dues were always late and often paid in installments. Martha figured Becca made the payments using her measly allowance - another neighborhood rumor.

Martha waited anxiously for her assistant, Carolyn Jenson, who was due at one PM. Carolyn worked part-time at the center and taught morning classes at the high school. "CJ" was Martha's right hand woman and a favorite with the kids. When she walked in, Martha passed her on her way out with only a brief hello and warning to leave Andy and Tommy by themselves in the game room.

As she parked in front of the Schmidt house, Martha noted the place could use a little fixing up. The yard was mowed and trimmed, but the house needed the care of a handyman. Huge aspen trees on either side of the front yard had overgrown the second story roof and filled the gutters with leaves. Martha chuckled as she saw a second floor window screen bent and partially out of its fixture. Had to be Andy's doings, she thought. Missy was too young to sneak out at night, although her time would come. A big branch of one aspen lurched over near enough to the window for an enterprising young boy to climb onto.

Despair emanated from the house. Martha knew it was partly due to her knowledge of the unhappy family living there. Some feelings though were stirred up by the austere look of the yard. There were no toys, no bicycles, no playthings for kids anywhere in sight. Most houses with two kids like Missy and Andy overflowed with signs of happy children within. Here, there was a strictness, an orderliness apparently stemming from one man's twisted ideas about being lord and master.

Martha rang the doorbell and waited. She counted to twenty, then rang it again. Again no answer. Perhaps the bell didn't work; batteries had run down. She knocked loudly, frustrated. She felt driven to comfort the family inside, yet no one came to the door.

Must be out back, she thought. She followed the side yard around back to the gate of a six-foot high, stockade fence. Lots of privacy. Nearest neighbor an acre away to the side or through the woods. The place was secluded. Her mind returned to what she knew about this family now. She had been affected by the boys talking; she had to talk with Becca.

Martha opened the gate and walked into the backyard. Becca was lying on the lounge chair, her face concealed behind gigantic sunglasses. She wore a straw hat to shield her eyes from the spring light sifting between cottonwoods. Missy and Katie were busy over in the corner of the yard swinging on the jungle gym. Strange, they were very quiet about it for being six. There was no giggling, just quiet play as if they were two ladies enjoying each other's company after a game of bridge. Neither smiled. They looked grim.

"Becca, hello." Martha announced herself, trying not to startle her. "May I visit? No one answered the door, so I decided to be brash and walk around back. Hope you don't mind." Martha approached the deck where Becca rested, and motioned her to stay seated.

"Please don't get up. I had to come see you. How are you?" Martha's eyes searched the dark lenses of the sunglasses hoping for some sign of acceptance or friendship. She sensed a hollowness from the woman sitting before her.

"I, I'm just fine, Martha. Right now I don't have much time. We were, uh, we were just going over to Jack's to have a joint family cookout."

Martha held up her hand. "I don't want to keep you. And I don't care if you think I'm an interfering old fool. It's just that I overheard Tommy and Andy talking about what happened last night. I can see you're not feeling well." Martha scooted closer. "But I had to tell you I want to be your friend. When you're ready, you can talk to me."

Becca turned her head away and shuddered. Tears eased down her cheeks. Instinctively, Martha understood her shame and embarrassment. She quickly got up and sat down beside her, taking Becca's hands into her own, holding them gently. Then a desolate Becca turned her head into Martha's shoulder and sobbed. They sat this way for long minutes, holding each other, sharing grief and pain in their embrace. Finally, Becca pulled away and began to speak in whispered fragments that only her confessor could hear.

"Malcolm hit me again last night, Martha. I'd gotten used to his verbal assaults. They no longer affected me, I thought. He hit me once before in a drunken rage and hadn't touched me until last night. I'd hoped he was over his anger, but I guess not." Becca paused to wipe her nose and gather some more courage before she spoke again.

Martha listened as Becca revealed her struggle with severe feelings of guilt for not being a good wife, whatever that had meant to Malcolm. At the same time, she felt terrible for not standing up to him sooner to protect her children.

"He was crazy about me at first, Martha. I had done some modeling for this department store and he saw me in a newspaper ad. He told me he pulled strings to find out who 'that beautiful model was so he could marry her.' He was passionate about me. Insistent. Wouldn't be denied. A 'no' answer was unacceptable. He wore me down until I agreed to go out with him. I was flattered. He courted me like I was a princess. On our first date, he swore he would marry me. And he never touched me until we were officially man and wife. It was like a fairy tale, except there was no happily ever after." Becca glanced over to the girls, then focused on Martha again.

"I look back on it now and wonder, how could I have been so stupid? He took control of my life, and I let him do it. He wanted to move. We moved. He didn't want me to work. I quit. He wanted a child. I got pregnant several months after the honeymoon. That changed everything. Malcolm began traveling more out of town for days, then weeks at a time. When I went into labor I had no idea where he was and a neighbor took me to the hospital. Malcolm showed up two weeks after I came home from the hospital, stayed a day, and left."

Martha listened and nodded. She had seen this happen to other women; it had happened to her. Once the perfect family had been acquired, the head of the household went his way, seeking other excitment, unable to bond with children or be a parent in any sense. Of course, when problems arose, he was quick to find fault with the mother and homemaker who was supposedly there to deal with those matters. Martha shared this with Becca, and the younger woman's eyes widened in surprise.

"Not you, Martha. Who on earth would treat you like that?"

"The man who married me as his fairy princess and left me to carry the blame when our son was killed. That man. Oh, he never struck me, but his cruel words went straight to the heart."

Becca felt the power of her friend's emotions sweep across the deck and encompass her. Someone else was just like her. This woman the whole neighborhood looked up to as strong and willing to take on any task. Becca reached up and removed the sunglasses. She looked at Martha out of beautiful violet eyes. Her left eye was bloodshot, almost swollen shut. Dark smudges stretched across the bridge of her nose, touched part of her cheek, and ended near her left temple.

"Bastard." Martha mumbled, trembling with rage.

"His rules became stricter as time went on," Becca said. "I tried for another child, hoping that would draw him closer, but the opposite happened. Finally, I didn't care anymore." Becca looked out at the woods lumbering into the greenbelt beyond her backyard. "Last night, I decided to get out and have a life without him. I went to a soccer meeting at Jack's house, even volunteered to help coach the team. I felt good about myself again. Then I came home, and, and he was here...."

She told Martha about Jack's role, now wishing he had beaten Malcolm to a pulp. She wished Jack had been there to back her up three years ago.

"So, you and Jack are friends?" Martha queried in a neutral way, smiling with a twinkle in her eye. "He's a different sort of man, a good one in many ways. He can relate to your situation since you are both virtually single parents."

"Yes, I can see that, Martha. You're right. He is a good man and a very good friend. We are close neighbors. Our kids have always been best friends. They play together every day. He has invited us over several times for cookouts, but up to now we had to decline. Now, though, I think we might just go over there and begin to enjoy life a little more. I am truly numb from what has happened and realize I have to reach out to friends and neighbors. Doing that will help me survive and protect my children."

"I can understand that's how you feel at this moment, Becca. I grieved the loss of my son and that was quickly followed by my husband's desertion. It's too soon for you, but eventually, I began to think about the possibility of another romance now and again."

Becca was surprised at first to hear this, then she thought, why not? Martha was young middle age, and a vibrant woman. Why shouldn't she consider another relationship? But that was for Martha, not her. True, her marriage to Malcolm had really been over for years. Even though they had lived under the same roof since his first attack, it had not been as husband and wife. But today she hurt physically and emotionally. This was a time to heal and be there for her kids.

FOURTEEN

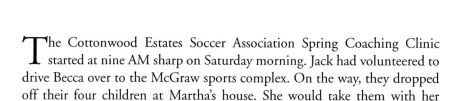

The Cottonwood Estates Soccer Association Spring Coaching Clinic started at nine AM sharp on Saturday morning. Jack had volunteered to drive Becca over to the McGraw sports complex. On the way, they dropped off their four children at Martha's house. She would take them with her when she opened the rec center later that morning.

Jack watched the kids go into Martha's house and waved goodbye. Then he stole a glance at his assistant coach.

"You feeling better today, Becca?" She still hid behind those massive dark glasses and had barely said a word getting into the car.

"Sorry to be so quiet, Jack. Just a little nervous I guess. Honestly, this is like a coming out party for me. I'm not much of a joiner. For the past ten years I have done little more than be a homemaker." Becca drifted off to her vague thoughts again, then smiled. "Oh yes, I do like to play tennis and garden. I guess those things count as far as keeping active, don't they?"

"Well, you must be in pretty good shape if you've been playing tennis regularly. So, the physical exercise shouldn't be a problem. And since we both know absolutely nothing about this game, it ought to be fun."

Jack found himself glancing more and more to her side of the car, soaking up her striking profile. Frankly, he had never paid attention to how she looked until the incident the other night with Malcolm.

Becca was very attractive. No. She was beautiful, once he looked past the glasses. No wonder Malcolm, the control freak, had tried to keep her home for so long. Her coal-black hair looked silky. It was shoulder length, very full, and straight. No need for any curls or fancy do with gorgeous hair like that, Jack thought.

Yikes! Gravel pinged off the bottom of the car as Jack veered onto the shoulder. Eyes on the road, buster, he scolded himself. Jack wasn't paying attention to his driving and drew a puzzled look from Becca. He blushed, caught fantasizing about running his fingers through her hair.

The McGraw Complex wasn't too far away, but Jack still wanted to sneak little peeks at his new assistant coach. Her arms and legs were tanned perfectly, probably from all the gardening she did. Her white shorts and top contrasted quite nicely with her golden skin. It had been a long time since he had thought about another woman besides Helen. Becca was medium height and a bit on the slender side, he reckoned this was due to lack of sleep and constant worry about her abusive husband.

Yes, she does have a husband, he reminded himself, pulling back to reality. Even though Malcolm had forfeited any right to the title, at least in Jack's mind. Becca was still married and he would respect that. Still, Jack discovered he was attracted to Becca. Yet he knew very little about her except that she was physically a knockout, and she had raised two wonderful children mostly by herself.

"Earth to Jack. Earth to Jack. Are you going to pick a parking space or just sit here in the middle of the lot?" Becca's question broke his reverie. Jack had driven into the complex parking lot, then stopped in front of a row of empty spaces, hands at the ten and two o'clock positions, eyes focused on the mountains ten miles away. He wore a grin that disappeared rapidly when he saw what had happened.

"Sorry, Becca. My mind wandered a bit."

They parked and got out to join a few dozen adults bunched around a soccer goal in the middle of the fields. As Jack and Becca got nearer to the group, he noticed an almost equal number of men and women there. Good, now Becca won't feel so out of place. CESA had printed up a flyer on their program stating that although more boys than girls played soccer, the number of girls was increasing rapidly.

Skip Hawkins introduced himself as their instructor for the day. Skip was a familiar figure in the metro area, because he coached the Rockets, Denver's minor league soccer team.

All Jack could think of was how neat it was to have a professional teach them the game.

"Okay, folks," Skip began. "Line up facing me along this line, here and let's start. This is recreation soccer. That means everybody plays at least half of every game. This morning we're talking about six-a-side rules, which are somewhat different from regular soccer. Colorado is one of a handful of states to allow this form of the game. The field is cut in half, goals are smaller, games shorter. Only six players are on the field for each team, versus 11 for regular soccer, and there is no goalie."

Skip glanced around and saw puzzled looks staring back at him. "Yes, that's right, no goalie. But most coaches keep a couple of fullbacks on either side of the goal who fall back to defend it when the ball enters their side of the field. Soccer purists don't like this, but it gives each child more chances to touch the ball with only twelve kids running after it. The fullbacks also get more exercise than a goalie would, and that's one of the purposes of recreational soccer - exercise."

"First off, we'll go through some stretching exercises you can do with the kids." Most of the adults appeared in good shape, Jack thought. Yet, there were groans coming from the group as most didn't start their Saturday mornings off with so much vigor. Then the fun began as Skip started the instruction.

"Today we'll work on drills to develop the basic soccer skills of kicking, passing, and throw-ins. I'll demonstrate each drill, then have you break into small groups to practice on each other. Remember one important rule. Never allow one of your young players to get in the habit of kicking the ball with a toe. Teach them to use the side of their feet, always. When they get older, they'll learn an instep kick with their toe pointed forward and under the ball. Another important point is to teach them to use both feet to kick and pass the ball."

Becca was enthralled with the sport. It was simple and fun. She and Jack were in a group of eight men and women, all new to the game. They learned how to kick watching Skip demonstrate. Then they got in a circle and used the same techniques to kick the ball around the circle to each other. She could do this! Her tennis footwork was helping out since foot placement was important getting in position to hit the ball. Using your feet was the core of soccer. That and running.

After a few minutes of drills, Becca was laughing with the rest of the group when one of them goofed and missed the ball or stubbed a toe on the grass. Heck, they were all novices, yet she was beginning to feel that after this clinic she and Jack would be at least a few steps ahead of their girls.

Often, she and Jack were paired up to work on a drill together. Becca found herself watching Jack more than the ball, and she missed it completely the next time he passed it to her. They both laughed, then exchanged friendly smiles. Hmmm, she thought, there's something more than soccer going on here. She sensed a frisson of excitement, somewhat like butterflies in her stomach when she got nervous. Except this was a good feeling, and she decided to let it play out.

Skip led them through enough drills to get them going with their teams the following week. Then he divided them into teams and ran a mock game exercise, explaining the roles of coaches and referees.

"Remember folks, the refs are volunteers and parents just like you. Your team ref will never work one of your games, but treat the refs with the respect you would give a parent from your team. Now, coaches, listen carefully to me. Gather around." Skip got down on one knee and looked seriously at each new coach in front of him.

"Soccer is not like football or baseball in this country. It's especially not like basketball. For example, what do you see the managers and coaches doing on the sidelines of those games?"

Jack volunteered. "They are yelling and screaming. Most of them feel robbed by the refs or umpires and get into arguments with them. Frankly, I wish the TV guys would quit showing them on the sidelines. They set bad examples for the younger kids."

"You stole my script last night, didn't you, Jack? Gang, he's right. They set bad examples, and you'll see players emulate those examples on the field. It takes away from the fun of the game and shows a lack of sportsmanship. We teach soccer coaches differently in CESA. Once a game starts, do all the yelling you want to encourage all the kids, not just your own. Compliment good play on either side. Be positive. Don't gripe and complain. And don't try to coach from the sidelines. The kids won't hear you. Coach during practices, then let them play the game. This will be hard at first but lots more fun."

Skip then handed out packets of information that included diagrams for running the drills and basic game rules. He wished them good luck and let them go for the day.

Jack felt invigorated. What a great sport. He was energized and didn't want to get off soccer yet.

"Becca, how about a cup of coffee and a donut while we plan our first practice session?"

"Sounds fine to me, Jack." She replied, sounding in a much more positive frame of mind. Jack knew Martha would manage the kids quite well if they took a few extra minutes to develop strategy.

He pulled into the parking lot for the Yummy Donut store near the entrance to the neighborhood shopping center. Inside they got coffee and donuts and found a booth away from the doorway. Becca sat down and removed her sunglasses for the first time.

Jack wanted to wince at her eye but stifled any outward reaction so she would leave the glasses off. Becca's deep violet eyes mesmerized him as she peeked over a half-eaten donut and smiled back. Her cheekbones were delicate planes under large eyes that crinkled at the corners as she merrily ate her donuts, while Jack only sat and stared. He watched her lips as she sipped gingerly at the steaming coffee. Be nice to trade places with that coffee cup, he mused. Her face was perfect, softly rounded in just the right places. He noticed slight color on her cheeks from the exercise and sunshine of the morning clinic. The damaged left eye had turned from a semi-circle of black smudges to faint green and yellow tints. The swelling had receded to a slight puffiness above her cheek.

"Are you going to eat those, Jack? If not, slide them over here, I'm starved. Where is your mind today anyway? That's the second time I've found you on another planet." Becca gave him a dazzling smile. One morning out of the house and learning a new game with adults had created a metamorphosis. It was as if she had blossomed like the spring flowers popping up throughout the neighborhood, casting her troubles to the wind.

Jack couldn't help himself. He reached across the table and gently caressed her left cheek, all the time never taking his eyes from hers.

"Such a beautiful face to be hurt so badly." He dropped his hand down to the table, covering hers. Jack knew they were in a public place, but at that moment he felt alone with her. He experienced a light ringing in his ears. The presence of other customers, and the clinking of cash registers and burbling of coffee machines faded away. She returned his gaze with an astonished look.

"How can you be so kind and gentle for such a big man, Jack? You give me a feeling of comfort and security when we're in the same room. It's a warm feeling." Becca broke off her sentence and looked embarrassed.

Jack removed his hand and sat back in his seat, pulling back in body and mind. "Uh, I guess it comes from being a single dad and trying to play the role of mom on occasion. It's been good for Katie and me especially. We've gotten very close. But, uh, I don't think what I feel at the moment has anything to do with parenting." Jack looked around the shop and realized he had been acting a little fast, letting his thoughts out in the open. When he glanced back at Becca, he grimaced at her sad smile.

"My children weren't so lucky, I guess. I didn't make a very good choice with Malcolm." The spell was broken as bad memories replaced the golden moment they had shared.

Jack gulped down his donuts and coffee, then they talked about soccer. It was a safe subject revolving around their children. Yet, their earlier conversation had opened up much wider possibilities.

Martha had a nice surprise for them when they went to pick up the kids.

"Found a place to practice yet, Jack?" Martha snickered a bit and couldn't help grinning like a Cheshire cat.

"Haven't given it a single thought," Jack replied, now curious about his friend's smug grin.

"Don't you know, Jack, that finding a place to practice is the next hardest thing to getting decent fields to play on? Why, this morning alone I've had a dozen requests from soccer coaches to use the open field next to the picnic grounds by the pool. Yep, sure have. Turned them all down, though." Martha was actually chuckling now as she looked from Jack to Becca, waiting for one of them to catch on.

Understanding hit Becca right away. "Oh no, Jack," she said. "We don't have a place to practice, and now everyone has a head start on us. What'll we do?" Becca sounded as if all her hopes for a fun season of soccer had just been dashed. Jack's expression had turned grim as he mentally kicked himself for not planning ahead.

"Come over here, you two." Martha opened the lower half of the Dutch door to her office and guided her friends to a big chart on the far wall. The top of the chart was sectioned off to form a reservation schedule for the tennis courts and other parks and open spaces under control of the center director. Martha grabbed a pointer and moved it to the space by her pool that was in such high demand. All afternoon time slots were marked "Reserved."

"As soon as you come up with a name for your team, I'll put it in this reserved space." Martha said, joyfully.

Jack and Becca whooped together and grabbed Martha in a bear hug. The three hugged each other at once. Heads came together in the middle, touching, laughing. Jack planted a big smooch on Martha's cheek. He paused suddenly and looked at Becca's face in anticipation. Then he stepped back before he was tempted to kiss his assistant as well. He would have to settle for the camaraderie he shared with Becca as they prepared to coach their team. He did notice that her cheeks were a slight pink and Martha had a smug expression from the closeness of the triple embrace.

FIFTEEN

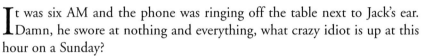

It was six AM and the phone was ringing off the table next to Jack's ear. Damn, he swore at nothing and everything, what crazy idiot is up at this hour on a Sunday?

"This better be good," Jack grouched into the receiver. When he heard the voice on the other end he knew it would be.

Senator Conley used his most authoritative command voice on his former intelligence officer. "Get out of that bed, and stand at attention, mister!" Jack heard a low chuckle. "Hey there, Jack, hope I didn't wake you. But, too bad if I did. How's things in our beautiful state this morning?"

"Things were great until the doggone phone woke me up, general, senator, sir. What the hell do I call you anyway, Bill? And where are you?"

"Master, will do nicely," Bill Conley joked. "Couldn't make it home this weekend. Elizabeth is not too pleased either. So I need you to go down to the Springs and take out my storm windows for me. Okay?"

"That's what you called me for?" Jack played along with the bantering. The senator usually softened the bad news with some trifling assignment before he unloaded with the heavy stuff.

"You know better. Jack, something is up in your neck of the woods, and I need you and Dave to check it out. I sent out a packet of information through Strothers' office. He'll have it first thing tomorrow and expect you two downtown for a briefing. Say nine AM. I figure you can drop the adminstrivia for a few months and do some real work for a change. Call Dave and work him into the scheme for me, please."

"Can you tell me anything beforehand, Bill? You know getting Strothers to come to the point will take all morning. The guy speaks gobbledygook fluently." Jack already dreaded the meeting and he hadn't gotten out of bed yet.

"Yeah, all right. I had a little briefing from some friends in the FBI and Secret Service last week. In a nutshell, land developers out there are laundering counterfeit money and grabbing open space designated for parks and recreation. Any of that sound familiar?"

Jack recalled exactly what was familiar. He remembered Helen's death, an avalanche, and a big bastard who had tried to blast him off the side of Douglas Pass.

"We never caught the guy making the payoff out in Mesa county. You think he might be moving his operation to the front range, senator?"

"Could be, Jack. Could be. If so, let's bag him this time. Have a nice rest of the weekend, friend." The senator hung up, leaving Jack with too many memories for a pleasant spring Sunday.

Jack's mind wound itself around the events of three years ago and kept repeating miserable scenes, passing through an endless loop. He sank down into the bed, feeling his loss all over again until Tommy and Katie bounced into the room and jumped him, forcing him out of bed. They wanted their weekend favorite, big fluffy pancakes made from scratch, then a bike ride into the park. What a miracle, he thought. Just when he was ready to slide into his private chasm of grief over Helen, his kids happened by and pulled him back from the edge.

Downstairs, Jack started mixing up the batter. He had already cooked the bacon and poured the juice when the idea hit him. He still needed a referee, and he knew Dave Mendes goofed off every Sunday. Time to knock off two birds with one undercover agent. Jack called his best buddy.

"Hey lazy. Get up and come over for pancakes." Jack yelled in the phone. Then he held the receiver away from his ear to avoid hearing loss as Dave loudly protested being awakened. But, in the end he gave up, like Jack knew he would. Dave's condo was over on Baker Ranch a quick five minutes away.

"Don't let those two ragamuffins eat my share, Jack. Can I bring anything?"

Jack remembered his plans for the day. "Yeah, Dave. Throw your bike in the back of your truck. The kids want to ride into the park after breakfast. When we get back we can do a little cookout. How's that sound, pardner?"

"Great. You know I hate to cook. Be right over."

Jack's mind went into overdrive. He had a full pound of bacon all fried up. He could add more flour and eggs to increase the batter. He dialed another number.

"Becca, hi. It's Jack. Had breakfast yet?"

Thirty minutes later Jack had a house full of pancake eaters. Dave Mendes, Becca, Andy, Missy, and his own two kids were gobbling up pancakes faster than he could flip them. Finally he got to sit down with them and eat.

Andy looked across the table at him and took a breath after chomping through his last mouthful of the golden cakes.

"Mr. Marshall, how did you do these? I didn't know guys could cook. Can I come over again next Sunday?"

Missy wasn't going to be left out. "Me too, Mr. Marshall. Can I come too?"

Dave decided to get in the act. "Me too, Mr. Marshall. Pretty please," he added with dripping sarcasm.

Jack saw his opening and went for it. "First of all, Andy and Missy, now you can call me Coach Jack. And yes, you can come over any Sunday." Jack glanced at Becca to include her and received a warm smile in return. Criminies, he'd cook pancakes every day to get smiles like that.

"But Dave, you can only come back on one condition. Our soccer team is in dire need of a referee. We need someone who is tough and fair. What do you say, my friend?"

"Oh no, my friend," Dave replied. "I don't even have a kid on the team. I don't know how to referee soccer. Sure, I used to ref some high school football, but soccer's beyond me."

Missy saved the day. She looked up at the big man sitting beside her and spoke magic words. "But we have to have a referee, Mr. Dave. My mom says if we don't have a referee, we can't play." For added emphasis, Missy fluttered her eyelashes. She looked like a miniature Becca with her pony tail of black hair and her violet eyes. Jack thought there must be some gene in little girls that gave them this power over grown men.

Dave melted on the spot and was hooked. He couldn't let this pretty little girl down and everyone at the table knew it, especially Missy.

"Okay, you win, Missy, but I'm doing this for you and Katie, understand?" Dave was rewarded by hugs from both girls. He grinned from ear to ear.

Jack gave Becca a thumbs-up sign and then a curious look that asked, who had taught Missy that trick. Her return look warmed him all the way to his toes.

The bike ride caused a few problems. Becca didn't own a bicycle. She was embarrassed to admit that Malcolm hadn't given her the money for bicycles. She had paid for the kid's bikes by giving piano lessons and never had enough left over for a bike of her own.

"You all go ahead. I'll stay behind and clean up the kitchen." Becca rolled up her sleeves and started to gather the dishes, not noticing that everyone else stood still.

Tommy ended the short moment of embarrassment. "You can use my mom's bike," he blurted. "It's almost brand new, and she hardly ever rode it. Right, dad?" Tommy pleaded with Jack, his face giving away the crush he had on Becca. It was apparent to Jack that his son was determined to have Becca join them, and so was he.

"Of course," Jack replied, giving each of his children a happy smile. His look told them it was okay to move on. There was no need to build any shrine to their mother's memory.

•••

Hours later Jack and Dave settled on the deck after a successful ride and cookout. Becca and her tribe had gone home to get ready for the coming week of school. Tommy and Katie were in their rooms upstairs.

"Okay, spill it," Dave muttered in a friendly tone. "What's the real reason you asked me over here today? And I'm not talking about being introduced to the gorgeous woman next door that you obviously have big plans for." Dave winked at his best friend.

"She's nice, huh?" Jack knew he could talk to Dave about Becca. He had felt something changing inside all weekend, especially after the moment they had shared in the donut shop. Now he couldn't seem to get Becca out of his head.

"What's her story? Where's Mr. Schmidt?"

Jack brought him up to speed about the abusive Malcolm Schmidt. "After that night, all my innocent neighborly feelings towards Becca changed, Dave. Yeah, I took the guy's head off for yelling at my kids and hitting his wife. Felt protective, I guess. Then Becca and I went to this coaching clinic together yesterday, and, well, things changed." He saw Dave's smirk and hurried on. "But, I'll make it clear to you, pal. I'm trying hard to step on the emotional brakes." Dave shot him a skeptical look. "Okay, I understand what you're thinking, but I do have to play it slow and easy, at least until the dust settles."

Jack laughed out loud as he watched Dave's mime act. His big friend pretended to cast an imaginary fishing rod into the backyard then jerk back as if he had hooked a big one. Smiling, Dave pointed to Jack and covered his heart with both hands.

"Go for it, my friend. You deserve some happiness, and it's time."

Jack changed subjects and told Dave about the new assignment from Senator Conley.

"Jeez," replied Dave. "I wish Bill could just give us the work directly. I can't stand Strothers. He's some desk jockey who's never been out in the

field, doing the deed. He's a bean counter always looking to save a buck."
Dave took a swig of beer and shook his head.

"Looks like we have to put up with this creep for another morning at least,
Dave."

•••

Dave and Jack had been sitting in Henry Strothers' outer office over
twenty minutes, waiting for their assignment. They had been on time,
getting to the joint FBI-Secret Service complex at the federal office building
precisely at nine Monday morning. Both men were ready to strangle
Strothers. He did this every time they were called in for another assignment.
It was a power play, pure and simple. Strothers had information they needed,
thus control over them, if only for the few minutes it took to brief them and
let them go do the dirty work.

Finally, they heard a buzzer on the receptionist's desk. A distant voice
scratched out the words, "Send them in, Miss Melindez." The efficient secretary turned and smiled sympathetically at her two visitors. Her look trans-
mitted feelings about her supervisor that paralleled those of Jack and Dave.
She nodded towards the closed door.

The two agents exchanged a look of disgust and entered the office. It was
empty.

"This some kind of joke?" Dave was losing his patience with these games.

"Let's grab a chair, Dave. The SOB did this to me once. Took a potty
break so he could make a grand entrance to show me who was really the
boss." Jack turned sarcastic. "I suppose we must try to get in his shoes and
understand his perspective."

A voice drifted from the side door as Henry Strothers made his grand
entrance. "I heard that, Marshall, and it was not appreciated. I do run things
around here, you know. You would be wise to remember that."

Strothers crossed the room and took his seat behind a plain metal desk.
He turned his back on the agents, ignoring them, and began shuffling papers
on his credenza.

Jack spotted the packet of information for them on the front corner of the
desk and picked it up to read. He and Dave had worked their way through
half the material before Strothers deigned to speak again.

"Give me those documents," he whined. His face had turned crimson at
the audacity of the two agents. "The next time Senator Conley comes here
for a visit, I will speak to him about your insubordination."

Jack and Dave kept the papers. They returned Strothers' glare with neutral
expressions designed to push him over the edge.

"We know what to do, Henry." Dave spoke using the balding bureaucrat's first name. This tactic usually got him sputtering with indignation and ended their meetings quickly.

Jack and Dave had little regard for Henry Strothers. He was a low-level political appointee in charge of the combined FBI/Secret Service office in Denver. Bean counters in Washington thought the combination made economic sense. No one in the two agencies agreed. But as usual, jobs saved by the combo in Denver had been transferred back to the White House. There, after a period of several months to let hard feelings cool off, those same jobs were handed out to friends of the party in power.

This was usual procedure following an election. FBI and Secret Service agents ignored the whole mess, and continued to work together when necessary, and go their separate ways as required.

Henry Strothers puffed out his chest and gave his usual spiel. "I'll expect weekly reports on my desk each Friday by COB - that's close of business, or five PM. Monthly summaries are to be generated by the third working day of the following month. Is that clear?"

Jack and Dave exchanged looks. Dave spoke for both men. "Is that all, Henry?"

Henry replied indirectly. "I have followed my instructions thoroughly. You may leave now." But, he was speaking to an empty room as the two agents had already walked away, both muttering about political appointees taking jobs from career workers who knew what they were doing.

They turned left outside the receptionist's office, walked the length of the corridor to an unnumbered door, and entered. Inside they greeted their old friend Max Gonzales, the FBI techno-wizzard and senior agent who would give them the real briefing.

Last night, after several beers, Jack had called Max for the skinny on his new assignment. Now he and Dave would form a team with the FBI agent and gather whatever support was necessary to do the job.

"Guys," Max began, "it's good to work with you again. We've been watching several places around the state." Max rolled down a wall map and pointed to towns and counties with big red circles around them. Most were far from the heavily populated Front Range metropolitan area.

Max continued. "Used to take a shady developer years, sometimes decades to grab land that supposedly no one wanted. You know the deal. The feds cede what they call excess land to a city or county, say for a park. Local officials declare they're broke and can't use the land because it'll cost too much to develop. Then, *voila*, pardon my French, the parcel of land goes up for bid, and wonder of wonders, a kind-hearted, civic-minded construction company relieves the taxpayers of an undue burden, paying pennies to the dollar. By then, everybody has forgotten about parks, recreation, greenbelts, wetlands, wildlife, and all the other factors that were used to justify ceding the land in the first place."

Max took a breath, saw that his two friends understood everything so far, then continued. "Tract housing and strip malls cover the bull-dozed parcel before somebody realizes there's no money to set up services like utilities and police and fire protection. Out here in our semi-desert, they also conveniently forget these new homeowners and businesses will need drinking water. Then folks who move here to escape crime and glut in California and back east, demand that farmers on the Western Slope give up their water rights, and the court battles go on forever."

This all sounded too familiar to Jack. He had worked the Western Slope for years before Helen's death.

"Who are you watching, Max?" Dave said.

"There are a couple of big companies that have worked large developments in Ridgway and Montrose, small communities with lots of land but no money for development. It's tough to catch them. One commissioner stood out like a sore thumb in Ridgway, though. He went out and bought a Mercedes, tried to pass a bogus fifty at the a local deli, messed up big-time. We convinced him to join the witness protection program and nailed his benefactor."

Max handed over a list of people his agents had under surveillance. "Fellows, we need to watch out for these guys popping up over here. It takes too many people to keep them under 24-hour watch and we've been doing background checks on local politicians as well. We hope something will break. Or maybe you two characters will come up with a new twist."

"We'll work on it, Max," Dave responded. We'll be talking to you."

The three men stood and shook hands, silent with the understanding that this scam could affect their own neighborhoods.

SIXTEEN

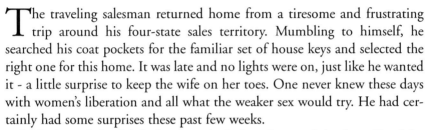

The traveling salesman returned home from a tiresome and frustrating trip around his four-state sales territory. Mumbling to himself, he searched his coat pockets for the familiar set of house keys and selected the right one for this home. It was late and no lights were on, just like he wanted it - a little surprise to keep the wife on her toes. One never knew these days with women's liberation and all what the weaker sex would try. He had certainly had some surprises these past few weeks.

Malcolm quietly slid the key into the lock and opened the door. Good, he thought, not a sound. Yes, a surprise tonight would be delicious, add to the excitement. He smiled and began removing his clothes as he climbed the stairs. At the top, he moved down the hall to the left, heading for the master bedroom. The door was open, an invitation.

Malcolm stripped away his remaining clothes, shaking and rigid with anticipation. He stopped by the closet to retrieve the silk scarves. Sometimes he wanted his wife under control, under his command. At the side of the king-sized bed, he glared down to ensure his rules had been met. It was a game they played at the end of each work week. She slept naked under the satin sheet, on her back, legs slightly parted. Prepared for his return. She was teasing him, eyes hooded in pretend sleep.

He pulled the sheet away revealing her beauty. Silky black hair framed her adorable face. Full lips pursed in a sleep-smile. Flawless creamy skin invited his touch. His gaze wandered down gentle curves, resting on the slender, erotic flaring of hips. Rising and falling with each breath, her perfectly formed breasts sloped to the side, their tips were relaxed now, but that would change soon. She feigned a deep sleep, something he required to satisfy his need to watch and control.

"Now." He signaled with one word for the scene to unfold. His gaze fixed on the curling hair between her legs.

She stirred, moaned, and began stroking herself with light, fingertip caresses. Malcolm stared at the juncture of her thighs, which moved apart, allowing access for her touches and his vision. His breathing quickened as he worked to stifle his own groan of anticipation. Surprisingly, he found that he was panting now, like a dog salivating for a scrap of meat. He frowned at this lack of control, squelching his weakness immediately. Still, he was frozen to the sight of his sexy wife stroking herself as if in a trance. Her movements were feather-like, delicate, arousing. It was her turn to breathe quickly, then utter small sounds of pleasure, as she increased pressure and speed. Her hips rose slightly, mating with an invisible body. Too quickly, her body arched then collapsed in release. Her hands slid back to the surface of the bed in contentment.

Malcolm shuddered in surprise. No, not yet. This was outside the rules, not part of the game. For the first time in minutes he checked himself and found his body hunched over the side of the bed. He had lost control and had begun to mirror the self-gratification he had just witnessed. Malcolm trembled. The giddiness of a growing orgasm threatened to overwhelm him.

"No, not this way," he said aloud. Maintain control. He forced down the mounting pleasure in a spasm of intense pain, then turned away from the erotic sight of his wife.

Malcolm hesitated no longer. He lunged onto her roughly, ignoring the grunt of pain as her breath was forced out. She pushed up on her elbows to offer a greeting kiss, but he pressed her shoulders down viciously, then forcefully buried himself in her. Not with sensitivity. Not even looking into her eyes.

It was over quickly. He collapsed, panting, and rolled away, oblivious to her fists clenched in anguish. He had found release, and nothing else mattered.

He compared. Rebecca had never had passion like this. She had turned into a frozen bitch years ago. That's when he decided to marry Audrey. She was younger, more pliable. He controlled her easily, and the vasectomy after Rebecca's second pregnancy, a mistake, guaranteed there would be no children to spoil his fun.

Boise, Idaho was a nice enough town on the western edge of his territory. After tonight, Malcolm decided he would spend more time with this wife and ignore the other one back in Colorado. For a while. Then the time would come to take charge of Rebecca again.

Audrey hurt inside and out. She struggled to stifle her emotions and allowed only a few silent tears to fall. This was no longer exciting. Her husband's sex games had become too rough and one-sided.

SEVENTEEN

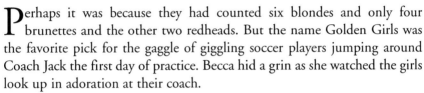

Perhaps it was because they had counted six blondes and only four brunettes and the other two redheads. But the name Golden Girls was the favorite pick for the gaggle of giggling soccer players jumping around Coach Jack the first day of practice. Becca hid a grin as she watched the girls look up in adoration at their coach.

She was well aware of the pedestal on which little girls this age placed their daddies. It was a bittersweet recognition for Becca because she knew her daughter wanted a daddy to love, and there was no one for her. Becca took in the angelic faces of innocence, each straining to be the closest to this big bear of a man smiling down at them. They would do whatever he told them and that presented a problem. There was complete trust, and yes, even hero worship that would require some restraint on Jack's part. If not, the upcoming separation a few years from now when they entered adolescence, would be very painful.

Jack was quite aware of all this, as he had told her just last night while they were planning today's practice. It was not that he held back in loving his daughter Katie. But, he tried to blend in discipline and education about having too much of a good thing. He told Becca that Katie needed to learn that her daddy was human and made mistakes. He wasn't perfect, but he tried hard to do the right thing. Not all boys and men did. He didn't want Katie to be afraid, just cautious. It was a difficult line to walk.

Becca thought back to how she had felt while Jack related his feelings about his daughter. Had her own father tried to teach her those lessons? Had she ever loved him unconditionally to the point of overdoing it? Had he let her? Was that why she had run away with Malcolm? Today, she worried. Who would guide Missy? Certainly not Missy's father. It took a dad to do that.

"Okay, Coach Becca, let's show these Golden Girls how to kick a soccer ball." Jack called her out of her questioning fantasy. Becca joined the group and went through the drill she and Jack had practiced during the clinic.

Jack did the talking. "Girls, I'm going to roll the ball to Coach Becca. Watch how she stops it with the side of her foot." The girls bent over and didn't take their eyes off the small soccer ball as Jack kicked it to Becca. All twelve heads were trained on the ball as it rolled. Becca stopped it, turning her body sideways to Jack. She stepped back and approached the ball, taking one long stride with her right foot, then a short hop that placed her left foot just behind the ball. Becca kicked it with the side of her right foot, shooting the ball straight for Jack.

Twelve mouths dropped wide open as the girls watched the ball head directly to their coach. When he stopped it, miraculously it seemed to them, they jumped and shouted hooray for Coach Becca. Pony tails bobbed as they exchanged high-fives.

"We want to try. Can we? Please?" came the chorus. Jack and Becca laughed. They had so much enthusiasm and unbounded energy. This was going to be a blast.

Each coach formed a circle with six girls and stood in the middle with a ball. They explained that the girls were to kick the ball only with the side of their feet, and stop it the same way. No hands allowed. No toes, either. Then Jack and Becca worked their respective teams, rotating inside the circles, kicking and stopping the ball in exchange with each girl.

Next Jack and Becca set up small cones for goals and corner posts. Jack called the girls over to the center of their field. He counted off six girls for himself and six for Becca, moving them into separate groups.

"Let's have some fun and play a practice game, girls," he shouted. Their response was deafening. "Look around and make sure you know who is on your team." Becca handed out colored practice vests. Jack pointed to Becca's group and said, "Coach Becca has the blue team today and my gang is the red team."

"Coach Becca and I are going to be the goalies. Your job is to try to score on us. I'm the Red Goalie, and Coach Becca is the Blue Goalie." With that, he threw the ball high into the air and ran back to defend his goal. Becca retreated to her goal, and both coaches watched chaos unfold between them.

Skip Hawkins had used the term *cluster ball* to describe six-a-side soccer. Beginning players all chased the ball. When they cornered it, they would surround it and start kicking at it. This led to a cluster of players encircling the ball and bouncing it around from kicker to kicker. A few stragglers would wait for the ball to squirt outside the cluster, then joyfully kick it back into the melee. Playing positions and passing to an open player to shoot on goal was a concept yet to come.

Today, Jack wanted the girls to run and play, enjoy some exercise and maybe figure out how to kick the ball. At the next practice they would cover passing off and staying on an assigned part of the field. Maybe. Becca and Jack stood alone at their make-believe goals as the girls joyously yelled, screamed, and bunched around the little ball.

Surprisingly, Sharon Huff broke out of the cluster with the ball bouncing from her pointed toe - a definite no-no. But she paid no mind of that and ran away from the rest of the girls towards Jack's goal. He stood ready to defend his goal, legs apart, arms out to the side. Hell, he realized, this was something they hadn't covered in the clinic. Then zap! Sharon punched the ball straight at him from about mid-field. He feigned an attempt to stop it, then at the last second let it go through for a goal.

Sharon jumped for joy, and her teammates surrounded her, patting her on the back, yelling and high-fiving. They had won. Sharon had kicked the ball past the coach.

"Great shot, Sharon. That's just fantastic." Jack praised her several times before taking her to the side for a little chat. "Sharon, that's a goal for sure, but what did you do that I asked you not to?" Jack knelt in front of the girl, who stood a head taller than anyone else on the team. She was flushed and breathing hard, exhilarated by her shot and the praise of her teammates.

Then she looked at Jack, exasperated. "I know, I know. Don't kick with my toe." Then she took off to get in her mother's car parked near the field. Jack watched her go. He saw Priscilla wave and then drive off.

Becca had come up at the last minute of the one-on-one coaching clinic. "So much for technique," she commented. "But, wow! What a kick. And she's very fast, too."

"Yeah, she's fast all right. She's also headstrong, stubborn, and spoiled," he replied. "She won't like playing only two quarters either."

The coaches gathered the remaining girls around them and complimented them on a good practice.

"Everyone played really well today," Becca said.

"See you here at four PM, Wednesday," Jack reminded, and the girls took off, scattering to the station wagons and vans pulling up to take them home.

Jack and Becca gathered up the cones and bag of balls and started for his car where Katie and Missy sat, chattering away about their team. Jack started to get in the driver's seat when he noticed one slender girl, Gina Ashworth, he recognized, sitting on the curb by herself.

Jack walked over to her. "Gina, do you have a ride? Somebody picking you up?"

"Mom said she would be here as soon as she got out of work." Gina spoke in a dreary voice, as if she didn't expect things to go well.

"Well come on over and sit in our car. We'll wait until your mom gets here." Jack saw the little girl's eyes light up. He walked her back to his car and they got in to wait.

Thirty minutes later, Gloria Ashworth drove up. She was in a hurry, and angry to boot.

"I'm sorry, Jack," she gushed, out of breath. "Got tied up at work and lost track of time. Thanks for staying with Gina. Come on sweetie, let's go get supper."

Becca and Jack watched them drive off. Maybe, he thought, they needed to increase their carpool by one more girl.

EIGHTEEN

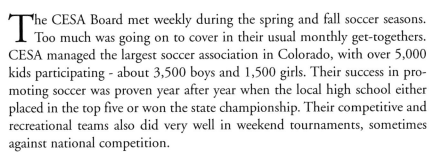

The CESA Board met weekly during the spring and fall soccer seasons. Too much was going on to cover in their usual monthly get-togethers. CESA managed the largest soccer association in Colorado, with over 5,000 kids participating - about 3,500 boys and 1,500 girls. Their success in promoting soccer was proven year after year when the local high school either placed in the top five or won the state championship. Their competitive and recreational teams also did very well in weekend tournaments, sometimes against national competition.

Fred Tompkins, CESA president, always worried about the field situation. For all the open space in Colorado, there were few athletic complexes available to schedule practices and games for the several hundred teams CESA fielded each season. Soccer also faced fierce competition from softball and baseball in the spring, and of course, dreaded football in the fall.

Fred had become a regular at Madison County Commissioner Board meetings, where he often pleaded for more fields for his kids. Tonight he was excited. He had great news for his CESA members. They were going to get more fields for the fall season without competing with other sports. And, the new fields would be right in their own backyards! He had heard the proposal in last night's county board meeting from Mr. Conninger, someone he never met but who was going to become a fast friend.

According to Conninger, the county owned a golf course alongside the South Platte. Part of the course had been leased to a sand and gravel company. That part had been closed off to golfing and mined out for months, but the rest of the course remained usable, just not for golf. Fred had missed the part about why the county opted to lease the course for commercial use in the first place. But he lost interest in that trail once it was announced that the county was looking for a neighborhood sports association to maintain the fourteen fairways that remained. Conninger explained that most of the land involved was suitable for some kind of playing fields.

Fred's heartbeat had increased to double-time at that news. After the meeting he went right up to Conninger and requested a shot at the fields for soccer. The little man had seemed positive about Fred's proposal, and so had his associate. Fred had forgotten the man's name, but he couldn't forget the guy who'd towered over everyone at the meeting. Ugliest SOB he'd ever seen.

It was time to start the meeting, and Fred called the members and guests to order. The guests were all the new coaches for the season. They were invited to see how business got done in hopes that some could be convinced to fill vacancies on the board. Turnover for the difficult jobs of registrar, training coordinator, and referee recruiter was high. Few people worked more than two four-month seasons before burning out. The pressure of scheduling and the many confrontations with parents who wanted to switch their children to better teams at the last minute was aggravating.

There was electricity in the air tonight, as word had already spread through the neighborhood about Fred's news. That rumor alone had drawn Jack and Dave to the meeting.

The coaches and board members waited anxiously in the overcrowded conference room through the routine registrar's report, treasurer's report, training clinic report, and status of referees report. This last report was a key item since, a shortage of referees could endanger their season.

At the call for new business, Fred cleared his throat.

"Folks, I have some good news about fields. The county has some land and they need somebody to maintain it for them. It's the first fourteen holes of the old Rabbit Creek golf course. And -" Fred had to pause as the buzzing and conversation picked up - "we have first shot at getting it."

The group broke into applause. Someone hollered, "Where do we sign?" And got a big laugh. Fred held up both hands for silence and explained the deal.

"We'll have to spend some money to hook up the irrigation system and mow the grass. I need some volunteers to go out there with me to mark off boundaries for playing fields. Anybody game?"

Jack stood and introduced himself. "I'm Jack Marshall. Dave Mendes and I will be happy to help out. We're free during the day and welcome the opportunity."

This was a first, Fred thought. He always struggled for help and these two guests just popped right up. His wife had mentioned seeing Jack Marshall running through the neighborhood. He was a single dad who worked out of his home. He was coaching his little girl's team for the first time this season. Mendes was a puzzle, though.

"Thanks fellows," Fred replied. "Meet me at the gate to the golf course about nine tomorrow morning. Wear some scruffy clothes, and we'll get to work."

Jack and Dave slipped out when the meeting turned to a discussion of CESA's lease agreement with the county.

"Smell something, Jack?" Dave knew his partner was working his mind around the evening events, off in another world.

"Could be our first break on this assignment just got dropped right in our laps, Dave. If this is a scam, it's a common one. A developer could be laundering the land through CESA, then convince the county to pull the rug out from under us so they could start building."

Dave considered this line of thought a moment. "Wonder how much it will drain the CESA treasury? They can't have too much money in the bank. The county parks department charges them a hefty five bucks for each kid who plays. Or, half the cost to register your daughter, Jack."

Jack nodded. "Let's call Max and get a line on background checks being done in Madison County. Be interesting to see if they're watching anybody on the board."

The next morning Dave and Jack walked through the greenbelt across the bike path in back of Jack's house. The golf course entrance was less than a half mile through the woods this way. Jack had bought his place just for that reason, to be near the trees and open space. Later on, lotto money had been used to build the bike paths leading from Denver all along the river to the park grounds inside Cromwell Dam Recreation Area.

When he wasn't jogging through the neighborhood, Jack liked to run to the dam and back on the bike path. He often took the kids bike riding there as well. The greenbelt was a jumble of wetlands and hideaways for smaller animals escaping the onslaught of development. Ponds and lakes dotted the landscape, most the result of digging and scraping by the sand and gravel company. Once they had finished carving out their money's worth, only minor reclamation had been needed to create a useful habitat for wildlife. Ground water had seeped in, and the ever-present cottonwood trees had sprouted automatically.

Tommy and Katie loved to watch the cormorants swim and dive like miniature seals. When they surfaced there was usually a silvery fish in their beaks, which was swallowed immediately. The kids got bug-eyed watching the lump of fish slowly inch its way down the bird's hungry gullet.

Jack's favorite birds were the great blue herons that nested on top of dead tree trunks in the middle of the larger lakes. The herons had made a successful comeback largely due to the money dumped into parks and recreation from lotto profits, and the hard work of many conservation groups.

Colorado was an outdoor state. Everyone did something outside like fly fishing, hiking, camping, hunting, bike riding, and the list was endless.

The two agents met up with Fred at the gate to the golf course.

"Hey, fellas," Fred said. "You surprised me. I kept looking for a car, and here you come popping out of the woods like spies or something." He added a nervous laugh.

"Not today, Fred," Jack replied, exchanging a grin with Dave. "Today, we're soccer volunteers. Now tell us more about this great place you captured for CESA."

"This is a great deal, Jack, although not cheap. We'll have to pay a higher user fee - eight dollars per player - and shell out money to hook up the irrigation. One of our board members owns a landscaping business and he has donated some industrial strength mowers to help trim our expenses. Still, this land will cost us close to $20,000 a year for the next three years to lease on top of the user fees."

Dave took a turn at questioning Fred. "What happens after three years? Do we have options to continue the lease? Can we buy this land eventually? Or, is all this going to be lost, or sunk costs as accountants would say?"

Fred had a look of concern now. Dave didn't need an outright answer to his questions. Fred's facial expression said it all.

"Sorry, Dave, but there are no guarantees. CESA's total investment could blow away easily. There's also a quit clause in the lease agreement spelling out the county's right to terminate the contract for *cause*. This can mean whatever local politician's want it to mean, if the right opportunity comes along."

With this sobering information out in the open, Fred took the volunteers on a tour of the grounds. There was a small clubhouse that would work perfectly for storing game equipment like extra balls, nets and corner flags. It even had a couple of restrooms that could be cleaned up and used. The available fairways would convert into odd-size soccer fields, but beggars couldn't argue too much. The half-size 50-yard fields used by the six-a-side teams would fit about anywhere. Parking would be plentiful along the first fairway.

The three men spent the morning pacing off sides and end lines. They drove stakes to mark boundaries. There was one problem they hadn't counted on, though. Rabbit Creek bisected the golf course, keeping them from using much of the flatter fairways closer to the river.

They mulled it over all morning, until Dave thought of something. "Guys, I say we go to the lotto commission and ask for a footbridge across the creek. This is a perfect application for them. We might even be able to talk them out of some picnic shelters as well." Dave was on a roll now, spending lotto money like he had won the jackpot.

Fred's face broke into a big grin. "Dave, do you think it matters that the lotto commissioner has two sons playing in our association?"

Jack took in the conversation from another angle. They had spent the morning working in a vacuum. He thought back to Dave's questions and knew this deal was a possible rat hole for chicanery. With land at such a premium, it was too good to be true. He and Dave needed to do some leg work, with Max's help, to figure out who stood to profit. If they didn't, another great property could be gobbled up and covered over by development. Worse, the kids would have no place to play. Jack made some mental notes on follow-up actions he and Dave would take when they finished with Fred. Meanwhile, his two companions were busy drafting a letter to the lotto commissioner asking for lots of goodies.

NINETEEN

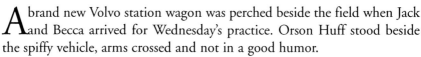

A brand new Volvo station wagon was perched beside the field when Jack and Becca arrived for Wednesday's practice. Orson Huff stood beside the spiffy vehicle, arms crossed and not in a good humor.

"Howdy, Orson," Jack called out. "Come to help out or just observe?"

Orson drew in a big breath and approached Jack with determination. "It's about my daughter, Mr. Marshall. Apparently you're not aware that we sent her to a soccer camp last summer where she excelled. So, you can imagine my surprise when she came in the house after your first practice and complained about getting scolded for kicking the ball too hard." Drops of perspiration appeared on Orson's upper lip and he clenched and unclenched his hands nervously. He seemed to be waiting for Jack's explanation and apology.

Jack stared at the overindulgent father and paused before he spoke. "That's great, that she went to a camp. I didn't know you could do that before the legal playing age of six." Jack tossed the ball back to Orson.

"Well, we managed to work out a suitable arrengement with the company running the camp. But I need to return to my original point. Why did you scold her? Seems to me that's a parent's job."

Oh brother, thought Jack. "Orson, Sharon didn't kick the ball too hard, and I didn't scold her. She really is good, you know. She's fast, runs a lot, and can kick the daylights out of the ball. Almost took my head off when I played goalie. But whatever camp you sent her to didn't teach her to kick the ball right. I just took her aside and did a little coaching, that's all." Jack could see that Orson was confused.

"What do you mean by 'kick the ball right,' Mr. Marshall? Kicking is kicking, isn't it? And, we paid good money as an investment in Sharon's future."

Jack had heard enough. "Orson, do you want to spend a bundle on orthopedic surgery when her feet get damaged from broken bones during her biggest growth period? She kicks the ball with her toe, and that will damage her feet. Becca and I spent last Saturday morning learning how to kick a ball from the coach of the pro team in town. Evidently your camp, in which you so wisely invested, taught Sharon incorrectly." Jack started to walk away, then stopped and returned to the flustered father.

"If you don't want me to coach your daughter, find another team for her. Otherwise, either get out on the field and help us, or take a seat and watch us practice."

Becca already had the girls in circles practicing kicks, stops, and passes with alternate feet. She saw steam coming out of Jack's ears when he approached, and knew his confrontation with Orson Huff had not been pleasant. Becca liked this man, Jack Marshall, maybe more than she should allow herself now. Was she attracted to him after only a few weeks working with him? That was an easy one. The answer was yes. Should she be? Harder question, but she couldn't ignore her feelings. Besides, he was super with children. How could a dormant yuppie like Huff take exception to somebody trying to teach his child how to play soccer? She found herself arguing mentally with the ignorant father, defending Jack. Didn't everybody see how nice he was? He was generous with his time and helped out doing so many things for his neighbors. Especially her.

She knew he liked her as a good friend. She wondered if there was more going on. They got along well, and working on the soccer team together was fun. Both were positive people, even though it had taken Jack some effort to bring out that side of her. They shared a love for kids and always complimented the Golden Girls on their play. Every little nudge of encouragement went so far to build self esteem and confidence in children this young. Heck, she thought, children of any age.

"Becca, please take a crack at teaching Sharon the right way to kick. I need to work with someone else today. Okay?"

"Right, Coach Jack." She answered with a smart salute that got him in a better mood.

The Golden Girls did the rest as they whooped and scampered over the field, chasing the ball during their practice game. Jack stayed busy breaking up one cluster after another. Finally, he yelled, "Time-out!"

"Everybody over here in the center of the field. Hurry!" The girls gathered around him expectantly. "Okay. See what you're doing? You're all chasing the ball. Let's learn some positions to play." The girls all clapped and jumped up and down. It didn't matter what he said. They were all for it.

Jack and Becca marched the girls to different parts of the field and spent the rest of practice trying to keep them in position relative to the location of the ball. It was slow-going, like trying to run in waist-deep water. Of course, Sharon ran everywhere as if she were a rover linebacker.

At the end of practice, Jack figured the girls would need some "incentive" to stay in position at Friday's session. Maybe extra laps around the field would do the trick. Then he noticed Missy over at the far goal practicing by herself. Jack watched the slender little girl as she approached the ball. She looked serious and determined as she kept her head down and eyes glued to the top of the ball. Missy planted her left foot perfectly and punched the ball squarely into the net with her right foot. On the next approach, she kicked with her left foot. Pow! The green and white ball swished into the back of the net. Jack saw no difference in her technique with either foot.

"Hey, Missy." He hollered. "Those are really good kicks." She broke into a big smile of appreciation as he walked over. "Why don't you try some corner kicks, and I'll stand in front of the goal as your target."

"That's great, Coach Jack." Missy hustled after the ball and ran to the nearest corner. But she surprised Jack when she left to get the entire bag of balls that Katie and Gina had just collected. She dumped them on the ground and looked up at him, grinning, ready to practice into the night.

Jack had to laugh. Such determination. She was only six and her desire to excel and compete was already extraordinary. He turned to see if Becca had noticed their special practice session. She was with Gina and Katie who were drawing dirt pictures by the car. Becca waved at him to take all the time he wanted.

Missy kicked, and Jack caught the balls and rolled them over to the opposite corner. After her last kick in one corner, she trotted across the field to work on her opposite foot. Jack was amazed. He didn't have to move, as Missy placed ball after ball right into his hands, squarely in front of the goal.

"Missy, come here, sweetie. You've worn me out today. We'll do this again after next practice."

She ran to Jack and gave him a big hug. "Thanks, coach. That was really fun."

Jack looked down into her smiling face and felt instant love for the child. She wanted so much to be loved and appreciated, and no dad was there for her. It took so little effort to please her. On impulse, Jack reached down and picked her up. Her arms went around his neck in a tight bear hug.

Wow! He thought. No amount of money could equal this. Malcolm was an idiot for giving this up.

Jack and Missy retrieved the balls and joined Becca. As they approached her, Jack noticed a sheen of tears in her eyes and a bittersweet smile on her face. Perhaps, he thought, there was more to her tears than joy for her daughter's sake.

Gina was joining them after practice to go to Becca's to wait for her mom to pick her up. This arrangement had been worked out by the two mothers.

Becca had offered to help out Gloria Ashworth, who was practically a single mom too. Her husband, whose name Gloria never spoke, traveled most of the time.

Friday's practice was smoother. Jack and Becca began to see the difference their constant drilling had made. Some girls now loved to stay in position and relished the chance to get an open pass and shoot on goal. The rest of their teammates were still bunched in one corner of the field. Of all the girls, Missy was the most coachable. She could watch Coach Jack or her mom demonstrate a kick or drill, then copy them exactly. It was uncanny. After three practices, Missy was the best at all the skills. She just couldn't kick as hard as Sharon.

After Friday's practice game, Jack and Becca found their daughters huddled on the ground near the picnic area. They had Gina there as well, and three ponytails bobbed as they held a secret meeting.

When Becca approached the group to collect them for the ride home, Missy jumped up. "Mom, can we have a sleepover tomorrow night? Could we, please, Mom? Gina's mom needs a baby-sitter, and she wouldn't have to get one if Gina came over to our house. And Katie is my best pal, so she's gotta come too. Please, Mom."

Becca looked down at her daughter's adorable face. How could she refuse? Malcolm had never allowed sleepovers when he was home - too much noise and prancing around for him and his staid routines. She would have a lot on her hands keeping Andy away from the girls, though. He always wanted to pester his little sister, and a target of three giggly girls would be a great temptation to him. Then again, Andy wanted to have an overnight with Tommy over at Jack's. Maybe they could work out a swap.

When they got to Becca's house, she invited the girls inside for a snack, promising to send Katie over to Jack's before supper. Before he left, she worked out the plan for the sleepovers.

Once the girls devoured their snack, they hustled outside to take advantage of the remaining daylight and kick a soccer ball around the yard. Becca watched them run for a few minutes before she called to Katie.

"Katie, honey, come inside a minute. I want to show you something." Becca noted the puzzled expressions of all three girls. "Don't worry, team, I'll send her back out shortly and you can continue your game."

Becca led Katie straight to the piano in the living room. She was pleased to see the little girl's face shine with delight when she realized why she had been called inside. Becca sat on the bench in front of the beautiful instrument and beckoned Katie to sit beside her.

"I think it's time you started lessons, Katie. I have an open spot this time of day, and we can surprise your dad when you feel comfortable with your playing. How does that sound?"

"Gosh, that sounds great, Coach Becca, uh, Mrs. Schmidt. But don't I have to pay you something for the lessons?"

"Not yet. Let's see if you like to play and want to keep up with it. Sometimes I think kids see the money their parents spend on them and feel they have to perform out of duty. Let's just ease our way into this and try to have fun." Katie's answer came in the form of a big hug as she turned to Becca on the bench and threw her arms around her. Both pulled back smiling. The teaching had begun.

TWENTY

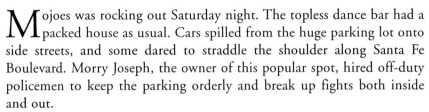

Mojoes was rocking out Saturday night. The topless dance bar had a packed house as usual. Cars spilled from the huge parking lot onto side streets, and some dared to straddle the shoulder along Santa Fe Boulevard. Morry Joseph, the owner of this popular spot, hired off-duty policemen to keep the parking orderly and break up fights both inside and out.

Patrons could get a little worked up, especially on Saturday nights. After several drinks, some of the men would pick out a dancer and claim her for his later on. Morry didn't discourage this. What his dancers did off the premises was their affair, and they all knew to take their men elsewhere. Still, he couldn't have people suing him for fights and damages caused by overzealous patrons. Especially since he had added the hottest dancer on the Boulevard.

Silver had made Mojoes her own after her first dance. She was a tall honey-blonde with gorgeous hair to her shoulders. Her body was perfectly proportioned and well-developed. Her breasts were large, firm, and always covered by a filmy, shimmering, gauze-like fabric that allowed enough of a tease to set the customers on fire. Still, she never took anything off, top or bottom. Her legs were those of a chorus line dancer. They were long and tapering, seeming to have no end as they disappeared into the fringe of her super-micro skirt. Her face was beautiful - what one could see of it behind her silver mask. That never came off either.

Fact was, Morry was glad she had insisted on the costume and her unwillingness to remove either her clothes or the mask. He could tell she had a great body, one that even everyday business clothes couldn't disguise. But her insistence on not stripping had led to his request for an audition. He had to see what kind of dancer she was.

She had been stunning. Morry was reminded of the fluid, erotic moves by dancers in the movie "Flashdance" a few years back. She spun and twisted sensuously, showing off the skilled dancing of a professional Las Vegas showgirl, which she had actually been. Yet, the lady Silver was much more than a former showgirl. Her sensuous dance routines always told a story and were done to classical music. She managed to work in ballet moves and gracefulness that mesmerized the normally rough and rowdy crew Mojoes attracted. Silver was the class act of the joint.

Tonight she was dancing to music from Tchaikovsky's "Romeo and Juliet." Silver enthralled the crowd, though 99 percent of them had never heard of Tchaikovsky. She knew the men didn't pay attention to the music anyway. They just stared at her body. Typically she did her number three times, and was the final act of the night. This evening, the beautiful and gifted woman retied her mask to keep her identity a secret. She was a single mom, and her reputation meant a lot to her. She didn't want her daughter laughed at or scorned by neighborhood kids. And who knows where William had gone off to? Her errant husband - soon to be ex in another 30 days - had decided he didn't want to be married to anyone. He had packed his bags and left her last year. She smiled grimly. The drooling characters out front couldn't possibly understand any man leaving their top dancer. But William had.

She had worked at Mojoes upstairs in administration for six months trying to make ends meet without her husband's paycheck. Most of her furniture had been sold, along with whatever valuables she had. She no longer invited anyone in her home out of embarrassment. There was nothing to sit on anyway.

Silver dropped her worries and took her cue for the last performance of the night. When she appeared onstage, the customers stood and applauded. They stayed standing but would remain silent until she finished. It had become a ritual, like the main event at a boxing match or the conclusion of a rock concert.

She smiled and began to move to the heartbreaking music of the greatest love story in history. Yet, no prima ballerina ever moved quite like Silver. She missed no opportunity to stretch her profile at an angle that best displayed her luscious body, adding a caress beneath a breast, brushing her hand down a provocatively flared hip, and parting the frilly skirt enough to draw groans from the men.

At the end, construction workers, ranch hands, miners, and even a few stock brokers out for a lark, stomped their boots and clapped their hands, clamoring for more. She never did an encore. By that time the crowd was too shifty and rowdy. Too many hands reached for her on the tiny stage. Her tips were enormous. Enough to help pay the bills, for now.

Entering her deserted house, the captivating Mojoes dancer was exhausted and glad that tonight her daughter was sleeping over at Becca Schmidt's. Gloria Ashworth needed some time to herself to rest and to think. She didn't know how much longer she could do this without someone finding out who she was. Regardless, she would probably have to move soon. Cottonwood Estates was an upscale neighborhood and beyond her means, even with her night job.

TWENTY ONE

The big-screen TV in Jack's family room blared with the noise and excitement of the Denver Broncos' back-to-back Super Bowl victories. Andy and Tommy sat on the floor as close as their eyes would let them, watching a video of the hall-of-fame play of John Elway. The comeback champion was guiding the Broncos to victories over Green Bay and then Atlanta.

Jack used the opportunity to remove the chilled bottle of Chardonnay from the fridge and slip over to Becca's. He would offer some reason to be there - probably just checking on the girls - and oh, by the way, how about a glass of wine on the deck, just the two of us? He was nervous. Becca was becoming a good friend, yet he didn't know how far and fast to go with her. Tonight she was like a magnet he couldn't resist.

Becca was a fascinating woman. Any normal man would be attracted to her physical beauty right off the bat. But there was much much more. Her days as a model had instilled in her a graceful way of moving that was sensual and flowing. She didn't just walk or run somewhere, she arrived there fluidly, attracting his attention every time. Her face had healed completely now, and he knew she slept better with Malcolm at least temporarily gone from the home. Coaching the Golden Girls and playing practice games had brought out her vivacious side. Surprisingly, Becca was opening up, displaying her own special feminine brand of humor that cracked him up every time. Whenever he asked her if she were ready to coach a drill, or collect the balls to go home, or whatever, her reply was a consistent, "Buster, I was born ready." This sly expression was followed with a sexy smirk that warmed him to the toes. Yes, Becca was a funny woman. She was also flirting easily, and Jack found himself attracted to her more every day.

It was like a treasure hunt to discover the hidden talents and interests of Becca Schmidt. Each layer Jack uncovered just led to a deeper and deeper person beneath it all. It really is a shame and a waste, he thought, that so many macho men wanted their women to stay at home and tend to the children. Was it a false sense of protectiveness? Something left over from hunter-gatherer days? An inherent weakness in the male psyche that refused to understand women's potential to do anything other than cook and bear children? Whatever the cause, the Neanderthals were missing out.

Maybe all husbands should experience the loss of a lifemate like his Helen. She had been his other half. She would never claim to be his better half, but she probably had been. He had put her first, and she had done the same for him. They made decisions together. He never considered acting like a macho man, one who demanded to be treated as the master of the house. No, Jack and Helen deferred to one another so much they often had to flip a coin to make choices. It didn't matter whose desires were met first, as long as they did everything together.

Jack never understood other men demanding a night out with the boys either. He had left that behind with his single days in the army. That was for high school and college fraternities. Heck, if you had a partner you cherished like his Helen, why go out with boys?

Jack realized that he missed Helen, yet he treasured the time they had been given. It seemed that after only a few months of marriage, a calm, contented feeling had settled over them that nothing could break. They had talked about the phenomenon often and saw the same look in other couples who had found the secret. They had been comfortable together, growing to love each other more every day. It was not a romantic love, although each managed to spice up the relationship in spite of having small children around. They simply always thought of each other first in every situation. Their marriage had been easy. It had not been work, as they had heard some describe their formula for success. Those couples who said, "We work hard at our relationship," lived in another world from Jack and Helen.

As he unlatched the gate to Becca's backyard, Jack didn't know what to expect. He didn't know what she would think of his visit either. Did he actually expect to start anything with her? Could be, he answered his own question. Yet, he felt sympathy and compassion for her and the immediate problems she faced alone. He felt she needed time. If his visit upset her and caused anxiety, then he would leave and drop the whole thing. Still, he was there, his inner compass pointing in her direction, so he started across the yard to her back door.

Jack had taken two steps before her voice stopped him.

"Who's there?" she called out, her voice quavering with an undertone of fear.

Then Jack's face was braced by a beam of light so bright he felt daylight had returned. He put up his hand to shield his eyes and called out, "Hey, it's just me, your friendly soccer coach, come to check on the Golden Girls." Jack felt relief when the light was switched off, but he stood still. His night vision was ruined and he saw only little blue and black spots swimming in front of him.

"Sorry, Jack. I don't take chances anymore. Did I blind you?" Her voice got stronger as she closed the distance between them. Then she took his arm and began guiding him to the deck.

Jack enjoyed being led and continued to let her guide him long after he could see again. It had been so long since he had been touched with care by any woman, even if she had scared him first.

They sat on the lounge chairs she had recently rescued from the garage. There was a slight hesitation of silence when neither knew how to begin, then Jack held up the bottle of wine.

"I thought we deserved to celebrate a successful week of coaching, Becca. Do you like wine?" He saw her smile widen in the moonlit shadows. He could see her clearly even without lights shining from inside the house.

"Oh, yes," she replied. "Fits my mood totally. I left the three gigglers to themselves in the master bedroom, where they can watch videos, play games, and talk all night if they want. I just came down to exhale and do some thinking by myself. But, some wine and your good company sounds like a better offer. Wait just a minute, and I'll get a corkscrew and a couple of glasses."

"Sit down and relax, Becca. I came prepared." Jack reached in his shirt pocket and pulled out his corkscrew, then began working on the chilled bottle. He filled two glasses, appearing magically from another pocket, and slid one across the table to her.

"Ah, so you came to ply me with wine did you? Chilled wine, opener, and glasses all in one neat package. Very efficient indeed." Becca added a sexy chuckle that had Jack wondering who was doing the plying. Jack knew her well enough now to realize she was kidding around. Her quick comebacks and dry humor had drifted to the surface all week during soccer practices. Wine did have marvelous side effects, and who knows where the evening would go, but Jack felt he wanted to learn more about this multi-layered woman sitting here in the dark with him.

They sat in silence for a time, comfortable in the quiet spring night, content with their unspoken thoughts. He would wait for her to speak, if she wanted to. After all, she had expressed her initial desire to be by herself and to do some thinking. Jack knew this was an important phase in her life. Perhaps in his too. He felt his own foundation shifting, though, resettling to accept something new. It took a leap of faith to sit and wait, but then she spoke.

"I've tried to figure out how this all came to be. You know, living like this, having a husband turn out so cruel and hurtful after I worked so hard to create the kind of home he demanded. I can't understand why people can be so mean, Jack."

He didn't respond. She was just getting started and seemed to want no answers to her questions. Her voice was blandly neutral. She appeared to hide any emotion, sadness or fear, about the life she had been trapped in. Yet her words implied all that.

"First I think, how could I let somebody do this to me? How did I become such a weakling? I didn't start out that way. I was taught early on that I was responsible for my own success, no one else was going to support me in that. I look at this family and see that the strong, independent young woman I used to be succumbed to whatever her husband demanded, without argument. I accepted Malcolm even though he turned into a demon and a bully."

"What do you mean when you say no one was going to support you, early on?" Jack had detected bitterness aside from Becca's growing dislike of what Malcolm had done.

She sipped at her wine and looked at him. "Did you have brothers and sisters?"

"No, I was an only child. One of those rotten, spoiled brats," he replied with a grin. "I think back to growing up and now realize that my parents sacrificed everything for me. They both worked and saved all their money to send me to college. I think that was their life; my success was theirs too."

"I had a younger brother, Robert. I was five years old when he was born and attention sort of shifted away from me then. My folks both worked too, but they came from the traditional southern family where girls worked in the house and boys went out to play. Girls were raised to get married, have children, and be supported by their husbands. Boys were raised to be the breadwinners, the masters of the house." Becca drained her glass and handed it over for a refill.

"I was expected to clean the house and help Mom cook. Daddy sometimes dried the dishes, but most of the time he collapsed in his rocker and slept off the bourbon he'd drunk for an appetizer before dinner. Robert was always outside playing with his friends. As he grew older, I could see him watching dad and mom and me. He learned early to emulate his father and soon expected things to be done for him, just because he was a boy."

Jack listened in amazement. He had no idea what it was like for a girl in her situation. True, his father had done pretty much the same as Becca's every night. But Jack had been required to do chores and housework - he had even learned to cook some things. His father had been exhausted when he got home and rarely helped out. But he made sure Jack did.

Becca was just getting warmed up. "I grew to dislike Robert. I feel a seething inside me today for how he acted and his taunting. And, more and more, my parents took his side in our arguments. Piano lessons I had begged for were stopped for Robert's college fund. An afternoon art class was canceled for the same reason. My folks made it clear to me that I would get married and become somebody else's responsibility. They were putting their money on Robert. I skipped a grade and graduated early, then left home at 17. Moved into my own apartment. Took a job in a department store. Saved enough money to buy my own damned piano, then a sewing machine so I could make my own clothes." Becca's voice trembled with anger she had stored away for years.

Jack was shocked. "How could you do that back then? Weren't you too young to just up and take off? Couldn't they force you to stay at home?" He had never heard of anyone doing that at her age. Not girls right after high school. His friends only left home when they went off to college.

Fortified with another sip of wine, she continued. "My mother came to see me once. She wanted to know if I needed anything. I said no, and she left. See, Jack, they came from a culture where young girls married in their early teens anyway back in the hills of Tennessee. They saw my age as no obstacle to moving out and looking for a man to support me. True, Mom had no one to help her around the house, but she and dad didn't have to feed me or buy my clothes anymore either. Lots of pluses, I guess." This time Becca refilled her own glass and took a long swallow.

Jack saw a sheen of tears in her eyes, reflecting the bright moon. He recognized tonight had turned into a necessary grieving process for her. He could see that her life with Malcolm was just one of several bad experiences. He had to touch her, to add his assurance. Jack reached for her free hand, and she gripped his fiercely in return.

They sat silently, Jack patiently waiting for her to continue, Becca gaining control over her emotions.

"After a few years, I moved to Detroit. Took a job in a large store and somehow got noticed by the women's department sales manager. She asked if I would model a new line of clothes for her, and I agreed on the spot. After that I did nothing but model, and did well. I enjoyed my single life - modeling by day, teaching myself the piano and sewing and drawing a little at night. It was a full life. Then Malcolm showed up."

She described how Malcolm had courted her, captured her. He made her the center of his life, placing her on the highest pedestal he could find. She found herself overwhelmed with attention, what she now felt was an obsessive infatuation. They were married within three months. Then Malcolm began to demand changes.

"He insisted I quit work. I stayed home and waited for him. His meals were to be at set times. In the evening, he needed time to wind down - we called it his time. I left him alone to read the paper and drink several martinis. Eventually, his time lengthened to more than several drinks, and dinner wasn't eaten until about ten PM. This didn't change when the children came along. Then, I had to keep them away from him or he would yell at them. Gradually, he had nothing to do with, with either child." Becca choked as she spoke these words, then sobbed.

Jack moved and knelt in front of her. He took her hands and massaged them, just to let her know he was there as support.

After a minute or so, she sniffed and sat up straight. "Looks like I had too much wine. Sorry to spill all this on you, Jack. It's not fair for you to have to listen to this awful mess."

"Maybe I need to listen, and you definitely need to spill it." He stroked a hand across her silky hair, smoothing it back from her face, damp with tears. He touched her face with care, letting her feel his tenderness and concern. Healing hands wiped away her tears, stroked her hands comfortingly.

Jack pulled his chair around to face her and spoke softly. "What do you want, Becca? Are you going to continue this or make a new life?"

"I called a lawyer yesterday. Martha recommended him. I have an appointment Tuesday to discuss a divorce and separation agreement. It is over with Malcolm."

"Then I suggest you and that lawyer work on a restraining order right away. Get those papers served to keep him away from this house. You should also change the locks and keep the house locked from now on."

Jack felt his heart tripping over a few beats. This was going faster than he had expected. He was riding along on a wave of emotion, and his timing had become irrelevant. The foundation shifted a bit more.

"What about you, Jack? What do you want?" There it was, the opening that would change everything. She was vulnerable, and they both knew it. Someone had to apply brakes, and do it now, but carefully.

Jack took a deep breath and plunged off the high board. "When Helen died, I grieved for what seemed like an eternity at the time. Then I decided I had to move on. I put all my energy into Tommy and Katie. Good friends like Dave warned me to be careful of rebounding into a quick relationship to replace what I had lost. Others suggested I go out and get laid every night to get it out of my system, sort of take advantage of the women who would be there as temptations."

"Instead, I closed myself off. I became superdad. I brought home the bacon, cooked it, kept house, and tried to be mom and dad. I haven't considered another woman." Jack looked into her eyes. "Until now." He wanted her; there was no secret about it. His stomach tumbled when he realized her slow smile expressed approval. Shaken, Jack rushed on.

"Becca, everything I have seen and heard tells me someone in your situation needs to settle one issue before trying on another one. I've had three years to deal with my loss. Divorcing Malcolm will be a loss, even though you can't wait to be rid of him. So, what I'm saying is, uh, I'm a patient man. Give yourself some time to discover the old Becca and enjoy yourself."

Becca gave him a challenging look. She caught his hands, holding them tightly when he tried to pull back. "You are such a gallant gentleman, Jack Marshall. What if I don't want any time to be by myself? Maybe I've had enough of that. What if I told you outright that I'm starved for affection? What if I dragged you to bed right now? Said to hell with settling any issues?" Becca slid her chair forward, scooting her knees between his legs. Jack sat frozen in place as she pulled his head down and kissed him. Then, just as quickly, she pulled back and looked up at him. His mouth was open in shock and his eyes had a stunned look in them. He was speechless.

"I thought so. You're a big chicken, coach." Then they both laughed, breaking the romantic spell.

Jack's brain searched frantically for the right words. He realized he was trembling when he tried to pick up his glass and sloshed wine over the side. He set the glass down signaling for a time-out.

Finally, he spoke. "Emotional overload. I don't know how to answer you. Yes, I am a big chicken. But you sure aren't any rooster. How did the roles get switched around? Isn't the guy the one to make the first move?" Becca had thrown down the gauntlet, offering herself instead of a duel.

Jack started out slowly. "I like you very much. I'm thrilled to think you might feel the same about me. This will sound funny for a guy, but I need some time to think it over. You do too, and you know it."

"Okay, Jack. Have it your way. But I'll be thinking about you while I'm trying to put my life back together, moving towards a final break with Malcolm. I realize you're a sensitive man. You feel you're doing the right thing by being noble, patient and kind, all those Boy Scout things. But maybe, just maybe, I don't want patience and kindness. Maybe I just want you." Becca paused to let this sink in. "And soon." She pulled Jack up with her and kissed him again. This time he returned her gentleness with passion.

Their bodies seemed glued from shoulders to toes, each shivering in the emotional pull and excitement, alive with deepening feelings. Eventually they pulled apart and just looked at each other. Both smiled and turned to go separate ways. For now.

TWENTY
TWO

When the phone rang this Sunday morning, Jack was already frying bacon for two starving young boys. "Morning, Senator. How's it going?"

"When did you get Caller ID, Jack?" Bill Conley answered with surprise.

Jack laughed. "I don't really have it, Bill. See, no one else is up at this crazy hour on a Sunday but you, and that also happens to be the only time you ever call. So, did you read our report?"

"Yeah, Jack, I did. I expect you'll be getting a visitor soon because of it. Why don't you check out front?" Three loud knocks sounded on Jack's front door as if on cue from the senator back in Washington.

Jack was used to tricks like this from Bill Conley. He was probably trying out some new techno-wizardry. Jack turned down the bacon and went to the door to find Dave standing there with his cell phone stuck in his ear, his free arm spread wide and an expression that said he didn't know what was going on either.

The senator did not keep them waiting. "You two birds in the house?"

"Yes sir," they replied together. There was a change in tone over the line on Jack's phone and he was transferred into a three-way conference call with Dave and the senator.

"Other than sending this big mooch over here for some free breakfast, what's on your mind, senator?"

"Jack, I'm going to talk to Dave directly, but I want you to hear everything. Okay?"

"Fine," Jack answered. "Shoot."

"Dave, I have a career opportunity for you that's too good to pass up. There's some pluses and minuses to it, so I want you to hear me out before you interrupt."

"Go for it, general, senator, sir," Dave replied, trying to lighten the atmosphere with humor.

"I want you to be the next DA for Madison County. The governor owes me a big favor, and I'm calling him in on it. He needs a sharp, young,

Hispanic hot-shot lawyer and hasn't the slightest notion where to find one who's qualified. Now, before you go off on the quota bit and being picked just because you're Hispanic, I sent your background file to the governor's office, and he was impressed. I also included the newspaper clippings about the drug task forces you have led. I told him about several capers in which you were identified as an unknown source."

Dave had plenty to say about this when Conley finally let him. "What makes you think I want this job, senator? I mean, I kind of like what I'm doing, and we both know DA's are very political, and I have no background for that. There's got to be a catch in here somewhere."

"Yeah, and I get left by myself dealing with land grabbers," Jack added.

"Fellows, who said you couldn't still work together on this? Maybe it'll be an advantage to have a *bona fide* prosecutor on hand to deal with the crooks when you catch them. Dave, there's two years left on the incumbent's term. But he won't be around to finish them. He'll be leaving quickly to avoid prosecution. Seems he had a little trouble filing tax returns in a timely manner. After two years, you can decide if you want to run for re-election or come back to Jack's world. You may not be aware of it, Dave, but you have a solid reputation for straight, honest work. Your legal work is impeccable. The police departments you have worked with give you the best marks possible. And, above everything, it is to your advantage that you have no experience as a politician. The governor needs someone who will stick to the job and not run up big out-of-state travel bills on local government credit cards. Here, inside the beltway, we call that going on boondoggles. In other words, he needs an honest man, someone who is unknown to both parties, and he is under lots of pressure from the Hispanic community for more high-profile appointees."

Senator Conley and Jack heard nothing from Dave. It was clearly his turn to speak and either agree or nix the proposal. Jack thought the post would be great for his best friend, who had given up any family life for his career.

"Sorry, senator. I just can't do it." Dave replied half-heartedly.

"What!?" Jack and the senator shouted together.

"I have a major conflict of interest. A time constraint that requires me to be unavailable for certain, uh, activities, at, er, specific times and, uh. Well, I'm just tied up, that's all." Dave barely kept a straight face, and a chuckle gave him away.

"Okay, spill it, Dave," growled Jack. "What's so all-fired important that you can't accept this terrific offer? Man, this is super for you. I don't care what activity you have going, probably some dame anyway, you need to take this job."

"Well, since you put it that way, Jack, I guess I will. Of course, that means you'll have to find another referee for the Golden Girls." Dave laughed at having cornered his pal into letting him off easy.

"Ouch, that hurts, Dave." Jack said. "Thanks a lot, senator. You've really made it a great weekend."

"My pleasure, Jack," Senator Conley replied. "So, Dave. I need a straight answer."

"Definitely yes, senator. And, much thanks for looking after me."

"Son, you deserve this opportunity. I just happened to be in a position to give you a boost. Give the governor's office a call tomorrow and go see him. He'll be expecting you."

"Yes, sir. Will do, senator."

"Fellows, your report looks promising. Keep on it. This kind of case is hard to crack, since very little paperwork is around to create an audit trail. You know we almost need a video of the actual payoff to take anything to court." Senator Conley let this sink in before continuing. "Jack, what did Strothers think of this report?"

Caught off guard, Jack hesitated a bit. "Strothers, oh yeah, uh, he felt the same way, sir. Complained about it not being on time, though."

"Never showed it to him, eh?" replied the jovial senator.

"Sir, I'll send him a copy tomorrow, I promise." Jack sputtered, feigning remorse. Strothers, he thought. Why couldn't the senator replace him as well?

TWENTY THREE

B uffalo Bill would surely have rolled over in his grave on Lookout Mountain had he witnessed the transaction taking place just to the right of his nose and six feet up. Bartles Conninger had requested a down payment from Rafe Stalker, and the two were haggling over price next to the wrought-iron fence surrounding old Bill's resting place.

"I have some good news, Stalker," Conninger said. The big man had not been pleased to have his Sunday morning interrupted. It was apparent to Conninger that his payoff man was hardly ever pleased at anything.

"This better be good, Conninger. I got people watching me, and they might spot you as well. You said you had something important that couldn't wait, but this little impromptu meeting out in the open puts us both at risk."

Conninger pulled out a map of southern Madison County and spread it over the hood of his car. "Look here." He pointed to a blue line representing the South Platte as it trickled northward from Cromwell dam. "About a third of the property you have targeted is right there along the river, covered by an eighteen-hole golf course. Fred Tompkins, head of a local soccer association, called me yesterday to say that his board has agreed to our terms to lease the golf course. Next, I'll work with county administration in Taylor City to draw up a development plan they will drool at. Only thing is, once they condemn the land and take it from the county, they'll run out of money and come back to us to dispose of it. Then you're set to pick it up cheap."

Conninger watched Stalker's lumpy face contort and shift under the flappy skin. Finally a glimmer of a smile appeared at the corner of the man's mouth, then disappeared just as quickly.

"How long do you figure before I can bid for it?" he grumbled.

This guy asks for the impossible, Conninger thought, and when I deliver, he brushes it off like there was nothing to it. But, the county commissioner recognized this tactic as a way to diminish his contribution. It was a power play used by politicians every day.

The stubby politician gathered up his courage and replied. "I don't know, and I'm really not interested until I see some money up front." Conninger flinched as the big man jerked back in anger.

"So far, Stalker, I've been the one taking risks, manipulating county codes to make this arrangement possible for you. Yet, all you can say is when do you get your goodies and how soon? Well, I go no further until I see some green stuff." Conninger stood as tall as his five feet, eight inches would allow and puffed out his chest for added measure.

Stalker said nothing. He glared at Conninger, his menacing bulk towering over the commissioner. Finally, as if all the wheels of a sluggish slot machine had finished spinning and rolled into place, he spoke.

"Meet me at the Sagebrush Inn. Tomorrow night. Eight PM." Abruptly, Stalker turned and went to his SUV.

Conninger's mind began calculating whether he had overstepped and pushed too hard. He had made a few calls to friends in the western counties of the state. Some knew of Stalker. No one liked or trusted him. Two comments stood out from the rest. Mr. Stalker seemed to feel the government owed him something, and his construction company did not do very good work.

Max Gonzalez retracted the antenna of his listening device and grinned. It was not often he could track one rat to another and get plans, names, and the mention of money simultaneously. Jack Marshall needed to be there for the initial payoff tomorrow night. And it looked like other payoffs were coming down the line. At least now Max knew whom to watch for the big grab.

•••

The loud bar was crowded with heavy drinkers, unusual for a Monday night. The week was hardly a day old, and Jack couldn't believe the people soaking up suds just a few blocks up from Boggy Creek, the source of water for the local micro-brewery. Jack laughed to himself, thinking about those delightfully clean and crisp TV commercials showing crystal pure water cascading down the Rockies right into a glass of effervescent beer. It made for great ads, but folks around here knew better. They drank it anyway, despite walking by the muddy creek every day.

Jack watched Bartles Conninger who had been sitting alone when Jack and Max arrived. That had surprised the two agents. Yet Conninger sat by himself, quietly in a corner booth. Max was on the other side of the room at the bar, pretending to be on the lookout for a one-nighter. Hell, with Max's luck recently he might record the payoff and get another phone number for his black book too.

The meeting time of eight PM passed and no one showed up to join Conninger. Jack began to wonder if the dirty politician had been cut off from the rough construction manager. He watched as a waitress approached Conninger's booth and spoke to him. Then she leaned over closer to him, looked at him and screamed.

"Help! Call 911! This man is bleeding!" The waitress backed away from the booth and the bartender rushed over to help her. Jack went over to get a closer look.

Conninger sat slumped in the corner of the booth, a trickle of blood oozed from the corner of his mouth. His body had been wedged tightly between the table and the seat. Someone had obviously pushed the table at an angle to hold him in and give the appearance he was just sitting there. By the time the waitress had checked on him though, his aorta, ruptured from a gut shot, had pumped blood to the top of his esophagus and out the side of his mouth.

Jack and Max saw that their man was dead, and probably had been before they had arrived. They left quickly before anyone could identify them. Sirens indicated local police were on the way.

Bull watched the scene from outside. He remembered the tall man and thought he had been killed by an avalanche years ago. He knew who to look out for now.

TWENTY
FOUR

Tuesday morning, Becca met with Jasper Mackey, the lawyer recommended by Martha Riddle. His twelfth-floor suite of offices was located in the Union Square Tower across from the Federal Center in Lakewood. Mr. Mackey was apparently a successful lawyer, if his plush reception area was any indication.

Becca admired the heavy, dark paneling and lush maroon carpeting. The solid oak executive desks were quite impressive, and each one probably cost more than all of her living room furniture. The receptionist greeted her cordially. My, my, Becca noted. She could have been on the cover of *Cosmo* or *Playboy*. Wonder what this guy charges? she thought. Yet, Martha had said this was definitely the man she wanted. So, here she was.

The receptionist smiled at her and showed her to Mr. Mackey's office. Jasper Mackey stood to greet her warmly.

"Mrs. Schmidt, welcome. Martha Riddle told me to take good care of you. Please sit down over here, and let's get acquainted."

Becca felt at ease right away. Jasper Mackey was a pleasant man. He looked to be in his mid-sixties and was a bit stoop-shouldered. His sandy-gray hair was thinning on top, but no baldness showed yet. Thick, reddish eyebrows - their graying a little behind the hair on top - capped bright blue eyes. His suit coat was hung on a corner rack, and Jasper's shirt sleeves, rolled to his elbows, revealed forearms that might belong to a man twenty years his junior. Becca also noticed a gym bag behind his desk and dusty Nikes on his feet.

Well, she thought, Martha had warned her that Jasper was more than he seemed at first impression. He was attractive and fit, yet informal, approachable. In one simple greeting, his manners showed her respect without being patronizing. Becca felt immediately that he was on her side. Martha had given her good advice.

Becca had second thoughts though when she noticed the buttery-soft leather sofa and matching chairs surrounding a marble-top coffee table. She hesitated to sit at first, then accepted Mr. Mackey's assistance, his hand guiding her gently to a comfortable chair.

"Mr. Mackey, I appreciate your time, but I'm afraid Martha and I are in different leagues when it comes to paying for legal support."

Jasper smiled kindly at her and touched her hand in reassurance.

"Don't be so impressed with this eye-wash, Mrs. Schmidt. That's for the high-flyers. Those guys I charge a hefty fee so I can offer lower rates to people like you who happen to fit into my specialty. For your case - which Martha, uh, Mrs. Riddle, has given me some background on - the fee will be $500 total. And that will come nicely out of your soon-to-be ex's funds. I require nothing up front."

"I don't understand, Mr. Mackey. I expected to pay much more than that, really."

"But, you don't know what my specialty is, Mrs. Schmidt. Can I call you Becca? And please, I'm just plain Jasper. Okay?"

"All right, Jasper, what do you specialize in?"

"Tough guys, Becca. Men who like to beat on their women. Those women hold a special place in my heart, so I give them a special rate. Besides, these are easy cases for me to work."

"It doesn't feel easy to me, Jasper." Becca said. "It feels like my life is being torn apart, like I've stepped over some taboo line in society, like people are looking at me differently." She looked away, struggling to remain composed as tears stung her eyes.

Jasper handed her a tissue and continued. "You can't blame yourself for this, Becca. You're a devoted mother and don't deserve what this guy has done to you. I guess I need to explain something else too. Martha and I see each other socially, and I have heard about you. Our relationship is more friend to friend than friend to lawyer."

Becca noticed a sparkle in his eye, and took a leap of faith. "Where do we start, Jasper?"

"First, in cases like this, we need to get a restraining order from the county sheriff. That tells Mr. Schmidt your home is off-limits. He crosses that line, and it's jail time. So, I need his full name and an address where I can serve papers on him."

"I don't know where he is. My neighbor, Jack Marshall, stopped his last attack and threw Malcolm out several weeks ago. I haven't heard from him since. Best I can do is give you information for his employer."

Jasper and Becca spent another thirty minutes exchanging information so that he could draw up a separation agreement and the final divorce papers. Becca felt ashamed that she knew so little about Malcolm's life away from their home. Yet, Jasper assured her he had more than enough to go on.

"Becca, this should be over in 90 days at most. When he hit you, he was the one who crossed the taboo line in society. There is no sympathy for his kind anywhere in our legal system." Jasper paused to consider another avenue they hadn't discussed.

"You say he gave you an allowance. You never knew about any checking or savings accounts?"

Becca nodded. "Yes, and of course I haven't received anything for this month's expenses. Malcolm always said the big bills came directly out of his paycheck at the company. Things like the mortgage, utility bills, anything he could have done electronically. Food, clothes, and my basic household expenses came out of the allowance."

"Did he ever mention a retirement account, a 401(K) pension fund at his work? Any IRAs or other investments?"

Becca was astonished at how little she knew about their - Malcolm's - finances. "I'm sorry, Jasper, he never mentioned any of those things."

"Don't worry about it then. Let me take care of it. Now, what is your monthly allowance?"

"I get $300 for everything, Jasper. I supplement that teaching piano lessons out of my house. It just isn't enough."

"Bastard," she heard him mutter under his breath. He opened his business check book, wrote a check, and handed it to her.

Becca was overwhelmed. The check was made out to her for $1,000. "Jasper, this is so much. Why are you doing this? I don't understand."

Jasper slid forward in his chair and took her hands in his. "Look at me, Becca. You have everything on your side. It will take one well-placed phone call to his company, a faxed copy of the restraining order and separation agreement, and you won't have to worry about money anymore. This is my specialty, remember?"

Becca's bottom lip quivered as she tried and failed to keep from bursting into tears. Jasper had more tissues ready. "Why, Jasper?"

He spoke in a soothing voice that got husky with emotion. "I do this partly for you and partly for my mother who went through the same situation. Her torment, inflicted by my father, is why I became a lawyer. Go home and take a breather. Let me do my job."

Becca gave him a hug, thanked him again, and walked to the door.

"Oh yes," he added, "Jack Marshall is a neat guy." Again a friendly sparkle touched Jasper's eyes.

"I think so too, Jasper," she said, and walked out of his office on a cloud.

Twenty minutes later, Becca parked in front of the Recreation Center and went inside to see Martha. She found her puttering away behind the counter adding up receipts for the previous day's activities.

"Don't let that man slip away, Martha. He's marvelous." She bubbled over and the two chatted for the next hour about Jasper and Jack.

"I swear, Becca, I have asked that man to marry me every month for the last decade it seems. He keeps stalling and saying he's too old. He says I need to find me some young stud! Of all things. Next time I'm taking a two-by-four along to make sure I get his attention."

Becca told Martha about her night out on the deck drinking wine with Jack. Becca got a faraway look.

"Think it's too soon to get interested, Becca?" Martha said.

"If you mean do I still have feelings for Malcolm, then no, it's not too soon. It wouldn't have been too soon several years ago when he first hit me. I made it clear he could divorce me if he wanted to make it official. But I also insisted that I was no longer his wife. I kicked him out of the bedroom but didn't leave the house. Today, I can't understand why I didn't file for divorce myself. But, I was so dependent on him, and scared to leave. It's strange, but Malcolm never said a word about my decision and the ultimate conditions. He just stayed away longer on his business trips. When he did show up, I never knew he was coming, and he only stayed a night or two."

Becca stopped talking when she realized she had gotten off track. "My head tells me to slow down and get used to being single. My insides right around here," - she brought her hand over her heart - "tell me to go for it. I'm afraid I may have come on too strong for Jack the other night. I probably scared him off, I was so hungry for affection.

"By the way, Martha, what does Jack do? Except for coaching soccer and being a great neighbor, I know little about him."

"Ah, the million dollar question, Becca. I haven't a clue."

Becca left Martha to doodle up her figures. On impulse she decided to surprise Jack with a visit. She drove the half mile from the center and turned down his street. Jack's house was centered at the end of a cul-de-sac, just like her own on the next block.

She felt so good about how her day was going she didn't notice the blue Volvo station wagon parked in front of Jack's house until she got out of her car. Hmmm, she thought, that looks like the Huffs' car. Wonder why they're here? No, her thoughts continued, Orson commuted to Denver. That's the car Priscilla drives to pick up Sharon after practices. Why would she be here today? Practice isn't until tomorrow. The kids are in school, so she didn't bring Sharon over to play with Katie.

Becca's mind raced away looking for all things negative. Not one positive idea came to mind that was a justifiable reason for Priscilla Huff's car to be parked in front of Jack's house. Why that two-timer! Brings me wine last Saturday, then invites Priscilla over for a little afternoon fun on Tuesday. Becca stood beside the Volvo fuming. She breathed deeply, gathering her anger up in a big ball. Damn, she thought, must be jealousy. This is awful. Couple glasses of wine, two kisses, and I've staked my claim. Still, she was angry for letting Jack lead her on so slyly. Men! Ugh!

Becca got out and slammed her car door, then stomped up the walk to have a shootout. She rang the bell several times, but no one came. Aha! Too involved to answer the door, is he? Becca opened the door and entered. She walked around in search of someone to take a swing at, namely that big lug, Jack double-timing Marshall. But she found no target anywhere.

She stormed out onto the deck, an angry glare plastered all over her face, and became instantly embarrassed. Jack, Dave, and Priscilla were practicing the techniques of refereeing in the backyard, and all three looked up at her simultaneously.

Jack took one look at her facial expression and grinned. Becca grinned back and stammered, "I'll, er, just come around some other time, Jack. Uh, I just wanted to go over some strategies for the first game. You know." Her face got redder the more she talked. Becca turned to run away from any more embarrassment, but Jack's voice stopped her.

"Becca, meet our new referee. Priscilla was gracious enough to take Dave's place and we're showing her the ropes. Right, Dave? The three of us have been at it for about two hours now. I'll give you a call later."

Becca had her back to Jack. She stomped her foot and turned to face him. "Damn it, Jack Marshall, wipe that smug look off your face!" Then she fled, hearing their laughter all the way to her car.

TWENTY
FIVE

During the last practice before their first game, the Golden Girls began playing team ball. Jack and Becca were proud of the girls who worked hard to keep in position and pass the ball to an open teammate. They had come a long way since that first practice only two weeks ago. At that time, their cluster-ball play had Jack thinking his coaching career was hopeless.

Jack was also cheerful at an unexpected benefit of volunteering to coach Katie. Another bonus had been the closeness that had developed between him and Missy. The little girl seemed to thrive on their extra sessions after the team practices.

He had gotten to know Becca during these practices and they found working together fun. Neither mentioned the wine and kisses of the previous Saturday night, although anticipation was certainly in the air.

Fact was, Jack had been pre-occupied with the suspicious murder of Bartles Conninger. He and Max had lost their payoff man and felt he had gone underground. Fortunately, Jack had Tommy, Katie, and now Becca to keep his mind occupied. A very pleasant occupation, he thought, as he watched Becca correct a player who was out of position.

Becca had seemed to come alive after the meeting with her lawyer earlier in the week. Jack noticed she smiled more often and appeared to have filled out some of the hollowness in her cheeks. Probably getting some needed sleep, he figured. She surely looked good now in white shorts and T shirt. Her black silky hair was bound in a short ponytail to match the Golden Girls, who all seemed to have adopted that style when they played soccer.

Today, Priscilla Huff had agreed to referee the practice game to introduce the girls to real game situations, and to give Priscilla some experience. Her whistle blew often to award the ball to the other side, usually when someone made an incorrect throw-in or forgot and swatted at the ball with her hand. Jack and Becca added their own whistles to the commotion when they wanted to correct a bad kick or pass or get players in better positions.

Sharon Huff was going to be their star player. There was no holding her back when she broke out with the ball and raced down the field. Yet, Jack could tell that she was beginning to look for teammates in the clear who had a better shot. Fact was though, she was usually so far ahead of the rest there was no one to pass off to, so she shot. Her kicking had improved to the point where she used her toe only half the time.

Missy was the heart of the team. The other girls watched her unselfish play and tried to copy it. She used both feet to kick and pass, and she took all the corner kicks because they required accuracy. Jack was proud of Katie as well because she was not far behind her best friend in skills.

It was time for a pep talk by the coach and Jack blew his whistle to gather the girls. He sat on the ground and they formed a circle around him.

"Okay, Madame referee," Jack said, nodding to Priscilla Huff, "how can these wiggle worms improve?"

Priscilla blushed and thought for a minute. "Coach Jack, they look pretty good to me. Girls, be careful on those throw-ins. The refs will watch to see if you use both hands and throw the ball straight over your head, Okay?" A chorus of "yes ma'ams" rang out from the girls. "Also, don't be afraid to ask the referee in your game tomorrow if you don't understand what to do. The referees are like on-field coaches. We're there to help you learn the game."

Priscilla smiled at the girls, and Jack noticed Sharon's look of pride and admiration for her mom. He knew volunteering to referee had been a big step for Priscilla, and after only a week it was already bringing mother and daughter closer.

Jack took over the meeting. "Thanks, Mrs. Huff. I mean, thanks, ref." He grinned at Priscilla and she blushed again. "Does everyone understand the must-play rule?" Puzzled looks came over the girls' faces. Jack had talked briefly about this at their first practice, then let it slide as he struggled to teach them the game.

"The must-play rule means that everyone gets to play. So, if twelve girls show up tomorrow, each of you will play two of the four quarters." The girls looked from one to the other. All kept their puzzled expressions.

Becca took a shot at it. "Girls, all of you will play in the game tomorrow. We'll try hard to have each of you play the same amount of time, but with twelve players no one will play the whole game. Anyway, you'll get out of breath and need a rest, won't you?" Again, there was a chorus of "yes ma'ams."

Jack followed up. "Our goal tomorrow is to play and have fun. If we win, that's icing on the cake, but no one is going to fuss at you if we lose. Remember, play and have fun. Don't worry about who wins. Got it?"

"Yes, Coach Jack," they all responded.

"Go home and get lots of rest tonight, and we'll see you at the field tomorrow."

The team meeting broke up, and girls scattered to their waiting parents. Jack and Becca collected Katie, Missy, and Gina and headed for their car.

"Jack, could I speak to you a minute, please," Priscilla said.

Jack came back to where she stood. "Sure, ref. By the way, you did a good job today. We really appreciate your volunteering to do this on such short notice." She blushed again and Jack wondered what was going on with this lady.

Priscilla looked up at him with big moon eyes.

"You really know how to work with kids, Jack. I watched you coach them and correct them out there. It's obvious you care for each one of them. I, uh, I just wanted to thank you for encouraging me to do this. Sharon needed to see me as a person as well as a mother. I tried hard today not to favor her and I could see that she pouted a few times about that but it was good for her."

Jack suddenly discovered she had covered his forearm with her hand as she spoke. Priscilla glanced down and quickly jerked her arm back, turning a deeper red than before.

Uh oh, thought Jack. What we have here is a little short-term infatuation building up. He turned to locate Becca and saw her looking their way with her lower lip pushed upwards in a sort of sarcastic expression. Her arms were crossed under her breasts and one foot was tapping the ground. When her eyes met Jack's, she turned abruptly and got in the car.

Jack thanked Priscilla again and went to the car now full of tension. The ride home was quiet. Even the usually chattering girls sensed something was up and kept their mouths shut. When Jack pulled up to Becca's house, she got out and left without a goodbye.

"Mom's mad at you, Coach Jack," Missy snickered from the back seat.

"Yeah, Dad," Katie piped in. "What did you do to upset her?" Jack looked at his daughter with some surprise. Her defensive tone implied she'd gone over to Becca's side and deserted him. He had mixed feelings about that, yet smiled at the possibilities.

Gina had the answer. "My dad used to get that look from mom when he didn't pay enough attention to her, coach. I bet that's it, huh?"

Jack chuckled. Such wisdom, he thought. "I think you're right, Gina. But hey, tomorrow is another day, and what are we going to do?"

"Beat the Green Dragons!" shouted the three Golden Girls in the back seat. Then all three girls raced to Becca's front door and went inside for their afternoon snack.

Jack hurried from the garage to answer his kitchen phone, ringing off the hook.

"Hello," he said, slightly out of breath.

"I'm sorry, Jack. I feel like a schoolgirl in a snit over nothing. This is the second time this week I've acted this way and I don't like what I see myself doing."

"Forgiven. Becca, listen to me. I can understand your feelings. Give yourself some breathing room. Relax. I'm not going anywhere or with anyone. Poor Priscilla may be looking at me as some kind of hero right now, but the fact is, the two of you have a lot in common. In a way, being our referee is her sort of coming out party. Orson is a bit of a stuffed shirt and wants his woman in the home, period. I have a gut feeling that I'll be hearing from him soon enough about my supposed attention toward his wife."

"I guess I don't know how to act about anything, Jack. Some things are moving too fast, others too slow. Meanwhile, I'm stuck here with three giggling girls who are ravenous and I'm hungry myself."

"Come on over and I'll cook up some pasta. Bring everybody. We'll stuff them with spaghetti then set them in front of a video and have a glass of wine on the deck."

"That sounds wonderful, Jack. Just how many different things can you cook anyway? We may have to come over more often." Becca teased him then hung up to round up her young charges.

Jack put a huge pot of water on to boil and fetched a giant bottle of his "homemade" sauce - the one with the Ragu label still on it. He laughed to himself. How many things can I cook, ha? Maybe ten if you count several kinds of pasta. There was "homemade" Ragu with meat sauce, vegetable sauce, extra mushroom and pepper sauce - heck that's three right there. He tried to count up the number of salads to add to his sum total but was interrupted by Andy and Tommy as they burst into the house. Looks like two more for pasta, he reckoned.

The house was a bedlam of shrieks, yelps, and shouts as everyone devoured the pasta and salad. He glanced at Becca at the opposite end of his extended dining room table and grinned. They didn't try to speak with all the noise, but they exchanged a knowing look: whatever was going on around the table was not only great fun, but it felt good. The girls had congregated at Jack's end of the table and were talking incessantly. Missy had scooted her chair close to him and kept asking him about kicking and whatever else she could think of to get his attention. It was obvious she doted on every word he said.

Andy and Tommy gravitated towards Becca and ignored the pests around Jack. Becca smiled at Tommy, who still couldn't seem to stay away from her. Jack was intrigued at the attention his son paid to her. Poor guy, he thought. He really misses the nurturing only a mother can provide.

After dinner, Jack assigned the girls the task of bringing the dishes to the kitchen counter. The boys were ordered to rinse them off and load them into the dish washer. Their reward had been to go to separate rooms and watch videos. Jack knew peace between the boys and girls couldn't last much longer.

When all the kids had settled into their movies, Jack poured two glasses of wine and grabbed Becca's hand to lead her onto the deck.

"Come with me for a grand tour of my backyard, Madame. I have something to show you." Jack gave her a sly grin as they walked down the steps to the sloping yard.

"Not your etchings, kind sir?" She queried, feigning naiveté with a perfect southern belle accent.

"No, too many kids around for that," he replied. "It's a little chilly out here, don't want you to catch cold." Then he draped his arm around her shoulder, bringing her close to his side, enjoying her softness.

Becca smiled up at him. Jack was glad she enjoyed his corny humor on this balmy summer-like evening. He led her to the far edge of his property, to the back side of a mammoth hedge growing around an ancient cottonwood. He stopped before a bench he had strategically placed to be invisible from the house. Here they could share privacy and a view of the greenbelt.

They sat close. Jack set his wine on the ground and pulled her to him. It was his turn to initiate the kiss. He started out gently at first, tasting, nibbling at each small portion of her lips, savoring her luscious mouth. Then he eased back and looked into her eyes.

"This feels right. I could do this all night, but only with you. Please understand that." He brought her close again and felt her heart pounding rapidly against his chest, echoing his own.

"I'm sorry again, Jack. I think my hormones are in overdrive or something. I've never behaved this way before."

"Let me tell you a funny story. Something that will clue you in on my point of view about this." But he never got the next word out, as Becca pulled his head down and kissed him passionately, searching his lips for an opening with her tongue. Jack gave in to a kiss that turned him inside out.

This time they both eased back and smiled. "Wow. You do that really well, lady. I had something to say, didn't I? You blew my concentration away. Oh, yeah," he continued, "about that story. I'm determined to tell, it so don't interrupt me, okay?"

Becca pouted. "I'm not promising a thing, buster. But go ahead. You're wasting time."

Jack had to search his memory for an instant to remember why he wanted to tell a story and exactly what that story had been. Finally it came back to him.

"I had this psychology professor my sophomore year who told us about his clinical work at a mental hospital. Each month they took the patients into the city for some excursion. His first turn at this was to escort two men to the ballet. One was a schizophrenic, the other manic-depressive. The manic patient was overanxious and constantly pulling my professor's arm out of the socket hurrying to get to the ballet. The poor schizophrenic slunk back and didn't want to go anywhere. My professor said he had to practically drag the man along. So you get this picture of a guy in the middle, being pulled forward and backward by these two mental patients."

Jack paused and looked at Becca. "So, do you get it?"

Becca stared at him as if he had grown another set of ears. "Get what, Jack? Is this some kind of parable? Are you trying to tell me I'm nuts. Are you nuts? Maybe we both are, and you're trying to let me down gently. Explain, please."

"Okay, okay, I admit I left out some of the transition. I see your emotions like the actions of the manic, racing ahead, dying to get to the performance. Me, I'm the schizophrenic lagging behind."

Becca snuggled up to him and reached her arms around his neck. She got nose to nose with him and breathed her next question. "Can't we just pretend we're normal and go for it?"

Jack replied, "To hell with psychology. I'm -" but again, Becca didn't give him the chance to continue.

Andy and Tommy had paused their video and turned off the lights in Tommy's room. They sneaked over to the window to spy on Jack and Becca.

Andy spoke: "What's going on? Tommy."

Tommy: "I don't know. They disappeared behind that big bush."

Andy: "Yeah, they were looking kinda goofy at each other all night."

Tommy: "I saw that too. Maybe they're out there smooching in the dark."

The movie was forgotten as the two boys searched the darkness for some hint of what the two grownups were doing. It was a puzzle to them, also confusing. Andy wanted a dad. Tommy wanted a mom. They talked to each other all the time about it. But now both wondered if this meant they would become brothers?

"Your dad's a neat guy, Tommy. I like him a lot. He treats me like I'm his kid. You're lucky."

"So are you, Andy. Your mom is super nice to me. And wow, is she pretty!" Tommy hesitated to say what was on his mind, then decided to ask anyway. "Andy, do you miss your dad?"

"Naw, not at all, except that I never see him, so it's hard to say. He's never around, and when he does come home he isn't nice to mom. Do you, uh, miss your mom?"

"Yeah, sort of. Now and again I think about her always being there, but when she died my dad started staying home a lot, and that helped both me and Katie."

The video still ran in the girls' TV room, but they paid no attention to it. They were too excited about their first game in the morning. Gina was sleeping over the entire weekend with Missy, and so was Katie. Tomorrow was going to be super!

Saturday morning dawned crisp, cool, and sunny. It was going to be one of those famous Colorado blue-sky days. No clouds, no humidity. The air was so fresh and clear the top half of Pikes Peak could be seen 75 miles to the south. It was a perfect day for soccer.

Jack had spent two hours setting up his substitutions so he always had a good mix of players on the field. It would have been nice to put his best six girls out there at once, but when it was time to substitute in the next quarter, he would have been left with a much weaker team.

At the field, Jack and Becca had the girls going through stretching and warm-up drills. With just a few minutes until the start, Jack left Becca to watch the team and walked over to the nervous parents on his side of the field. It was time to coach the moms and dads.

"Folks, gather round me for a minute here, please." Jack put on his best smile and enjoyed the multitude of expressions that greeted him, some puzzled, some smiling, most uncertain.

"I just wanted to repeat something I said at our initial meeting. Each child here today will get to play at least half the game. That means we follow the rules so everyone can participate. Above all, we want these girls to have fun. They'll become competitive enough once the game starts, but we need to remember this is not a competition for the World Cup. We can all teach some sportsmanship this morning by cheering good play by everyone on the field, not just that of our Golden Girls. If a girl makes a mistake, tell her nice try and forget about it. By all means cheer when they do make a good play."

The crowd of parents appeared to be with him on this. The one exception was the frowning face of Orson Huff at the back of the group. Jack could feel the confrontation coming on. It was just a matter of time.

At last the girls lined up for the kickoff. Missy passed back to Katie, who rifled the ball laterally to Sharon on the right wing, who took off dribbling through the Green Dragons towards the goal. Parents from both sides began to yell instructions: "Run. Pass. Kick it harder. Center it. Watch out! Oh no, not that way!" Jack laughed. It was impossible to tell what anyone was saying. Skip Hawkins had correctly predicted that would happen.

The Green Dragons were shocked at Sharon's speed and size. She dribbled down the side of the field quickly. Missy kept to the center, and Katie miraculously stayed on the other wing. Becca jumped up and down in glee and grabbed Jack's arm to draw his attention. Their girls had a perfect formation to score. Zap! Sharon kicked the ball hard, and it went in! It was 1-0 Golden Girls, and less than a minute had elapsed in the first quarter.

The girls were jumping for joy and hugging each other. All were patting Sharon on the back. Their parents shouted encouragement and gave each other high-fives. Jack watched the other team, though. The Dragons were crushed, and some were crying as they walked over to their coach. The short little man berated them for sloppy play and began fussing at them to play harder. Their parents were silent. Not a word of support.

The Dragons kicked off this time, but they had no set play, and their best kicker simply pummeled the ball into Golden Girls' territory. Kelly Hatcher intercepted the loose kick and passed it to the side for Missy, just as they had practiced. Then it was *deja vu* all over again. Missy passed to Katie, who turned it over to Sharon who was off to the races again. This time Jack shouted at her: "Center the ball, Sharon!" But she either didn't hear or didn't want to let go of the opportunity as she kept on dribbling without looking for her teammates. She at least used the side of her foot, and a resounding thump was heard as she shot the ball into the Dragons' net.

Again the parents for Jack's team cheered, and the Golden Girls were ecstatic at their success. Jack motioned to the ref that he wanted a conference with his team and called the girls over to the side of the field.

"You guys are playing great," he said. "But, I want more passing." He looked directly at Sharon. "Honey, when I say center the ball, I mean to pass it back to the middle of the field in front of their goal. Missy and Katie were both in position to score on that last play." He watched her begin to pout, then said, "You're playing great, Sharon. I'm not being critical. I just want you to pass off so you're teammates can score some goals too." Her face perked up, and she nodded with a big smile.

The next quarter held much the same for the Golden Girls. They could do nothing wrong. Jack's second quarter team was weaker but still managed to score two goals. At half time, the Golden Girls were up 5-0. Jack and Becca sat the girls in a circle around them and passed out quarters of oranges, the traditional half-time snack. Soon bits of orange clung to faces, ears, hair, and dozens of fingers. It was a successful mess. Gloria Ashworth passed around wet cloths to help with the cleanup.

Their reverie was broken by a sharp voice to the rear. "Coach, I'd like a word with you." Jack turned and saw the Dragon's coach standing a few yards away fuming. He got to his feet and shrugged his shoulders at Becca's concerned look.

"Sure, Coach. What do you want?" he said as he ambled over to the upset man.

"That big girl is too good. How old is she? I think she should be in an upper age bracket or something. What's her birth date?" The outraged man spit out questions and demands like a commanding general as he stared angrily up at Jack.

The Golden Girls' coach looked around to see if anyone had heard the boisterous fellow. Everyone was busy eating oranges and chatting about their success. "Come with me and I'll show you something." Jack led the man to his duffel bag containing all the paperwork for the Golden Girls. He pulled out his official roster giving names, addresses, and dates of birth. Then he sat down and looked at his antagonist glaring down at him.

"Sit down and read this." Jack's sharp tone caught the man by surprise. He had spoken with quiet authority that demanded compliance, yet Jack had smiled when he said it. He passed the roster over to the irate coach and pointed to the line with Sharon's name on it. The coach read the information slowly and his angry look turned to one of chagrin. The roster showed that Sharon was one of the youngest players on Jack's team, and all were the correct age.

"She's an exceptional player," Jack continued. "Her parents sent her to a soccer camp when she was only five. I'm trying to get her to pass the ball more, though. When she learns to be a better team player, I think we'll be able to score 20 goals on your team." Jack paused when he saw the opposing coach flinch at his challenge. "We'll do that because right now we're a better team. And, I haven't seen your girls do more than play cluster ball. Your parents, and you as well, only yell at them for mistakes. You never offer any encouragement. In fact, the only cheering for your team has come from our side of the field." Jack continued to smile, even though he was seething inside.

"We practice at the Recreation Center field at four PM Monday, Wednesday, and Friday. You're welcome to come out and watch. My assistant coach and I will be happy to show you some drills." Jack got up and offered his hand to the man, helping him off the ground and shaking his hand simultaneously. "Good luck in the second half."

"Thanks, coach." The chastened man walked back to his side of the field. Jack could tell the man was still disgruntled.

The second half was a repeat of the first, except that Sharon actually passed off to Missy several times. Missy scored on both chances and was elated. The tally was 12-0 when the whistle blew, mercifully ending the game. Jack gathered his team at the center stripe of the field and readied them to march across and shake hands with the Green Dragons. But when he turned around, he was astonished to see the other team slogging away to their cars.

"Wait here, girls. Becca, keep them in line." Jack ran after the other coach and called to him. "Hey, coach. We're supposed to shake hands out there as a show of sportsmanship." The coach shrugged his shoulders and walked away. Ah well, Jack thought. You can't win them all.

Jack returned to his team. "Great game, girls. Let's go get that can of pop." The girls squealed and ran for the cooler of pop Gloria Ashworth had dragged over to the side of the field. Jack also noticed Becca and Gloria having a serious conversation away from the ruckus. He joined the girls, congratulating each one. Finally, he could relax.

"Coach Marshall, could I have a word with you." Jack turned around to see Orson Huff standing a few yards away with a concerned look on his face. Here we go again, he thought.

Jack walked over to join Sharon's father. "Sharon played a great game today, Orson I'm glad you could be here to see her. What's on your mind?"

"Yes, well, that's what concerns me somewhat, Coach Marshall. I expected to see her play the entire game and score more goals. But you didn't let her play half the game and she is obviously your best player."

"Did you see how she passed the ball off so one of her teammates could score, Orson? Did you notice how proud she was to assist on a goal? Did you see her learning how to be a team player? Any of that cross your line of vision, or did you just pick out the negatives, of which there were precious few?" Jack was steaming.

"I also want to know what you're up to with my wife? It's absurd, talking her into being a referee, of all things." Huff was red in the face from anger and embarrassment.

Before Jack could fire off an answer, Becca walked up and put her arms around him from behind, giving him a bear hug. Then, right there in front of the team and all the parents, she spun him around and planted a big smooch right on his mouth. Jack was stunned.

Becca broke off the kiss and turned to Orson.

"Mr. Huff, I think it's great that Priscilla is our referee. I watched Jack and Dave train her the other day. She's going to be terrific. Wow! What a great game Sharon played, huh? You should be very proud of her." With that she turned Jack around and walked him off the field to their car.

"Jack, sweetie, you can't solve everybody's problems in one day. Come on, let's go have some lunch." Jack glanced back at the rest of the parents, who were standing around with their mouths wide open. Okay, he figured, guess there are no more secrets in this neighborhood.

TWENTY
SIX

Excitement was the word of the day after the lopsided victory over the Green Dragons. Missy, Katie, and Gina worked up a game of two-on-one soccer in Becca's backyard. From the looks of it, they would be playing out there the rest of the afternoon.

Jack tackled handyman chores around the house and started his spring cleaning projects in earnest. Between the land grab caper and his coaching duties, he had neglected maintaining his home and yard. He couldn't let this go too long or his neighbor, Larry Thigpen, would come over and complain. Larry did nothing but work on his lawn which looked like $20-a-yard green carpeting. Jack could count on a complaining phone call if Tommy or Katie ran through Mr. Thigpen's yard. Jack could also expect a call if he didn't control the dandelions in his yard. He had received lectures in the past about how his weeds were infecting Larry's precious grass.

Andy and Tommy were at a loss for what to do with themselves this afternoon. It was too early for swim team and the pool didn't open for another two months. The beautiful sunny weather might change quickly. Rocky Mountain spring weather could bring Chinook winds causing warm, summer-like days, followed by snow, sleet, thunderstorms and even tornadoes and hail. And all of this could happen within a 24-hour period. The boys wanted to do something. Only, what?

Andy had an idea. "Tommy, let's ride our bikes over to the new shopping center and look around in KMart. They have lots of stuff in the sporting goods section we can play with. What do you say?"

"Sounds like a winner to me, Andy. There's no good movies showing anywhere, just more of that mushy kissing stuff and we have enough of that around here now."

The boys ran off to tell their parents where they were going, then hopped on their bikes for the ten-minute ride to the shopping center. Tommy raced ahead of Andy, his longer legs and bigger body pumping away. Andy caught up quickly, though, with his wiry strength and determination. When they had first become fast friends, the boys had been clear opposites, with Tommy's chunky body contrasting greatly to Andy's undersized, wiry frame. Now they were closer in size, yet Andy remained the smaller boy and had a more reserved personality. This characteristic made him a good quarterback, a position that required calm thinking in game situations. Tommy just went for it and let his actions speak for him.

They coasted along slowly, enjoying the great sunshiny day. Tommy brought it up first.

"Andy, what's going on with your dad? I haven't seen him for a long time. My dad told me about what he did to your mom."

Andy hesitated at first. They were best friends, but he felt awkward talking about his father. Andy was mad at him for hurting his mom, yet he wanted a dad to do stuff with, especially on days like today.

"He hasn't been back, and mom got a lawyer so she could divorce him. She told me and Missy all about it the other night at dinner. They haven't gotten along since the last time he hit her."

"You say he hit her before? That's so stupid. Did you see it? Was she hurt bad? Golly, she's so pretty and nice, why would he hurt her? That's dumb."

Andy no longer felt like defending his father, even when Tommy called him dumb and stupid.

"I saw him do it both times. I don't like him anymore. Really, I hate him, Tommy. I don't want him to come back."

Andy had a lot on his mind and decided to talk about it with his pal.

"What do you think about my mom and your dad, Tommy? I know they like each other, 'cause mom told me so when I asked her."

"I don't know how to feel about it, Andy. I haven't had a mom for so long. I was the first one to see her after she died, and it's something I'll never forget." Tommy hesitated and seemed to have a hard time finding words. "I really like your mom, Andy. Dad hasn't said anything to me and Katie, but we both saw him kiss her last night. Geez, his eyes get really big whenever she's around him. It's just like one of those movies. But. I don't know. Mom's been gone a long time though."

The light changed, and they walked their bikes through the crosswalk to the KMart store. Inside was a kid's dream of toys and sports equipment. The blue-light special wagon was blinking away over in ladies underwear like a warning for them to stay away. Andy pulled Tommy along to the back of the store to the sporting goods section.

Both boys loved football the best and ogled the shiny helmets and new cleated shoes they would be getting for the fall season. Tommy's dad had been their coach last fall, and he had promised to do it again. Andy was the quarterback, and he really liked the wide-open plays Mr. Marshall designed. He got to pass the ball a lot, which was his favorite part of the game.

Andy picked up a spongy football, and the boys looked around for any store personnel, but as usual, there was no one nearby, so they tossed the ball up and down the aisle. They had to stop abruptly when an old lady pushed her cart through their playing field to look at basketballs. Tommy gave Andy a look that said, what would a grandma want with a basketball?

Next, they wandered down the water sports aisle, and Andy spotted the newest style swim goggles in small plastic cases. He needed a pair for the summer season, but he knew he would have to make do with his old ones. That was another reason to hate his father. Mom always had to scrimp for everything, so Andy had learned not to ask for new stuff.

Andy looked around the store. There were no workers in sight. Most of the customers were over buying yucky ladies stuff or out in the garden department checking out fertilizer and lawn tools. He whispered to Tommy.

"Hey, come here. See this?" He picked up an orange set of goggles and handed them to Tommy. "I could really use these. I think I'll try to slip them in my jacket and take them home with me. What do you say?"

Tommy's reaction was immediate. "No way. No. Don't do it, Andy. My dad works with the police sometimes. He told me I could get in a bunch of trouble taking stuff." Tommy vigorously shook his head from side to side. His eyes had gotten big and frightened.

Andy was determined, though. He was worked up, angry. He wanted new goggles, but mostly he was mad at his father, who was never around. Who would care if he stole something?

"I'm going to do it anyway. Stand over there and check for people."

Again, Tommy's reaction was swift. "Wait, I gotta go to the bathroom. It's over there. I'll be right back. Don't do anything until I get back, okay?"

"All right, but hurry. I want to get out of here." Andy pretended he was just looking around and wandered to another aisle, still holding the goggles. He figured he could carry them all over the store, then sneak them in his pocket when no one was looking.

Being on call twenty-four hours of the day irked Jack Marshall. Officially, he wasn't supposed to take out the trash without wearing his cell phone on his belt. After carting it wherever he went this afternoon, the damn thing finally decided to ring just when he was at the top of a ladder cleaning out the gutter.

"Marshall here," he answered curtly, ruing the day Henry Strothers had insisted he use this thing.

"Dad, it's me, Tommy. You gotta come quick. Andy's going to get in trouble. Come quick, please Dad?"

Jack felt the hair on his neck prickle as he listened to his son calling for him in tears. "Where are you, Tommy? What's going on? Is somebody hurt?"

"KMart, Dad. Come quick. Just get over here to the sports department. I got to go." The phone went dead, and Jack noticed the low battery light had come on.

"Shit." Jack skimmed down the ladder and jumped into his car. He left a trail of rubber going up the cul-de-sac and drew the ire of Larry Thigpen, who was aerating his lawn. Larry waved his arm in anger and Jack flipped him the bird. "Take that asshole," he muttered. "And get a life." Jack smiled, though. He and Helen used to have a standing joke that the guys who spent all day working in the yard or in the garage had probably pissed off their wives and never got any. He and Helen would take long walks through the neighborhood, see some poor slob slaving away late in the day and wave, and mutter to each other, there's another one.

Jack's daydream lasted until he slid into a parking spot near KMart's garden shop. This was the quickest entrance to the back of the store where the sporting goods were. He slammed the door and took off running, expecting to see an ambulance parked nearby. There was nothing outside, and when he barged past a long line at the garden checkout stand he still saw no sign of trouble.

Jack rushed into the store and down the main aisle to sporting goods. He slowed to a fast walk and picked up the sound of two boys arguing. He peeked around the corner of a display and saw Andy and Tommy toe-to-toe, each holding onto an end of a slender plastic package. Tommy was the bigger of the two and seemed to be winning the argument.

"Don't do this, Andy." Tommy repeated again and again. "If they catch you, you'll be in big trouble.

Aha, thought Jack. Some shoplifting in progress. Tommy has learned his lessons well. For a split-second, Jack felt very proud of his son. However, he also knew he had to deal appropriately with Andy. He coughed, loudly interrupting the squabble.

"Hey, fellas, what's going on here?" Jack used a neutral but slightly stern tone of voice. Andy jumped and Tommy slumped in relief. Tommy came to him and put his arms around Jack's waist as if he would never let go now that his dad had saved the day. Andy held both hands behind his back, hiding the goggles from view.

"It's okay, Tommy. Wait out in the car. It's parked near the garden shop entrance. Andy and I will be along soon." Tommy gave his dad another hug and left. Jack turned his attention to Andy, who was beginning to shake. Tears welled up in violet eyes that matched Becca's.

"Let me see what you have behind your back, Andy." Jack got down on one knee in front of the scared boy and held out his hand. Andy slowly brought his hand around and gave the goggles to Jack.

"These are nice goggles. Let's see, not cheap either. Price right here says $8.95. How much money did you bring with you, Andy?"

Tears streaked down Andy's face and his voice was so small Jack could hardly hear his reply.

"I don't have any money, sir." Andy broke into a full-blown cry and sagged to the floor. He placed both hands over his face and wept so hard his shoulders jerked up and down. A clerk came over to check on the disturbance in sporting goods.

"Is there a problem here? What seems to be the matter with your son, mister?"

Andy's head jerked up with terror on his face. Jack could read the boy's mind. Andy probably thought he would be arrested and sent to jail.

"There's no problem," Jack responded. "Nothing I can't handle." The clerk gave him a strange look and started to say more just as an older woman stepped into the aisle and asked for assistance with basketballs. The clerk excused himself and walked away with her.

Jack tossed the goggles back up on the shelf and helped Andy to his feet.

"Let's go outside and have a little chat, son." Jack held Andy's hand as they walked though the store. "Hold your head up, Andy. It's okay now. You stopped in time, and we'll work this out, just you and me." He smiled down at the frightened boy and saw total gratitude reflected back.

Jack waved to Tommy sitting in the car. "Wait here on this bench, son, I'll be right back." Andy quickly sat to wait. Jack went over to Tommy and opened the car door to talk to him.

"Everything's going to be fine, thanks to you, Tommy. You did a very smart thing. You're a good friend. When Andy gets over the shock of this, he'll thank you, but for now, let me deal with him. Don't mention anything about it unless he brings it up. Got that? When I finish talking to Andy we'll go get something to eat." Tommy responded with a big grin.

Jack returned to Andy and sat beside him to talk. Sometimes it was easier to say serious things to kids this way. Look them straight in the eye a time or two, but give them a chance to watch you from the side without being seen doing it. It took some of the fright out of the situation.

"Tell me what happened, Andy. From the beginning."

Andy started off slowly but soon gathered speed and spilled out the whole truth. He said most of this glancing away from Jack, but when he turned to look at him again, he saw a friendly face.

"So you knew it was wrong, but you wanted to try it anyway?" Andy nodded his head. "You're a smart guy, Andy. You knew that was stupid from the start, yet you took a big risk getting caught. Can you think why you did it?" Jack looked up as the same older woman walked by pushing a cart with her purchases, with a basketball loose on top. He recognized her and smiled. She gave him a wink and continued on. He realized she had run some "interference" with the store clerk earlier. Andy had had more than one friend in KMart that day.

"I'm sorry, Mr. Marshall. All I could think about was how we never have any money and mom is always saying I have to wait and I got mad at my father all over again and I needed new goggles so bad and I just took them. But Tommy wouldn't let me and he got mad and we started talking too loud and then you came. I'm sorry." Andy hung his head and started crying again.

Jack placed a comforting arm around the distraught boy's shoulders.

"There is a way to get those goggles, you know. The right way. You can earn money working, like most folks do. Save it up, then come back and pay for them honestly." Jack shifted over on the bench and hugged the sobbing boy to his side. I just happen to have lots of work to do around the house and I'll pay you fifty cents an hour to help me do it."

Andy looked up at Jack with wonder in his eyes. "Really, you got something for me to do to earn money?"

"Yep, sure do. But you have to save most of it. Then when you have enough, ask me, and I'll bring you back here to get those goggles." Andy was overjoyed and broke out into a big smile. "But. I catch you trying something like this again, and I'll string you up, pardner." Jack used a stern but friendly voice and got Andy's attention on the spot.

Jack held out his hand. "Let's shake on that, son." Andy shook hands then wrapped his arms around Jack and hugged the daylights out of him. "Okay, time to eat." Jack and Andy walked to the car to join Tommy.

Andy was thrilled and walking on a cloud. He would never try anything like that again, he promised himself. Yet, that was a fleeting thought. Mostly, he was thrilled that Jack Marshall had called him son. Tommy was sure a lucky guy, and today, Andy reflected, he was too.

TWENTY SEVEN

The beautiful spring day had turned into an early summer paradise of warm air and soft breezes that continued into the evening. Trees boldly exposed new growth. The entire neighborhood had that fresh scent of cut grass. Flowers nudged blossoms into the sunshine. Rocky Mountain springtime was mostly turbulent and totally unpredictable. Today had been so nice, though, that Jack had announced he was firing up the barbecue grill for a cookout. The Golden Girls success called for a celebration - with steaks, no less. He had called Becca to come over and help with the salad.

Tommy and Andy had worked all afternoon hosing off the deck, cleaning the summer lounge chairs, scraping the grill, and doing just about anything Jack had asked them to. Andy had been like a puppy, following him around and jumping at the chance to earn his approval. Meanwhile, the girls played soccer the entire day, only stopping for a quick peanut butter sandwich, forced on them when Becca took the ball and refused to give it back until they ate. When Becca got ready to go over to Jack's, the girls insisted on taking the ball with them to challenge the boys to a game. They had so much confidence they were ready to play anyone.

Jack saw the determination in their faces as they came out of the woods, shouting their challenge to the boys for a game of soccer. He wondered what kind of game they could play in his little back yard. True, the whole back side opened out into the greenbelt, but even so, the boys could kick much harder than the girls. They would spend a lot of time fetching the ball from his neighbors' yards. He motioned to Becca to come with him to the old cottonwood tree.

"My, my. Are we getting an early start on tonight?" Becca kidded as they sat on the bench.

Jack pulled her to him and kissed her tenderly. He let the kiss linger a while, then opened his eyes and looked into her smiling face.

"I just needed a small reminder. Lately, I find myself thinking about this all day long. Problem is, we always seem to have a passel of kids around, so I have to watch my step."

"I think about us all day too, Jack. It feels right. You make me happy. Sometimes I find myself walking around the house whistling. Do you do that?"

"You whistle? Gee, I didn't know women did that. You must be happy. Lately I'm whistling more than ever. But, I didn't call you over here to whistle. Tell me what's going on with Gloria and Gina. You seem to have Gina every weekend, including Friday nights."

"You saw us talking at the game, didn't you?" Jack nodded. "Well, I trust you to keep her secret. Gloria has a weekend job with really late hours. Her boss just started making her work Friday nights too. She is in a bind financially, and has to keep the job to support herself and Gina."

"What about Mr. Ashworth. She never says anything about him. Doesn't he work?"

"There is no Mr. Ashworth, Jack. He skipped out on them eighteen months ago. He doesn't send them any money, and Gloria lost track of him when he moved out of state. She and I discovered we have a lot in common, so I volunteered to watch Gina for free." Becca looked out over the greenbelt wistfully. Jack could tell this was hard on her.

"I went over there this afternoon just to talk and be supportive. Jack, there's hardly any furniture in the house. She has sold most everything to pay the bills. This job, which I swore not to tell you about, barely helps her make ends meet."

"Such a shame," Jack said. "How could a red-blooded American male skip out on a gal like that? Must be some cards missing in his deck." Jack started to grin, but knew he was in hot water as soon as his words were out.

"Oh, so you think Gloria is attractive?" Becca got that pouty look and slid back from him. "Just what appeals to you, coach? Is it the big boobs again? You men! Come on. You dug this hole, let's see you climb out of it."

Jack tried to change the subject quickly. "The reason I wanted to talk to you was about the game the girls want to play. Now, I have some ideas -" But Becca stopped him with a strong grip on his shoulder.

"Give, Coach Jack. Let me in on gossip you guys snicker about in the neighborhood. What do you say about women like Gloria?"

"Okay, so she has a great body. So what? We all just look and don't touch anyway, what's the harm in that, huh?"

Heating up for battle, Becca jabbed her finger in his chest. "You men. Do you ever think about the person in that body? Gloria is a smart woman with a lot going for her, but guys will never know that because they can't see past her appearance.

"You're right. You win. Guilty as charged. From now on I will only think about your lovely personality. Yep, it's hands off for me."

"Well, that may be correcting your attitude too much the other way." Becca slid back to him and wrapped her arms around his neck. She had started to nibble on his mouth when the sound of giggles came from behind the bushes, breaking the romantic moment.

Jack backed off quickly like a teenager caught kissing his girlfriend, and glanced over her shoulder. "Okay, hold the thought," Jack said. "Back to our contest. I was thinking we need to handicap this game of soccer the girls want to play to cut down on the kicks sailing into Larry's precious yard and denting his grass. What if we make every player kick with their opposite foot? If they usually kick right-footed, they can only use their left."

"Great idea," Becca added. "I have another suggestion. You get the girls, and I'll take the boys."

"Sounds fair to me," Jack agreed.

Once the game got underway, Becca saw that Jack was not handicapped at all. It soon became apparent that Missy and Jack were both ambidextrous. They could kick equally well with either foot, while she and the boys kept stubbing their toes and kicking nothing but air. Finally, Becca got an open shot and whaled away at the ball in frustration, using her right foot. Unfortunately, the ball took off and sailed right over the fence onto Larry Thigpen's carpeted lawn.

"Oh, no," she groaned.

"Quick," Jack whispered, "go around the end of the fence by the greenbelt. Sneak in there. He won't notice you. Hurry up now."

Becca hurried off, and Jack gathered the kids over by the fence so they could all watch what happened. Jack knew that Larry Thigpen could tell when a sparrow pooped on his grass. Nothing got by him. The girls were giggling, and Jack shushed them. He pulled benches over to the fence so the girls could see over it.

Becca had really kicked the ball hard. It was almost to the far side of Larry's yard. Jack's audience snickered as they watched her tiptoeing over to fetch it.

"Who's out there?" a high-pitched voice hollered from the screened-in porch. Larry trotted out the door and stopped short as Becca picked up the ball and gave him her best smile.

"Hi, Larry. I'm so sorry. I guess I got a little excited and whomped the ball over here." Becca sidled up to him with a little sway to her walk that surprised Jack. He suddenly realized he didn't care for this turn of events.

Becca continued. "I promise, Larry, I won't do it again." She beamed at the professional landscaper, who stared back at her open-mouthed, speechless.

Finally, Larry managed to stammer a reply. "Okay. That's perfectly okay. Uh, whomp it, er, kick it over here all you desire, I mean want to." Larry glanced nervously back over his shoulder to check the location of Marvella, his ever present leash.

"You're so understanding, Larry." Becca gently touched his arm and let her fingers slide softly down to his wrist. Then she turned and ran back to Jack's yard. She pulled to a stop when she saw the grinning faces of the boys and girls lined up to watch her little show. One face was not grinning. Jack had a huge pout going and was trying to emulate her jealous stance, but he couldn't hold it and broke up laughing at her stunt.

The game ended with a tie manufactured by the parents to save face for the boys, who struggled to get anything past Jack. Dinner was fantastic, as Jack grilled steaks to perfection and served them with baked potatoes and Becca's salad. Jack timed his cooking so they could feed the kids first, then he grilled his and Becca's steaks so they could enjoy a quiet meal out on the deck.

The kids raced for the game room in Jack's basement, leaving the adults alone at last.

"You sort of claimed me for your own this morning with that very public kiss," Jack said. "Are you really ready to tell the world about us?" Jack gave her a wink. They both knew the team parents had probably long since spread this story through the neighborhood.

"I couldn't help myself. At first, I was overjoyed at our success, then you needed to be rescued from Orson, who was spoiling everything. We had worked so hard, and I just thought how nice it was to have your support and all. At that moment, the kiss seemed like the most natural thing to do. We do make a pretty good team, don't we?" Becca glowed with happiness, her feelings quite evident.

"It's quick, isn't it?" Jack said. Becca nodded. "We've been stealing kisses and short moments like this one for several weeks. We see a lot of each other almost every day, and I find I want to see even more of you. After being alone and a single dad for three years, it's wonderful to be with someone supportive. Have someone to talk to."

Becca placed her hand over Jack's and intertwined their fingers.

"You'll think I'm rushing, Jack, but I don't want to wait. I'm ready to go to the next step. More than ready after today. I know you're giving me time to adjust to what's going on between us, and I appreciate that. If you need some sort of signal from me that it's okay to go further, here it is." Becca leaned over the table and kissed him lovingly. "Come to me tonight after the kids are asleep. I want you in my bed."

Jack was swimming in her deep violet eyes. They had stepped over the edge together. He was ready too.

"Dad, telephone for you. It's Senator Conley." Tommy hollered out the back door. "Come on, dad, he says it's important. He wants to talk to you right away."

Jack and Becca exchanged grimaces laced with frustration. This would delay any romance for the evening.

"Just what exactly is it that you do, Jack Marshall?" Becca shot him a look of puzzled anger. "I asked Martha about your work the other day, and she said it was the million-dollar question."

Cornered, Jack looked out at the greenbelt, at nothing. His mind churned over the right way to handle this situation, trying to find the right words. The answer hit him in the gut - be straight, no secrets.

"I guess it won't do any good to say that I would rather be with you now, but that's the truth. I do police work and really shouldn't talk about it. Fact is, you now know more than anyone, except Dave." He looked back at her and could tell his story was not very popular at the moment.

"I'm about to get divorced from a secretive husband, Jack, and keep discovering I know less about him than I should. I have to think about taking on a relationship with you when I don't know what's going on. I don't think I can handle any more secrets." Becca slid away from him and took a turn staring out at the greenbelt.

Jack was shocked at how her reaction affected him. Parts of him were numb with the fear that she might slip away over a small misunderstanding. She had come to matter so much in such a short time. And he could see her point of view. Still, there was so much to talk about, but now he had to go find out what the senator wanted.

Tommy cried out again. "Dad, come get the phone."

"I'm sorry, Becca. I promise to tell you more later. I'd better go see what the senator wants." He stood and pulled her to him, but Becca had stiffened and did not return his embrace. Reluctantly, he left her and went to answer the phone.

"Hello, senator. What's up?" Jack's enthusiasm for this conversation was low, and his tone didn't go unnoticed.

"Sounds like I interrupted something, Jack." The voice on the other end took on a slightly inquisitive mien.

"Oh, yes, sort of. We had a little victory party going on over here and, I had to leave at a, shall we say, a critical time." Jack was sorry he had started down this line of talk and looked for a way to extricate himself. He knew Bill Conley was too sharp not to see through his ramblings.

"Sorry, Jack. Please tell the young lady I am in her debt." Conley chuckled. Jack sighed and joined him, breaking the tension.

"Jack, Dave and I are coming over there to see you in a few minutes, and I just wanted to give you a little notice. I made the trip out here for the weekend and need to hear about your investigation. We'll be there in a jiffy." Click. The phone went silent, and Jack was left standing without getting in a reply.

This was great timing. He had a house full of kids and a lady he was falling for who may or may not be waiting for him in the backyard. He turned to go back to Becca and found her facing him across the kitchen table.

She fixed him with a stern look.

"Let me guess. You have to go out - wherever it is, that's no concern of mine, and you want me to watch the kids." She assumed her familiar pose with arms crossed beneath her breasts, left foot forward and tapping, upper lip pouting, eyes unblinking.

Jack was speechless at her ability to read him so easily. He also realized he adored her. It had seemed forever since a woman had craved his attention like this, or, made him want to be with her, eager to return that attention. Even though he was being tattooed by her glare, he was deeply affected by how much she obviously cared about him.

Jack never took his eyes from Becca's as he crossed the room to her. "Don't go away mad. There's someone I want you to meet, and then you'll have to go watch the movie with the kids while we talk. Afterwards, I'll tell you everything. Promise me you won't leave?" He gradually enfolded her in his arms and kissed her. He heard a little sigh as she softened and returned his embrace.

"Just as I figured," came a voice from behind them. Jack and Becca slowly broke their clinch and found Senator Conley and Dave standing in the kitchen.

Jack didn't miss a beat. "Becca, this is Senator Bill Conley, who owes you big time for interrupting our celebration. Senator, this is my friend and neighbor, Becca Schmidt. She is also my assistant soccer coach," he added proudly.

"A pleasure to meet you, Becca." Bill Conley let loose one of his beaming smiles that came naturally and guaranteed him a friendship with anyone whose hand he shook.

Now it was Becca's turn to be speechless. She was rescued by Dave.

"Just give us a half-hour with the big guy, Becca. We promise he'll be returned in one piece." Dave shot her a huge grin.

Becca turned a bright crimson and finally replied after searching the faces of each man. She saw only friendliness and sincerity. Her face gradually returned to its natural color.

"Nice to meet you, Senator. I'll just go roust the kids out of the game room, and get them upstairs to bed, Jack." She smiled then left the men to their high-powered talk.

Jack started. "Senator, I'll make this short. Most of our work has been waiting and watching for someone to make a move. We did have a prime suspect, Bartles Conninger, but he was murdered right under our eyes. We don't know who shot him, although we're watching a few suspects. Like you implied at the start, this is a tricky business. The local politicians and developers involved manage to keep their dealings close to the edge of legality.

"The best incriminating evidence would be locating the murder weapon or the source of the counterfeit bills being passed during the bribes. But the recipients of the money we've traced are dead: the Mesa County Commissioner I tailed to Douglas pass three years ago, and now Bartles Conninger. We can't even link their murders since the commissioner's body was never found."

Dave took a turn next. "I'm settling into this new job with relish, senator. Thanks again for the opportunity." Senator Conley waved him off with a big smile. Dave continued. "My official confirmation is in another month or so, but your friend, the governor, issued an executive order granting me interim authority to perform the duties of the Madison DA. Now, if our world-famous secret agent here can break this case, I stand ready to prosecute it."

Senator Conley concluded the impromptu meeting. "Good work, Dave, and congratulations. Fellas, it is frustrating, but I'm satisfied you're on top of this. Just a word of warning, though. If they dared kill Conninger out in the open, then their next target could be anybody, anywhere. Be careful out there." Then he turned to Jack, his eyes shining with mirth.

"Son, I loved Helen like a daughter. But it's time for you to move on. I liked that young lady we shushed upstairs right away. I forced myself into your private celebration like an ornery old military man, and she just let it roll right off her back. That shows character, Jack, that and some deep feelings I'd say. She's also very pretty. You deserve the best. Good luck with her." Conley slapped Jack affectionately on the back and strode out the door behind a still-grinning Dave.

The tone of the evening had changed. Once Jack and Becca got the kids settled in bed, they began talking. They sat facing each other on the living room floor. It was a time for truth-telling. Physical and emotional desires were put on hold.

Becca spoke first to clear the air. "This is all new and strange to me, Jack. Again, I find myself acting like a jealous kid. But there are some gaps in our relationship. It frustrates me, I guess because I care deeply about you. Not knowing everything hurts. I don't want to repeat any of the bad experiences I had with Malcolm. You must know you matter to me. I must care about you, else I wouldn't be getting into these snits all the time."

Jack took a deep breath and settled himself.

"I never told Helen much about my work. She knew I was supposed to keep it a secret and didn't ask. She worried a lot, though. Right after she died, I felt tremendous guilt about my job and the worry she suffered which may have aggravated her headaches, causing her death. Maybe that didn't help her condition. It's hard to tell, but I find myself wanting to share everything with you, no matter what the rules say." Jack paused and drew another deep breath.

"I had secrets from Helen because that's the nature of my job, Becca. On paper, I work directly out of the joint FBI and Secret Service office downtown. I have also worked for Senator Bill Conley for over 20 years as an undercover agent, doing whatever he asks me to do. Same goes for Dave."

Jack stopped talking and let this information sink in. Becca had gotten very still. She seemed to be shrinking away from him. He reached for her, gathering her back to him.

"Breathe. It's okay, really." He smiled at her to break the serious mood and took her hands in his. "Most of my work involves chasing phony paper money and shutting down illegal printing presses in somebody's basement. Sometimes, probably twice in the last three years, I got to guard the president when he came out here. Best assignment I had for that was to taste the food before he ate at some big political rally in Denver." Becca looked puzzled. "You know, see if someone wanted to poison him."

"That sounds like fun, Jack. Can I help out the next time he comes to town? I could write a cookbook about what the President eats. Who knows? I could become a White House chef." Becca was getting into her fantasy role, but the serious look on Jack's face stopped her.

"What comes next isn't fun to talk about," he continued. "Three years ago I had an assignment over on the Western Slope. Tracked payoffs to a local politician. Even trailed him one night up Douglas pass in a blizzard. Then, just when I had the crook and politician together at the top of the pass, an avalanche almost did me in. Next morning Helen died."

Becca grew still in front of him. Jack's voice came softer, quieter for the next part of his story.

"Senator Conley saved me, Becca. He pulled strings with my Washington bosses to get them to assign routine administrative projects I could do from home. I was able to become a full-time single dad to Tommy and Katie and keep my sanity doing some worthwhile work. Yet, I'm tired of it. Lost my edge, as they say in the trade. I rarely go out on dangerous field assignments - maybe a stakeout once in a while. My skills are getting rusty. That means I could put another agent in jeopardy if I don't react properly. And, honestly, I may have done that already." Jack went over the incident at the restaurant where Bartles Conninger was killed. He took the blame for not protecting the man, not scoping out the situation better.

"I've not talked to anyone about this until now, with you, but I don't really want to do this kind of work anymore. Yet it was a key factor in pulling me out of a depression after Helen died. For that reason I had to keep at it, even though as I put more time into being a dad, doing all those household chores, going to PTA meetings, the works, I began to change."

"What do you mean?" Becca asked softly, understanding showing on her face.

"The changes came in subtle ways I think. Little things like getting immense pleasure out of preparing a meal for Tommy, Katie and me. Sitting down and eating together. Making sure they got to school on time. Keeping their clothes clean. Accepting the awesome responsibility as their only guardian. And through those kinds of things, I began to discover why women can make a career out of raising a family, never working outside the home. I also started realizing that dangerous work assignments endangered my family."

Jack looked away to gather his words, and realized he felt better baring his soul to Becca. This was how he felt. His therapist three years ago had pushed him. "Get in touch with your feelings," the man had urged. Perhaps he had done that internally, but until tonight, no one else knew what he truly wanted, how he saw himself.

"Go on, Jack. You needed to unload this." Becca's smile encouraged him, built up even more intimacy. Her tears formed small pools and slid down her cheeks as she tenderly reached a hand to his face, and caressed his own damp cheeks.

Jack continued. "I know myself pretty well, Becca. There has to be a dramatic change lined up for me to take, one that will match my insides with the world I could be comfortable in. So far, I haven't found it, haven't looked hard or cared much, until lately. Perhaps that's the underlying reason I never attempted a relationship with another woman after Helen. I was coasting in neutral, with no goal in sight, nothing to offer for the future. Most guys are still stuck in that mode of being the breadwinner, you know."

Becca was shaking her head side-to-side in disagreement. "You know better, Jack. You have so much to offer it's hard to know what part to take up first. But keep talking. You have me interested, seriously."

"There probably isn't much more to it. I did realize some time ago that if I ever had another serious relationship, I had to be completely open. There would be no secrets; it just wasn't fair to the other person."

Becca smiled coyly at him. "So, you're telling me this because you think we have a serious relationship?"

"You know we do," Jack responded. He lost his serious face, letting a slow grin take over. "That look you gave me in the kitchen when I got off the phone with the senator said so." Now he got serious again. "I felt, overwhelmed, bombarded - no that's not the word, thrilled and excited with your concern. Someone was on my side, in my corner, rooting for me after all these years facing everything alone. That look said I was no longer on my own. I took it as a much stronger declaration of your feelings than the big public kiss at the soccer field this morning."

Becca smiled at Jack's words. Although outwardly calm, her heart was racing with excitement, anticipation. She had never known anyone so perceptive. Here was a "tough" government agent who had tapped into his sensitive side, something most women seemed to come by naturally. What a combination! How could she not care about him when she felt his concern for her?

"So, what are we going to do about this?" Becca scooted as close to Jack as she could get and kissed him. They sat, bent over, heads resting together.

"It's your turn to spill the beans, lady." Jack said as he pulled back an inch. "I want to hear what you want for *Becca*. You must have a dream or two in that beautiful head of yours. Tell me what I need to aim for."

"Just like that? You make me feel like I've been granted three wishes, and, knowing you, you'll find a way to make them come true."

"I'd sure like to try, but you know what I'm getting at," Jack replied. "You have listened to me patiently. I need to hear your story, too. What makes you tick? You've had a bad time of it with Malcolm. If you had the perfect relationship what would it be like?"

It was a first for Becca. This man wanted to know her feelings, her desires, everything about her, and she believed him. He was serious, so she thought back to the start.

"My brother Robert was always treated like a prince. I was made to feel second class around him. I thought Malcolm was going to be my knight on a white horse and treat me right, give me the attention I missed as a child.

But, he turned out to be, well, not what he appeared to be. A total jerk - no, that's not strong enough. Malcolm was controlling, abusive, secretive, manipulative, mean to the kids, certainly no dad in any of the ways I have seen you be."

She paused. Becca knew what she wanted, she just had to say it. "I need to be equal in my perfect relationship. Nobody's princess, not a slave either. No patronizing. No pats on the head and being told not to worry about the details of my life like I'm some fragile crystal vase that will shatter if exposed to the truth."

Jack nodded. "Go on. That's a good start."

Becca felt empowered, energized. The words came easier now. "There's got to be trust. Period. I always wondered what it would be like to have someone I could rely on, the way you described before. Someone who was there for me, in an equal partnership, who wasn't demanding that I keep to the house, be his to command. Oh, wait! That's all taken care of if I'm allowed to be myself. That would be a first." Jack's face took on a puzzled look, and Becca rushed to explain.

"See, here it is in a nutshell. Both people in a relationship must want freedom for themselves and each other. Each must want the best for their partner at all times, think of the other person first, every time. That's why trust is so important. If someone cares about me no matter what, then I know I can do just about anything. First, though, I have to feel that freedom. There would be no control, no coddling, no restraints, just certainty that I would always do the right thing for myself and the other person. To me, that would be the most powerful feeling ever. Of course, it takes lots of love and understanding, and empathy, sympathy, or whatever reassurances necessary if I did screw up. Yeah, that's it. The freedom to fail miserably and know you -" she blushed, "- he would stand by me."

Becca stopped to catch her breath. Her eyes were bright with excitement. She had never said these words to anyone. While talking, she had gazed past Jack and fixed her concentration on some distant point, now she came back to earth and focused on the silent man sitting in front of her. He was smiling confidently, as though he felt he could deliver her dreams. She took a second to check for any arrogance or macho conceit popping loose. She saw none.

Becca continued on. Jack listened to this marvelous woman as she told of her dreams while revealing what she would contribute naturally to her perfect relationship.

He found himself thinking of her as a treasure and stopped short. He had placed Helen on a pedestal, and Becca wanted no part of that. Her needs were simple: equality, trust, freedom. She had used the "L" word only once, but they both knew it was the foundation for a successful relationship. He felt confident, comfortable with what they had started. It was time to move from the floor.

"Let's take a walk and get some air, shall we?" Jack stood and pulled her to her feet. They did a quick check upstairs and found the kids totally zonked out. Then he walked her through the greenbelt towards her house.

Becca pulled up short halfway there and faced him. "You suddenly got quiet, Jack. Cold feet?"

"I like everything that's happening around us and to us, but yes, maybe I feel like I have to catch my breath a bit. Right now I want you to go to your bed, and I'll go to mine. My mind is churning with so many thoughts that I don't know if I can be much good in your bed. I want us to be perfect, and I know tonight might fall short. Give me a day or so. Okay?"

"Fine, Jack. Here's something to help you concentrate." Becca took his hands and placed them on her hips. She kept her eyes locked on his as she slid his hands under her T-shirt, resting them on her bare breasts. Then she grabbed his head and pulled it to her hungry mouth and devoured his lips. They stood glued to each other until Jack managed to come up for air.

"Good Lord, woman. Go home quick, before I tear off your clothes. I feel like the kids are watching us from their bedrooms." Becca fixed him with a sexy smile, turned, and walked away. Jack watched her disappear into the woods and enter the gate to her yard. She had come fully alive in these past weeks. It took every bit of his will power to return to his house and not follow her, but he had sleeping children to watch over.

TWENTY EIGHT

After a long Sunday of household chores and some reflection on his deepening relationship with Becca, Jack needed his Monday morning run to clear his head. He had argued with himself again and again about why he had been reluctant to go to bed with her over the weekend. Why was he hesitating? The answer was simple this morning. At age 40, and as a devoted single dad, he was not willing to try a fling or have an affair. He had too much respect for Becca to play around with her feelings or with his own.

This meant serious business. One step past heavy kissing, and he had to be ready to make a commitment. He knew himself well enough to recognize that. So, he asked himself as he ran down the bike path through the greenbelt paralleling the South Platte, was he ready to join his life with this woman's? His mind racing, he decided to run as far as possible and walk back, relishing the calm such exertion always brought. When he got back to his house, he would know what to do about Becca. His mind would also be ready to tackle the mystery of his assignment for another week.

The concrete path he traveled was eight feet wide and crossed several pre-constructed wooden bridges over runoff gullies and dry creek beds that emptied into the river when heavy spring rains filled them. Jack passed a dormant pool eddying alongside the river where beavers had dammed the water and built a home. Cormorants swam around the thatched beaver home and dove deep in search of silvery fish for an early breakfast. When they surfaced, their sleek black heads and long necks resembled water snakes. Jack slowed as he neared an old dead cottonwood near the edge of the pool where a great blue heron had set up her spring nest for her brood.

The path narrowed as it crossed under C-470, the infamous state-funded beltway around Denver's southern suburbs. Jack laughed to himself every time he ran under the super highway that had helped spawn excessive development. A former governor had promised to stop the vampire-like construction on this roadway by driving a silver stake through its heart. Must have been a mere superficial flesh wound. The city of Fullerton had been one result, planting six houses per acre for a total population nearing 100,000.

Rumors of scandal still circulated about where the Fullerton Development and Planning Office had gotten the water to support such frenetic expansion and burgeoning population. Payoffs and bribes were not uncommon in this arid state when water was at stake.

Jack's mind wandered as he entered Cromwell State Park, yet some sixth sense told him he was sharing the path this morning. A glance back over his shoulder revealed a lone bicyclist a few hundred meters behind, pedaling at walking speed. Not usual for bikers at this hour, he thought.

He followed the curvy path as it neared a large copse of cottonwoods between a bend in the river and the wetlands north of the dam. Another glance, and the biker was speeding up. He was huge and obviously stripping gears as he pedaled harder. Not usual, Jack thought again. Neither were the baggy pants, heavy coat and construction-type boots that kept slipping off the pedals.

Jack turned to scan the path ahead and saw another sharp curve going to his left. Red twig dogwoods lined the right side. Their whip-like branches reminded him of the switches his mother had used on him when he misbehaved as a child. Jack's perusal was cut short by the grinding sound of thick mountain bike treads scudding along the rough concrete, gaining speed. The hair on his neck stiffened. No recreation rider would barrel full-speed toward a sharp curve. He turned to glance over his left shoulder just in time to see the biker's bulky arm cutting a huge arc on its downward swing at his head. The descending hand held a three-foot long steel rod bristling with spikes.

Jack jumped straight back as the modern day mace sliced at him, ripping a gash in his shoulder. He landed in the dogwoods and rolled away from the path into brambles filled with winter tumbleweeds. His bare arms and legs were scratched and cut form the thistles, but his head was intact. The biker's aim had been a few degrees too low to put Jack out of commission.

He rolled to a stop and held his breath to listen for the tires. A resonant drumming noise faded away as the attacker made his getaway. Mistake number one, Jack thought. There was no quick way to exit the park except to come back this way, and the next half mile of path contained more sharp curves through the heavily wooded area.

His shoulder burned from the deep slice and was bleeding profusely, but Jack used his anger to ignore the pain. He ran across the marshy ground bordering the wetlands. He knew this trail very well. The biker had to make a big circle out to the left then come around at a 90-degree angle to Jack's position. Less than a football field in length separated Jack from the other section of the pathway, but took him across sink holes and swampy terrain. Jack was oblivious to these obstacles as he gritted his teeth against pain and raced to cut off his assailant. He hurdled fallen trees and sloshed across mossy, slick pools, ignoring his aching shoulder and the blood running down his arm. He'd deal with that later.

As he approached the return loop of the concrete path, Jack saw the biker streaking up the long straightaway, head down, legs pumping. He kept looking back to see if he was being pursued. Jack never stopped running as he crashed through more brambles and collided with the man, tackling him shoulder high. The bicycle continued forward a few yards then carried both men down a slope and into a pool of sludgy water.

Jack landed on top as surprise gave him the advantage over the larger man. He heard a low-sounding whoompfh as the breath left the man beneath him. Jack's solid 200 pounds had struck like a battering ram. He reached for the lapels of the bulky coat to pull the man out of the water and smash his face. Then, Jack's anger drained away at the sight of fixed, staring eyes of his victim. His neck had been snapped in the fall, killing him instantly.

Jack dragged the heavy body out of the water and collapsed beside it. The moment of surreal silence following Jack's attack, and the crash into the pool was broken by the cacophony of screeching wetland birds settling back into their morning ritual. In less than 90 seconds, Jack had been sliced open, brutally scratched by thistles, attacked, and had accidentally killed a man. And now all was right with nature again. Just another day in the park. Survival of the fittest.

He sat up and drew in deep breaths to fight the dizziness nipping at the edges of his mind. Something wasn't right. He scratched at the stinging on his left shoulder and his hand came away sticky, smeared with blood. Lots of it. He tore off his T-shirt and wrapped it around the wound to staunch the flow. His world was throbbing in slow motion as he looked around to find help. Damn. Where was a yuppie jogger with a cell phone when you needed one? Jack managed to crawl backwards up the slope to the path using his remaining strength, and then lost consciousness.

The man on roller blades cruised down the steep hill that sliced along the face of the dam and streaked towards the wetlands. He could attain speeds near 30 MPH and coast most of the way to the picnic grounds where his car was parked half a mile away. After that, he'd check his messages and let his office know he would be a little late today.

He ended his free coasting and began pumping his arms and legs to finish his run. Fortunately he was looking down when he almost creased Jack Marshall's arm, which was splayed out in the path. He hopped over the arm and began toe-stubbing to brake and check out the scene. Probably some homeless person sleeping it off in the weeds, he figured, as he slowed and made his turn back to the arm.

•••

Malachi Hamilton only had nine head of cattle, and by damned if he was gonna lose his best one. He followed her tracks and occasional splotches of dung up the winding ravine that roughly paralleled the Douglas Pass road. Malachi walked slowly in the high altitude to keep his breath and not scare off the errant beast. Whatever possessed her to take off up the steep slope, he'd never know.

There she was, just rounding an outcropping of mud and rock slide from the upside of the hill. He hurried quietly to rein her in before he ran out of air. Malachi didn't need to worry. The lumbering animal halted near the edge of the slide and nosed around the ground at something sticking out from the rocks. Malachi approached easily and slapped the animal on the rump, turning her downhill, back toward his fenced pasture. He glanced down to see what had attracted the dumb beast and jumped back in surprise. The dry climate and tons of icy snow had preserved the head of a man. The shifting dirt and mud slides had finally given up the remains of Willard Shupe, former Mesa County Commissioner.

•••

Dave watched his best friend struggle to claw his way into semi-consciousness. He was one tough hombre, but it had taken several pints of blood, and multiple stitches to stabilize Jack Marshall. X-rays showed a concussion. He had been the lucky one. Jack's "mild" concussion had been the killing blow to the man the FBI had identified as Samuel Baldridge, project superintendent for the Stalker Construction Company.

Jack Marshall looked like he had run into the back end of a porcupine. His face was covered with scratches and small punctures from the mad scramble to overtake his assailant. Jack had mumbled this much to the ambulance attendant before passing out on his way to the Urgent Care Center on Clydesdale Boulevard. His legs looked equally bad under the sheets. Dave had watched the nurse when she checked. There were many patches of abraded skin.

Dave was thankful, first for the relative safety of his friend, and second for this new link in the chain of events. Baldridge was directly connected to Rafe Stalker, and a revolver found back at his car was being tested for a match to the weapon that had killed Bartles Conninger. Dave shuddered thinking of the twisted mind that had chosen the mace attack over just using the revolver. Jack had paid a price for this lead, but now they knew who to watch, and evidence was mounting against the aggressive developer from the Western Slope.

"Oh God, I feel like shit." Jack Marshall spoke to the world at large for the first time in hours. He tried to scratch at his shoulder and found bulky padding preventing his fingers from relieving the incessant itching. Puzzled, he attempted to crane his neck and head down to see what was going on with his arm, and pain shot up his head like a Roman candle. Stars in his vision and a loud ringing in his ears became his whole world for a few seconds.

"Hang on there, good buddy," Dave murmured gently as he pushed Jack back down and fluffed the pillow under his head. "The doctor says to keep still for the next day or so. I told them you had the hardest head in Colorado, but they still want to check you out in that department. Don't know how they'll be able to figure out what's normal though."

Jack laughed through clenched teeth as his head started ringing again and more fireworks touched off. This batch lasted only a second, and he looked up at Dave, his friend and tormentor.

"What's the scoop? How did I get here? Where's the guy who took a swipe at me?"

"Be quiet and I'll tell you. The guy worked for a construction company. He's DOA at the Denver Morgue. We found a weapon that may connect him to Conninger's murder. You got lucky when a roller blader almost ran over you in the park. Now shut up and rest."

"Hold it!" Jack tried to shout, and his head exploded with another blast. "It's coming back to me. I was hit by this guy on a bike, and he had to have been following me from near my house. Dave, they're watching the house. You need to put some guys over there and warn Becca." Jack was getting agitated and tried to sit up, but Dave pushed him back down.

They both froze at the voice from the doorway. "So, this is the carefree life of the Secret Service agent who has not been in a threatening incident for lo these many years, eh?" Becca taunted both men as she nervously eyed Jack's scratched up face. She moved unsteadily across the room to stand by the bed opposite Dave.

Dave backed out of the room before she threw him one of those unmerciful glares she now aimed at Jack. Besides, he couldn't take the electric connection between the two. Dave had not seen this in his own life for too many years. The attraction between his best friend and the woman glaring down at him was too powerful for Dave.

Jack looked into Becca's sad and worried eyes. His spirits rose as he recognized the depth of her feelings for him. It was almost enough to lift him out of the bed. At least in spirit. The flesh was not going anywhere for a while.

"Wish I could tell you what happened, but I seem to have a slight memory loss."

"Uummm hmmm, sure you do," she murmured. "Slight everything. Memory loss, sliced arm, scratched body all over, I'm told by your nurse, who winked as she described damage to places I've yet to see. Let's see, there was also something about the transfer of several pints of blood? Sure is a pleasant way to make a living, pushing paper out of your home."

"Give me a chance here, lady. I'm not thinking too straight now. But, I swear, what I said to you Saturday night was the truth. This attack came out of nowhere."

"Well," Becca continued, "right now my biggest concern is finding someone to run the soccer practice this afternoon." She tried to smile, but couldn't quite pull it off.

"You know, Tommy does this sometimes. Katie too. When they get really scared they act like they're mad to cover it up. I think it's some kind of defense mechanism that started around the time they lost their mother. What do you think your reason is?"

Becca found a spot on his right arm that wasn't too badly scratched and stroked it. She fixed him with a look that melted his irritation. "Maybe I almost lost something precious today too, Jack. Just when I thought I'd found a perfect match, you go out and get attacked and almost die." She didn't try to stop the tears as they washed down her face.

"Damn it, Jack. You scared me so bad I hurt. I know this is part of the package and I have to accept what you do. That's why you opened up so wonderfully the other night. You included me in your life, and today I thought I'd lost you. I'm crazy about you. Fallen overboard without a life-jacket. Cross-eyed. Smitten. Hell, I've run out of words."

"That's enough, Becca. I love you too."

"Yes, I left those out." She stopped suddenly with a sharp intake of air. "You do?"

Jack smiled up at her beaming face. "It's the only diagnosis I can come up with to describe my condition, other than the superficial stuff that's all bandaged. Come here, closer."

Becca bent over him and brushed her lips gently across his. "Ummm, Jack. This is a predicament, isn't it? There's no place I can touch you except right here." She continued to make love to him with little caresses on his lips and small pecks on his face where there was a clear spot.

"I must admit, this is a new position for me," he groaned in mock agony. His brain was sending extremely erotic messages to significant parts of his body, but there were no return signals. Must be drugged, he thought. Either that, or he was paralyzed for life. Nah, they would have said something by now.

"Lady, you're driving my brain nuts, and I'm helpless to do anything in response." He pleaded.

Becca stood back and smiled. He could see she was overcoming her initial fear quickly. He returned her smile, their eyes locked until the doctor came in.

Becca started to leave the room, but Jack stopped her. "Stay. You need to know." She smiled grimly at him, and they waited for the prognosis.

"Your friend alerted me that you had come around, Mr. Marshall. He assured me you were doing fine and to give you two a few minutes alone. Something about a different kind of therapy being administered." The doctor glanced over his shoulder at Becca with a sarcastic smirk. Then he checked Jack's eyes, blood pressure, and other vitals quickly.

"I'm amazed, Mr. Marshall. Just an hour ago you were much worse, nearly slipping into a coma. I expected gradual improvement, but nothing this fast. Other than an elevated heart rate, which I think probably applies to both of you at this moment, there doesn't seem to be much to worry about. You'll be up and out of here tomorrow. But, take it easy for the rest of the week." The doctor shook his head and walked out of the room muttering.

"Guess he noticed the lipstick all over your face, Jack. It's a special brand designed to cure anything."

"Getting cocky are we? I'm not amazed at all. I felt better as soon as you walked through that door. Now get out of here and go coach our girls."

TWENTY NINE

Jasper Mackey had seen cases like this before. He could always find an audit trail to fiddle with and ferret out the truth. No one just disappeared completely. Neither did anyone successfully run two households with two different wives without some incriminating paperwork. In the situation surrounding the Schmidts though, he wondered. He couldn't find a thing wrong with Becca Schmidt. She was a good mother, and a smart and beautiful woman whose qualities were more than skin deep, at least as far as Jasper had observed.

Malcolm Schmidt had a nice home in a nice neighborhood, two healthy, adorable children, and Becca. Yet, it wasn't enough. Why? Jasper reviewed the private investigator's report one last time. It looked like Malcolm had grown discontent shortly after moving to Colorado. His second, illegal marriage to Audrey Hammaker in Boise took place a scant six months after he started work for the Gondo Sports Equipment Company. Jasper was certain Gondo management was unaware of the dual life of its top salesman, since Becca and the kids were listed on their records as Malcolm's official family.

The case was going to be easier than Jasper had expected. The Fullerton judge would schedule a hearing, but he felt sure she would grant an immediate dissolution at the hearing, and Becca would take possession of all family assets and property in Colorado. Plus, she had first claim on any other financial assets yet to be discovered, and Jasper figured Malcolm had squirreled away plenty in Boise. Audrey, the other Mrs. Schmidt, would lose, big time. Jasper felt pity for Audrey. In most cases of bigamy, neither wife knew about the duplicitous second life of the husband. Malcolm deserved and would get jail time.

Jasper glanced over the photo his investigator had taken of the second Mrs. Schmidt. She was a knockout brunette, and almost a carbon copy of Becca, though 15 years younger. Audrey had been a clerk in a local Boise sporting goods store, and fresh out of high school when Malcolm had married her. Probably, Jasper thought, another vulnerable woman prone to the let-me-take-you-away-from-all-this syndrome.

He finished signing the sheaf of papers his secretary had generated for the case. There were going to be some surprises out in Boise tomorrow when Mr. Schmidt received this packet.

"Annie, would you please send Mrs. Schmidt in now?" Jasper didn't relish the next few minutes when he would tell Becca about her double.

Shock, surprise, bitterness, and then overwhelming joy registered on Becca's face in the few seconds it took for her to focus on the photo of Audrey and hear the news of Malcolm's double life.

"Jasper, why did he do this? I did everything in my power to make a happy home." Becca's anger diffused to mirth as she giggled out loud. This was not the usual response to such news, she supposed, but now there were no legal roadblocks for her and Jack. Jasper sat silently with a puzzled look.

"Don't expect me to complain about this, Jasper. It was over with Malcolm and me three years ago. I always wondered why he put up with being cut off so easily. He never said a word, just packed a bag and took off on a business trip. This photo tells the story, doesn't it?"

"Becca, I expected you to be angry, maybe a little sad, then show some relief that we can settle this matter rather quickly. I must say, you have recovered faster than anyone I've ever seen."

She turned pink and looked down at the plush carpet for a moment before responding. "Let's just say I have a few secrets of my own, Jasper. Where do I sign?"

•••

Two thick packets were placed on the entry hall table for Malcolm to see when he returned from Sun Valley Friday night. He brushed by them, in a hurry to meet Audrey in bed upstairs. He had called ahead and told her to get ready for him. It was to be a special night. He had reminded her what it meant to disobey his orders, and anticipation was eating at his groin.

It was his favorite fantasy, and one he demanded every Friday night regardless of her mood. She would be blindfolded, naked, freshly bathed, and covered with scented massage oil. Her lithe, young body would be splayed across smooth satin sheets, receptive to his whims. Tonight he heard the demons talking in his head. He might have to get the scarves and play a little bondage. Audrey always protested at first, but then she turned frantic with passion and moved under him like she was on fire.

He stopped at the top of the stairs and stripped off his clothes. Malcolm watched his image in the full-length mirror at the end of the hall. His excitement and anticipation had already created a stone-hard erection. Malcolm trembled. He was so into this scene that he might need Audrey to relieve him quickly before he got into the role-playing any deeper. The thought of her pert little mouth on his body caused shivers as he walked toward their master bedroom.

A soft, fearful voice drifted across the room from the oversized bed.

"Malcolm, is that you? Please speak to me. I'm frightened. I don't like this game anymore."

Audrey lay under the covers. As he approached silently, Malcolm noted that she was blindfolded but wore a cotton nightgown that covered her neck and probably went all the way to her toes. He started to get angry at this violation of his directions.

"Who else would it be?" he shouted. "How many others do you entertain while I'm out working, earning the money to pay for all this?"

"Nobody. There's no one. Please Malcolm. You scare me when you get like this. It's so impersonal, I -" Malcolm slapped her hard and tore the covers off.

"No, don't!" she screamed. "You're hurting me. Stop it, Malcolm!" He ignored her and tore at the neckline of the nightgown, ripping it down the center. Audrey tried to cover her body, crossing one arm over her breasts while reaching the other between her legs. That left her face exposed and Malcolm slapped her again.

She gave up and lay still. Malcolm spread her legs and plunged into her without warning. He didn't notice or care that her arms lay by her sides. Neither did she wrap her legs around his hips in a passionate embrace. He rammed into her so forcefully that her head knocked against the solid oak headboard. Still, she said nothing and didn't move. Tears ran down her face as Malcolm roughly grappled with her breasts and kept up his thrusting.

Mercifully, he didn't last long and exploded inside her quickly. She lay still under his weight until he slipped out abruptly.

"Don't move an inch. I'm not through with you." He moved to his dresser and reached inside the bottom drawer for the restraints. "Perhaps some time alone might straighten up your attitude."

Malcolm tightened the wide cloth bands that encircled her arms and ankles, securing her to the corner posts of the bed. He noted with a satisfied grin that she was totally helpless. There had been no struggle or protest this time. Instead, Audrey seemed apathetic, almost as if she were in a trance. Silent.

Malcolm padded into the bathroom to wash himself. He slipped on his silk dressing robe and went downstairs to get a drink, leaving Audrey to wait for his next move. Good, he thought as he crossed the room and saw her silent tears. This will teach her a lesson. The next time she'll be ready and hot. His body was recovering quickly just thinking about what he would do later. He was in total control.

Downstairs, he poured malt whiskey over a few cubes of ice and went to check on his mail. The two thick packages intrigued him. They had been sent overnight and were covered by signed receipts dated several days earlier. Malcolm's traveling took him out of town Monday through Friday each week. He had given Audrey strict instructions not to touch his mail, so there was no way she could have done anything about these items. She also didn't know where he went or how to contact him.

The first package was the thicker and showed a return address of some lawyer in Colorado. Curious, Malcolm tore open the envelope. He took a soothing sip of the whiskey and began to read the first document. By the second line, he had turned red in anger. *Colorado Judicial District, etc. - Hearing, - Dissolution of marriage between Rebecca Schmidt, plaintiff, and Malcolm Schmidt. physical abuse - bigamous relationship in Boise, etc. All assets to Plaintiff. Respondent's wages garnished, - pay child support. Sole custody of the children to plaintiff, - no visitation by respondent. Restraining order against respondent. Etc. Patricia Langfelt, Chief Judge*

Malcolm choked and spit out his whiskey, then threw the glass tumbler into the fireplace. How could this be? She was trying to screw him out of a house and everything he owned in Colorado. Malcolm was blind with rage, and ignored the notice to appear at the hearing. This was ludicrous. Impossible! Nobody could do this to him. He would have to get even. That lousy, stinking bitch, Rebecca and her loverboy neighbor who had threatened him in his own house. They were to blame.

Malcolm shook with fury and paced back and forth in his living room. He threw down the obnoxious order from the judge and scanned the attachments. Cold sweat ran down his back as he began to comprehend his situation. Someone had discovered the checking account he kept in Denver. That money, along with the investment fund for his retirement could soon belong to Rebecca. He turned shakily to the second attachment, which required him to pay all current expenses to run Rebecca's house and raise "her" children. They were certainly no longer his, and that part didn't bother him so much. It was the money he hated losing. His one consolation was the retirement fund at Gondo, and that was a sizable chunk of change.

Malcolm staggered to the bar and filled another tumbler with whiskey, this time without ice. He tossed the drink down and filled the glass again. Then he spied the remaining package. Opening it, he learned the courts of Idaho had also reached out and grabbed him by the balls. *Idaho, First*

District - Hearing on the Estate of Malcolm Schmidt, etc. - division of property equally between Mr. Schmidt and Rebecca Schmidt of Colorado. Including the retirement fund and checking account managed by the Republic Federal Savings Bank of Sun Valley, etc. Answer charges of bigamy. Harry Birdsong, Associate Judge

Trapped. God damn it! He was trapped. He couldn't go to hearings in either state without being charged with bigamy. He had been found out, and he'd be left with nothing except this puny house mortgaged 100 percent and a dumb slut of a wife tied up on the bed upstairs. His mind raged as he looked for something his anger could devour. Another glass went sailing into the fireplace. Malcolm grabbed the bottle of whiskey and stomped up the stairs. Someone, everyone would pay, he vowed. Jack Marshall and Rebecca were out of his reach for now, but not forever. He growled under his breath as he stormed into the bedroom. Audrey would beg him to kill her before he was through tonight.

•••

Sergeant Sally Mayfield could barely make out the words of the emergency call. It was a weak signal and growing fainter, but a tiny voice was asking for help.

"Caller, please talk to me," she said. "We'll send help, but I need to know what's happened."

Again, only that single word came feebly over the line - "help." Then silence, yet the line stayed open, and caller ID had pinpointed the source. Just before three A.M. Saturday morning, Sergeant Mayfield sent paramedics and a squad car to the address of a Mr. and Mrs. Malcolm Schmidt.

When Officer Bobby Harrison approached the home, the front door was ajar. No lights were on, and no sound came from inside. He drew his weapon and entered the house slowly. Jim Murphy, a paramedic, followed closely with his medical treatment bag.

Harrison called out, "Anybody here? Police. We're here to help." Silence greeted the two men as they checked the ground floor. "Let's go upstairs, Jim," Harrison said. They turned and headed up.

Both men reached the entrance to the master bedroom at the same time and stopped short. The slight figure of a woman, scrunched into a fetal position, lay on the bed. Naked. Unmoving.

"Stay here, Jim. We may have a homicide on our hands." Harrison quickly crossed the room and took in the horrible sight. He jumped back as two frightened eyes popped open to stare at him. A soft moan came from her lips.

"Jim! She's alive! Let's go."

Murphy darted across to the bed and felt for a pulse. It was weak and slowing. The woman's eyes were dilated but alert.

"Bobby, call for an ambulance. She's going to need a doctor and emergency room care immediately."

While Harrison radioed for help, Jim Murphy began checking for broken bones, and head and neck injuries. Welts covered her backside. Bruises were beginning to color her ribs and face. Soon, he thought, the swelling would close both eyes. Her nose was fractured and bleeding slightly. All in all, her body looked like someone had thrown her off a rocky cliff. She flinched away from his lightest touch and cried out whenever he tried to check her injuries.

Together the men gently rolled her on her back once they determined she could move her head and neck. Jim Murphy covered her with a gown and then a blanket to help reduce the shock sending tremors through her body. She was becoming more alert now and trying to talk to them.

"Husband did this," came out in a slurred mumble through swollen lips, cracked and bleeding. She struggled to sit up. "Malcolm did it. Said he was going to get even with Becca, his wife." She looked pathetically into the eyes of Jim Murphy. "Don't understand. Thought I was his wife." Murphy caught her as she fainted back onto the bed.

Bobby Harrison grimaced and bit his lip to stay calm. If they ever found this guy, he and Jim would have a few words with him before they put the cuffs on.

Jim Murphy tried to separate his job from the people and circumstances he came across daily. Thankfully, he worked three straight days and was off the rest of the week so there was usually a span of time to help him wipe out bad scenes like the one this morning with Audrey Schmidt. Yet, when his shift ended at six AM Saturday, he stayed on at the hospital. He was drawn to this young woman like no other patient he had treated.

He stayed with her the entire weekend and then took her home, his home, to protect her and give her the care she needed. Miraculously, he had earned her trust in the hours spent by her bedside. When she was released, she had nowhere else to turn, so she let him lead her to safety. It was a quiet place where she could sleep with the lights on.

Officer Bobby Harrison spent most of Saturday morning on the phone with the Colorado Bureau of Investigation in Denver. Although the western

United States was big country and easy to disappear in, Idaho and Colorado police were working to shrink it rapidly for Malcolm Schmidt.

THIRTY

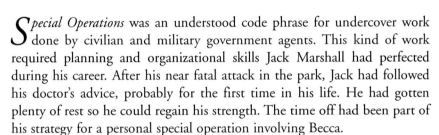

Special Operations was an understood code phrase for undercover work done by civilian and military government agents. This kind of work required planning and organizational skills Jack Marshall had perfected during his career. After his near fatal attack in the park, Jack had followed his doctor's advice, probably for the first time in his life. He had gotten plenty of rest so he could regain his strength. The time off had been part of his strategy for a personal special operation involving Becca.

On Sunday, he had asked Martha and Jasper for help, and they had eagerly agreed to watch the kids this coming Saturday night. On Tuesday, he had gone downtown to arrange dinner reservations and hotel accommodations in person. Finally, he decided to be entirely presumptuous when he bought a nifty little gift to top off the evening.

Only one task remained: talking Becca into going out to dinner with him on a date in the first place. It seemed silly to be nervous about it. After all, Becca had made it clear she wanted him. He was a grown man, yet felt like a teenager asking for his first date. Everything was in place. The baby-sitting was set up. The four star Continental Plaza had reserved a suite on the fortieth floor, and the Broker restaurant had reserved their finest private booth for dinner. All that plus Victoria's Secret had promised to deliver his presumptuous gift directly to their room at the Continental. This time there would be no interruptions, and the setting would be perfect.

The Golden Girls had played games through March and April and were still undefeated. Word had spread that this was a special team from Cottonwood Estates. Sharon Huff was the star, scoring almost four goals each game, but she was finally becoming a team player and having just as much fun. With two weeks rest behind him after the attack, Jack had been a spectator at last Saturday's game. Becca had coached the girls to a victory over the Brown Bombers from Aurora. It had been fun to sit back and just enjoy the game. Becca had planned all the substitutions and had even gotten some help from several parents during practices and for the game. In fact, whenever the Golden Girls practiced, their coaches could count on three or four adults to participate in drills, chase down loose balls, and act as referees during practice games. The Green Dragons' coach had also watched several practices and taken notes on his coaching clipboard.

This week Jack had gone back to work and resumed his job as soccer coach for the Monday, Wednesday and Friday practices. When Friday rolled around, he decided it was time to speak to Becca about tomorrow night. Katie, Missy, and Gina were busy collecting practice cones, balls, and other loose items. It was the perfect time to ask.

"Becca, come over here a second." He tried to look confident and cool, but his palms were sweaty, and he didn't know quite what to do with his hands.

"Sure, Jack. Say, what are you so keyed up about? You've been on another planet the whole afternoon. Still recovering from the so-called minor incident?" Becca added a heavy dose of sarcasm to this last statement. She had continued to bug him about his "serene" life as an undercover agent.

"I want you to know that I'm completely healed, everywhere, according to the doctor who checked me out three days ago. Yep, fully functional and ready to dance, er, rumble. Or, whatever." Jack turned red and looked around for cover but found none.

"Spill it, fella. Something's up, I can tell." She stepped up close and grabbed his sweatshirt with both hands, pulling him forward. But her tough guy act mellowed quickly at his next words.

"Would you like to go out to dinner with me tomorrow night?" He huffed out the invitation quickly then let out a breath in relief that he had finally said it. After all, it was one thing to tease around and steal a few kisses, but quite another to take the first step towards a whole new future. They both understood the significance of his request.

Becca loosened her grip on his shirt and stood on tiptoe to plant a big smooch on his mouth. Then she beamed.

"Great idea, Jack," she said coyly. "There's a new Italian restaurant over on Stanley Boulevard that has excellent veal parmigiana. I could call them in the morning and get reservations for the six, no, make that seven of us counting Gina. What do you say?"

"Uh, no. No kids allowed this time. I've already arranged a sitter and I'll order pizza for their supper. This will be just for you and me, Becca."

But she continued on, planning a frugal night out for just the two of them anyway.

"Wonderful! Reservations will be much easier if it's only two of us. Hey, Jack, this will be our first night out alone won't it?"

"Yes, it will, and I already made dinner reservations. You need to wear a slinky cocktail dress so I can show you off. We're invited to a small party afterwards and may end up dancing a bit too. Some sort of political campaign soiree for Senator Conley. Thought you might enjoy it."

Becca watched his handsome face as he continued to make up stuff as he went along. With each fabrication his eyebrows shot up in exaggeration as if he were being surprised himself with what he had invented to say.

"You know, Jack. You get this wild look on your face when you get excited. Are you making this up?"

Caught, Jack's face turned a shade of pink, and he felt the heat of embarrassment intensify around his neck and down his back. "No, of course not, Becca. You'll just have to wait and see for yourself tomorrow night. Leave everything to me." Then he turned towards the waiting girls and yelled.

"Everybody in the car, let's go." Jack walked back to the car and didn't dare look back at her. One more of her truth-serum glares, and he would mess up all that wonderful planning.

Saturday morning promised another beautiful Colorado day. No clouds. No humidity. And best of all, no wind. Jack had seen beautiful days like this ruined by constant winds that often changed direction on the hour and wreaked havoc with weekend landscapers in the neighborhood. On those days it was useless even to think about raking leaves because a gust of 50-MPH wind would redistribute them all over again. These winds also carried chilly weather and often a late spring snow as well.

Today, though, there were clear skies for another Golden Girls victory. In this game, Sharon passed off consistently to Katie and Missy, and both girls scored two goals each. Jack watched Gloria marking down the scores on a pad and walked over to see what she was up to.

"Hey, good looking. Whatcha doing?" Jack had gotten to be good friends with Gloria. Gina spent the weekends with Becca, and most of that time Becca and the girls ended up in his back yard for a picnic.

"Hey, Jack." She smiled back. "I'm trying out a new scoring system Becca dreamed up. We wanted to reward the girls who played well but didn't score any goals, so we worked up this score sheet." Gloria showed it to him. It was a matrix with all the girls' names going down the left side of the page and columns across the top edge.

Jack was amazed at the information Gloria recorded. There was a column for goals scored, of course, but that was followed by ones for assists, good defensive play, good pass, great kick, and finally plain old good sportsmanship.

"How in the world do you keep track of all that during the game, Gloria?" Jack looked out to the field, where twelve tiny little girls scampered every-where as if some giant had poked a stick into a big ant hill.

"I have my methods, Jack." Gloria gave him a friendly smile. Jack grinned back, then lost her as several parents nearby called out player's names and what they had done. Gloria wrote furiously, jotting down marks under the correct columns.

Aha, he thought, a surreptitious scoring system had developed under-ground while he wasn't looking. What a great idea! he thought. In too many recreational sports activities the superior players got all the attention. The quarterback, the home run hitter, the pitcher, the fastest runner. The list was endless. Attention centered on those kids who developed faster than most others their age. Other children were left out of the glory, or, in the worst cases, sat on the bench and never played.

Jack realized his team parents had taken the "must play" rule one step further by ginning up a scoring system every player could point to with pride. As the first quarter ended, Gloria poked him in the ribs and handed him a piece of paper.

"Stats from last week, Jack. See how we do it? The list is in alphabetical order, and every element counts the same. The total column adds up every-thing for the game. Of course Sharon, Missy, and Katie have more points than the others, but everyone has points. Neat!"

Gloria turned her attention back to the game, while Becca lined up the team for the second quarter in his absence. After she sent the girls back onto the field, she nodded to him as a signal that he had two seconds to get back to the sidelines and do some coaching. Her pouty, jealous stares were gone.

He laughed out loud, and several parents looked at him curiously. He walked over to Becca and hugged her with one arm. "Everything's Okay, chief. Gloria was just showing me her new scoring system. That's all, I promise."

"Good, Jack. Now get back to work." Becca smiled up at him as she stepped on his foot and began cheering the start of play.

"Ouch!" Jack moved away and reached down to rub his offended toes. Tonight couldn't come soon enough.

Jack was relegated to baby-sitting Saturday afternoon as Becca sent the girls to his house to play. Martha and Jasper arrived around six and Jack ordered pizza. He had already taken the kids aside and told them he and Becca were going out dancing and would see them in the morning. He had been surprised when Tommy and Andy gave each other high-fives and the girls just giggled and ran off to their room to whisper.

Jack took Jasper aside and brought him up to speed on the undercover work that required a 24-hour watch on his house.

Jasper was astonished. "This is just like right out of a spy novel and happening right in our own neighborhood. You really think this guy will try to come into the house, Jack?" Jasper's eyes were wide with excitement, and his expression was a strange mix of fear, anticipation, and adventure.

"Now just hold on, Jasper," Jack said. "The suspect is over on the western slope working on a project in Moffat county. That's as far away from here as you can get and still be in Colorado. Still, someone will be close by and they'll keep anyone from bothering you. If one of the kids gets sick or has an accident, you know where to reach us."

Martha came up beside the two men and gave Jack a big hug. "One would think you were going out on your first date, Jack. A wee bit nervous, are you?" She gave him a motherly smile of assurance. Jack smiled at her and kept quiet.

"You are two of my favorite people, Jack, and you both deserve all the happiness life can afford. I'm betting it'll be a happy life together as soon as Jasper can clear the legal hurdles for you."

Jasper wore a smug expression, and the other two looked at him with curiosity.

"I know a few things, my friend, but it's Becca's news to tell, and I'm sure she will when the time is right. Lawyer/client privilege, you know." Jasper had a slightly cocky look about him until Martha elbowed him in the stomach.

"Ooff!" Jasper bent over as the air left him from her jab. "Boy, I'll tell you," he coughed, "women are getting more assertive every day around here, Jack. Watch your step tonight, young fellow." He turned on Martha, wrapped her in a bear hug and kissed her silly before she could stop him. "Hey, Martha," he said with a wink, "did you know Jack's got a big king-size bed up there?"

"Let go of me you lecherous old man," she protested. But her complaints were smothered in another kiss, and they both chuckled as Jack waved goodbye on his way out.

Jack pulled in front of Becca's at precisely half past six and sprinted the short distance to her door. Before he got to the porch, the door opened and Becca stood there ready to go. Jack stared at her wondrous transition. Wow! She looked beautiful. Becca, his athletic assistant soccer coach that morning, had changed into a gorgeous lady for their evening out.

Becca had her hair up in a French twist that allowed a few strands to dangle sexily over her brow. Her dress was a simple black sheath that seemed to cling provocatively, yet leave everything to his imagination. Spaghetti straps lightly caressed each shoulder, but they had little work to do as the filmy gown seemed weightless. Becca wore little makeup; her skin was flawless. Her single piece of jewelry was a silver chain that dipped enticingly between her breasts. A large black pearl nestled on the end of the chain, capturing his gaze.

Any man would have judged her beautiful, and yet Jack sensed an inner glow radiating from her directly to him. Without words he knew that she wanted to be with him and no one else mattered. He was a lucky man.

Jack gazed at her as she stood in the doorway. "You are absolutely beautiful, Becca. You make me proud to be with you."

"Thanks, Jack. You look pretty special yourself with that fancy suit and tie. I've never seen you all dressed up." She kidded him because he usually worked in sweats, blue jeans and whatever casual clothing was clean at the moment.

They embraced and walked to the car holding hands.

Becca turned the ride downtown into a pleasantly erotic experience. She slid close to Jack, sitting sideways so she could drink him in fully while he had to keep his eyes on the road. Her first thought was simply that Jack was a good man. Yes, and he was great to look at, too. Very masculine. Protective yet sensual, with an enticing mix of gentleness and strength. When everything was added up, he was just plain good, through and through. Being a single dad must have had a great influence on him, she thought. No one knew the sacrifices a parent made unless they had kids, and single parents did double duty. She took her time to see every bit of this man she had fallen for.

His reddish brown hair was clipped short and brushed straight across. It was thick and inviting. She tangled her fingers in some hair that edged over the back of his shirt collar. Becca let her fingers curl around the nape of his neck and massage the tense muscles leading to his broad shoulders. She noticed a grin edging around his mouth and knew he was excited about tonight too. Now that they were alone, away from kids and neighbors, she felt free to touch him lovingly and admire him.

His face was strong with a nose that had been broken playing football, so he said. A small vertical scar over his right eye edged into the brow. This had been the result of a foolish car accident when he was young, Jack had confessed.

He had soft green eyes that sometimes looked blue if he wore certain colors. Those eyes smiled constantly, and always made her feel comfortable. Sure, she might kid him and play at being jealous of other women, but she knew he had a particular look that was reserved for her. It was a look that said she was as special to him as he was to her.

Becca gazed down the length of his muscular arms to his hands. They looked rugged and athletic, yet she had experienced their gentle touch. She realized that her perusal of his body had the effect of warming her own. Becca looked back to see his grin just as Jack stole a glance at her.

"A penny for your thoughts, my lady. You keep up that massage technique on my neck and I'll pull over into a 'no-tell' motel that rents rooms by the hour."

"My thoughts are X-rated and censored, mister," she murmured. "At this moment I don't need to eat or dance or meet a bunch of politicians. I could ride here all night, just touching you, keeping you all to myself."

"Well, that's a very tempting offer, but I'm hoping we'll both need lots of energy for later on, so we'd better eat something."

Jack's timing was perfect as they pulled up to the front door of the Continental Plaza. He opened her door and placed her wrap around her shoulders for the short walk to their restaurant.

Becca looked puzzled when they passed the entrance to the hotel.

"Where are we going, Jack?"

"There's this quaint little place around the corner where we can get a bite to eat before the party. It's not far."

Jack led her to the steps descending to the Broker and watched the expression on her face when she saw the name of the place.

"Little bite to eat, eh? No wonder you had me get all gussied up." Her eyes lit up and a look of wonder appeared on her face as they were shown to their private booth. The Broker is famous in Denver's history. Bankers, stock brokers, and businessmen meet in these same private booths to conduct business deals, trade stocks, buy and sell land, while eating the best food in town.

Their waiter opened the curtains to their booth to reveal a table set with a chilled bottle of wine and a huge bowl full of shrimp ready to peel and eat. This appetizer was the specialty of the house, and many diners never had room for their entrees afterwards.

Jack and Becca toasted each other, their children, and the Golden Girls, all credited with getting them together. They nibbled on their shrimp, then Jack pulled a cord that hung down on his side of the table to signal for the entrees.

Five minutes later their waiter appeared with Orange Roughy, mesquite grilled, and salads lightly flavored with honey Dijon dressing.

"Jack, this is too much. If I didn't know better I'd say you were trying to seduce me." Becca had kicked her shoe off. She stretched her foot under the table to rub the inside of his calf. Her gaze never left his face.

He looked cross-eyed back at her with a semi-pained expression.

"If you don't quit it, you'll have us thrown out of here. Now eat up, I don't want you to be weak and defenseless."

She giggled and dug into her fish. Then she stopped eating, raised her glass and offered a toast.

"Here's to you, Jack Marshall. You're the best. This is all very sweet and special to me. I will never forget this evening."

Jack returned her toast with one of his own. "Here's to you Becca Schmidt, for giving me a new life to look forward to. I won't forget this night either, and it's just begun." He sipped his wine and held her eyes with his look of desire.

After dinner they walked back to the Continental Plaza. Jack led Becca to the elevator, where he pressed the button for the penthouse level. Becca attacked as soon as the elevator door closed. She kissed him feverishly, and Jack's arms went around her in a passionate embrace.

Jack deepened the kiss and moaned.

"Ummmm, lady. You kiss great, but hold off until the elevator stops. You're driving me nuts."

"My plan exactly," She murmured.

They remained glued together just enjoying the feel of each other, until the elevator stopped and the door opened. They stepped out into a small vestibule leading to several doors. Jack inserted a key card into the nearest door, opened it, and stood aside to allow Becca to enter first.

She stepped into a dream world. Soft music floated around the room from hidden speakers somewhere above their heads. Ahead, a floor-to-ceiling window provided a breathtaking view of the city. Colorado's golden-domed Capitol Building, bathed in spotlights, provided a glorious focal point. A small fountain gurgled in the center of the entry way and directed their vision to an elongated atrium stretching to the very top of the building. There, a skylight revealed a clear night, sprinkled with stars.

Plush sofas and lounge chairs were arrayed within the space to encourage small groups to form and chat or just relax in the exceptional atmosphere. That is, groups would form if there had been a social gathering as Jack had promised. But they were alone. Becca gazed from one corner of the room to another, noticing only a single door off to the left. She turned to Jack with a puzzled expression.

"You've done it again, haven't you? Tricked me. There's no party for the Senator's campaign. If we're his only support, he might as well pack up and leave Washington tonight."

Jack said nothing as he pulled her into his arms and brought her head up to meet his kiss. This time there was no pulling away. They took pleasure in each other's mouths greedily. Jack held her face between his hands and kissed her with tenderness. He started at her eyes, gently kissing each lid, then her nose. He continued on, nibbling his way over to an ear, running his tongue around the rim and then down to the tenderness of her throat.

Becca moaned softly and turned her head to give him free access to her neck. Jack hungrily took advantage of her offer while she worked her hands under his jacket and massaged his broad back, kneading the muscles. Then she began pulling his shirt out of his trousers to feel his warm skin.

Jack took a breath and moved away from Becca for a moment.

"Let's see what's behind door number one, over there." He led her to the side door and opened it. Inside was yet another fantasy world. A gigantic circular bed was centered under another skylight. A Jacuzzi bubbled in a corner. A small dining table sat off to the right near another wall of glass. On the table was a white linen cloth and a bottle of wine in a chilling container. Two dozen red roses lay beside a silver-papered gift box encircled by gold ribbon.

"You devil. This is way overboard. Jack, it's lovely, charming, exotically romantic, thrilling. Yet, all I wanted tonight was you."

He stopped her before she could start another kiss and pointed to the silver box on the table.

"Since we're staying here all night, I thought you might need a little something." He handed her the gift box and watched her gleefully tear off the paper. Thank goodness, he thought, she's not one of those women who save every scrap of paper and all the bows and ribbons.

Becca opened the box and gaped at the diaphanous negligee inside. She felt its silky smoothness and held it up to her body. It reached from her neck to mid-thigh. Its deep red matched the roses on the table.

"This will be great for later. However, I think it's time for you to open *your* present, Jack." She presented herself in invitation. "If I remember correctly, we were in the middle of the greenbelt, and I told you to concentrate on me real hard, and I did this." She stepped up to him and took his hands in hers, then placed them on her hips. Then she guided his hands up to her breasts, mimicking the seductive scene in the woods a few weeks past.

Jack's eyes glazed with the sensation of touching her. He leaned down and kissed the soft flesh above the neckline of the scanty dress, then slid his arms around her back and reached for the slim zipper. His eyes never left hers as he slid the zipper down. Then he flicked the spaghetti straps over the sides of her shoulders and watched the dress slither down her body with a cool swishing sound. His breath caught. Becca wore nothing beneath the black sheath. Proud of her body, she stepped towards him, naked, glowing with his look of admiration.

She helped Jack remove his clothes until he stood before her fully aroused. Becca rested her hands on Jack's shoulders. "Touch me, Jack. Please. Everywhere. I want you to know every part of me, just as I want to know you."

Jack moved his hands softly over her shoulders, smoothing the skin of her arms lovingly. Her breasts filled the palms of his hands. He bent to kiss each nipple as Becca arched her back. Her arms went around his back and she hugged him, pressing into him, feeling his excitement against her thigh.

Both felt the side of the circular bed and rolled onto it still embracing, not willing to let any space come between them. Then there was a frenzy of touching, loving with hands and mouths, an exploration by two lovers imprinting their physical and emotional commitment on each other, like a map designed for endless journeys.

"Now, Jack. Please, now." Becca rolled over pulling him with her and urgently reached out to guide him inside her. Now one together, she hesitated, looking up at him when he lay still.

"I just want to see your eyes, your look of love, Becca. You feel incredible."

"You too. Love me, Jack. I can't be still another moment."

Rational thought left him as he felt her hips rise up, at once submissive and capturing. They touched from head to toes, sliding over sensitive skin, slowly at first, relishing, cherishing. Sensations came to them as if both were discovering lovemaking for the first time. They lost track of where one body stopped and the other started. Then urgency overcame their coupling as each sped to please the other.

With the luck of fate, they climaxed simultaneously, both crying out in joy. Jack no longer had control over his body as he collapsed on top of her. Becca gloried in his heaviness with a feeling of complete invulnerability.

"Jack, my toes are tingling and my arms feel numb. I think my whole body has melted. Jack, darling, say something. Are you awake?"

"Mummmpfh, … yeah, I think so. It's been a long time, and I just went away somewhere, dreaming, floating. Wonderful place. Cozy. I didn't want to leave. Got to get some air, though." He started to roll to the side but Becca stopped him.

"No, stay. I don't want you to go away just yet. You feel too good. Whoa! What are you doing?" Becca felt him shifting his weight and suddenly found their positions reversed; she was looking down into his sly grin.

"How do you like it up there in control?"

"Gee, this is quite nice, but I thought I was in control before." Becca beamed down at her conquered lover, who nodded his head in agreement. Then her face turned quickly solemn. "Hold me tight, Jack. I'm new at this. I've never had someone to cuddle with afterwards."

"I'm yours for the whole night, Becca"

"That's right. I still have you captured, don't I?" His look of total pleasure was her answer.

"Relax, lady. Put your head down on my chest and be comfortable. We have plenty of time until dawn."

Becca did as requested and drifted into a cozy place of her own as Jack smoothed his hand down her back and over her bottom. She felt like her own private masseur was working on her, drawing magical artwork on her backside.

The new lovers talked for a while about everything good that would result from this night. Sexual tension and urgency had been replaced with deep contentment. Becca thought she could sleep like this all night, but Jack had other ideas, as a part of him quickly forgot about relaxing.

Jack reached down the backs of her thighs and gently brought her knees forward so that Becca straddled his middle, still connected to him.

"Time for you to enjoy the ride up there."

"Interesting arrangement, mister. Something else new for me. What happens now?"

"Oh, just about whatever you want. Wiggle around a bit and see how you like it." Jack pushed her into a sitting position and again filled his hands with her breasts. "Perfect. Beautiful. You have a marvelous body, and from this vantage point, I get to see it all. Watch your reactions. What do you think?"

"I think you talk too much. Just lie back and let me do the work." She moved awkwardly at first, then discovered a graceful rhythm that drove him wild. She ignored his pleas to go faster, teasing him, pleasuring them both. Then it was her turn to collapse in a heap. Sated. Thoroughly loved.

It was the most realistic dream she could remember. Becca saw herself looking up at blue sky framed by leafy boughs of cottonwoods. She floated, naked, perhaps on a raft, across the center of a lake reflecting her surroundings upwards as if there were a picture within a picture in the sky. She felt nothing, sensed everything. The sun began to warm her face, then her breasts, then lower to her center. She may have spoken or murmured in her dream-state and opened herself to the welcomed warmth.

Loving tendrils tickled her intimately, encouraging, stroking. Unhurried. The lake was wide, and Becca felt timeless as her imaginary lover continued like an incoming tide, filling her then receding, filling again, falling away.

Gradually she felt a liquid pressure increasing. It was irresistible, growing stronger, overwhelming her dream.

Jack rested his head on her trembling stomach. The damp, soft hair between her legs tickled, turning him on even more than her thrusting had. Aftershocks from her orgasm continued, gradually decreasing until Becca drifted awake.

Jack snuggled up to her back and spooned her body while his free hand roamed easily over her front. They slept again. Woke often, and sought comfort in their pleasure with the endurance lovers gain from trust and freedom.

Becca lay still. She felt sexy all over and enjoyed Jack's sleeping embrace. She felt secure and loved, impressed by everything jack had arranged - dinner at the Broker, a penthouse suite, even a scandalous piece of lingerie she had yet to wear. He had thought of all her needs for a night away from the kids. A special night where their love-making had gone over the top, sealing their commitment to each other. Yes, that was the contentment Becca realized she was experiencing now. They were together, mind and body from tonight on.

Becca gathered her strength and rolled Jack over on his back. She stretched her body on top of his, switching their positions so she could look down at his sleeping face. She couldn't help inviting herself to nibble on his lips and then began to kiss his eyes, cheeks and mouth, waking him gradually. Finally his eyes opened.

"Whoa, how did you get up there?" his voice drifted up at her lazily, suggestively, as if her maneuvering opened the way for further experimentation. His pursed lips and cheeky grin said he was far from through for the night. His hands reached her backside and stroked.

Becca caught her breath as she felt his excitement stirring. The man was insatiable. But she had something to say before they reached another point of no return.

"Time out, coach." She sat back on his middle enjoying the feel of him trapped beneath her. She leaned forward and captured his wrists in her hands and pinned them on either side of his head. But her tactic backfired however, as Jack managed to raise his head just enough to tease her breasts which were within inches of his face.

She still had serious words to get out and sat back again, bringing his hands together in hers, resting them on his chest to avoid further temptation.

"Jack, I have to say this entire evening was wonderful. You're wonderful. I feel wonderful, satisfied, loved." Becca brought his hands to her mouth and kissed them. "I love you, Jack Marshall." She looked into his smiling eyes and saw his love returned equally.

"I love you too, Becca." Jack answered and sought to free his hands to reach for her, but she held him back again.

"I have something to tell you." Becca drew in a breath then blew it out, ruffling the strands of hair over her brow. Seemingly fortified, she continued. "It seems I have a crackerjack lawyer who knows the ropes when it comes to dealing with husbands like Malcolm. Anyway, Jasper wrote up papers setting me free by the end of the month, unless Malcolm appears in court and appeals. I just wanted you to know that, well, I'm practically a single woman again." She stopped, wanting to say more but couldn't. Maybe she had gone too far as it was. She knew how she felt at this moment, and she knew she wanted him more than anything. But would he think she was being too pushy? Did she sound like she was looking for someone to support her? Was she taking advantage of him?

"I see millions of little calculations going on in that gray matter up there, Becca. You look happy and perplexed at the same time. Bend down here where I can kiss you and tell you something." Jack slowly guided her down, her cheek resting on his heart, eyes soft and puzzled gazing into his.

Jack continued. "I have loved exactly two women in my life. Telling somebody I love them is special for me. I don't toss those words around lightly. I can see you find yourself in a predicament here. You want to let me know that you're practically free, yet you don't want to appear too eager. Am I right?"

Becca answered with a slight nod, tickling his chest with her chin. Her worry lines began to smooth over with his words of encouragement.

Jack moved suddenly and sat up, holding Becca in place on his lap. He wrapped his arms around her and stared into her gorgeous violet eyes.

"Please marry me, Becca. I want you for my wife. I don't want to spend another night away from you."

"Yes, Jack. Oh, God, yes." She kissed him deeply, encircling his back with her arms, never wanting to let go.

They sat like that for a minute, exchanging kisses, sealing their commitment. Slowly they moved into a lazy coupling that would last a lifetime.

THIRTY
ONE

The Fullerton Economic Development Office was a beehive of meetings, ringing phones, and drafting tables overflowing with blueprints. There were busy, busy people everywhere. Rafe Stalker stood in the doorway of the cacophonous bull pen and stared. His business would never run like this. He made decisions and people moved accordingly, decisively straight ahead, no curves, no modifications, period. He made lots of money that way.

Rafe had an appointment with the director of this mess he saw before him. Friends in the business had told him this director, a woman, liked to make deals and could be easy to work with. Her name was Margo Turner. Some name he thought. Well, he was eager to see just how much this Turner woman would turn in his direction.

"You must be Mr. Stalker," a voice from below his left elbow squeaked. Rafe craned his head downward and saw a meek clerk squinting up at him with a phone stuck in her ear. She held one hand over the mouthpiece so she could listen to the speaker on the other end and give him a portion of her time as well.

"Ms. Turner is expecting you, sir. Her office is across the way, over there in the corner." The double-duty clerk hunched her shoulder towards an open door. "She will be with you in a moment. Can I get you -," She was talking to herself though, for as soon as Rafe knew where to go, he went there.

He walked into the cluttered office without knocking, and shut the door behind him, cutting off the roar of activity in the outer room. The director had her feet propped up on the corner of her desk and a phone held to her ear. Must be some defect in all the people around here, he thought. He listened as she ignored him and continued her personal call.

"Jerry, I never said that I wouldn't go out with you. It's just that, uh, I wasn't sure about, you know - OOPS! Hold on, Jerry. Someone just came in." Margo Turner lost her composure when she looked across the desk at the imposing glare of Rafe Stalker. "Call you back in a while, Jerry."

Rafe checked out the flustered blonde who was scrambling to stand up and straighten her skirt and blouse, fix her straying hair, and greet him all in one movement. Not bad once he saw past the schoolmarm exterior. One of those librarian types in her mid-thirties. The type, he figured, who went wild when they took off those ugly glasses and let their hair down. Built pretty good, too. Chest was big enough. She had wide hips and probably carried a cushy ass around back. Rafe changed his tactics on the spot.

"Sorry to barge in on you, miss. Your receptionist said to go right in, so I did. I could come back later if you prefer. Oh, excuse me. My name is Rafael Stalker, but friends call me Rafe." He held out a big paw and gently smothered her clammy hand, never taking his eyes from hers.

Margo gulped in a deep breath.

"Nice to meet you, Rafe. Just call me Margo. Have a seat and tell me what the City of Fullerton can do for you."

"Oh, Margo, I think you'd call my proposal something I can do for the community, not the other way around. Could we step down the street to get a cup of coffee, maybe something to eat? I just got in from the Western Slope and didn't eat lunch. My treat, okay?" Rafe didn't wait for her answer as he reached for her coat on a corner rack and held it for her to step into.

Margo smiled and acquiesced.

•••

An emergency board meeting of CESA had been called for tomorrow night. Fred Tompkins had sounded depressed, angry, exasperated, and just plain worn out when he had called Jack asking him to attend and bring any parents willing to do volunteer work in a hurry.

"Hello, Gloria. This is Jack Marshall. How are you tonight?" When in need, soccer coaches always relied on their team mothers to work the phones.

Another frustrated voice responded to his cheerful greeting. "Hi, Jack. Things are so-so over here, I guess. Just trying to pay some late bills again." There was a slight pause. "Pardon me, Jack. It's not your job to listen to my personal problems. What can I do for you?"

Now it was Jack's turn to hesitate before speaking. He thought about giving her some encouragement but decided against it. Financial woes were something he could do nothing about. Too bad Gloria couldn't meet up with some well-off, handsome stud to solve her problems, but Jack knew that was the typical male chauvinist attitude, and Gloria would skin him alive if he started down that road. Anyway, Becca had told him Gloria's secret and he wasn't supposed to know about her situation.

"Gloria, I need some parents to attend a special soccer board meeting tomorrow at the Rec Center. CESA needs volunteer help right away, but I don't know what for. Would you call around and try to get some folks to attend the meeting? It's at seven PM."

"Sure, Jack. I'll get right on it. And thanks for helping Becca watch Gina on the weekends. I know she spends more time at your place than at Becca's. All she does is talk about what a great dad you are when she gets home." Gloria's voice trailed off into a sigh. "Talk to you later, Jack." She hung up.

That is one sad lady, Jack thought. He couldn't help feeling a stirring in his chest with the feedback about being a great dad. It seemed only natural to him to step in and be a dad to any kid within range. So many parents worked and left their children for others to parent, like during sports activities, or down at Martha's Rec Center. After school activities had become the unofficial daycare centers of suburbia.

Cottonwood Estates was a tough act to live up to. Just about every household had one parent in a professional career making upper middle-income wages. A short walk down Jack's cul-de-sac revealed wealth on display in all forms. There was a spiffy houseboat across the street. Next door, the Stones owned mountain property on which they were building an A-frame cabin for weekend retreats. Janet and Tubby Hanks, next to the Stones, had installed a pool last summer - heated, of course. Each driveway boasted late-model SUVs or other gas guzzlers.

All Jack had was a big backyard and lots of trees that fed onto his property from the greenbelt. He hadn't even built the typical stockade fence, since his neighbors had almost surrounded him with theirs. He had one car, no pool and no mountain property. If he wanted to keep up with his neighbors, he figured his income would have to double. He calculated that when his neighbors wanted to keep up with each other, usually both parents had to work.

His thinking led back to Gloria. No matter how hard she worked as a bookkeeper, even factoring in a second weekend job, she would have trouble maintaining a home here. He figured her best asset was the house she could no longer afford and would have to sell in order to rent an apartment. Single parenting was tough, especially for a woman without professional qualifications.

Jack felt very lucky tonight. He and Becca had spent the rest of their weekend dreaming, planning, and fantasizing. They would wait until she had the final papers from Jasper, who was waiting for a reply from Malcolm or his lawyer. Apparently it was simple. Jasper had wrapped the case into a nice little package and handed it to the judge, who had signed the orders readily. Malcolm now had less than a week to respond to the court or appear on a set date the following week. If he missed both chances, his goose was cooked.

Tuesday night's CESA board meeting turned out to be the flash point for the Cottonwood Estates neighborhood. Word had spread that Fullerton had taken steps to annex their greenbelt and even fringe parts of the neighborhood. Although this was not unusual in Colorado, the neighbors who gathered at the Rec Center were incensed. They had watched the City of Denver slime its way into the very middle of Monroe County, to their north, during one of its annexations. Denver's rationale had been to claim a slim, vestigial spur along one city block that somehow connected it with a special district in Monroe County containing very profitable shopping centers. If one used greatly exaggerated imagination, it was possible to see a physical connection, albeit a slight one.

Fullerton was apparently making a move for their greenbelt, if the rampant rumors were true. They were after several cul-de-sacs as well, including Jack's and Becca's.

Jack walked into the crowded room and was astonished at the community's reaction. His team was well-represented. Priscilla and Orson Huff were there with Gloria. Next to them were the Stones, and Betty and Michael Batchelor. Jack knew Becca would love to see this, but she had volunteered to watch the kids back at his place.

Fred Tompkins stood before the buzzing room and asked for quiet.

"Hello, neighbors. Am I glad to see you. Let's get right to the point." Fred walked over to the wall and pointed to a map of their neighborhood he had borrowed from Martha. She had come along as well and dragged Jasper with her. They sat to the side of the crowd holding hands.

Jack didn't have to ask them if they had enjoyed their night of baby-sitting.

"Folks," Fred continued, "I know the rumors have already reached some of you, so let me set the record straight. Fullerton has petitioned the Colorado Secretary of State to annex this strip of land you see along the river here." Fred skimmed his finger along the South Platte from the wetlands, scene of Jack's battle with the biker, up through the golf course CESA had been upgrading to use as soccer fields. It was a bold and audacious maneuver that continued right up to the southern city limits of Taylor City, their own county seat.

Orson Huff was livid and jumped up to speak.

"They can't do that! That land is in Madison County. Somebody paid somebody off, that's what I think. We have to fight this." Orson angrily looked around the room for support. His outburst generated a loud buzzing of conversation from the crowd. Jack noticed that everyone seemed upset at this sneaky political chicanery by Fullerton.

Fred interrupted. "I was hoping for this reaction, Orson. I've invited a special guest tonight, someone from the neighborhood who may be able to give us some pointers on fighting this. He's a little late, so we can at least pass around a sign-up sheet for people who are willing to start a petition drive against this." There was more buzzing as folks turned to speak with their neighbors and argue about the whole idea. Fred didn't need to go into the details about why such an annexation wasn't good. These people had given up weekends to work at the golf course. They appreciated the wetlands and knew the effects of development on such property. It would be a death blow to the greenbelt.

"Sorry I'm late, Fred." A voice boomed from the back of the room. Everyone turned to see Dave Mendes entering the meeting room carrying a bulging briefcase chock full of papers. "Had to stop by the Capitol building to pick up these forms and then get them copied." Dave walked to the front of the room and turned to greet his neighbors.

"Howdy, folks. It's nice to see you all here." Dave shot Jack a smile as he looked around the room for familiar faces. He wore his new office well as the DA for the county. Dave wore a dark gray suit with navy pin stripes, a white shirt, and a red silk tie. He cleaned up well, Jack thought.

In his short tenure as top prosecutor for Madison county, Dave had already begun to earn an excellent reputation for straight shooting. He was respected by the police as one of them, which he truly had been on numerous raids and stings done under cover. Back then Dave had gone farther than the average team leader for drug raids and special operations. He had taken many of the cases into court as a prosecutor and won. Now his operating policy was to be tough and fair.

Dave Mendes was an imposing physical figure at an even six feet and 225 pounds. He looked like a big V with broad shoulders and size 32 waist, the linebacker physique that had served him well at Colorado State University. Dave's Hispanic heritage gave him a soft bronze complexion that contrasted with his bright smile and flashing white teeth. He smiled at the group and won them over immediately as a friend and neighbor. All curiosity about his strength and physical abilities vanished when he spoke to his neighbors gathered in the room.

"Today I took the time to do some research on the annexation process and talked to the Secretary of State down in Denver. Seems there is nothing to stop a local government - city or county - from filing to annex property that is even vaguely near it. Best example we have around here is the insertion of the City of Denver five miles into the center of Monroe county near the big shopping malls." Dave acknowledged the grim nods of the crowd.

"The only way to stop Fullerton is to rally the community against them and force an election. And that will take lots of work by volunteers like you, starting a petition drive and educating your neighbors about this." Dave glanced around the room again and recognized Orson Huff, who had a question and was waving his hand frantically.

"Yes, Orson. You have a question?"

"Right, Dave. I haven't been here very long, but it seems to me that this part of Madison county is sort of like an orphan child to our county seat 20 miles north in Taylor City. What are we going to do when Fullerton starts telling our neighbors about how much greener the grass will be on their side of the fence?"

Jack was amazed. In all his dealings with Orson Huff this was the first sensible thought the man had uttered. He had a valid point too. South Madison county had been a stepchild and everyone knew it. He was interested in Dave's response to Orson.

"You hit the nail on the head, Orson. Very good point. Maybe there are some good arguments for annexation. We already get fire protection from Fullerton in a special district financing arrangement. So why not go whole hog and tie in with another local government altogether? Why fight the annexation? Don't forget, Madison county was formed out of the southern half of Monroe county not that long ago. Who's to say we couldn't split away and join with Fullerton across the river over in Hamilton county?"

The buzzing in the crowd picked up again, and neighbors who had come into the meeting ready to fight annexation became less sure of their positions. Then Gloria stood to speak, and the hush was immediate.

"I know Orson's question was designed to educate us on the complexities of the situation and get us to thinking about it. But, annexation is pure bullshit." Gloria spoke with deep emotion and fire in her eyes as she stared at the crowd, daring them to challenge her.

"Fullerton's track record is abysmal. If they follow their regular pattern, they will be out to strip the greenbelt and make money for developers. Pure and simple. They don't want to provide us with better services. They want our property taxes and our land. If you ask me, some developer has gotten cozy with officials across the river and probably paid them off to start this whole thing." Gloria sat down as if she had finished talking, but she got back up again before Dave could continue the meeting.

"And another thing. Maybe we should send a strong message to Taylor City that this time we will fight annexation because we know it stinks at its core. But. But, next time maybe we'll organize and go looking for a better partner than this county." Gloria was magnificent in her anger, and her neighbors were stunned by her rhetoric. Before tonight she had been a gorgeous blonde with a great body, ogled by any man who caught sight of her. Now everyone was surprised to learn there was much, much more under the surface. They applauded her loudly. Gloria turned crimson and wrapped her arms across her body.

Dave spoke to rescue her.

"Gloria that was fantastic. You should lead this rag-tag bunch to victory. You guys don't need me except to hand out copies of the petition forms." Dave beamed a smile at her and received a shy one in return.

Jack watched the exchange and slapped himself mentally. What a match! He had never played Cupid before, and until tonight the thought had never crossed his mind, especially with Dave. The man had practically sworn off women and driven himself to excel in his dual career as undercover agent and prosecuting attorney. Gloria worked two jobs to barely support herself and Gina in an overpriced neighborhood. They were both attractive, single, and smart. It was right there in front of his eyes, and Jack hadn't seen it. Still, before he had gotten together with Becca, he hadn't been much of a romantic either. Now he felt so good about his relationship that he wanted other people to experience the same good fortune. Besides, Dave was his best friend, what could be better!

For the rest of the meeting, Jack kept close watch over the two people he intended to bring together. Yes, he could see it. Gloria was surrounded by friends and neighbors talking excitedly about canvassing the neighborhood and protesting to Taylor City and their representatives in the legislature. Dave was surrounded by another group, just as animated. Jack noticed that occasionally their heads would come up and look across the room, checking on each other's progress. To Jack, it was like watching a slow-motion tennis match. His head turned from Dave to Gloria and back to Dave again. He couldn't wait to get home and scheme with Becca. This was better than any Secret Service caper he'd had in years.

•••

Of the fifty-some people who had crowded into the CESA meeting to organize against the annexation that night, a handful determined the results of the petition campaign. Jasper had a client, James Burrows, who was connected with Channel 10 News. James Burrows also lived in Cottonwood Estates. Within 24 hours, minicam crews from all the networks were camped outside Margo Turner's offices demanding interviews and generally causing a disruption.

Emily Charles, an enterprising reporter for the *Denver Post* and another concerned neighbor, took investigative reporting to a new level. She dug up records showing the Stalker Construction Company's plans for the greenbelt. These same plans had been squirreled away in the offices of the deceased Bartles Conninger. Similar documents magically appeared in Margo Turner's office as well. Ms. Charles pressed for interviews with Rafe Stalker and Margo Turner. She wanted some answers and started a daily series in the paper that drew statewide attention to the political morass of the annexation process. Shortly thereafter, Mr. Burrows' minicam crews began camping out at the Stalker Company too.

Through it all, Gloria was the star. She was on the phone constantly at work, and at home in the evenings. If she got a busy signal, she visited that home in person to get a signature. Emily Charles wrote about her. James Burrows interviewed her live on the evening news. Dave Mendes gladly stepped back from the limelight and let Gloria take the lead. Meanwhile, Jack kept watching for his opportunity to get them together.

•••

Jack sat in a plain brown van across the street from the gated subdivision where Margo Turner lived. He had been tailing her for the past week, hoping to connect her to Stalker. However, the woman was a stickler for routine and so far had not varied from her drive directly to or from the Fullerton County office building where she worked. She ate at her desk and went directly home after work each day. Contacts who trolled the hallways inside reported no significant meetings during the time period. She led a boring life, judging by appearances.

This morning was different. Jack watched Margo Turner exit the gated drive and turn left instead of right. He followed easily and smiled to himself when she made a beeline for the Stalker offices.

Turner stopped by the Stalker company headquarters and went inside. Jack contacted the FBI agent who was watching the Stalker offices to let her know what was up.

"Alice, go inside and make up an excuse to see Stalker personally. See if Turner went to see him."

"Roger that, Jack." The lady FBI agent left her compact parked up the street and headed for the building entrance.

Jack waited another ten minutes until Turner appeared, leaving the building. Alice followed discreetly behind and gave Jack a thumbs-up sign as she went by his van. Jack started the van and followed Turner, who drove straight to her bank. This was going to be easy, he thought. It was Friday morning, apparently payday.

He parked and went inside a few minutes after she did. Jack noted the teller she had chosen and went to the lobby receptionist.

"Morning ma'am," he flashed the young woman a smile and showed her his badge. "I need to see the branch manager right away."

"Of course, sir." She turned shaky right away and got up to lead Jack to her boss.

"Mr. Crandall, this gentleman asked to see you." The balding manager looked up from his spreadsheets at the interruption then settled down when Jack showed him his credentials.

"I'm Jack Marshall, Mr. Crandall, from Secret Service. I've been tracking a person who we think is mixed up in some unsavory business and need your cooperation."

THIRTY TWO

Most of Colorado's population consists of fairly conservative farmers, ranchers, and suburbanites. Denver contains the largest population of minorities, mostly Hispanic with a small percentage of African-Americans. Still, the big city seems staunchly conservative when compared to Boulder. Home to the University of Colorado, Boulder's free-style atmosphere makes it seem more like a refugee from the "left coast," than a bastion of higher education in the old west. It is helter-skelter, liberal, socially active for the latest causes, environmentally conscious to a fault, and full of students and bicycles.

Jack cringed when he saw the Boulder Blasters on his Golden Girls soccer schedule for the coming Saturday. It was an away game, and he hoped to get in and get out before any of his kids became enamored of the place and wanted to go there after high school. Boulder was too wild for his blood, yet he was confident his team would do okay up there against the backdrop of the Flatiron Mountain range.

All week long he had checked the weather for approaching Pacific coast storm fronts moving in. Wind storms were a big problem in Boulder. The city was located in a trough between the mountains and plains. Storms slipped over the front range of the Rockies and blew down through this trough with wind speeds often approaching hurricane strength. Only last fall, Jack had watched his football team struggle to play in a Boulder gale. On one occasion his punter had kicked the ball only to see it rise straight up then sail back over his head into the end zone. You had to see it to believe it.

A thousand-foot-high antenna had been erected by the National Oceanic and Atmospheric Administration, whose offices were located in Boulder. Local folks had laughed at the monstrous erector set plopped down just east of the city. Its main purpose was to allow scientists to peek over the mountains for an early warning of bad weather. Yet, everyone along the Front Range knew that if a weather forecaster said it would snow an inch on Wednesday, you could count on a blizzard at least 24 hours earlier. And weather arrived like a freight train roaring down the mountains, loud and powerful enough to flatten new construction in the framing stage.

Up-slope conditions brought on the trickiest kind of storms though. Moist warm air would blow directly from the eastern plains up against the foothills along the Front Range and collide with cold air traveling down from Canada. Without warning, the wind could reverse itself and a storm front would blast from just above the high peaks of the Flatirons west of Boulder and rush out onto the plains. Jack hoped for a calm day with sunny skies.

The Golden Girls routinely started each game with Missy gently rolling the ball back to Katie, who would strike it hard across the field to Sharon. This was their standard play and they had scored in every game with it. But the Blasters had the wind to their backs on a field that stretched east-west. Jack knew weather would be a factor when Missy's soft pass back to Katie was hit by a sudden gust of wind. The ball picked up speed, and before anyone could react, it streaked into their own goal! His players were surprised to see the opposition score on them, especially when the Blasters hadn't even touched the ball yet. This was not a good sign and seemed to forecast the remainder of the first half. Each time the Golden Girls got the ball rolling the right way, a Blaster defender had only to stick her foot out to send it sailing downwind at lightning speed.

Sharon had bullied the ball upwind for their only goal to leave the Golden Girls behind at the half 3-1. At the break for oranges, Jack gave his first pep talk of the day. He was alone today, because Becca and Gloria were busy canvassing the neighborhood for the petition drive against annexation.

"Okay, girls, listen up. This wind is terrible, but you're still playing great. And we'll have the advantage in the second half when we switch ends of the field. Then those Blasters will have to work extra hard to stop our shots. Now eat those oranges and get ready to win this game!" He was greeted by a chorus of cheers and optimism. Now if the weather would only hold true to its first half form.

Jack looked up at the roiling clouds and shook his head. The day had started off bright, clear, and sunny. Over the peaks of the Flatirons, numerous angry clouds were forming like black cotton balls writhing in mid-air. The air had turned chilly, and the wind died down suddenly. That's okay, he thought. We're a better team and can beat them when the weather isn't choosing sides.

Jack's luck lasted barely five minutes into the second half. His Missy-to-Katie-to-Sharon combo took the opening drive right through the Blasters. The score was 3-2 and the Golden Girls were pumped up with enthusiasm.

Then the winds changed abruptly into the familiar up-slope condition. Ferocious blasts of cold air blew from west to east, right in the faces of the Golden Girls.

Jack was proud of his girls. Even facing certain defeat, they played harder than they had all year. Gina made several key saves in her defensive fullback position. Katie headed the ball into the Blaster net when the wind miraculously stalled on one of Missy's corner kicks. The odds were stacked too high against them, though. The Golden Girls lost 6-3.

They came off the field broken-hearted, heads down, lips trembling. Jack would have none of this. He looked over his shoulder at the parents and started clapping.

"Come on, folks. Let's hear it for these girls. They played a great game." The parents suddenly seemed to realize it had been just a game, and started cheering and clapping for their children, who were, after all, just six years old.

Jack watched faces brighten and tears vanish. He reached for Katie and gave her a big hug. Then he grabbed Missy under his free arm and held her close too. "Okay, girls, let's go congratulate the winners." He turned them around and marched them across the center of the field to shake hands with the Blasters. Jack shook hands with the opposing coach and they watched the traditional slapping of high-fives as the two teams shared sportsmanship.

"See you this fall when there's no wind around, coach." Jack chided the lady coach with a big grin.

"It should be a good rematch," she replied. "See you then."

The team gathered around him and Jack realized they needed to hear him say something to make it all better. It was as if they had a team booboo and wanted him to kiss it and make it well. He got down on one knee and brought them in close.

"I'm really proud of you today. You played your best game ever. The Blasters are a good team. The wind helped some, but let's don't blame the weather. You played hard and never gave up. We couldn't ask for more from any of you. Now go get your can of pop!" He stood and watched them romp over to the cooler he had brought. Today he was subbing for Gloria as the team mother.

Jack turned to collect his equipment and found Orson Huff waiting for him. Oh boy, I don't need this today, he thought as he approached the father of his best player.

"Some game, eh, Orson?"

"Those girls are lucky to have you for their coach, Jack. I needed to tell you that to your face since I got on your case early on. Sharon talks non-stop about you, and Priscilla has really come out of her shell since she started reffing. Who would have thought this could happen to my family? Thank you, Jack." Orson shook hands vigorously and walked away to congratulate Sharon and take her home.

Jack watched Orson trot over to his daughter and give her a big hug. He stood in the center of the field long after most of the players and parents had gotten in their cars for the trip back home. He felt ten feet tall. They had lost a game, but it had been no setback. It was more like taking one step back to leap forward a hundred. His first thought was to share this with Becca. Lately, it seemed that was the way he felt about everything.

THIRTY
THREE

Waiting for her cue to dance, Gloria wondered how much longer she could keep this up. She was working her regular job - plus sneaking in personal calls to neighbors. She was canvassing the neighborhood at night, and still dancing at Mojoes Friday and Saturday nights under the lecherous supervision of Morry Joseph. Bills were piling up. Everything she earned went right back out to pay them.

Her dancing was a two-sided coin with plus and minus sides. Yes, she earned lots of money for the time she worked. Yes, it was a great outlet for her frustrations, balancing her complex life. But, there was a big drawback staring her right between the eyes. The crowds were getting unruly now. Many men came to see her every Saturday night and they wanted to really see her. Topless. Morry was losing patience with her modesty.

At first he had agreed to let her keep on the mask and her gauzy top. Now he was squirming out of the deal. Gloria knew she couldn't remove the mask. Her face had been on TV news shows for the past week. She was quite well-known as the blonde bombshell with brains who was fighting the Fullerton annexation bid. She also couldn't remove the top of her costume either. Her insides told her she couldn't do it. But Morry couldn't care less about her scruples. He wanted his customers to keep coming back and pouring money into his pockets.

"Let 'em get a gander at them hooters, babe. They'll go wild over you."

Her music started, and Gloria walked unsteadily to the side of the stage, still unsure of what to do. For the last several weeks she had danced to Ravel's Bolero, and the place had gone bonkers with her conclusion. She had spun in a tight circle, collapsed in a full split, thrusting her breasts forward. Then she arched her luscious body, touching her head to the floor behind her. Security guards had to tackle guys who had scrambled over the stage to cop a feel. Several bruises were still healing where some drunk had grabbed her.

Gloria was going to calm things down tonight with a movement from Vivaldi's Four Seasons. Her cue came up, and she glided onto the stage. But this time music designed to soothe and calm the drinking patrons had the opposite effect. Cat-calls and whistles punctuated her performance from the first notes.

"Hey baby, show us something tonight."

"Come on, baby. Take it off."

Gloria tried to block out the sounds of the raucous crowd, but they started to get wild towards the end of her dance. She twirled too near the edge of the stage and a drunk redneck grabbed her ankle, pulling her down and triggering a minor riot. Gloria hit the floor hard, and drunks flew out of their seats to see what she had hidden under that scanty costume. Security guards managed to jump into the fray and push back some of the earlier arrivals, but an eager fellow managed to squirt by them and rip off part of Gloria's top.

She fought back, kicking and striking at anything that moved, aiming at the closest groin. Morry ran to the stage to take a gander but froze at the sight. Then he ran outside to get the additional cops he had hired to patrol the parking lot.

•••

All work and no social life had some professional rewards. Dave Mendes put in long hours and got results. Days blurred into weeks, and he lost track of time. He didn't believe in weekends or days off. Every day was a Monday, and Dave hustled to catch up. His assistants and the top managers in the county sheriff's office knew to call him at any hour to help set up a case or handle a touchy situation. Like last night when he had been up thirty-six hours straight working a bust out in Tiny Town. The taxpayers were getting more than their money's worth.

Tonight Dave had watched a video at home and gone to bed around midnight. Deep in sleep, he didn't grab for the phone next to his ear until the seventh ring.

"Mendes," he barked. "This better be good." He growled into the receiver.

"Sir, this is Desk Sergeant Murray, Englewood police. Your staff said I could reach you at this number and it was okay to call at this hour."

Englewood? That was out of the county. Who did he know in Englewood?

"What's going on, Sergeant?" Dave tried to lose some of his initial gruffness. The poor guy was just a cop doing his job.

"It's hard to explain, sir. We had to arrest a bunch of people over at Mojoes on Santa Fe an hour ago. One of the strippers got the crowd agitated, and a riot broke out. She's this real hunk of a dame, if you get my drift, sir, and she wouldn't take it off, so the guys charged the stage."

Dave lost his cool. "Does this have anything to do with me, Sergeant Murray? You got ten seconds to tell me why I shouldn't hang up on you and go back to sleep." He sat up in bed and wondered why he had taken this job.

"Give me a chance, sir. It's kind of complicated. We had to arrest this stripper cause she assaulted one of our men when he made a grab, er, tried to restrain her, sir. He'll be okay, though. Probably walk a little stiff-legged for a day or so, but nothing permanent."

"Murray, get on with it!" Dave yelled into the mouthpiece.

"So, this dame refuses to identify herself and for her one phone call she asks for you. Says you and she are real pals, sir."

"Huh?" Dave was speechless. For sure, he had woken up in the twilight zone of DA hell. Then he realized the sergeant was talking again.

"...she's cold, sir. Says she needs some clothes, and could you stop by a friend's house and get her something to put on."

"Hold it!" Dave exploded. "Where is she? Let me speak to her, sergeant. Now!"

"I'll get her for you, sir. Be right back."

Dave sat in the middle of his bed fuming. His mind methodically cataloged the relationships he had - friends, foes, people he had arrested. He tried to remember the last woman he had gone out with, but that had been years ago, and he thought she had gotten married. Why wouldn't her husband take her some clothes anyway? Strippers? He didn't know any. He had heard about Mojoes, though. Word on the street was the owner looked the other way when the women did a little hooking on the side, sometimes right inside the place. His getting involved with a stripper who might be a hooker would really appeal to the public.

A soft voice whispered on the phone, and Dave strained to make it out.

"Dave, are you there? Hello? Dave? Please come get me, I'm desperate. Dave? Hello? I'm cold, too. Please, can you bring me some clothes?"

"Please talk louder," Dave shouted in frustration and growing anger. "Who in hell are you anyway?"

A clear response came over the line. "Wait a second, Dave. I need to ask the sergeant to leave the room."

Dave blew out a breath in exasperation. He stood and began pacing the room, waiting for someone, anyone to give him a straight answer.

"It's okay, now." Her sultry voice spoke clearly. "Dave, you there?"

"Ready when you are, sweetheart," he replied sarcastically.

"I'm really sorry this happened, Dave. This is Gloria Ashworth, Jack's team mother, the woman running the neighborhood effort against annexation. I've been busted, big-time."

Dave sat down, stunned.

"Gloria, of course I know you. But, what are you doing in a strip joint and getting yourself arrested?"

"Please, Dave, can you help me out of this? Then I'll explain everything. I'm afraid the longer I stay here the better my chances are of being discovered, and the whole campaign could go down the tubes."

"Of course I'll help you," he replied, his attitude completely different now. "But what about clothes? What happened to yours, if that's not too personal a question to ask?"

"Just bring me an old raincoat and a big floppy hat, something to help hide my face. Oh, and make up a name for me. I can't tell them who I am, and I won't take off my mask either. They don't like that so much. Okay, Dave?"

"Don't worry, Gloria. I'll think of something to get you released to my personal recognizance." He searched his brain for a solution. A light bulb went on. "Gloria, I'll tell them you're a protected witness on a drug bust. How's that? I'll be right over. Now, let me speak to the desk sergeant again."

"Okay, and thanks a bunch, Dave. You really are a nice man." There was another pause and the sergeant came back on the line.

"You wanted to speak to me, sir?"

"Yes, Sergeant Murray. As it turns out, the young lady you have arrested is in the witness protection program. I can't tell you her name, but I'll be right over to have her released to me personally." As soon as he said this, Dave heard a muffled chuckle from officer Murray. There was a palpable *wink* of macho understanding coming from the cop over the phone. Murray might as well have said, "Sure, DA Mendes, if you say so. The boys at the station house will get a real charge out of this."

Dave dressed and grabbed a bulky overcoat and old cowboy hat he had worn once on a stakeout. Then he drove the few miles over to Englewood's main police station. As he pulled up in front to park, he spotted trouble. There was a TV minicam crew on the scene already, anxious to record this big news event. Must have been some riot at Mojoes, he thought. Instead of parking in the visitor's lot out front, he drove around back to the entrance used to bring in prisoners.

Several policemen recognized him and greeted him as he entered the building. Was that a smirk he saw on their faces? Word spread quickly, probably. Going farther down the hall, he heard a loud commotion from the front desk. The clamor of angry people getting hauled in drunk and disorderly clanged into his consciousness. This wasn't going to be easy.

But, his luck changed. Ambling down the hall towards him was a sergeant with a familiar face. Yes, he knew the guy from a caper they had run last year!

"Sergeant Janson, how you doing? Good to see you again." Dave greeted the man like a lost brother.

"Well, well, well, if it isn't our famous Madison County DA come to free his personal protected witness. Hiya, Dave." Janson shook Dave's hand and smirked all the way to his receding hairline. "The guys can't wait to hear all about this one. Boy, she's some looker, Dave. Where did you pick her up? Uh, I mean, how long has she been under government protection?"

"Okay, Sergeant Janson, I guess nobody's buying the story. The lady is a friend of mine, but that's all I'll say for now. If you help me get her out of here, I'll let you in on it when I can. Right now, pal, I need a big favor."

"Sure, Dave, what do you want me to do?"

Their exit had been successful. Dave drove slowly down Santa Fe Boulevard. Gloria slumped against the passenger door, crying softly. He figured he would find out eventually what was going on, but for now he just let her cry out her fear and the shame of being arrested. At least she had taken off the mask when they were a few blocks from the police station and out of sight of the minicams.

Gloria cried all the way to her house. Dave pulled up in front and helped her out. At the front door, she stopped and turned to face him.

"I'm so ashamed of myself, Dave. Please come in and I'll put on some coffee and tell you everything."

Dave nodded and followed her inside. He pulled up short when he saw the empty living room. He followed Gloria back to the kitchen, which held a table and two chairs, but little else.

Gloria started the coffee and excused herself to go put on regular clothes. She returned in a few minutes wearing a blouse and a pair of beat-up sweat pants. They faced each other across the table.

"First off, Dave, thank you for saving me. Second, I'm no hooker, and actually, I really am a dancer, but I'm not much of a stripper. That's kind of why I got into trouble tonight."

Gloria started at the beginning and told him about her days as a ballet pupil and professional dancer. That was before she became a single mother whose husband had run away. He sent no support money and Gloria was trying to make ends meet by holding down two jobs, one she had kept secret until tonight.

Sometime during her recounting of events, Dave had reached across the table to hold her hands. Gloria struggled to keep back tears of shame and gratitude.

"So you danced, but refused to strip, and always wore a mask to hide your identity?" She nodded. "Why didn't you ask for help?" Have the courts track

down your husband so you could get support? Divorce him? I don't understand."

"I was ashamed, Dave. Devastated. I didn't want to embarrass Gina. I love
this neighborhood and wanted to stay here. Looking back, there were all
kinds of reasons I guess, none really smart. The whole neighborhood is well-
off and out of my league, yet I kept hoping I could work things out." Gloria
brought her hands up to hide her face as tears came again.

Dave pulled his chair around to her side of the table, and gathered her
into an embrace, trying to absorb her grief. Gloria's head sought the comfortable nook between his head and shoulder, and she let out her misery.
Eventually her arms went around his neck. They sat, linked head to head.

She stopped crying, sniffed once, and looked sheepishly up at his sympathetic smile. Gloria grinned back at him with a face of innocence and adoration. At that point, everything changed for Dave. He felt an electric
attraction that overwhelmed his senses. Yes, he admired her courage, and her
ability to balance the many facets of her complex life as a single mother. He
respected her tenacity and take charge attitude in the petition drive. All those
feelings had been there before this moment, though. He looked at her beautiful face and wondrous brown eyes and realized he had deeper feelings for
Gloria, emotions that went far beyond admiration and respect.

She was vulnerable and so was he. Yet, he realized he wanted her. Tonight.
He also wanted to protect her, to care for her in every way possible.

Gloria sensed a change in his touch, his look. She sat still as his eyes
explored her face and settled on her mouth. She nodded, understanding, and
returned his gaze expectantly. They drew closer. Dave kissed her softly, as if
she were a fragile doll. He lingered there, placing eager kisses all over her
mouth. Then he drew back, smiled and gathered her close in a loving
embrace.

"I want you, Gloria." He felt her shiver and held her tighter, relaying a
feeling of trust and security.

Gloria shifted in his embrace. She took his face in her hands and kissed
him passionately.

"Oh, Dave. I want you too."

Dave returned her passion equally, deepening their kiss into a well for two
thirsty lovers.

They sank to the floor, trembling, hands frantically searching, caressing,
tearing away clothes. Their overheated bodies ignored the unyielding floor,
numbed to anything but pleasure. Gloria opened to him, then guided,
accepted freely.

Dave moved cautiously at first but quickly gave in to an uncontrollable
urge to claim her. Gloria's body seemed to melt under him, encircle him

everywhere, push him to completion. Together they cried out, spent, gasping for air.

Dave rolled onto his back pulling Gloria on top. Both were breathing hard, unable talk. Dave found his voice first and started to speak.

"You're incredible, I -"

"Sshhh, don't say anything. Hold me." She sealed his mouth with her kiss then collapsed, atop him.

Dave had to speak.

"How did we end up down here? One minute I was being a good listener, the next we're lying here lusciously naked, and I feel incredible." He stopped. "Gloria, look at me. I didn't rescue you tonight to get you into bed. This is more than a quick roll in the hay for me."

Gloria rolled to the side and pulled him up, into her arms.

"I didn't call you to come rescue me so I could get you into my bed either, Dave. But that's exactly where we're going." She stepped back to look at him , all tenderness. Dave admired her body, his eyes glazed at the sight of her. He freely took in what had caused the Mojoes customers to riot, what he had not seen in their passionate coupling minutes before. Her body, flushed with the sheen of sex, was perfectly proportioned and breathtaking.

They reached for each other, touching sensitive places they had possessed freely only minutes ago, but never seen. He held her breasts tenderly. She caressed him lightly, then turned and led him down the hall to her bed.

It was a night of discovery. Dave talked about his wife and his loneliness since her death, years ago. Gloria shared her embarrassment and disappointment at being left by a husband who just didn't want to be married any more. They searched each other's bodies for pleasure, overjoyed in their lovemaking, holding back nothing.

Towards dawn, Dave held Gloria gently, nestled against her back. They were like two spoons facing the breaking sunrise out her bedroom window.

"I don't want to leave, Gloria."

"Then stay."

"Do you care what the neighbors will think?"

"No. Do you?"

"No."

"Don't go, Dave, ever. I'm certain about this."

"I won't. I'm certain too."

"Did Jack invite you over for dinner tonight?"

"Yes, did Becca invite you?"

"Yes. Let's surprise them."

THIRTY FOUR

Judge Langfelt's courtroom was deathly quiet. Jasper Mackey sat at one table with Becca. He shuffled papers, trying to look calm. No matter how many divorce proceedings he went through, he always got nervous. One never knew what a hot-headed, soon-to-be ex-spouse with a background of physical abuse would do, even in an open courtroom. For certain, Malcolm Schmidt had a short fuse and violent temper to go with it.

Jack sat behind the railing that separated the lawyers, litigants, and judge from the rest of the courtroom. He was directly behind Becca, watching everyone entering and leaving in the small, brightly lit room. He was wary of anyone suspicious who took a seat. The court would be in session in another ten minutes, and Becca would have to face her husband one last time.

Jack craned his head around to check out two men who had just come into the courtroom. They stood at the back and searched the room as he had been doing. Cops. There was no doubt in his mind the second he saw them. But not local. Maybe they were the guys Dave had told him about last Sunday. Boise police were working with the Colorado Bureau of Investigation to track down and extradite Malcolm for beating up his second wife. These fellows would provide an interesting conversation, he thought, as he left his seat to introduce himself.

Jack walked up to the two men, both young, tall, and lean. Unsmiling. All business. He showed them his Secret Service ID and shook hands.

"I'm Jack Marshall, Mrs. Schmidt's neighbor. You guys from Idaho?"

The cops from Boise smiled in recognition of a fellow law enforcement professional and greeted Jack leisurely.

The taller man spoke. "I'm Bobby Harrison and this is Larry Showalter. We thought there might be a chance this guy would show up here today. His other wife, Audrey, showed us the court papers. We don't know where Schmidt is, but he knows about today's hearing."

"You got papers to extradite him to Boise?" Jack wondered how much cooperation the states were showing each other. He thought Colorado might want a shot at Malcolm first.

"We coordinated everything through CBI, Jack. We had clear sailing once we showed the guys in Denver pictures of Audrey Schmidt. She was a very pretty young woman, before Schmidt tied her up and beat her. I was the first person on the scene. I thought she was dead."

"Tell me about her, Bobby. What's she like?"

Bobby and Larry glanced up to the front table at Becca. Jack saw their eyes go wide with surprise and then admiration at the pretty brunette sitting there.

"It's amazing, Jack. Is that the first Mrs. Schmidt, up there with her lawyer?" Jack nodded. "She could pass for an identical twin to Audrey Schmidt in Boise. Slender, beautiful, fair skin, black hair. Unfortunately, Audrey had no one to protect her from Malcolm Schmidt. She'll never look the same. She's also younger, about 22, and still naïve enough to believe Schmidt's lies about what a great life he would give her."

Jack saw more than professional detachment in officer Harrison's demeanor as he spoke of Audrey Schmidt. There was an underlying tremor to the man's voice that raised the hackles on Jack's neck. Harrison had set his jaw with clenched teeth. A ripple of muscle scooted across the man's cheek as he spoke about Malcolm. Jack was convinced that Malcolm would not escape this man.

"All rise. The Seventy-ninth District Court of Colorado is now in session, the honorable Judge Patricia Langfelt presiding." The Bailiff sang out the ancient chorus, and Jack left the Boise police for his seat close to Becca. There was still no sign of Malcolm.

Judge Langfelt entered her courtroom austerely. She commanded respect, immediately serving notice that she was the boss. Her face was sternly set, her features as bland as the black judicial robe she wore.

"Is the plaintiff, ready, counselor?" Judge Langfelt looked at Jasper Mackey without smiling. They were good friends outside her courtroom, but this was her domain. Judge Langfelt had her own set of rules, some 20 single-spaced typewritten pages worth, and every lawyer who came before her had better abide by them. There was no resemblance to the Perry Mason style bantering in this judge's court. No strutting about, posturing, and making speeches for the evening news or a future political campaign.

"Yes we are, your honor." Jasper stood to address her and sat back down, complying perfectly with another rule.

The judge leveled her glare at the defense table across the aisle from Jasper and Becca. It was empty.

"Bailiff, where is the other party to this case?" she snapped. The small group of participants in her court stifled grins and chuckles as the bailiff cringed visibly.

"Uh, your honor, as you can see, no one is there. We have no motions from the defense counsel asking for a delay, either."

"There wouldn't be a delay in any circumstance, bailiff," she snapped again. The judge paused and considered the situation for a minute. Then she began riffling through the case folder in front of her, reviewing the charges and settlement figures Jasper had prepared.

Jasper and Becca watched intently. He had told her before the proceeding started that the judge might continue the case until there was a response from Malcolm. Or, she might decide it today.

They had their answer quickly.

"Before I make my ruling, does the plaintiff's counsel have anything to add to this matter?" Now Judge Langfelt's countenance was softer, her tone friendlier, and she gave the slightest hint of a smile at Becca.

Jasper stood up.

"Yes, your honor, I do. If I may proceed to the podium, please?" This was another rule. Anything past a simple yes or no required permission to approach the center podium to speak, and the message had better be short and to the point.

"Your honor, I would like to call Officer Bobby Harrison to the stand. Officer Harrison is from the Boise, Idaho, police department and has important information about Malcolm Schmidt, that I believe may impact your ruling."

"Proceed," replied the interested jurist.

As it turned out, the impact was remarkable. Officer Harrison recalled the scene in Malcolm's bedroom when he and Jim Murphy first discovered Audrey. He offered a manila folder of telling crime scene photographs documenting the brutal beating Audrey had suffered. Harrison started to continue his testimony, but stopped when Judge Langfelt raised her hand for silence. She shuffled the photos quickly, then looked directly at Becca, communicating an understanding compassion that stirred the courtroom.

"Proceed, Officer Harrison." Her voice noticeably affected.

Harrison also reported the charges against Malcolm and presented the extradition papers authorizing release of the defendant to his custody for transport back to Boise. Included in the packet of papers were documents authenticating the duplicitous second marriage of Malcolm Schmidt to Audrey.

Jack was impressed as he watched the lady judge shuffle through the photos and papers handed her by the policeman from Boise. He had never seen someone's ass nailed to the wall quite as effectively as Jasper had done to Malcolm.

Suddenly, Judge Langfelt lost her stern composure.

"There will be a five minute recess." She turned away from the courtroom and quickly hurried to her chambers.

Everyone stood as the judge rushed out. Jack leaned over the railing and caught Jasper's attention.

"What happened, Jasper? I thought she was about to give us her decision."

"Don't worry, Jack. I've known her a long time and try to bring all my cases to her court. But, this is the first time I have seen her lose it in open court. Once or twice in chambers she has let off steam or gotten watery-eyed, but nothing like this. The photos did it." Jasper turned to Becca who had gotten emotional herself, and dabbed at the corner of one eye with a tissue.

"I know this is hard, Becca, but it will end soon. I'm thankful you had a friendly neighbor to protect you." He winked at Jack. "Here she comes. This ought to be good."

Judge Langfelt took a moment to sign a few papers immediately after she sat down. This was yet another departure from her routine. Any papers signed by a judge became court orders. The judge usually announced her ruling, then took the papers to her chambers and signed them within a day or two. Not today, though. Jasper turned to smile at Jack and patted Becca on the shoulder.

The judge cleared her throat and spoke.

"The marriage between Rebecca and Malcolm Schmidt is dissolved immediately. The settlement agreement prepared by the plaintiff is so ordered, in addition to the requests to garnish wages from the defendant's employer for the support of the children, Andy and Missy Schmidt. The defendant is found to be in contempt of this court and is hereby fined $5000 and ordered to serve 90 days in jail, the maximum penalties I can impose. Further, sole custody of the children is awarded to Rebecca Schmidt. Mr. Schmidt is ordered to seek visitation rights through this court. Otherwise, the restraining order against him remains in effect permanently."

The judge ordered another 15 minute recess before the next case and everyone stood as she left the room. The bailiff gathered the signed court orders and handed them to Jasper.

"Mr. Mackey, the judge said you knew what to do with these. She would like to see you and Mrs. Schmidt, plus Mr. Marshall, in her chambers now."

Jack overheard this and was surprised. He didn't realize the judge knew about him and shot a glance at Jasper who grinned in return. He went to Becca first and gave her a hug. She turned her face into his shoulder and let out the tears that had been building all morning. Jack held her for several minutes until he sensed her relief take hold.

"It's okay, darling. You won. He's out of your life for good." Becca looked up at him and smiled with a mixture of sadness and love. Jack knew it would take time for Malcolm to leave her thoughts as well as her life. He also knew she was recovering quickly as their relationship strengthened.

"Come on, folks," Jasper said. "Let's go meet the judge."

Jasper led them through a side door and down a narrow corridor to the inner offices that constituted the judge's chambers. He knocked gently, and a strong voice welcomed them in.

Jack and Becca were greeted by a diminutive lady in a flowing, cotton dress that covered her from ankle to collar bone. It was bright green and splashed liberally with blue and gold flowers. She was all of five feet tall and probably weighed a hundred pounds counting her granny boots. Her hair - an equal mixture of salt and pepper gray with a few strands of red - was tied in a loose pony tail and hung down to the small of her back. Her face was soft and kind now that the case had been resolved, yet she had on no makeup to liven her appearance. Probably did that on purpose, thought Jack. She was an attractive woman when greeted face to face, but Jack could not remember noticing any of these features in the courtroom. Even her size and the lengthy pony tail had been disguised by the high bench and her robe. The hair must have been stowed under a wig of some sort, everything done to neuter her appearance and exude strength. Here, she looked like an escaped hippy from the sixties.

Jasper handled the formal introductions, even though they had just left the courtroom where the judge appeared to know everyone.

"A pleasure to meet you, Becca," Judge Langfelt said. "I'm sure this is a relief to you."

Becca beamed.

"It certainly is, your honor. I never thought it would be so easy or happen so fast. Thank you."

"Call me Patty, now we're outside my bright little chamber of horrors, dear. And, don't thank me. I just did my job out there. Frankly, this is unusual for me. I rarely invite litigants back to talk right after I decide their case. Right, Jasper?" He nodded and she continued. "But, I had to meet this hunk of a guy who sat behind you like a mother bear protecting her cub."

Judge Langfelt turned her 100-watt smile on Jack, and he went red down to his toes.

"Mr. Marshall, it is a delight to meet you at last. Jasper spoke of you the last time I went to dinner at Martha Riddle's house. The same night I married them."

It was Jack and Becca's turn to be shocked as they looked at Jasper, now redder than Jack and sputtering.

"What about that secret you promised me, Patty? Where's that judge/lawyer/client confidentiality stuff we discussed over that same dinner? Huh?"

Judge Langfelt bore into Jasper with her stern courtroom demeanor and silenced him immediately. Then she broke into a huge grin and punched him on the arm. Her laughter broke the tension in the room as Jack and Becca congratulated Jasper. They continued to talk about happy things, ignoring the sordid revelations of the testimony by Officer Harrison that had upset everyone.

"So, Jack." Patty Langfelt fixed him with a sardonic smile. "You'll let me know when you two are ready to tie the knot, eh?" Becca sidled over to Jack and held his arm. His mouth moved like a fish out of water, no sound emerging.

"I only have one rule, Jack. I do marriages. Detest weddings. They're a waste of time and money. Also, I expect to be fed royally in place of a fee. Oh yes, and call my secretary for some written guidelines on the words you want said, vows and all that stuff. Or, make up your own, just don't try to slip in any malarkey about wives being subservient to their husbands. Got that?"

Jack looked from Patty to Jasper to Becca. He was outnumbered and out-maneuvered. It had to be a setup. He figured to fight fire with fire and faced the judge again.

"Sounds great to me, your honor. What I want to know, though, since you obviously put a lot of thought and planning into this, is what kind of instructions you have for the honeymoon?" He turned on the charm and got satisfaction as the neutral face of the lady judge turned pink.

"Touché, Jack. I leave that entirely up to you." She laughed along with them, then excused herself to dress for her next case.

•••

Bear. That's what Thomas Corbett looked like, and that's what folks back in the mountains called him. Bear was hairy all over, from the top of his head to the ends of his nine fingers, having lost one to a grizzly, some said. No one knew how the grizzly came out of it, but Bear was alive all right. He stood six and a half feet high, not counting another four or five inches of frizzled, mangled wildness atop his head.

Regulars in the Tank Top bar in downtown Taylor City saw him each spring when the weather softened and he came to town to have a little fun. He was almost four hundred pounds of fun, not counting the size 20 boots that tracked mud all over Ed Burton's linoleum floor this chilly, rainy evening. The locals knew to give Bear at least a bar stool on either side for clearance to get up in case he needed to go out back and take a leak. The women offering a good time managed to skitter out and find it somewhere else whenever Bear showed up.

Ed, the owner and bartender, returned Bear's grunt of greeting with a nod and placed a bottle of Jim Beam and a glass of water in front of him. Bear tossed a fifty on the bar and cracked open the bottle. Patrons eased back into their routines, each keeping a wary eye on the giant hunched over his bottle.

Malcolm sat at the end of the bar, unrecognizable in a scraggly Van Dyke dyed an orangey red to match his hair. He had avoided the Idaho police for weeks and knew he was in deep trouble for what he had done to Audrey. Still, his anger fueled an arrogance that demanded revenge. He was searching for the right man to take out Jack Marshall. He took one look at the giant who had just rumbled in and thought he might finally be in luck tonight. The man was certainly big enough. He looked twice as heavy as that bastard, Marshall, able to handle anyone up to the right tackle for the Denver Broncos.

Malcolm strolled confidently down the bar and sat next to Bear. He took in the raw, wild scent of the outdoors and guessed Bear lacked indoor plumbing. Malcolm waited for the hairy man to lower the half-empty bottle before he spoke.

"Hello there, the name's Malcolm Schmidt, nice to meet you." Malcolm offered his hand to the man and didn't even receive a grunt in return. Ed Burton inched towards the other end of the bar and pretended to dry glasses that hadn't been washed. Regulars at the bar cautiously slid off their stools and stole away into darker corners.

Bear turned his mammoth head in Malcolm's direction and exhaled a long, gut-rumbling belch that hit Malcolm full in the face. Slowly the big head turned back to the bottle and raised it for another slug of whiskey.

Undeterred, Malcolm decided to raise the stakes. "Well, friend, how about I buy that bottle for you and interest you in a little proposition?" Before Bear could respond to this intrusion, Malcolm had turned to Ed and motioned him over, waving a hundred dollar bill for everyone in the smoky bar to notice.

"I'd like to buy my new friend a drink here and set up one for the house as well." Malcolm pushed the big bill across the bar to Ed and smiled at his new friends around the grimy place. He was oblivious to their nervous smiles.

A few minutes passed, then Malcolm took up his cause with Bear once again.

"Say, friend. I need a special job done, and I'll pay you good money to take care of it for me." His heart skipped several beats when Bear turned his head suddenly and glared at him.

"How much? What for?" The rumbling voice came from a tunnel miles under the ground. Malcolm's skin puckered around his balls.

"Five thousand dollars. I have an enemy who needs his nuts cut off. He stole my wife."

"Hummpf!" answered the hairy giant. Bear got up and turned to Malcolm. "Got to piss. Stay." This last command came out like the man was training a wayward hound. Malcolm was rooted to his seat, sweat ran down his face and his feet were ice cold.

Bear went into the restroom and took a stall away from the door. He flipped open his cell phone and dialed 911. He gave simple, straightforward instructions and went back to his seat to listen and pry more details from the idiot trying to talk him into murdering someone. Bear listened for another 15 minutes until he got a signal from a newcomer to the bar. He got up and went back to the restroom for a little chat with the man. Five minutes later Bear took his seat again, this time wired for sound.

Bear spoke. "Tell me again how much you'll pay, and who you want me to de-nut?"

Malcolm sputtered. "I'll give you $5,000 to castrate, er, de-nut, Jack Marshall. His address is on this piece of paper." Malcolm slid the paper across the bar and waited for Bear's reaction.

"Where's the money?" came his gruff reply. The little man reached for his wallet. Bear signaled the newcomer with a nod, as Malcolm counted out hundreds right on the bar. This was rich. How stupid could he get, thought the retired policeman.

The newcomer had heard enough and approached Malcolm from behind, pausing at another nod from Bear.

"Just so I completely understand," Bear said. "This guy, Jack Marshall, stole your wife, and you are paying me five thousand dollars to cut his nuts off, right?"

"Exactly," said Malcolm gaining confidence. "Here's the money. Cut off his balls and stuff them down his throat."

Bear reached out with one mighty hand and grabbed Malcolm's shirt front, hauling him off his feet.

"You're busted, asshole! Get him out of my sight, officer."

The undercover cop had Malcolm cuffed and dragged outside to the waiting patrol car before he could comprehend what was happening.

Two men slid away from the side of the building and approached the officer and his prisoner. The officer released Malcolm at once. As expected, he bolted for open space.

"Oops," said the Taylor City policeman. "Looks like he's getting away. Darn." The three men watched Malcolm stumble down the sidewalk then trip over the outstretched foot of a fourth man who had stepped out of the alley.

Malcolm splattered face down on the concrete, scraping the skin off his forehead, nose and chin. The man tripping him, helped Malcolm stand up.

Officer Bobby Harrison snarled at Malcolm Schmidt as he slammed him against the brick wall and kneed him in the crotch. Malcolm doubled over only to meet Bobby's other knee rising to crush his nose.

The three men near the entrance to the Tank Top let Harrison have his way for another five minutes before they stopped him. There had to be a live body to fly back to Boise, and it appeared the fugitive had been effectively subdued after resisting arrest.

THIRTY
FIVE

The stakeout of Margo Turner's office and townhouse had become a daily routine for Jack over the last month. Her trail of deceit had been easy to pick up once he gained the cooperation of her bank. Jack watched Turner's house from his plain vanilla van down the street. Her phones had been tapped by court order, and Max Gonzalez was in the back of the van recording her latest conversation with Rafe Stalker.

How could a fairly intelligent and attractive woman end up in bed, literally and figuratively, with a man like Stalker, Jack wondered? It was probably the money. Had to be, since Stalker was about the ugliest human around. Local government didn't pay much, and Turner's bank account had gone up rapidly since the city of Fullerton had started its annexation push. Every Friday, government payday or not, Jack and Max had trailed Margo Turner to the Stalker Constuction company and then to the First Commercial Bank, where she deposited a stack of crisp fake fifties.

Jack would wait until she had left the bank and then meet with the manager to retrieve the money as evidence. The total before this Friday's deposit came to $25,000, not counting her regular salary, which she kept in a separate account. Jack could only describe Margo Turner's actions as dumb.

He and Max had decided to confront her today and present their evidence downtown at FBI headquarters. Their goal was to seal their case against Rafe Stalker with her testimony, and then go after the big fellow himself. He was currently over on the Western Slope and was expected back in Denver next week. By then, his counterfeit money and development scam would be history.

As Margo Turner's garage door began to open, Jack alerted Max.

"Here we go, Max. Close up shop back there. We're on the move."

Turner drove down the street by their van and turned left at the intersection, heading straight for Stalker's. Jack breathed a sigh of relief. She was sticking to her routine and making it easy for them. He followed at a greater distance than usual since he knew where she was going. If she had a change of plans, Max would likely pick it up on her cell phone.

They had nothing to worry about. Turner came out of Stalker's office and drove to her bank as usual, parking near the front door. Jack pulled up beside her car and waited for her to go inside. He and Max followed and stood in line behind her. This deposit was going to take a little more time, though, as a little old grandma was filling out her deposit slip at the teller's window to put her monthly Social Security check in the bank. Wish she had used electronic deposit, Jack thought, as Margo Turner started to fidget and look around nervously.

Finally, Turner reached the teller and opened her oversized black purse. She retrieved a fresh stack of fifties topped by her completed deposit slip.

Jack spoke first. "Margo Turner, you're under arrest." Turner straightened, then moved to take back the money. "Leave it on the counter and put your hands behind your back, Ms. Turner."

Max cuffed her, and Jack examined the stack of bills before a wide-eyed teller. The manager came up beside her and calmed her down.

"It's okay, Louisa. These men are federal agents. They warned me they would be here this morning. That's a stack of counterfeit money in front of you."

While bank employees and customers gaped at the scene, Jack carefully examined the bills to verify they were counterfeit.

"They're all bad, Mr. Crandall. Freeze her accounts as we discussed. Nothing in or out until we release them. We appreciate your cooperation." He turned to Margo Turner, whose complexion was growing whiter by the second. Her head had sunk onto her chest. She had gone into shock, trembling from head to foot.

"Let's get her out of here, Max, before she faints and we have to call an ambulance." The two men each grabbed an arm and walked Turner back to the van where they secured her handcuffs to a loop of steel on the armrest. Max sat in back as Jack drove them downtown. Neither noticed the dark green sedan across the street.

Bull pulled out to follow the van. He knew the big man already as a Secret Service agent. Guy must have nine lives, he thought. He had been washed over the side of Douglas Pass years ago and left for dead. Next time he would have to use more explosives to finish the job.

THIRTY
SIX

The Golden Girls ruled supreme the following Saturday morning. Jack, Becca, and a crowd of parents cheered the girls from start to finish.

This time the coaches had reversed the roles of their key players. Sharon now passed the ball back to Missy, who faked a pass to Katie on the left wing, but quickly switched feet and shot it to Gina on the opposite wing. Jack had figured correctly. Since they had already played the Green Dragons in their first game, he would have to mix things up. It worked perfectly. The Dragons' coach had trained his players to rush the wing on Katie's side. That left Gina open on the other wing. She dribbled straight downfield and centered the ball back to Sharon, who was standing in front of the goal. Score! 1-0 for the Golden Girls.

The rest of the game wasn't so easy though. The Green Dragons coach had actually watched some of Jack's practices and was using strategies Jack had dreamed up. At the half the score was tied 3-3. Jack had noticed his girls playing at a slower pace than in their other games. He decided to join their circle for a little chat while they gobbled down their oranges.

"Hey, girls. How many of you remember playing this team before?"

Sharon stopped sucking on her orange long enough to reply.

"We beat them really bad our first game, coach." She went back to her orange, seemingly without a worry about the outcome.

He looked around the circle at the unconcerned faces. Innocents each one, they hadn't a clue about being overconfident. They had played easier against the Dragons without realizing it.

Gina said, "Coach Jack, if we beat them so bad the first time, we must be a better team. How come we're not beating them today?" Gina had a perplexed look.

Jack smiled at her and waited for the other girls to pay attention.

"Katie, what do you think? Are we a better team? Why aren't we beating them just like last time?" He watched his precocious daughter swallow the rest of her orange. She turned her head to the side and back - just like her mother, Jack thought.

"Gee, dad, I guess it's because they got better and we're taking them for granted." She turned to her best friend for confirmation. "Right, Missy?" Missy nodded her head emphatically.

"Yeah, that's it, Katie! And their mean old coach even watched us practice, so they sneaked and stole our secrets." Missy was all bug-eyed and the rest of the girls started chattering at this profound observation. Jack let them simmer down.

"You're both right. They are better now. Fact is, they are in second place behind us." A collective gasp escaped the team. "And yes, their coach came to watch us practice, but that's because I invited him to. Want to know why?" Heads and pony tails wagged up and down all around the circle.

"Well, I thought it would be good sportsmanship, that's why. His team didn't play well, and they were all down in the dumps after we beat them. Some of those girls are friends of yours aren't they?" Again 12 wagging pony tails agreed.

"Listen to me closely, girls. It's okay for the Green Dragons to be successful and win games just like us. They need to have fun playing, and they weren't having any fun when we played them the first time. But look at them now." The Golden Girls all looked across the field. The other team was jumping up and down, chomping at the bit to play the second half.

Gina spoke for the group.

"Gosh, Coach Jack. What are we going to do now?"

"We're going to play harder in the second half. I want you to play like you did up in Boulder in the wind. Play the best you can, and I believe you will win this game." The girls' enthusiasm rose visibly, and looks of determination wrinkled their faces. "There's only one more thing to remember. Even if they win, you still get your can of pop." He was greeted by laughs and giggles.

The change in the next half was miraculous. The Green Dragons played their best, but the Golden Girls never let up. Gina took a centered shot from Sharon and scored. Missy raced down the left wing, crossed to the front of the goal on her own, and scored. Katie put a corner kick squarely in front of the Dragon goalie and jumped for joy as Sharon toed it in easily, then sheepishly looked to the sideline to see if Jack had noticed.

The Dragons scored as well, but they couldn't keep up with the rejuvenated Golden Girls, who won 10-6. The victory made them the champs of their division. Jack and Becca were surrounded by squealing and jumping girls. He hugged each one and got a big smooch on the cheek every time. Then Becca poked him on the shoulder and pointed to the center stripe where the Green Dragons were lined up to shake hands.

Well, well, he thought. They had come a long way since slinking off the field dejected after their first game. He hustled the girls over to the other team and they went through the sportsmanship ritual for the last time of the season. He came to the end of the line and shook hands with Greg Mallory, the Dragon coach.

"Good game, Greg. Your girls have really improved. The parents too. They did a lot of cheering today."

Greg beamed at Jack and clapped him on the shoulder.

"I owe a lot of our improvement to you, Jack. You helped set me on the right path early on. I really appreciate it. And hey, we came in second to you for the championship. How about that?"

The two friendly adversaries separated and went back to their respective teams.

Jack gathered Becca and the girls into a close circle around him.

"Your are truly Golden Girls. Coach Becca has something for you."

"Girls, our season is over but we have a special picnic set up for next Saturday. Here's an announcement with all the details for your parents. We're going to have a parent/kid soccer game. It will be kids against the parents with some special rules." She hesitated as the chattering began amongst the teammates.

Gina piped in.

"We're going to play against our parents? Wow! What fun. We'll totally beat them." The girls jumped up and down in their excitement.

"Okay, now calm down a minute," Becca continued. "After the game there will be a picnic over at my house, and all your families are invited." Again she had to wait for the excitement to simmer down. "Just make sure you give this invitation to your parents and tell them to call me or Gina's mom if they have questions."

When Becca finally finished, the girls took off across the field, scattering like a handful of marbles. Jack and Becca watched Gina run right up to Gloria and Dave. Dave scooped her up, gave her a big hug, then lifted her onto his back for a piggyback ride to their car.

"Nice how that turned out, isn't it, Jack?" Becca grinned at him. "It's great to see another couple find each other."

"You know, that means Gina won't be sleeping over at your house this weekend." He gave her a cocky grin."

"Oh, I see what you mean. Hmmmmm, I may just have to arrange for you and the boys to sleep over at my place this weekend. What do you say to that? I think I have a soft spot all picked out for you, too."

Jack was thoughtful a moment. Katie and Missy were occupied passing a ball back and forth over near their car. Now was a good time to discuss living arrangements.

"I think my gang should move over to your place." Her surprised look of pleasure encouraged him to continue. "It would be a good opportunity to see if we want to live in your house or mine or build another one. I would feel better, more secure really, with everyone under one roof until we wrap up this case with the crooked developer. Plus, the security detail would only have to check on one house."

"Are you seriously worried about that, Jack? I thought you had arrested some of the people involved?"

"Not all. The main guy will be taken into custody next week. Things should be pretty quiet this weekend, though."

Becca embraced him, then lifted her head to plant a kiss on his mouth.

"Then it's settled. We think so much alike, Jack. I was going to suggest this after dinner, but let's go for it now!" They collected their daughters and walked arm in arm to the car.

Dinner that night was a special affair. Becca had insisted on cooking a meal in her kitchen. She set the dining room table with her finest silver and china. Andy, Tommy, Missy, and Katie were a little upset at having to take baths and put on clean clothes. Usually they just played outside, paused briefly to snarf down hotdogs and hamburgers Jack cooked on the grill, and then played again until bedtime. But not tonight.

Jack had been curious about Katie all afternoon and evening. She was acting different, anxious almost. Jack had noticed Katie and Becca exchanging looks all evening. Something was up, besides the big news he would share tonight, and he wondered what those two were scheming. Becca had even run him out of the kitchen while she prepared her favorite lemon chicken with rice and green beans. The aroma was driving him nuts.

When dinner was ready, Jack and Becca sat at the head of the table holding hands. They were nervous, hoping for a good reaction, but with four kids one never knew what to expect.

Andy had it all figured out, though. He had watched his mom all evening. He had clued Tommy in on it too, so he could keep a close eye on his dad. Before Jack could get everyone's attention to start the meal, Andy burst out with his surprise question.

"When are you guys getting married? Tommy and I want to be brothers."

Katie followed his lead.

"Yeah, dad, what's taking you so long?"

Tommy jumped into the fray, seemingly delighted that he and Andy had taken over.

"How about it, huh?"

Missy was not to be left out. "We could have a big picnic out back. Huh, mom? Couldn't we, please?"

Jack and Becca drew in big sighs of relief. There was no need to worry. Far from objecting, their kids had everything all planned out and were anxious to get the ball rolling.

"How about next Saturday?" Jack offered. There was absolute silence as the kids sat open-mouthed and stared at their parents.

Jack turned to Becca's children. "Andy and Missy, I love your mom very much, do I have your permission to marry her?"

Before her children could get out their answer, Becca turned to Jack's children. "Tommy and Katie, I love your dad with all my heart, may I have your permission to marry him?"

They were bombarded with a chorus of yeahs and shouts of happiness.

Hunger took over as they all settled into Becca's lemon chicken and devoured it quickly. The table was noisy with the kids talking back and forth about what this all meant. Jack and Becca discovered they were in a quiet zone at their end of the table and exchanged smiles.

"Do you think you can feed this bunch all the time, Becca? I can cook up a dish of pasta and grill anything to help you, but mealtime with this crowd could be a chore. They won't eat my cooking after they taste yours. This is scrumptious."

She smiled.

"You go out and catch the bad guys, and I'll do the cooking, Jack. When our lives settle down some, I'll give you a few lessons. Teach you how to cook too," she added mischievously, drawing a lecherous chuckle from him.

"Okay, listen up, gang." Becca raised her voice to get everyone's attention. "Before dessert there will be a short intermission, during which special entertainment will be provided. Everyone into the living room." She pulled Jack into her arms and gave him a big hug. "You are going to like this, dad. Come on with me."

Katie sat at the piano waiting for her new family to settle down. She beamed at her dad and waited for Becca to announce her first piece.

"Everyone, please give me your attention. A few months ago, Katie asked if I would teach her how to play. Since then, we have been secretly getting together so I could give her some lessons and she could surprise you. So, tonight's the night." Becca looked at her young pupil. "Ready, sweetie?" Katie nodded, eyes bright.

"Her first number will be 'Row, Row, Row Your Boat.'"

Jack sat on the edge of his chair. He was surprised, then suddenly nervous and proud.

Katie played softly, hesitantly at first. It was a simple piece, yet she stroked the keyboard exactly, not missing a note. Her playing was good enough to silence Andy and Tommy, who had started out squirming, anxious to go outside and play. But they listened, recognizing that she really could play the piano.

Everyone applauded when she finished. Katie stood and bowed like Becca had shown her. She couldn't contain herself and ran to give Jack a big hug. Then she hurried back to the piano for her next number.

Becca provided drama for her next piece, a tune that was familiar and a bit harder. "Miss Katherine Marshall will now give us her rendition of 'The Happy Butterfly.' It's something I teach all my intermediate students." Becca winked at Jack, then nodded her head in Katie's direction when he mouthed, "Intermediate?"

Again Katie captured her audience. Andy and Tommy were stunned. Missy bounced up and down on the sofa. More applause followed. Then Katie announced her last number for the evening: "I call this one Doodles."

Missy, Tommy, and Andy snickered at the title, but they sat back to listen anyway. Jack noticed there was no sheet music on the stand for her to follow.

If Jack thought she had surprised him enough for one evening, he was greatly mistaken. His daughter closed her eyes and rolled out music from her heart. The simple melody varied over and over. It sounded almost like a typical scale used to warm up, but got more complicated as she played. The lilting music only lasted a few minutes, but that was enough.

Jack and the rest of the others applauded when she finished. Jack shot Becca a questioning look again.

"Where did that come from?" he asked.

Becca walked over to Katie and hugged her, not ignoring Jack's question so much as including Katie in the conversation. She had to bring Missy along too, because she wouldn't let go of her soon-to-be sister's hand. The boys took the opportunity to head for the backyard and make use of the remaining daylight.

"Jack, Katie is a gifted child. All that time she had trouble focusing and kept getting into trouble in school was because she hadn't found her special gift. Now she has."

Jack hugged his daughter and tried to keep the tears from spilling over, but it was too late. Becca sniffled too. Then they saw the pouting look on Missy's face and drew her into their arms for a group hug.

"You're special, too, Missy." Jack said, soothing her feelings. "I watched you play all season, and you know what?" He paused as her frown turned into a smile. "You do things on the field none of the other kids do. If I tell you to pass the ball or center it or anything else, you just do it. Sometimes you do it before I even tell you to. That's special, Missy." She jumped into his arms and hugged him fiercely. Jack peered over her head at Becca with a look that said it was not going to be easy with the natural competition ahead between these four kids. When they got into their teens, all would be searching for their own particular identity, watching their parents to see if anyone was being favored.

Becca blew him a kiss over their daughters' heads. They would have to provide a united front, and it was an opportunity they both eagerly looked forward to.

Jack cleaned up in the kitchen while Becca helped the girls settle in for the night. He had a rule. Whoever cooked didn't have to wash dishes. He laughed to himself. Tommy and Katie were always bugging him to let them cook something. They were tired of washing dishes every night.

He called the boys inside around nine. Light was fading fast, and they would be starting swim team soon. That meant early morning practices and going to bed on time. They grumbled a bit but went to Andy's room, shutting the door emphatically. He chuckled again. Those guys would be up late for weeks to come talking about their new family.

He closed up the house and went upstairs. He wasn't sure which house to pick, and, if they built somewhere else, he would hate to leave these cul-de-sacs. They were perfectly positioned near the bike paths and the river. Fortunately, Gloria's campaign to stop the Fullerton annexation had succeeded. Her petition drive had galvanized the community into action. It would be a long time before anyone tried to develop near Cottonwood Estates. Tomorrow there would be a big neighborhood picnic and potluck at the Rec Center to celebrate.

Jack opened the door to Becca's room and found himself in total darkness, until a candle flickered to life over near the bed.

"What took you so long, fellow? I've been waiting for you. Come on over here and let me make you feel at home." Becca purred in a throaty voice Jack had termed her 1-900 come-on. It was so totally out of character they both broke up laughing. They had discovered that humor heightened their anticipation and enjoyment in bed.

Jack began removing his clothes as he sauntered over to her. He stood beside the bed, taking in her barely concealed beauty beneath the silky lingerie he had bought for their penthouse night. She was stunning, stretched lazily across the bed, arms draped over rows of pillows, openly inviting his admiring gaze, presenting an erotic view that took his breath.

The flickering candle shifted light to conceal then display Becca's body: the slight rise and fall of diaphanous material over her breasts, peaked with excitement, a seductively narrow waist, the erotic flare of hips tapering into gorgeously-shaped legs. Hints of an exotic treasure were obscured by the dimness, and Jack moved his head from side to side trying not to miss a moment. He was a lucky man.

Jack stripped off his remaining clothes then pounced on her without warning, breaking the sultry mood. Becca squealed and rolled with him across the bed and back again. They kept up this competition as had become their custom, struggling to see who would take charge. Tonight Becca sought to erase this week's tension and won quickly.

Jack was easy prey. He had learned to appreciate the subtle benefits of playing a deceptively submissive role. He was eagerly willing to let Becca take her pleasure, knowing they would be together regardless.

"Keep your hands to yourself, mister. Let me love you." He acquiesced, smiling up at his delightful woman, determined to please him. She swayed to and fro, using fingers, arms, legs, lips, even hair and eyelashes to massage his body, pleasure them both. Somewhere in the shifting about, she had captured him between her legs, and she instinctively rolled her hips rhythmically, in synch with an invisible tidal force.

Towards the end, she lost herself and pressed his hands to her breasts, shuddering in release.

THIRTY
SEVEN

The greenbelt provided ample cover for the big man carrying an over-stuffed backpack loaded with material from his construction site. His accomplice had created total darkness up and down the cul-de-sac by extinguishing the single streetlight in front of their victim's house. This early in the morning, the entire neighborhood was asleep. Not a single light shone from any houses the full length of the street.

Rafe Stalker walked up a gradual slope through brambles and thick woods to join Bull in Jack Marshall's backyard. It was a calm, unprotected home, a place considered off limits to great violence, but these men were about to change that.

"You checked for anybody moving around up there, Bull?" Rafe asked his driver one more time, just to be sure.

"Everything checks out okay, boss," Bull answered in an anxious whisper. He had walked around the silent home twice at Stalker's insistence. Nothing stirred. No lights were on, nor did he trigger any security lights.

Rafe Stalker looked into Bull's face in the patchy moonlight. This man had been with him from the beginning when they had fought and struggled to take old man Greenhault's construction company away from him. Bull had witnessed and committed many crimes for the sake of their enterprise. He had often been Rafe's trigger man, whether setting explosives or firing a weapon. He knew exactly what had been done to make Rafe's company successful, including the location of the printing equipment that kept them in bribe money and extra cash.

Yes, Rafe thought, Bull knew it all. He was the only one who did, and tonight that would end. There would be no turning back after what they were about to do. Bull had become a liability. Rafe knew government agents had ways of convincing a slow-witted man like Bull to turn against his employer. They would offer Bull a plea bargain and almost no jail time to get at the mastermind. Bull could be a key witness. But not if Rafe moved first.

He nodded to Bull to set the charges, then stepped back into the shadows. Rafe held the remote device they had used often in their construction business to set off blasts from a safe distance. Rafe could trigger the blast any time, and tonight he would not wait for Bull to signal he had left the danger zone. In one instant he would be gone along with that bastard Jack Marshall. Then it was off to Mexico to start over. After the Fullerton bribery had fallen through, Stalker's operations in this country were finished. Jack Marshall was solely to blame, and tonight he would pay. Blowing up Marshall's house and killing his family would not sit well with the government, so Rafe would be forced to flee south. Workers were cheaper down there anyway, and he could still print enough money to last a long time.

He watched as Bull came from around front and started setting the charges at strategic points along the back wall of the two-story house.

•••

Jack heard a tiny voice from another world, overlaid by frantic tapping on the bedroom door. Becca was wide awake and shook him gently.

"Jack, someone is calling to you out in the hall. Sounds like one of the boys."

Jack sat up in bed and listened. A muffled voice called out in a whisper bordering on tears.

"Dad! Dad, wake up. There's someone in our yard!"

Still groggy, Jack glanced at the bright illumination of the digital clock on his night stand. Two AM! What was Tommy doing up at this time?

"Just a minute, Tommy. I'm coming." He stepped into his Levi's and made his way to the door, opening it a crack to reveal two grimy faces. Tommy and Andy looked like wild Indians who had gotten lost in the swamp. They had brought in part of the greenbelt with them. Their clothes were stitched with twigs and branches; their shoes were covered in clay and mud from the woods and river. With a closer look, Jack realized their faces were smeared with camouflage paint snitched from his undercover stash he thought safely hidden in the garage. Other than four bright eyes wide with fright, both boys were practically invisible.

Jack stepped into the hall and confronted them.

"What are you two hyenas doing up, and where have you been?"

Tommy and Andy each grabbed an arm and started pulling him to their room down the hall, pleading with him to come and see what they had discovered.

"We're sorry, dad, really we are, but you gotta see for yourself. Someone is out in the woods looking at our house." Tommy breathlessly rushed on and dragged his dad over to the double window that looked out onto the backyard.

Andy chimed in with his own version of events.

"He's right, Mr. Marshall. We were scouting the woods for enemy soldiers and saw these two guys going up to your house. We came home as fast as we could to tell you. They looked mean and big, too."

"Okay, quiet down, boys. Let me take a look and try to focus on the woods over there. It's really hard to see anything." Jack scanned the barely visible edges of his backyard, letting his eyes slowly range from the back of his house to the beginning of the greenbelt. It was impossible to detect anything. All the trees had leafed out, and the moon was providing dim lighting at best.

"Guys, I can't see a thing." He turned to take in their scared faces. The two frightened little boys had obviously been in the woods playing around, and they had not imagined anything.

"Tell me again, slowly and from the beginning. What did you see?"

Tommy shook Andy's shoulder.

"You tell him, Andy. You were closer than me."

Andy gulped in a big breath and spoke.

"There were two guys, Mr. Marshall. Two big men, and one had a big pack on his shoulders that looked heavy. I was, er, hiding from Tommy over by the path from our house to yours, and they walked right by me. Then one guy walks up to your back door and starts walking around to the front while the other man stayed in the woods. I sneaked away, and me and Tommy watched a while, then we ran up here to get you." Andy drew a breath and looked at Tommy for confirmation. Tommy nodded back enthusiastically, and both boys looked frantically at Jack for assurance.

"Stay here in your room, boys. I'll go take a look outside." He returned to the master bedroom and started pulling on the rest of his clothes in a rush.

"Becca, call Dave over at Gloria's. Tell him to get over here on the double and bring his weapon. Tell him to come through this house and meet me near the bench where you and I used to smooch. The boys saw two men out back, and I'm betting we have some unwanted company." Becca's face turned ashen and her hand shook as she went to the phone.

"Jack, wait for Dave to come over. Please don't go out there by yourself." But he was gone, leaving her to make the call for help.

Downstairs, Jack was glad he'd decided to bring his weapon in a lock box whenever he and the kids stayed over. He retrieved the pistol, grabbed a flashlight from the kitchen cupboard, then left quietly through the basement sliding door.

Once outside, he stood still, listening for sounds from the woods. But there were only the usual creature noises and the occasional thrashing of a night hunter, probably an owl, successfully scarfing up a field mouse for its dinner. He slipped out of Becca's gate and vanished into the woods, circling away from his house to come up on his backyard from the direction of the river. Whoever had come from that way would be cut off when they tried to escape.

He knew these woods well. Spring rains had softened the floor of the forest, making it easy to walk without crunching branches or stirring the undergrowth. As he came to a point directly behind his house but a hundred yards out in the woods, Jack wished he had stopped long enough to wipe on some of the camouflage paint his boys had used. His boys - he smiled to himself at the phrase. He would have two boys and two girls soon. Then his anger rose at this threat to his family. Determined to protect them, he pushed on towards his yard.

•••

Rafe peered into the darkness at Bull. He was placing the last charge now. Rafe wanted to make sure the man was still by the house when the explosives went off. There! He saw Bull rising from his knees beside a support post for the deck. Rafe raised the remote and pressed.

Jack caught sight of a man under his deck and raced forward. Then his world went white, then bright orange. Jack was knocked backwards as a massive explosion sent shock waves through the greenbelt. He rolled into the undergrowth half-stunned and slapped at patches of his clothing that had caught fire from the sparks of the blast. He sat up in time to see his house engulfed by a huge, roiling fireball. The whole second floor had imploded and collapsed onto the first floor. Finally, the twisting, mangled catastrophe crashed into the basement, landing with a loud crackling and smashing of debris mixed with smoke and fire and the remains of all Jack's possessions.

Jack stood in the open, staring at the ruins of his house. Whoever had set the explosives knew what he was doing, because there had been little damage to houses on either side. Even the fire had been contained to his basement, now burning under control in a small area. The flames had been partially snuffed out by the smothering crush of debris from the upper floors. Thank God his family was safely over in Becca's house tonight.

Jack pushed thoughts of his family aside as he stood in the open, analyzing. The devastation had been skillfully done by someone who knew just where to place charges to effect maximum damage to a specific target. He knew one person who could have done this, and began scanning the woods for Rafe Stalker battling the smoke and flickering light of the fire.

He looked towards Becca's house and saw a man standing there not far from the gate to her backyard. Suddenly, the smoke cleared enough for Jack to recognize the giant figure of Rafe Stalker, arm raised and pointing at him. He heard a shot and dropped to the ground. He stayed flat and rolled into the brush. He had exposed himself out in the open, gazing at the fire one second too long. Jack crawled to his knees and watched in horror as Stalker ran towards Becca's house.

He tried to stand and found he was wobbly, still dazed from the explosion. His pistol still clenched in his hand, Jack started through the woods to stop this maniac before it was too late.

In desperation, Jack ran through the brambles and undergrowth to Becca's. Stalker had thrown open the gate and was advancing across the yard. Jack was only a few strides from the gate when help arrived.

"Freeze and put your hands up," Dave shouted from somewhere inside the yard. Jack had kept running, but he stopped short as two shots exploded in front of him. He focused his flashlight on the gate as it sprang open and Rafe Stalker burst through, coming directly at him.

Jack was through with warnings. He caught the man's face full in the flashlight, blinding him instantly. Then he aimed at his chest and shot point-blank, emptying his pistol into the raging maniac. Stalker kept coming even though his chest had been punctured and torn open with shots. Blood streamed down his body. His face was contorted with pain and anger as he tried to get at Jack one last time.

Jack stepped aside and used the flashlight to club the side of Stalker's head as the huge man stumbled by him. Stalker grunted and landed in a heap. Spent. It was over.

Jack looked down, counting seconds in his mind as extra precaution before he approached the body. Then he rolled the inert form over and grimaced at the deformed, angry face, locked in a death grimace filled with venom.

"He was a determined bastard, Jack." Dave came up beside him with his pistol aimed at the dead man's skull. "I drilled him with two shots, and he just turned and ran back out into the woods, charging at you."

The two friends sat down on a log and stared at the hulk of a man on the ground. Jack felt waves of relief flood his body, then he gave way to the after effects of the trauma, and began to tremble with the onset of shock.

"Come with me, Jack," Dave said gently as he supported his friend, helping him back inside the fenced yard. "An ambulance is on the way. You don't look so good. Sit down over here and catch your breath." Jack let his friend tend to him as if he were a child. His body continued its downward spiral into shock from the effects of the explosion.

Then Becca was there to wipe his face and wrap a blanket around him to help keep him warm. Her beautiful eyes, full of fear and love, overflowed with tears of relief. He pulled her to him and tried to soothe her.

Gradually, he noticed tiny little hands on his back and shoulders, comforting and calming him. His children surrounded him, loving him in the only way they knew how. They were still shaking and scared from the noise of the explosion and gunfire. Yet, they had to be with him despite Becca's orders to stay inside.

He and Becca exchanged a smile and kissed.

"We have great kids, don't we, lady?" He half mumbled in her ear, having trouble finding his voice with the sound of the explosion still ringing in his ears.

Becca shuddered in his arms and held him tight. Her embrace was joined by the children in a healing circle of love.

Dave went to the front of the house to lead the ambulance and paramedics to Jack. They checked him out briefly, then loaded him into the ambulance. Becca stared at the scene, unable to move.

"Becca," Dave said, "go with him. I'll stay here with the kids. I called Gloria to come over with Gina. We'll take care of your family. It's safe now."

"Thanks, Dave. You saved us tonight. That man looked like he would blast right through the house to escape. You really are his best friend. Mine too." She smiled at the big man and gave him a hug. Then she left to join Jack in the ambulance.

•••

The Madison County police had arrived with the ambulance. Detective Lewis scratched his head in wonder as he recognized the hulking figure of the DA standing in the yard.

"Evening, Dave." Lewis said. "I thought you told us not to call you any more late at night. Somebody passed the word you had gotten a life." Lewis joked. "Word sort of spread through the department that there was a special lady, a former protected witness, I believe.

"Very funny, Lewis. Yes, you're right about my good luck. But, for now, there's a dead body outside that gate you need to deal with. In my former life, I tracked this guy with Jack Marshall. It has taken over three years, but we finally caught up with him. I'm going to take a look at the remains of Marshall's house. Jack's boys told me there were two men out back, so be careful. We may have another one to take in."

Dave made his way along the path that was dimly lit by the dying flames of the fire. Several fire trucks were out in the cul-de-sac pouring water on the flames and on nearby houses to prevent any spreading. The heat was still intense, and Dave had to circle around the back of the yard, much as Jack had done earlier.

Dave was looking at the fire as he walked along and tripped over an object lying across the path. Then he heard a groan and looked down to see Bull's crumpled body writhing on the ground. Somehow, the man had survived the blast, although the burns on his body made for a gruesome sight. He looked thoroughly barbecued with segments of exposed and charred flesh partially covered by tattered and smoking clothing. Dave rushed back to Becca's to call for another ambulance. The man may be alive but Dave didn't want to see how the paramedics would get him on a stretcher without pulling him apart.

Stalker's accomplice probably wouldn't live, but Dave hoped he might give them some information on the location of the counterfeit operation. That much was still a mystery.

THIRTY EIGHT

The early morning explosion that demolished Jack's house was the talk of the Front Range all day Sunday. Fortunately, Dave Mendes handled the TV crews and reporters who flocked to the now-famous cul-de-sac in Cottonwood Estates to pick through the remains. He presented a simplified version of events, leaving Jack's name and identity out of most of his description. Yet, it was going to be hard for his best friend to work undercover in Colorado in the future. His photograph and those of his children were featured on all the TV news programs, and would run on the front pages of the two Denver newspapers Monday morning.

Becca, Gloria, and Martha had a busy week ahead of them and hoped the explosion would become old news quickly. The Golden Girls picnic had turned into something much bigger. Following a private ceremony inside, it was now unofficially referred to as a backyard wedding reception. The guest list had increased twofold and food was becoming an issue. Without Becca's knowledge, Gloria and Martha had told everyone there was more to this picnic than picnicking, and the response from team parents, friends, and neighbors was overwhelming.

Jack had complained about staying in the hospital Sunday night, but Becca had insisted on it. Jack's doctor was concerned about the overall effects of the shock wave and noise of the explosion that had shaken him internally. Once his minor cuts, scrapes, and burns had been cleaned up, he appeared fine. But his vital signs were erratic, and his balance was a little off. Generally, the doctor concluded, he needed to be still for a day or so and let his body work its way back to normal.

Becca stayed with him. The doctor ordered some routine tests Monday, and then pronounced Jack fit for "human consumption" and let go. Becca brought him back to her house early Monday morning. She let the kids skip school so they could be near him and convince themselves he was alive and healthy. All four children seemed to be experiencing their own kind of shock, as if they had stood near Jack when the explosion occurred. She could see that they needed to talk to him and touch him to get over their own fears.

Becca steadied Jack as he walked out onto the deck and stretched out in a comfortable lounger. He relaxed visibly before her as the sun beamed its healing vitamin C down on his aching body. Then the kids sneaked up on him in a tight little band. Becca saw them coming and knew it had been a good decision to keep them home.

Jack's was dozing in the bright morning sun when he felt little hands touch his arms followed by whispers.

"He's asleep, don't touch him, Katie."

"Go easy, you might hurt him." Another child warned.

He opened his eyes to see four very concerned children watching him. Such worried faces for little kids, he thought. Katie and Missy had their hands on his right arm, and Tommy and Andy had claimed the other, careful not to touch any bandages.

"Are you going to be okay, dad?" Katie spoke for the others, who had become too shy to say anything.

He tried to get out a response but his voice caught, emotion suddenly constricting his throat. He could only nod in affirmation as tears welled up. Jack looked from face to face and smiled. Then he gulped down the big lump stuck in his throat and spoke.

"I'm going to be fine, kids. Thanks. Don't worry. You can touch me. I won't break." Evidently this was the signal they needed and Jack was besieged by hugs from all four kids. Even the two boys quit trying to be brave and let their emotions show. Once again Jack felt their healing power. Becca and the children hovered over him, showing him how much he meant to them.

It was a special moment in another way for Jack, though. In the back of his mind, he felt sympathy and a deep, aching pain for them. Katie and Tommy had lost their mother. It had taken them years to absorb that trauma. This time they had almost lost him. They had come close to witnessing a shooting right in their own backyard. They had also lost their home, the only one they had known.

Missy and Andy had seen their father attack their mother and would never forget his rage. Becca had told Jack her children had never had a dad until he came into their lives. Now they had almost lost him before he could make it official.

Then there was Becca. He knew the strain this had put on her. She had not wanted him to go outside to check on the prowlers. Her whole body had shaken with fear as she embraced him in the yard that night.

What effect did his secret life have on Helen? He would never know. Had worrying about his safety damaged her own health?

His full concentration swung back to his new family, surrounding him on this beautiful and sunny day. He looked at Becca, who clearly knew he had drifted off to another dimension.

"We need to talk, sweetheart. Later when these kids are over their scare. Okay?" She nodded and smiled her relief as if she had read his mind. They had grown so close in such a short time. Jack wished he had known her all his life, and he was determined to make their life together a long and safe one.

Jack spent the rest of the morning retelling the story of the bad men to his kids. He left out some of the scarier stuff, but by lunch time they understood his job was catching counterfeiters, and that's why their house had been blown up. It was a big business, and over the years he had saved lots of money at the expense of the crooks. But, he emphasized, there would be no more mean guys coming near them again.

Becca made sandwiches and iced tea for lunch and happily watched her family swarm around the table to devour it as if they hadn't eaten in days. Afterwards, she ordered the kids to bed for a nap. Despite their ages and reluctance to leave Jack, she was surprised to see them all agree and go to their rooms. They were suddenly very tired and the adrenaline rush of the exciting weekend had drained them of any energy.

She came back to the deck and sat facing Jack, waiting for him to bring up what was on his mind.

He spoke after a long moment of reflection, gazing into her eyes seriously. "I have to get another job."

"Don't work for a while, Jack. I know you love your career. This is what you have always done. I'll get over this. I see those looks you've been shooting at me, worrying that I might break apart. Well, whatever you do that's fine with me, and I'll support you. So, stop worrying. Rest. You'll feel differently about this tomorrow or the next day."

"Okay, this day has been full enough and it's only half over. I'll rest, and we'll talk tomorrow when the kids are in school." He noticed her brave smile then continued. "I've made up my mind, Becca. You'll see."

Becca leaned into him and kissed him softly. She walked him upstairs to bed and made sure he was comfortable. Then she backed away when she saw his eyes glaze over with exhaustion.

Outside the bedroom she leaned back against the wall, her insides still in a jumble as she struggled to accept this trauma and be brave about Jack's work. He needed all his strength to heal, and find his way without worrying about her. Didn't he?

Jack clawed his way out of the nightmare feeling dizzy and sick to his stomach. He was locked in an agonizing loop with Rafe Stalker standing just beyond his grasp and pointing at him. Stalker held a pistol in one hand and a remote control in the other. Jack saw his house explode, heard shots. Bullets came at him in slow motion and struck him at the same time Stalker opened Becca's gate and began shooting inside her backyard.

He groaned and tried to scream, but the sound was strangled in the middle of his chest. He twisted about in the bed until calming hands soothed him and brought him out of the dreadful vision.

"Jack, honey, wake up. You're dreaming. Everything is fine." Becca leaned over him, smothering him with kisses and an embrace. She smiled and drew him up into a sitting position, then scooted closer until the entire length of his upper body lay beside hers.

"We'll have that talk now." He spoke in a tone new to both of them. Serious.

"Fine with me. You first."

"I'll find another job, simple as that. I can't put you and the kids in danger. It's eating me up thinking about what could have happened. I've done this enough. It's time for younger men and women to do the field work and get shot at." He hesitated to check her reaction. The lines of worry around the corners of her eyes and the deep creases on her forehead seemed to relax with his words. She smiled shyly. He grinned back, knowing this was the best news for both of them.

"Next problem. Where to live?" He noticed her look of puzzlement and forged ahead quickly. "See, the way I figure it, if we stayed here in your house there would always be some bad memories. And as the kids get older, they'll want their own bedrooms." Jack's tone lightened. "Personally, I'd kind of like a luxurious master bath with a Jacuzzi over in the corner." Becca's eyes went wide, and they both chuckled, remembering their tryst in the penthouse suite.

"So," he rushed on, his momentum building, "we'll just have to build our dream house where my old one used to be. Add a couple of bedrooms and allow for a really big master bedroom. What do you think?"

"Sounds wonderful to me, Jack." Becca was surprised at his renewed strength as he pulled her across his body so she sat astride him. "Hmmmm, say, what's that stirring down there?" Jack only grinned in response as she wiggled her hips.

"What do you say we consummate, er, seal our decision the old fashioned way?" He leered at her and raised his eyebrows suggestively. He framed her face in his hands and brought her forward for a lingering kiss.

"Hmmmmm, Mr. Secret Agent," she murmured. "You sure do heal up fast."

•••

By the middle of the week, the news media had finally lost interest in the explosion in Cottonwood Estates. Rafe Stalker's bribery of Margo Turner was also old news. The neighborhood was taking longer to settle down, however, especially since there was a gaping hole at the end of Jack's cul-de-sac. Larry Thigpen had filed a complaint with the sheriff's office for damages done to his lawn by the firefighters. In rolling out their thick hoses they had left huge creases in his grass and it was not springing back up. In fact, patches of Larry's yard had been singed by fragments of Jack's burning house.

In the early part of the week, insurance investigators were kept busy at every house in the neighborhood. They had been called out by anxious homeowners who thought perhaps they could scrounge a new cedar shake roof from the disaster. Couldn't the investigator see, they argued, that their curling and chipped shingles - the most expensive kind of roofing around, had been damaged by the explosion? But in the final analysis, only Jack's immediate neighbors got any satisfaction. Larry got replacement sod, but he still complained it didn't quite match the deep green of the rest of his yard. The Hammakers on the other side got the entire side of their house replaced and were quite satisfied.

Jack and Becca settled with his insurance company quickly and began doodling with floor plans for their dream house. They would have a big yard, and the basement had already been freshly excavated, though some large chunks of broken cement would have to be taken out. Financially things were not that bad either. They had the insurance settlement as a solid basis to start with, and soon the proceeds from the sale of Becca's house would add to their financial well-being. All in all, it looked like they would be able to plan and build their dream home. They were comfortable in Becca's house for now and would take their time, allowing the trauma to drift away before rushing into major changes.

Physically, Jack felt better each day. He was due compensation for his injuries and time off to recuperate. Yet, by Wednesday, Henry Strothers had called demanding an incident report so he could close out his case file. Strothers seemed to have no clue about the tragedy, and didn't care how it affected the people involved. In the end, Jack figured the stuffed shirt actually did him a favor by pressing for the report so soon.

He dictated it to Becca as best he could, and she typed it up on Thursday afternoon. Strothers hadn't considered the fact that Jack's computer and office files no longer existed. Their remains were no more than ashes that had drifted through the greenbelt to reside in the South Platte and float to Kansas.

But there was one record Jack had memorized: his personnel file. His job was definitely hazardous duty. His injury record proved that point and he was through getting shot at, blown up, and swimming through avalanches. As a field agent, he could retire after a minimum of 20 years service. This was a minor benefit for putting his life on the line over the years, and Jack figured it was time he took advantage of it.

Jack watched Becca set the sprinklers in the backyard Friday morning. Their next yard would have an underground automatic sprinkler system, he vowed. Dragging hoses around was a pain. Yet he enjoyed watching Becca work at it. She loved gardening, planting, watering, making things grow. Each tree, bush, plant, and flower under her care received a good talking to as she passed by. She touched each growing thing and encouraged it to succeed, using a low voice only the plant could hear. Funny woman, he thought, yet her yard looked like it was straight out of Better Homes and Gardens.

"Come here, gorgeous. I want to show you something." Jack called across the yard. He had taken to his usual lounge chair on the deck to soak up the morning sun while doing some calculations. Actually, he had lost concentration watching Becca out in her back-yard paradise. Her halter top and shorts were very stimulating this morning. He must be almost 100 percent, he thought with a grin.

Becca sat down at the table and gave him a big smile.

"Don't tell me you're ready to become a gardener, Jack? You've been really overseeing my work this morning. I'm happy to see you're interested."

Jack chuckled. "Oh yeah, I'm interested all right." He ran his hand up her thigh and teased a finger under the edge of her shorts. Becca just slapped his hand away as she would a pesky fly.

"Hitting a wounded man while he's down. Where's all that sympathy I was getting earlier this week?"

Becca returned the favor as her hand teased the inside of his thigh, then withdrew quickly. "You don't look much like a guy who's down today, Mr. Secret Agent."

Jack reluctantly turned serious. "Later, later. Now look at these figures I've ginned up." Becca scooted closer and rested her hand on his arm. She gave him her full attention, especially when he used his serious-mood voice.

Jack pointed to a column of numbers all neatly labeled as current income, hazard pay, and retirement income. After those came the monthly amount from her children's trust fund that had been created from Malcolm's resources. They could count on that for another ten years. Finally, he listed her income from piano lessons.

Her eyes widened when she reached the bottom figure, and Jack got a cocky smirk on his face.

"So, with all this money coming in," he said, "I don't need to work at all. I'll just enjoy the deck, maybe do a little gardening, while you slave away teaching piano."

"Damnation," she swore and punched his arm hard, right on the bony part. "Not a chance, fellow. And what's this about retirement income? I thought you were just going to quit?"

Jack explained the rules governing his occupation and promised he would go back to work when he found something more peaceful.

"Let's change clothes and pay a visit to Henry Strothers downtown. This will be fun. Afterwards we can get some lunch at the Deli Connection on Hampton Boulevard." Jack looked up from his figures and felt the full and sensuous gaze of his beautiful lady sitting beside him. Then he felt her hand on his thigh again.

"I don't think we'll make it downtown until after lunch, Jack." Becca gave him a throaty chuckle. "I have other plans for you this morning. Consider it part of your physical therapy." She smoothed her hand along his thigh and gave him a silent message he understood completely.

"Late lunch and then we visit old so-and-so downtown. I forget his name at the moment. Something else has come up."

Jack and Becca walked into the house holding each other close, treasuring their special time together. The demolition of Jack's house and the threat to his life had served to draw them closer and made them appreciate every moment together.

That afternoon they filled out forms for Jack's retirement and walked into Henry Strothers' office together to plop them on his desk. Henry sputtered a bit with the interruption and looked up reluctantly at his intruders in time to catch Jack's incident report as it sailed into his lap. They said nothing and walked out, leaving Henry gaping like a bass.

THIRTY NINE

Saturday morning was glorious. No upslope conditions had been forecast. Rain, snow, sleet, and hail were nowhere in sight, and no wind blew either. Just clear blue skies and plenty of sun. Perfect for a picnic and a parent/kid soccer game tacked onto a small wedding reception. At last count about a hundred well-wishers were coming to congratulate the Marshall family on their special day.

A few close friends had been invited for the private wedding ceremony to be held inside before the picnic. Gloria, Dave, and Gina arrived shortly before noon to help Jack and Becca get ready. Gina ran upstairs to talk to Missy and Katie. Gloria went to check on Becca and calm her down. That left Dave alone in the living room to greet the guests.

The doorbell rang, and Dave opened it, coming face to face with a giant of a man. He was shaped like a full-sized refrigerator and looked to weigh about as much as one, all of him solid muscle. He dwarfed Dave and blocked out most of the sunlight from the door. But he had a friendly face.

"This the Marshall wedding and picnic?" the giant said with a grin. Then recognition hit his face. "Oh, hello Mr. DA. Nice to meet you. I'm Moses Hawthorn and this is my wife, Patty." Moses turned sideways to allow a petite woman to step up beside him.

Dave couldn't help himself and laughed out loud. "Judge Langfelt, nice to meet you and your husband. He shook hands with them, grimacing from Moses' bone-crushing grasp. Then he stepped back and took another look at the big man. Recognition registered.

"You used to play offensive guard for the Broncos, right, Moses?" Judge Langfelt's husband nodded and followed his judicious wife inside to meet Jack and Becca.

Dave caught up with Judge Langfelt. "I've heard a lot of good things about you, your honor. Too bad your court isn't in my county."

The wizened jurist gave him a steady, no-nonsense gaze.

"Yes, that is too bad, Dave. I hear good things about you as well. Seems like we have a mutual friend in Bill Conley. He gave the governor good advice. But, I sometimes work in this county, you know. I make house calls for occasions like this one, and my fee is pretty reasonable. All you have to do is feed us." She winked at him.

Understanding dawned on Dave and he nodded in silent agreement just as they were joined by Gloria. Dave introduced her to the judge and her husband.

Patty Langfelt jabbed Moses in the side when she saw him admiring Gloria. "You're risking ten years house arrest, Moses," she warned. Moses chuckled as he turned pink. Judge Langfelt immediately struck up a close conversation with Gloria as if they were old college roommates. Then, arm in arm, they left the men standing in the doorway to greet any new arrivals.

Martha and Jasper arrived next. Martha entered holding out her left hand to display her wedding ring.

"Isn't it fabulous, Dave? Next week we're going on a cruise to Alaska, and we may just keep going and travel the rest of our lives." Jasper stood behind her beaming. He carried a folder under his arm brimming over with papers.

"Hi, Dave. This is my last official business before our honeymoon trip. When I get back, you and I can sit down and have a little chat." He gave Dave a conspiratorial wink and guided Martha into the house.

Dave smiled at all the obvious hints he was getting. He thought it was funny that he was being encouraged to take a step that he and Gloria had agreed to the first night they had spent together. Neither tried to explain their instant attraction, but both were equally smitten and steadfastly committed. They had only decided to wait so Gina and Dave could get to know each other. Fortunately, Gina had accepted Dave completely within just a few days.

Dave was drawn from his daydream when the doorbell rang again. He opened the door to Senator Bill Conley's back. The Senator was holding up his hands to gain the attention of the TV minicam crews now crowding into Becca's front yard. His wife Elizabeth stood beside him. They were framed by two guys in gray suits, easily recognizable as Secret Service agents.

Senator Conley grumbled at the throng of questioners all talking at once.

"Hold it, hold it. I told you I have no announcements. Nothing to say. There is no news story for you here today. We came here for a picnic. Now butt out. And move your trucks out of this cul-de-sac. We have a whole soccer team arriving soon, and they'll need room to park." The Senator scowled at the disappointed gaggle. He stood on the porch in shorts and T-shirt, but he glared at them in his best two-star-general mode. When they hesitated, he started to step off the porch towards them and they scattered to their vehicles.

Elizabeth and the agents stifled their smirks as the Senator growled at the fleeing journalists. When he turned around, his expression reverted to the image of an affable grandfather again, and they all had a laugh along with Dave.

"Dave, it's great to see you," the Senator said. Then he turned to the agents beside him. "You guys make sure the media circus is cleared out before the soccer parents arrive. Then come on out back and join the fun." He gathered Elizabeth to his side, and they joined the other guests inside so the ceremony could start.

Jack and Becca rounded up their kids and introduced them to the group of adults gathered in their living room. Tommy and Andy went bug-eyed when they met Moses. They got him to sign a paper napkin, then went into shock when he asked for their autographs in return.

None of the children seemed to know what to think of the small lady who had donned a long black robe. Judge Langfelt became the center of attention as she walked to the far end of the room and cleared her throat.

"Okay, folks. Let's get this show on the road, I'm getting hungry." Everyone laughed. "Let's gather around our special family. This is the first time I have done a ceremony quite like this. I'm very pleased that Jack and Becca and their children asked me to do the honors."

Jack and Becca placed the kids in front of them where they would be a major part of the ceremony. Everyone except the judge wore shorts and T-shirts so they could enjoy the picnic and soccer game afterwards.

The judge looked from face to face and smiled.

"Friends, this is an extraordinary occasion, and a very happy one. We have the privilege today to witness the birth of a new family." She paused and smiled down at the four children. "First of all, I congratulate these children. They are lucky to have such loving parents. I only wish all children who passed through my court could share in their good fortune.

"Next, I have to admit that I offered scripts to Jack and Becca, and they turned them all down." The group chuckled at this and Becca turned crimson. "It seems Jack likes things simplified, and the two of them really boiled this down. So I'll get right to the point."

The judge smiled down at the children and asked, "Who gives permission for this marriage today?"

The four children looked up at the petite lady judge and answered together: "We do." The girls giggled and the boys elbowed each other then tried to look serious. Then all four glanced sheepishly over their shoulders at their parents, and received approving smiles in return.

Judge Langfelt laughed.

"Great, kids. Now settle down for this next part."

"Jack, will you have Becca for your wife forever?"

"Yes," he answered with a smile.

"Do you accept Missy and Andy as your adopted children from this day forward, and do you promise to be a good dad to Missy, Katie, Andy, and Tommy?"

"Yes, I do." Jack squeezed Andy's shoulder and gave Missy a hug from behind as he said this.

"Becca, will you have Jack for your husband forever?"

"Yes," she answered.

"Do you accept Katie and Tommy as your adopted children from this day forward, and do you promise to be a good mom to Missy, Katie, Andy, and Tommy?"

"Yes, I do," she answered as she hugged all four children together.

"Then, I now pronounce you husband and wife - and family." The judge didn't have to give anyone permission to kiss or hug, because the new Marshall family was gathered in a tight circle doing just that.

Their friends clamored around to congratulate them. Judge Langfelt reached in her robe pocket and handed a tissue to Moses. The big man had tears streaming down his cheeks.

"He does this every time, folks," Patricia Langfelt announced to the room at large as she stood on tiptoes to plant a big smooch on his cheek.

The signing ceremony was next. Jasper had the papers all spread out along the dining room table in the next room. Jack, Becca, and the judge signed all the wedding papers. Dave and Gloria signed as witnesses. The children joined their new parents for the signing of adoption papers, somehow wrestled through the system by Jasper.

The kids had had enough of the formalities and sneaked out back to get something to eat. They were surprised to find the backyard full of friends and neighbors waiting to congratulate them. Forgotten were the tragedies leading up to this day. The girls ran to join their Golden Girls teammates, and the boys discovered most of their football team was there as well.

The chattering was hushed suddenly by the strong voice of Patty Langfelt speaking from the deck.

"Ladies and gentlemen and children, may I present Mr. and Mrs. Jack Marshall."

There was applause and cheering as Jack and Becca stepped out to greet their friends.

•••

The reception and picnic turned into the first big party of the summer. New friends were made, and old acquaintances renewed. The scene reminded Jack of a full-fledged *Renaissance* festival where people wandered about eating, drinking, and joining in games. He had gotten separated from Becca somewhere in all the hilarity and sought her out in the crowd.

Jack couldn't see her anywhere, and he turned to check back in the house. He found himself face-to-face with Senator Conley and Dave Mendes. The three men had come through a lot together and now seemed to be going in different directions.

"What's your next assignment, Jack?" Senator Conley posed the question on everyone's mind. "I figured old Henry Strothers would be chomping at the bit to pawn more work off on you."

Jack grinned at the gentle man who had been his mentor for several decades.

"I don't think Henry will be calling me anymore, Senator. You see, I retired yesterday." Bill Conley stopped drinking his glass of tea and straightened. A smile came to his face.

"Smart, Jack. Don't blame you at all. There's something about the law of averages that says the next bullet might be the bad one. You've given this country enough. I'm proud of you, son. I remember a wise old sergeant giving me some good advice years ago. He taught me more about leadership than any officer course I ever took. He said I always had to do what was best for myself, and be able to recognize that sometimes that meant doing what was best for someone else first."

The two old friends shook hands. Then the Senator spotted Moses standing by himself and walked over to chat with him about the fall football season.

Jack slapped Dave on the back.

"I have this sneaking suspicion you may be following me down this road pretty soon, my friend. What do you have to say about that?"

"Don't place any bets against it, Jack. Say, uh, are you looking for work yet?" Dave asked coyly, checking out his best friend's reaction with a sideways glance.

"In another week or so, Dave. I need to get this old body back in working condition. Why? You know somebody who needs a worn-out spy and under-cover man as a security guard?"

"No," Dave squared his body to face Jack straight on. "But, I do know a certain DA who needs a trained investigator to do, shall we say, a bit of free-lance work." Dave saw the pained expression on Jack's face and rushed to clarify his offer. "It's nothing bad, Jack. You've had enough of that for a lifetime. I'm talking about computer work from your home, some followup stuff, evaluating certain casework done by my staff, working directly for, - er, with me. As much work as you want. I have a couple years' backlog and no one to do it. What do you say?"

"I'll have to talk it over with my new partner, Dave. I believe you're beginning to get a feel for how that works now, aren't you?"

Dave returned a knowing smile.

"You got that right, Jack. And I don't mind it one bit. Anyway, the offer stands whenever you two get around to talking about it." Dave and Jack noticed Judge Langfelt heading their way with a determined look on her face. She had her eye on Dave, and Gloria was right behind her.

"Uh-oh, buddy. I think I'll leave you to discuss the situation with the judge and your new partner. They look like a pretty persuasive pair of women, and Moses gives the judge some pretty solid backup."

Judge Langfelt cornered Bill Conley after she had set a date with Dave and Gloria.

"What's your plan, Senator?" The fiery judge leveled him with her sternest look, one that made lesser men cringe just before she pronounced judgment in her courtroom. "Are you going to lead this country out of the quagmire those Washington politicians have created?"

Senator Conley admired her assertiveness

"Oh yes, your honor. I have decided to run, but it won't be like any campaign you've ever seen. To answer your next question, no, I will not join a major party. I started out independent and will remain so. Elizabeth and I have sketched out a plan, even thought a lot about a running mate." The senator let this sink in before he continued.

"I understand you have written rules for your courtroom on decorum and procedure, that correct?" She nodded with a big smile in return. "Well, I want to borrow a few ideas from you for my campaign. We just might have to sit down over dinner one night and talk about them."

The two friends locked arms and strolled to a corner of the yard where they could continue their chat.

Becca anxiously searched the yard for Jack. She had been talking with Martha and Jasper, and couldn't wait to share her news with her husband. Finally, she spotted him relaxing on the deck. As she approached him, Jack motioned her to be quiet and listen to their children, who were gathered in a circle at the foot of his chair.

Becca listened to the conversation which seemed to go around the circle from one child to the next.

Katie: "It's six of us now all in one family. And, we're all brothers and sisters."

Missy: "Yeah! It's really neat and we're best friends too."

Andy: "The best part is we all have a mom and dad."

Tommy: "Yeah, but we've got to figure some things out. How late does your mom let you stay up, Andy?"

Jack stifled a laugh and stood to go join Becca.

"Looks like we're outnumbered, four to two. We had better work out some strategy before these kids run right over us."

Becca dragged him over to a corner of the deck. She had some news to share.

"Guess what, lover? Martha is taking a leave of absence. She and Jasper really are going to continue traveling after the cruise, and she needs someone to take over at the Rec Center. It could turn into a permanent job. She wondered if you could recommend someone. Know anyone who might fit the bill?"

"Definitely," he answered, and covered her mouth with a searing kiss of commitment.

"Afterword"

Residents of Colorado's Front Range won't find Hamilton, Madison, and Monroe counties anywhere. Neither will they locate the cities of Fullerton and Taylor City. They do not exist. No doubt some developer has named their latest creation Cottonwood Estates, but that's not the place I wrote about. Western Slope folks will agree that Douglas Pass is just as nasty as I have portrayed it. Don't go there.

I made up this story. All the characters are fictional, although I borrowed characteristics from a number of people I ran into, some friendly, some not so. I was never a secret agent, but I did coach little girls and boys how to play soccer and baseball. I moved a soccer practice one day without telling all the parents, and got thoroughly scolded by a single mother who was in a panic to find her little boy. That incident and my own short tenure as a single dad gave me a world of insight into this difficult and noble role.

Over 25 years as a problem solver for the federal government left a bad taste for those more interested in power and aggrandizement than serving the public. Sadly, too, my observation of close friends in abusive relationships tells me fathers must set better examples for their sons. I know of no better way to get at this problem, except to describe Jack Marshall.

Bio Sketch

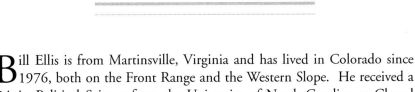

B ill Ellis is from Martinsville, Virginia and has lived in Colorado since 1976, both on the Front Range and the Western Slope. He received a BA in Political Science from the University of North Carolina at Chapel Hill, and a Masters of Public Administration from the American University, Washington, DC. His work life includes being a park ranger, toll booth operator, Army officer, consultant, instructor, technical writer, and runner for a law firm.

Bill and Joan have a combined family of six children and seven grand-children - at last count. They live in Fruita, Colorado, 18 $^1/_2$ miles from Utah in the near desert, with Max the adolescent farm dog and Charley the Velcro cat. Contact Bill at P.O. Box 571, Fruita, Colorado 81521, or email at billelliswrtr@aol.com.